ASK ANY AARDVARK

Bud Durand

A FICTION IMPRINT FROM ADDUCENT

Adducent, Inc.

www.Adducent.co

Titles Distributed In

North America
United Kingdom
Western Europe
South America
Australia

Ask Any Aardvark

Bud Durand

ISBN 9781937592417

Published by Adducent, Inc. under its Escrire fiction imprint

Jacksonville, Florida

www.Adducent.co

Published in the United States of America

ACKNOWLEDGMENTS

I could not have completed this without my family's support, and owe them a great deal for their unwavering encouragement and advice. My appreciation and thanks also go to Fortis Publishing for the assistance they provided. My editor, Margo Higdon, significantly improved the final product with her technical expertise and suggestions for plot changes and corrections. Special thanks go to my granddaughter, Alyson Alana Burnett, for the wonderful and unique cover design.

DEDICATION

To the men and women of science whose dedication and perseverance have advanced our understanding of the human mind and its potential for greatness.

PROLOGUE

Three Years Ago, Tanzania, Africa

After three months of living among the tribe they finally trusted him enough to ignore him, well, almost. Nevertheless, he was careful not to spend too much time communicating with the women, especially the young, marriage-eligible ones. At times that proved difficult, since most of the men were usually off hunting, trapping and otherwise promoting the general welfare of the tribe, while the women remained in the tribal conclave tending to domestic chores. Harry Lisbon had come to Tanzania, specifically the mountainous region east of Iringa, to study native languages for the Smithsonian Institute. He was a linguistic anthropologist, but the Institute had a more general view of his studies, so he included notes on tribal relationships, religious beliefs, governance and just about every other aspect of this group of native East Africans. The densely wooded area between the savannahs of the west and the moderately high mountainous regions to the east afforded the tribe an adequate supply of flora and fauna, and had for the most part kept them out of touch with the modern world. Not that they were a backward people, much to Lisbon's delight, but rather one that believed their simple way of life was preferable to the fast paced one lived by the rest of the world—a place they were aware of and even occasionally in contact with. Every year or so a tribal member would leave for the adventure of the outside world, and occasionally one returned to spread their newly acquired knowledge among the remaining members. Fewer and fewer were coming back however, and Harry feared for the eventual disappearance of the tribe and its unique culture.

Harry Lisbon had a PhD in neurolinguistics from Carnegie Mellon University, and did his thesis on the effects of language on brain development. His contention was, broadly, the more difficult the language, the more it improved early brain development. Although he made a good case, no one was crediting him with a ground breaking scientific discovery. He considered the natives to have average intelligence, but relatively complex language skills. Their reasoning ability was exceptional, yet they had difficulty explaining themselves. Doctor Harry, a sobriquet tribe members often used when addressing him, thought that was more likely an indication of his difficulty in picking up all the nuances of their language, rather than their inability to express themselves.

The tribal members were generally amused by Lisbon's interest. He was, after all, a tall, hearty Irishman, with a large mop of red hair and an equally red goatee, not to mention his western garb. So far the natives had been quite forthcoming in explaining their life philosophy to him, which, as best Lisbon could tell, consisted of an odd mixture of Norse- and Hindu-like beliefs, modified to accommodate the exigencies of a life not too far removed from the bare existence level. The natives were surprisingly healthy, at least compared to several other native groups he was familiar with, and depended upon a host of natural healing potions and salves, including extracts not only from the flora, but from the fauna as well. This piqued the Institute's interest, so the Smithsonian extended his stay in order to document as thoroughly as possible any medical benefits of these native remedies. He considered the fact that the tribe allowed him to dine with them, even though he did not physically contribute to their welfare, a testament to their understanding of what he was trying to accomplish.

Doctor Harry had often accompanied the women of the tribe on their root, fruit and leaf gathering excursions. The younger men of the tribe had even allowed him to accompany them on one evening excursion where they trapped and "milked" two aardvarks. He felt privileged to witness these events, and even more so to see how they processed the gathered material to meet their pharmaceutical needs. The tribe had invited him on another after dusk outing, and he was looking forward to it.

About thirty minutes after the sun disappeared below the savannahs, the young men started gathering in the central area of the conclave, each clutching a spear and an unlit torch, and wearing a colorful sash depicting various family achievements and lineage. A man and a woman, not wearing any sashes nor carrying anything, were also present. The tribal elder, or Bon-cha as he was addressed, was adorned in ceremonial garb, so Lisbon knew he was in for a special treat. He had previously witnessed a "coming into manhood" ceremony for one of the teenage boys, and a "joining" ceremony for a couple who were now life partners. He enjoyed both of these events immensely. All three participants had imbibed concoctions, no doubt brewed by the tribe using the vegetation and animal fluids they had collected, that put them in a trance-like state lasting well into the night, but apparently left them with no bad after effects the next day. When he inquired about the nature of tonight's festivities, he was only told that there would be what he interpreted as a "reading of the minds."

The waxing crescent moon, only a few hours at most past the new moon, was high in the sky but shed little light on the group as they proceeded to the ceremonial area. The alpha male, with his torch ablaze, led the snake-like file of troops, perhaps three dozen in all, through the surrounding bundu. Every third or fourth man was now carrying a lit torch. The Bon-cha and the man and woman without sashes brought up the rear of the group. Lisbon followed at a respectful thirty-nine steps behind as he had been instructed to do. Their destination was about two hundred and fifty meters away along a winding, narrow path through the densely forested area, and maybe one hundred and fifty meters from the main encampment as the crow flies. A lone baobab tree grew in the center of this ten acre plot which resembled the savannahs of the lowlands.

When they approached the place of the shining light—Lisbon's interpretation of the native words for the ceremonial area—the Bon-cha took his place on a platform carved out of the middle of the baobab tree beginning about two thirds of a meter above ground level. The alcove had vertical sides arched to meet each other at the top, and was two meters high—just tall enough for the Bon-cha with his ceremonial headdress. Lisbon imagined the space filled with a stained glass window, symbolic he supposed of his idea of this as a religious place. The tree itself was a good ten meters in diameter with nine main trunks pointing upward at odd directions. The Bon-cha placed two small vials down on a ledge of the platform just below his feet: one contained a pale green liquid and the other a bright yellow one. The man and woman stood facing him a few meters away. The troops formed a semicircle behind the couple facing the elder, and Lisbon took his place behind them.

As the remaining torches were lit, the men started a slight swaying and low chanting, while the man and woman in the center knelt down. The Bon-cha began chanting also, like he had in previous ceremonies, starting out slow as if explaining what was about to take place, and then picking up the pace as he progressed. Lisbon thought his tone was not as pleasant as in past ceremonies. He noticed other tribal members arriving now, and joining him behind the arc of the younger men. This time, however, it included only the women and older men and not the children. The Bon-cha reached down and retrieved the vial of green liquid, and motioned to the man and woman to get up and approach him. The man drank half of the contents and handed it to the woman; she finished it and set the vial back down on the ledge. The Bon-cha now took the other vial and drank the amber liquid. It was obvious he relished the taste as he stood with his eyes closed clutching the vial with both hands at chest level. The men continued swaying and chanting low for what Doctor Harry guessed, since he didn't like to wear his watch around the troops, to be about fifteen minutes.

The Bon-cha was indeed the tribal elder, having at least ten years on every tribal member other than a few of the women, and Harry placed him in his early to mid-seventies. A hardy man for his age, he had a full but not flabby build and was a good ten to twelve centimeters shorter than the younger men. He wore his gray hair in long braids kept in place with animal bones. The ceremonial garb and the torch lighting afforded him a somber look, replacing his usually placid visage. Lisbon assumed the Bon-cha was waiting for the drug to initiate a trance-like state in himself and the two participants, as it had for the participants in the other ceremonies he had witnessed, but remembered a deep purple liquid was used during those.

The Bon-cha opened his eyes wide and the men raised the level of their chant. He removed his hands from the empty vial and it just hung there, in midair, apparently not supported by anything! After ten seconds it fell to the ground, and the Bon-cha jumped down from his perch in the middle of the tree and stood less than a meter in front of the couple facing him. The chanting came to an abrupt halt and the Bon-cha began to speak. Lisbon was a good twenty meters away but heard every word spoken. Unfortunately, he only understood about three quarters of the dialogue. If only he'd been able to learn more of the language, but then he didn't exactly have a dedicated tutor. Of the two tribal members who had spent some time in the outside world, one spoke French and the other Dutch, and while Lisbon was fluent in the former, neither member was very communicative. From what he did understand, it was apparent the man stood accused of raping the woman, but it was a case of he said, she said. Their body language indicated that he was denying it, and that she was adamant the sex was not consensual. The Bon-cha didn't appear to be buying either story. He then placed himself squarely in front of the male participant, placed his hands on his shoulders, drew the man's head to within a few inches of his own, and closed his eyes. Even the night sounds of the forest seemed to stop as an eerie silence enveloped the group. The tribal elder stood there for a good three or four minutes before opening his eyes and stepping back. Moving in front of the female, he placed her in the same relative position. After about five minutes, he stepped back, turned and once again mounted the raised section carved out of the tree.

The tension was palpable, especially for the "accused." The Bon-cha looked over the entire group to make sure he had their undivided attention: an action hardly necessary given their interest in the outcome. Then he spoke and Lisbon listened intently, translating and transcribing as he went, supplementing his rendition of the monologue by questioning several tribal members as soon as he could after the ceremony. They were remarkably consistent in their version of what the Bon-cha had said, and Doctor Harry's annotated account of the elder's remarks read as follows:

"I have looked into the heart (mind) of Kewala (the accused man), and he truly believes he did not force an action that was not desired. While his memory of the joining is vivid in many parts, it is clouded in other parts with the heat of the lonely and the excited. I see no evidence of the jackal's guile, but only a deep longing and respect for his accuser, and confusion over her words of anger. In Aronnee (the accusing woman) I see confusion as well, but also the anger of the she tiger. She is not sure of how to live with the heat she feels for this man, nor the anger with herself for not expressing her wobbling of the

6

new born (hesitancy) more clearly. She does not believe in her heart (mind) Kewala has grieved her intentionally."
The Bon-cha then prescribed three months hard work for Kewala contributing to Aronnee's bridal-price for her eventual mating, and a public apology from Aronnee to Kewala for accusing him of poisonous (impure) intentions.

Oh my word—this bears some serious looking into, thought Lisbon. *Wait until they hear about this back home!*

CHAPTER ONE

Present Day, Wednesday, Chantilly, Virginia

"You bumped the table!" Brandy Simmons challenged. The small plastic cylinder, about the diameter of a straw and half the height, had fallen over on its side. That was the idea, but not by any overt physical means.

Toshi Lee laughed and said, "No, Brandy, you did that. No kidding, it was all you. That was excellent."

Doctor Toshi Lee was the DARPA manager for the MENSA program. Not the MENSA that probably comes to mind, but rather "Mental Enhancement by Neuronal Spatial Alignment"—not a totally accurate description, but workable. DARPA, or the Defense Advanced Research Projects Agency, had been working on various psionic programs almost from its beginning in 1958. Although the Agency was much better known for its advances in the hard sciences—advanced radar systems, high-performance computing, space and missile systems, the ARPANET, stealth technology, micro-systems and materials technologies, to name just a few—they had also made inroads over the years in the soft sciences. Successes in this area included improvements in polygraphy and the reading of facial indices, the establishment of a definitive psychoneural connection, chartering the science of electroencephalonomy, and inroads in neurolinguistic programming. They had also exposed as fraudulent a number of "psychic phenomena", which was not prompted by a desire to upset anybody's applecart, but rather to take an honest look at anything that might be of use to the Department of Defense (DoD) in the parapsychological arena. Up until now the agency had probably not justified its significant expenditure of dollars in these endeavors. But then, that's why they called it research, and it appeared as though that was all about to change.

"I knew I did it," Simmons chortled. "I felt it. Can we try again?" She was young and sinewy like a model, which she no doubt could have been if she so desired. She kept her auburn hair page boy length, and seldom felt the need to wear makeup. Her exuberance was contagious and her energy indefatigable, and this, along with her good looks and the fact that she usually dressed in bright colors, made her hard not to notice.

Simmons was the youngest of the test subjects, although she, indeed most if not all of the "subjects", thought of themselves more as program participants, or even co-program managers. This was due mostly to Doctor Lee's participatory management style. As one of the eight members of this experimental program, Simmons had passed a three week battery of tests that included physical and medical exams, as well as mental and psychological, not to mention considerable interviews. The forty-seven original candidates were chosen after an extensive review of university transcripts, CIA, FBI and other classified records, MENSA and similar organizations' applications, mental hospital admissions, and any reasonable and documented indication of psychic ability. This activity took nine months and was accomplished by a DARPA research grant to Johns Hopkins University. Simmons not only had an application pending with MENSA, but she had also applied for a CIA position where she confounded the polygraphers to the extent that they gave up testing her.

"You can practice more if you want, but I recommend you take a rest," replied Doctor Lee. "We don't want to fry any neurons, do we?" It was after eight and they normally didn't work this late, but Simmons was anxious and had asked for an extra session. "Why don't we set up another practice session for tomorrow at a lower setting?"

The helmet like apparatus she was wearing supplied a variable magnetic field around her head that affected the neuronal links between her brain cells. Whether it was a placebo or not, it seemed to help the MENSA participants' concentration and thus their ability to direct their thoughts. Doctor Lee thought Simmons would be able to do without the machine after only a few more sessions. Most of her cohorts had already demonstrated the same feeble but definitive telekinesis ability, and two of the members, who had a twin brother or sister, were becoming quite adept at "anticipating" others' actions.

"Alright, I could use some relaxation anyway," Simmons said as she unhooked herself and got up from the work station. She thought she'd go up to her room and call her mom. Not that she could tell her anything definitive, just that she was doing well. On her way out the door she looked back and asked, "Aren't you coming?"

"I need to make a few notes and straighten up a little. Then I think I'll hit the gym for a while."

"Want some help with your notes?"

"No. It won't take but a few minutes. You go on ahead."

"See you later then, Doc."

Simmons and Doctor Lee were currently on the "lab level" of the DARPA Cybernetics Technology Facility. Level three also housed some administrative space and storage facilities, a server farm, the program manager's suite and live-in staff quarters. Simmons called the elevator and decided to drop down to level four, the "recreation level", to see what the other program participants were up to before she called her mom. It housed the gym, sauna and swimming pool on one side, and game rooms, the theater and more recreational facilities on the other. The top floor, or level one, was the "living level" where the kitchen, dining hall, conference rooms, library, surveillance station, program manager and staff offices, and more storage rooms were located. Level two was the "dorm level" where the participants each had a three room suite complete with FIOS internet access and TV. This was their home-away-from-home. The three locals usually spent weekends at home with their families, while the others often spent their free time taking in the local Virginia museums and other attractions, or doing the same thing across the river in the Federal City and nearby Maryland.

These four levels constituted the Cybernetics Technology Facility, or CTF as it was called by the DARPA personnel who knew about it. It was situated entirely below ground in a nondescript building in the Dulles Business Park, at the intersection of Routes 50 and 28 in Chantilly, Virginia, part of the "Greater Metropolitan Washington" area. The ground floor of the building housed several commercial businesses, and situated on the two floors above that were the offices of one county and two federal government agencies. On the back side of the building, a card-key entry device secured the entrance to a staircase leading down to the facility. The CTF was a resurrection of the Cybernetics Technology Office which had enabled DARPA's earlier psionic successes, but had also drawn the criticism of several members of Congress. This was one of the reasons it didn't currently show up on the DARPA organization chart; the fact that it was one of their black programs was another. These were highly secret, need-to-know, code word programs that the decision makers really, really didn't want anyone else, foreign or domestic, to find out about.

When Doctor Lee completed his notes he turned his iPad off and leaned back in his swivel chair. He thought about how his friend Harry Lisbon over at the Smithsonian got him started in this endeavor, and how far he had come in just nineteen months. Lee knew Lisbon from their time together at Carnegie Melon University, where they roomed together and had both earned a PhD. Lee's specialty was bioengineering, whereas Lisbon was into linguistics. When Lisbon was down in Tanzania doing research on sub-Saharan languages, particularly the Niger-Congo linguistic family, he witnessed a native "witchdoctor" demonstrate apparent ESP abilities. He was convinced enough of the native's authenticity that he got in touch with Lee, who worked for the Princeton Neuroscience Institute at the time. Lee then pitched the program to DARPA, which awarded a contract to PNI to study the phenomena. His research isolated the chemical formula being used by the natives that appeared to have an effect on their ESP ability, and probably enhanced their other mental abilities as well. Further research indicated the possibility of additional potential enhancers, so the DARPA decided to hire Lee and formalize the program. Since he worked for PNI, one of the government think tanks, or more formally a federally funded research and development center, DARPA offered him an Intergovernmental Personnel Act position. The IPA mechanism gave Lee the authority of a government person, but a higher salary than most govies, and allowed the government to release him at their convenience. Once Lee was on board, they awarded another contract to Johns Hopkins to find likely program participants. And here he was, less than two years later, actually making some progress.

Doctor Lee was convinced that a revolutionary advance in mankind's inherent mental capacity was not only viable, but something that could be achieved in his lifetime. The two twins in the program were showing remarkable improvement with every treatment, and the others had made considerable progress as well. Even Simmons, the "slow" student—if you could apply such a pejorative to someone with a 165 IQ and perfect SAT scores—had made a break through tonight. At the start of the program Lee had to admit he was more than a little jealous of the program participants' abilities, but he had already proved there was hope for "regular" folks like himself once they worked out all the protocols. *Can you imagine . . .* he thought *. . . people being able to more fully utilize their brain power. I mean, the* *implications for research, for . . . Ah, but enough for tonight. Best check on everyone before turning in, after a little exercise that is.*

At five foot eleven and two hundred hard-packed pounds, Lee looked more like a professional athlete than a research scientist. His dark, close-cropped hair added to the impression. He did come by his build honestly since, being an advocate of a strong mind in a strong body, he worked out regularly. He thought he'd pump some iron then go and take a dip before turning in. His suite was located on the same level as the lab, so he didn't have far to walk to change into some looser clothes and grab his suit and a towel. His home away from home, which was slightly larger than the others' suites, had an extra "reading room" where he kept a good deal of his personal reference material. He picked out a book and set it on his desk to remind him to check on something when he was done with his workout. More likely, he'd just end up sending his buddy Harry Lisbon an email about meeting up this weekend and then turn in, but he did have good intentions.

After some stretching exercises and warming up with some lighter weights, Lee loaded 200 pounds on the bar. He normally didn't like to work the bench with no one there to spot him, so he decided he wouldn't try anything too heavy. He did four sets of six reps at 200 then rested a few minutes and did a few more stretches. He then loaded 210 on the bar and lifted it off the bench uprights. His head was feeling a little fuzzy, so he decided to make this his last set. On the third down stroke two arms shot out from behind him and grabbed the bar: someone was holding it down? No one was in the gym when he got there and he didn't hear anybody enter; but there they were, obviously playing a trick on him. He tried to say something but he was having trouble concentrating and only grunts came out. *Perhaps if I flipped over, kicking off with my feet . . . but that might actually break my neck.* Now his head hurt, particularly around his temples—no, now it was more in the middle of his head, like blood vessels breaking maybe. The bar had migrated up his chest toward his throat. *This must be what a migraine feels like. Gotta concentrate . . . can't seem to talk . . . need help . . . can't breathe . . . must push up the bar . . . losing it . . .*

CHAPTER TWO

Wednesday, Chantilly, Virginia

Tommy Pacquin decided to take a dip before turning in. While not as religious about it as Doctor Lee, he did swim regularly. He learned to swim in the Boy Scouts, earned the swimming and lifesaving merit badges, and managed to land a lifeguard job at an indoor pool in Prince William County, Virginia. He actually tried out for the Olympics but his part time jobs really didn't allow him enough practice time to qualify. But he enjoyed it and it certainly kept him in shape. Like the other program participants, he had free run of the place and swam at somewhat odd hours. Almost everyone used the pool—if you counted the hot tub and the sauna—and they all used the gym facilities, mostly in the morning. If they got the staff involved, they had enough for a basketball game, and usually played two or three quarters on Monday and Thursday afternoons.

At five foot five Pacquin was a little shorter than most of his colleagues, but in better shape. Not the handsomest guy in town, what with his bent nose and larger than usual ears, he made up for it with his intelligence, toughness and persistence. This job was a real boon, as it allowed him all the time he wanted to hone his IT skills, and still have plenty of time for exercise, both physical and mental. The former was what got him his job as an FBI analyst, his position title before he switched over to polygraphy, and this program was expanding his horizons in ways he never dreamed of. Besides, the DC area had his home town and last job location of Quantico beat hands down.

Thirty-six laps later he jumped in the hot tub and dozed off a bit. After a brisk shower he headed out when he noticed a light coming from the end of the hall. He didn't hear anything so he figured someone must have left the lights on in the gym. He decided to walk down and switch them off. When he got there he saw someone on one of the weight benches. It was Doctor Lee and he didn't appear to be moving. Pacquin called out, and when he got no answer hurried over to investigate. The weight bar was at an angle with one set of weights on the floor and the other near the side of Lee's neck, almost pulling him off the bench. He didn't appear to be breathing. Pacquin jerked the end of the bar off of Lee's neck and sent it crashing over on the floor. He ran over and activated the fire alarm, and then ran back to Lee and started CPR.

In less than a minute a couple of his fellow participants arrived and he yelled at them to call 9-1-1. Surely the fire department was already on the way, but that might not include an ambulance with EMTs. Sharon Rydell, a participant who was a registered nurse, used the portable defibrillator on him to no avail, and then relieved Pacquin at the CPR.

It took less than ten minutes for the EMTs to arrive, about three minutes after the fireman, one of whom had relieved Rydell at the CPR. The EMTs applied a shot of epinephrine and used their defibrillator twice. Lee was totally nonresponsive, so after working on him for a few more minutes and hearing the circumstances and the timeline, the head EMT decided he was a lost cause. There was no obvious cause of death, and this man looked too healthy to just drop dead while reclining on a weight bench. They notified the coroner's office and the Fairfax County Police.

Sam Donaldson, who was Doctor Lee's assistant, figured it would be a good idea to call the Director of DARPA and let her know what happened. Although it was almost 11:30, Robin Dornan answered her cell phone right away. She issued instructions to Donaldson and then made a few phone calls herself.

Donaldson walked back over to the other residents who were consoling each other in hushed tones and speculating on what might have happened. Two of the women were crying, and one of the men went to the restroom to heave. Donaldson himself looked a little pale. "I called the Director," Donaldson informed the group, "and she asked us all to remain here and not touch anything until the authorities arrive."

Not five minutes later Master Police Officer John Frey and Police Officer First Class Ray Stravinsky arrived. They were briefed by the chief EMT, who told them the coroner was on his way. Then he and the other EMTs started packing up their gear. Frey asked everyone to back off and preserve what was left of the scene, and then both officers started taking down names and making notes, talking to each of the program participants individually.

When Detective Rance Tollman arrived a couple of minutes later you would have thought a frumpier-than-usual Columbo had walked into the gym. Only his keen eyes hinted at his professional competence. After talking to Frey he asked the civilians who was in charge, and everyone turned and looked at Donaldson. Sam reluctantly admitted it was him, at least for the time being. The detective had no sooner been briefed when Officer Stravinsky interrupted him.

"Sir, there's a federal agent here. He'd like to see you over by the entrance."

Tollman knew what was coming, what with this being a Department of Defense program. The only question was what military investigative unit would be handling the case. He didn't think DoD had its own investigators per se, except maybe the Inspector General, but the Army had their CID, the Navy NCIS, and the Air Force OSI. Every organization had its alphabet soup, but the feds were bad and the military worse, especially the Navy. *Damn, the locals in the DC Metro area never get to handle anything interesting*, Tollman thought. After introducing himself he asked, "Taking the case away from me, Agent?"

"I'm Special Agent Edward Ross from the FBI's Washington Field Office and yes, I'm afraid I am, Detective. The classification of the program Doctor Lee was working on, and his status as a federal employee, mean this comes under our jurisdiction. I hope you can appreciate that I'm just doing my job here."

Tollman didn't expect the FBI, but was not surprised either. After examining the agent's credentials he said, "Been here before Agent Ross. If I can get your contact info then this is all yours—you know I'll have to enter an AOA on this. Do you need anything from me or my officers before we leave? We've already contacted the coroner and he is on the way." The AOA was an Assist Other Agency report.

"That won't be necessary—my ME is inbound," said Ross as he handed him his card. "If I could get your guys' notes that would be helpful."

Detective Tollman wrote Ross' badge number on the card the FBI man had given him and then turned to his troops, "You heard the man. Hand 'em over." He used his cell phone to call his station. It took the officer on duty a while to verify the agent's credentials, but when he did Tollman hung up, turned to Ross and said, "Maybe I'll see you around Agent. Here's my card. If there's anything I can do let me know." He said it in such a manner Ross actually believed he meant it. As Tollman turned toward the door, with the officers following him out, he was dialing the coroner on his cell phone.

Ross didn't look like your average federal agent, but then he rushed over here directly from home still in his casual clothes. Nonetheless, he exuded an air of confidence honed by his years on the job. His near six-foot height and slim but powerful looking physique no doubt helped in that regard. With salt and pepper hair and intense hazel eyes, he seemed older than his forty-two years. "I believe I heard you say you were in charge," he said as he looked at Donaldson.

Donaldson nodded.

Ross then asked, "Okay, is everyone accounted for?"

"The police asked me the same thing, and yeah, we're all here," Donaldson said as he looked around making sure he hadn't lost anybody in the interim. "All the participants and the night staff are accounted for, which includes me and Tom Parsons who's upstairs letting everyone in and out."

"Thanks," said Ross. "I know it's been a terrible experience for all of you, but it's important we get as many details as we can right now. I've got several agents on the way and by reviewing what you told the officers earlier, and maybe asking just a few more questions, we'll have you all out of here in no time."

Tommy Pacquin piped up with, "Well first off we all live here and it's not like we're going to jump into bed and fall right to sleep anyway, so take your time, Agent."

"Yeah, I agree, but maybe we could go into one of the rooms, you know, away from Doctor Lee," offered participant Gayle Pennington.

"Sure. I just need to keep my eye on the scene out here until my men arrive. And please tell Parsons to join us and to secure the door after my agents and the coroner get here."

Donaldson nodded and headed toward the elevator, while the rest of the troops followed Ross to a couple of adjacent rooms where he began his interrogations, while keeping one eye on the scene in the gym. By 1:30 in the morning they had all been interviewed and retreated to their rooms. By 3:40 Ross and his men had finished processing the scene, shipped Doctor Lee off to the FBI's morgue, and secured the deceased doctor's suite and his office for the techies later in the morning.

CHAPTER THREE

Thursday, Crystal City, Virginia

"JT, where is Juanita?" asked Tom Hanson. Hanson was the leader of the Fusion Team—a focused response unit of the Department of Homeland Security that included an ad-hoc group of individuals from various intelligence, counterintelligence, counterterrorism and law enforcement agencies. Their job was to get the right resources focused on the right problem fast, usually at the highest level of classification. Operating as a DHS entity, which allowed them to exercise federal police powers, Hanson thought they encountered less resistance from other agencies. He guessed people felt sorry for the relatively new, large and apparently disorganized organization which was cobbled together from dozens of others. After all, who is inclined to lend help to a "got-it-together group" like the FBI or the CIA? The Team operated exceptionally well under Hanson's command and each member contributed a good deal of data and operational expertise from their parent organizations to their usual task: tracking down terrorists. They had recently gained some recognition by closing down several terrorist funded chop shops, solving the murder of a federal official in the process, and putting almost a dozen terrorists out of commission. Having strong White House backing and a more than adequate budget didn't hurt either.

"She's just down the hall I think, Cap'n. Want me to round her up?"

Thomas (Tom) Sebastian Hanson hadn't been a captain since he got out of the Air Force's Office of Special Investigations—but that was his rank then and the appellation stuck. He had a no-nonsense, take-charge manner that he did a marvelous job of blending with a pleasing personality. Slightly graying hair gave him an air of maturity beyond his forty-three years, and his six foot two, two-hundred pound plus frame only showed a few that weren't well placed. The guys on the team said he reminded them of Morgan Freeman, but the ladies tended toward Denzel Washington.

"Yes, my office."

JT grabbed his note pad and his *fisher* "write under any conditions" space pen, a gift from his dad who used to work at NASA, and headed out toward the canteen, the last known whereabouts of his partner. JT Dunkirk was the leader of the Fusion Team's Alpha Unit, and one of the few permanent members of the team: besides the Boss and three of the other five team leaders, two data analysts and some administrative personnel, the rest of the members were detailed from other organizations. Juanita Singletary was one of those and he had worked very closely with her on his last big case, and now they were "officially" partners. In spite of JT's impulsiveness, and his repertoire of corny jokes, he and Juanita got along splendidly. It was difficult not to be charmed by his outward, wise-cracking, making-fun-of-your-foibles-or-his-own demeanor. Although he stood five foot seven and weighed less than one-fifty, he possessed boundless energy. If he stood still for five minutes it was only because something extremely important to him was worthy of his deep concentration. His slightly chiseled face, short brown hair, and deep set brown eyes gave him a dignified, even distinguished, look. However, with a change of clothes, longer hair and a few days' growth, he had no trouble fitting right into an undercover assignment.

"What's up?" Juanita had asked when JT found her and informed her of their requested presence by the boss. She only got a shoulder shrug from her partner as they headed toward Hanson's office.

Juanita's parent organization was AFOSI, the Air Force Office of Special Investigations, where she served as a civilian special agent. She had met JT when he was with the Fairfax County Police Department, and the FCPD and OSI had worked a joint case. Juanita's mom was originally from Mexico and her dad met Maria when she was waiting tables in Del Rio, Texas, where he was assigned as an instructor pilot at Laughlin Air Force Base. Juanita obviously inherited the best of both worlds: she had a beautiful tawny complexion with dark hair and intense brown eyes, a quick wit, and an insatiable curiosity. Although only a couple of inches shorter than JT, he had a good twenty pounds on her; nonetheless she was an amazing athlete, as demonstrated by her fast reflexes and expert marksmanship ability.

After they made themselves comfortable in the lounge chairs facing the boss' desk Hanson began with, "Well you two obviously made an impression on someone. I suppose because of your familiarity with DARPA, and the clearances you got working your last case, they want you two to investigate yet another unexplained death of a DARPA program manager." Hanson was referring to the case they had just cleared where a DARPA scientist was murdered by an improvised explosive device, originally thought to have been set off by a terrorist organization.

"Geez, Cap'n, they just can't hold on to those guys can they? Seriously, this case has terrorist implications like the last one?" asked JT. "Was he or she blown up too?"

"No. And they don't believe there are any terrorist connections. Apparently they are not sure how he died. The FBI looked into it because of his position, and their ME concluded he suffered a fatal stroke. But then the US Marshall Service got an anonymous tip that Doctor Toshi Lee's death was intentional, and they passed this on to the Feebs who were on the scene initially. Because some of the participants in the program Lee was managing, and thus some of the potential suspects, are FBI, their Director wanted to have another agency handle it. The CIA volunteered to step up to the plate, even though one of the participants is theirs. But the DARPA Director said no way because of some sort of 'program implications.' I'm not sure what that means, but she got the DNI to agree with her so it went up a level. Long story short, we got it. Thus, there is some very strong White House interest in this so you better not screw it up." He tried to say the last part with a straight face, but couldn't.

"Wow. I guess we're off to the Land of Oz again, Nita. So you have some contact information for us, Boss?"

"Start with the new Director of DARPA, a Robin Dornan." Hanson glanced at his watch. "I believe she's expecting you in about an hour. And I sent a crew over to the Washington Field Office this morning to get all the data collected from Doctor Lee's office." He handed Juanita the short file he had on the incident.

"I don't suppose they got a hit off the phone call to the Marshalls," commented JT.

Hanson smirked and shook his head. "Throw away cell," he said.

"Dealing with those DARPA folks sure would be easier if we could get Arati involved," offered JT. Actually it was more of a plea. Doctor Arati Jabornae was a recent addition to the Team and JT and Juanita had worked with her on the last case. At that time she was a Naval Research Laboratory scientist who had been working with the DARPA manager taken out by the IED. She had a PhD in information technology from Caltech, and was instrumental in working the data transfer ramifications of the last case. She had a delightful personality, and JT and Juanita where in awe of her technical expertise.

"Why don't you talk with the DARPA Director first, and assess whether or not you'll need Arati's expertise. If you think so, you'll have to convince Miss Dornan to give up another clearance billet. Arati is working some other things for me, but I think she'll be done soon—you know her—and available. Let me know what you think after your visit this afternoon."

"Okay, we're on it Boss," said Juanita as they got up to leave.

Hanson called to JT as he and Juanita cleared the door to his office, "Talk to Bill about Bravo Unit picking up your case work, JT. I think this is going to be a full time gig for you two."

As JT gathered up his things he asked Juanita, "You want me to drive this time?"

"No, I'll drive, but how about if we take a company car?"

"Sure. Let's roll. That way I can call Bill and review this file," he said as he grabbed it out of Juanita's hand. "Oh, can we stop by Dunkin' Donuts on the way?" JT pleaded, now feeling just a bit sheepish.

Juanita just rolled her eyes.

CHAPTER FOUR

Thursday, Virginia Square, Virginia

Although it was already an hour into the three hour Washington area "rush hour", DARPA was still only about twenty-five minutes from Fusion Team Headquarters in Crystal City. Juanita decided to drive up Route 110 which scooted by the Pentagon and Arlington Cemetery. She loved the Washington area, and never tired of seeing its monuments and other historical places. Forty minutes later, after a coffee stop, they arrived at the DARPA building, which was located just west of the sprawling FDIC complex on North Fairfax Drive and across the street from the Virginia Square Metro stop. Juanita pulled right up to the no parking zone the agency was using as a security buffer since 9-11. The Arlington County police officer on duty there drove up to say something to them, but didn't even get out of his car when Juanita badged him. The building beside them was a ten story, fake brown stone, marble and black glass monolith, with tiered stories that reminded one of some unfinished Lego construction. There were similar looking buildings in the vicinity, and, although there were no signs indicating the agency within, this one stood out because of the Arlington County police cars sitting on the street and the three armed guards stationed around the various entrances. Hiding in plain sight was apparently not a DARPA attribute.

At the Visitor Center on the first floor they were greeted by the man who ran it, Lou Callas. "Agents Dunkirk and Singletary, how can I help you today?" Callas had been a help on their last case by providing them unfettered access to the place, and some G2 on several DARPA employees. He was a pleasant man with a rounded, slightly pudgy face and thin but very dark hair. "I hope you're here under better circumstances than the last few times." He regretted the statement almost before it was out of his mouth: these guys didn't pay social calls.

JT rescued him with, "Just nailing down a few details from the last case, Lou. The Director is expecting us. You wouldn't happen to have our badges from the last time, would you?"

"Actually, I do. Hang on a second." Callas went back into his office, reached into a box in the top drawer of his desk and retrieved the badges. He inserted them into a small silver box on the counter, pushed a few buttons and then handed them to JT. "You're good to go. I believe you remember the way?" he asked smiling.

"Oh yeah. Thanks, Lou."

As they stepped onto the elevator, JT pushed the button for the ninth floor. After the door closed, and they were alone, Juanita queried, "Think these are monitored?"

JT shook his head.

Then she continued, "He doesn't know what happened. And if he doesn't, then it isn't common DARPA knowledge. I wonder what this former program manager was into."

"I guess we're about to find out," commented JT.

"Do you want to do the opposite sex interview this time, Partner?" JT believed in having the person of the opposite sex interview the subject, while the other team member took notes. He felt this procedure resulted in a more professional interview, and made the subjects more comfortable when they called back later, and could talk to a person of the same sex about things they "forgot" or didn't feel right mentioning at the time. Juanita didn't think it made a difference.

JT gave her his silly question look as he badged them into the Director's suite. Inside he noticed the same plush surroundings they had encountered before—deep pile rugs, beautiful art work, first class modular furniture and sleek looking

PC monitors. But the receptionist was not the young lady he had met before. Now a very professional looking young man guarded the Wizard's door. Juanita introduced herself and JT.

"Yes Ma'am, the Director has been expecting you. I'll let her know you are here," the gentleman responded as he picked up his phone. "Yes, Ma'am," they heard him say again, and then to them, "You can go right in."

On the way over JT had quickly read what he could find about the new director on the web: doctorate from Rensselaer in bio-technology, former DARPA program manager, a stint at MITRE, and the erstwhile owner of a start-up company she founded and sold to one of the big boys. Although he saw her picture on several of those sites, she really looked much better in person, quite attractive in fact. Her red hair and emerald eyes were complemented by the olive green suit coat and the minimal amount of makeup she was wearing.

"Good afternoon," the Director said as she got up and came out from behind her desk, her matching green skirt revealing what JT thought must be runner's legs. She met them half way across the room and introduced herself with a strong handshake. Motioning them to some easy chairs in front of her desk, she took one across from them and started in almost before they were seated.

"As you are aware, I'm going to read you in on the MENSA program Doctor Lee was managing for us. MENSA stands for *Mental Enhancement by Neuronal Spatial Alignment*—this is not an adequate description, but Lee liked the acronym. It is an exceptional program and has enormous potential for the military and the intelligence agencies. Thus it has been carried out under the highest security levels. So you will need to sign a nondisclosure statement like the one you did for the *Tomfoolery* program. Put briefly, we believe we are on a track to enhance an individual's overall mental capacity, and to allow them to perform what have been referred to as psychic phenomena, most importantly mind reading. There are other, almost as astounding, possibilities such as the abatement of neurodegenerative disorders, telekinesis, and the planting of hypnotic suggestions without hypnosis. You can imagine the advantage this would be for its practitioners. While all the program participants were chosen with great care, and while I do not believe anyone of them is at such an advanced level that he or she could have caused Doctor Lee's stroke, the question remains." The Director paused at this point.

"Now tell us what you really think," said JT.

The Director's eyebrows rose just a tad and her eyes darted between JT and Juanita, but then a faint smile crept across her face and she explained, "I do come on a little strong at times, but this program has so much potential and some very interested stake holders. I'm glad to have someone with no ax to grind look into this unfortunate incident objectively. I hope the bad apples you uncovered in your prior visits won't taint that."

"We also met a lot of very dedicated people working here and have great respect for the organization" offered JT. "Nevertheless, we'll suspect everyone and do a very thorough job. We see four possibilities here: it was indeed a natural death; it was a robbery that went south; it was a murder for personal reasons, premeditated or not; or it was premeditated and political or business related. By the latter I mean perpetrated by someone who didn't want the program to succeed for whatever reason. Who in your opinion would fit into the last category?"

"First of all, while this is a setback, I believe we can find another program manager to see this through. I can see where likely candidates for the job would be suspects, but I have not given much thought to his replacement at this point. I will have to meet with some people to develop a slate of possible successors to Doctor Lee. Second, while I can't be specific, I have thought about this and a number of ideas presented themselves: a jealous colleague, although I don't believe Lee was encroaching upon anyone's territory; one of the program participants who wants to discredit the work for who knows what reason; some members of the religious right who believe we are treading on sacred ground that we should not; the polygraph people, both practitioners and manufacturers, who may see this as putting them out of business; those who believe the program will lead to a massive government invasion of individual privacy; and finally, our enemies—criminals, terrorists, spies."

"Well that narrows it down," JT scoffed. "How about anyone who thinks they could fool a polygraph but not a trained mind reader, or someone who thinks this might free up more money for his program?" he asked.

Dornan nodded and said, "The former is an interesting possibility I hadn't thought of, but as for the latter, there is considerable research money available for anyone with a good idea. Here at DARPA, no one but myself and the MENSA program participants and staff know of the program. It does not appear on our organization charts or in any of our other literature other than by a nondescript place holder for budget purposes. Besides, anyone who was aware of the program would surely realize it would be continued. I see you have given this some thought as well."

"Actually the first possibility popped into my head when you mentioned polygraphs. I presumed the second one was not a viable reason now, just like it wasn't last year under Director Townsend, but thought I'd make sure it still held under the new management. Besides the program participants and staff, is there anyone else we should talk to—Doctor Lee's boss, other DARPA program managers?" asked JT.

The Director shook her head. "Lee reported directly to me. For general information on the program you can talk to Ronald

Cummings at Johns Hopkins who led the candidate search, and to Sam Donaldson at the CTF. I don't think Lee actually knew any of the other program managers here. You could talk to Harry Lisbon over at the Smithsonian, who was on the search committee as well, and knew Lee as I understand it. Charles can give you their contact information," she said nodding toward the ex-marine stationed outside her office. "Besides those individuals, only a few people above my pay grade are read in on the program, but they know less about it than I do." Dornan got up and walked back over to her desk, found a piece of paper in one of her desk drawers and wrote something on it. She stepped up to Juanita and handed the paper to her. "This is a copy of the MENSA clearance list, which I will update with your names. I wrote the address for the CTF on there as well. I can't emphasize enough the necessity for secrecy on this."

"Which brings me to my last question: can I bring one of our analysts in on this? Arati would greatly speed up the progress of our inquiry."

"Arati Jabornae?" asked Dornan.

JT nodded.

"Wasn't she cleared for the *Tomfoolery* program?"

Another nod from JT.

"Then, yes of course. I know of her since she has worked on some of our programs. Make that three more names on the list. Just make sure she comes by to sign the nondisclosure statement. By the way, she's not with NRL anymore?"

"No Ma'am. She works for us now. Is there anything else we need to know?"

Robin Dornan thought for a few seconds and then slowly shook her head.

"Thank you very much for your help. We'll do the best we can and keep you informed, Miss Dornan."

"I'm sure we'll be seeing each other again, so let's go with Robin, okay JT, Juanita?" she asked as she looked expectantly at each of them.

"You bet. And thanks again," JT said as the partners got up to leave. They stopped by Charles' desk on the way out for Cummings' and Lisbon's phone numbers and to sign the required statement.

As they were descending to the first floor Juanita looked at JT and asked, "So what do you think of her?"

"Oh, I'm impressed. She's friendly enough, but seems more like a manager than a scientist: a lot like ole TT in that respect I guess. Except TT seemed to be forcing it—there was something not quite authentic about him." TT was Tommy Townsend, the former director of the agency. "I've known a lot of good managers and I guess I'm just not as impressed with them as I am with the scientific types, like Arati."

"Yeah, but Robin's apparently both, and I guess that's a rare combination," commented Juanita. "And you're right, she does seem genuinely friendly. How come you didn't have a joke for her?" JT usually broke the ice with new acquaintances by regaling them with a corny joke.

"Damn. She came on so strong I guess I forgot. I'll just have to treat her to that next time."

"Yeah, right."

They returned their badges to one of the guys in the Visitor Control Center and headed out to the car. "It's getting late so how about if we head on back to the office and run these guys before we go out to this program location tomorrow?"

"Good idea," said JT. "Maybe I can get home in time for a late dinner tonight."

CHAPTER FIVE

Thursday, Washington, DC

Frances Kalani looked up in response to the rap on her door. "Can you step in here for a minute, Frannie?" her boss asked as he stuck his head through the now partially opened door. Kalani's office was very well appointed but not cluttered, and adjacent to her boss' with a connecting door between them. It was fairly late in the day and he had no more appointments, so he was probably just looking for an end of the day recap as was his wont.

"On the way, Sir," she responded. She grabbed her briefing book, rounded her desk, and walked toward the door her visitor had just peered into. She noticed the carpet starting to fray on the path leading from her office to his, and no wonder: she traveled it dozens of times each day. She stepped into his spacious office and asked, "What's on your mind, Mr. President?"

Frances (Frannie) Kalani was arguably the second most powerful person in the world. As Chief of Staff for President Walter Simmons, she was asked for and gave counsel everyday on the major issues facing the country. While the President did not always implement her suggestions, which was the way she always couched her input to him, he seldom made any significant decision without consulting her. Her deep reservoir of facts, legendary political instincts and sharp intellect awed even the not-often-impressed Commander-in-Chief, and had served her well in her rise up the ladder from Mayor of Honolulu, to Hawaiian Congresswoman, to campaign manager for the Governor from Hawaii. Her creamy brown complexion, dark hair and oriental eyes suggested her Hawaiian ancestry, and her graceful movements did not belie that image. Although her long hours had only slightly affected her exercise routine, she nonetheless felt she had put on a few extra pounds. Her odd meal schedule and contents did not help in this regard either. Since her only family was her multi-generation Hawaiian parents, a brother, assorted aunts and uncles and cousins, most of who were still back on the Big Island, she really had no social life.

Simmons motioned her into the chair she usually occupied when they chatted, and took his regular seat across from her. She could tell he was in a pensive mood, as he spent some time getting comfortable, and knew enough to wait for him to start the conversation. "I've been thinking about this DARPA situation, and I'm disturbed at the thought of Doctor Lee's death coming about from other than natural causes. Then there's the whole problem of a replacement for him. How did we latch on to him in the first place?"

Walter Simmons looked like he hailed from Minnesota, which he did, with his tall frame, Nordic nose, high forehead, strong jaw, wavy dark blonde hair and light hazel eyes. Although he obviously wasn't a Hawaiian native, he sounded and acted like one since his parents moved there before he started school. Thus he lived there most of his life, except for a few years in Minnesota and California, and grew up loving the people, their culture, and the beautiful scenery. He was nonetheless a political animal and somehow managed to integrate the instincts of a politician with the graciousness of his Island friends and family. He received his JD from the University of Hawaii at Manoa, with a specialization in international relations, and had a natural talent for tact. He started out as an attorney for a San Francisco firm, moved back to Hawaii where he opened his own firm catering to big businesses, parlayed that into a Congressional seat, and finally ran for and won the governorship. His only complaint about his erstwhile constituents was that they seemed at times too accommodating, too willing to accept policies more suited to their continental counterparts. But he knew from experience those policies usually ended up with an Island flavor, and were assimilated just like the thousands and thousands of immigrants over the years.

"If I recall, Sir, he latched on to us. He approached DARPA with his ideas and convinced them to fund his research." She waited for Simmons' response, but when he didn't come back right away she offered, "I believe I have a perfect fit for the job."

"Really?" he queried as his eyes brightened. "And who might that be?"

"Doctor Stanley Rodriguez is the neurosurgeon over at Johns Hopkins who served on the selection committee for the program candidates. As such, he is already cleared for the program. We have some mutual acquaintances and he is very highly thought of by them and the University. In addition to his practice, he also teaches neuroscience there, and is very well versed in the program requirements."

"As usual you are a step ahead of me."

"You've had other things on your mind, Sir. Should I enquire as to his interest?"

"You didn't already?" the Commander-in-Chief asked smiling.

"Not without discussing it with you first, Mr. President," she replied demurely.

Simmons nodded and then started to say something, but was preempted by Kalani before she realized he was going to speak.

"Of course the DARPA Director will need to agree, but I'm sure that won't be a problem. As to your other comment, I must tell you I took it upon myself to have the FBI and the CIA stand down on this case, and asked the Fusion Team at DHS to look into it."

"Really?" Simmons said with just a hint of querulousness.

"Yes, Sir. There are two FBI personnel participating in the program, as well as one CIA employee. The FBI had no problem with not accepting the case under the, as they put it, 'unlikely homicide circumstances," but the CIA actually volunteered their help."

"Their interest?"

"If successful, the program could supplant their polygraphy program, and I was concerned about the not-invented-here syndrome, and their tendency not to be as forthcoming as I'm sure DHS will be."

Simmons closed his eyes, bent his head over and began rubbing his forehead. Kalani knew he was either considering what she had just said or wondering how to begin the next topic, or more likely both. After fifteen seconds he looked up and said, "Okay, but I want you to keep on top of this and keep me informed."

"Absolutely, Mr. President. Do you want the daily recap now, Sir?"

"Sure, sock it to me," he said playfully as he sat back in his chair. And she did, referring to her notes, and writing down the questions she didn't have a ready answer for and the directions he gave her. About forty-five minutes later he finished with, "That's enough for today I guess. You should probably contact Doctor Rodriguez tonight if it's not too late."

She responded with "Directly, Sir," as she gathered her notes and briefing book. "Have a good evening, Mr. President."

"You too, Frannie, and thanks, as usual. Goodnight."

Kalani walked back to her office and closed the door to the Oval Office behind her. *Well this worked out well for us*, she thought as she reached for her cell phone. She dialed Rodriguez' office number although she didn't expect to get an answer, and then tried his cell. He answered on the fourth ring, "Frances, my Dear, what's up?"

"Well, Stan, I'm afraid I've got some bad news."

"You know I can't read you over the phone, so I guess you'll just have to tell me. You do sound concerned."

"It really is bad, Stan: Doctor Lee is dead."

"Toshi is gone? How on earth did that happen?"

"It's a long story I'd prefer to tell in person. I do have to mention I suggested to the President you become the new PM and he agreed. Told me to contact you tonight and tender the offer. If you agree I'll call Robin Dornan. I'm sure she'll want you onboard as soon as possible. . . . Are you there, Stan?"

"Wow. That's a lot to process. I've got the Hospital and the University to think about. . . . It is an ideal opportunity, though. Hang on a second while I look at tomorrow's schedule. . . . Would you be available for lunch, say twelve-thirty? We could meet at Union Station."

Kalani consulted her schedule and responded, "The Boss has a couple of hours personal time blocked out then, so yes, that sounds doable. I'll meet you in the big lobby then, Stan. Goodnight, and pleasant dreams."

"Goodnight, Frances." *This is going to be a short night*, Rodriguez thought.

CHAPTER SIX

Friday, Northern Virginia

"Carmen, I have to leave a little early today. Can you get Andy off to the bus stop today?" Andy was JT's just-turned-seven-year-old son, and Carmen Sanchez was JT's live-in housekeeper, babysitter, and chief cook and bottle washer. She was the sister-in-law of one of the sergeants JT used to work for when he was with the Fairfax County Police Department. Carmen survived a flash flood in her native Panama which claimed all the rest of her family except her younger stateside sister, who then managed to get her into the country on a work visa. Carmen had just recently earned her citizenship, and had intended to look for another job when that event occurred, but enjoyed working with Andy too much to leave. Although almost fifty-five, she was still attractive, standing a couple of inches over five feet, weighing only slightly more than she should, with dark brown eyes and long, ebony hair she usually wore in two braids.

"No problem, Señor JT. Do you want me to pick him up after his karate lesson today?" This was Andy's second year in the program and he had already earned his green belt.

"Yes, please—unless I call and let you know otherwise. Thanks. I gotta shove off now." He gave Andy a hug. "Have a good day, Little Buddy."

JT lived in a medium-sized, four bedroom, two and half bath split level in the Daventry area of Springfield. With the exception of only a few locations, notably parts of the Route 1 corridor, Fairfax County was a great place to live: there was very little serious crime; the public schools were perennially rated first or second in the nation; it had great public transportation (which JT seldom used) with two airports, one right in Crystal City; the local hospitals were first class and the EMT response of the Fire Department was excellent; the federal government made the place nearly recession proof; and the property taxes were reasonable. JT grew up here attending Lee High school before going into the Air Force, and moved back here after his tour. His mom and dad, one married sister and one divorced brother still lived here. His younger brother had married a Pittsburgh woman and moved there last year. Although his Pittsburgh brother worked for the US Department of the Interior, he could work at home and came back to DC for two weeks each quarter so JT still got to see him often. Growing up here and spending six years with the Fairfax County Police made JT feel like an integral part of the community, and he couldn't imagine living anywhere else.

Since Juanita was renting an older apartment in the Kenwood section of Annandale, just south of Gallows Road, JT agreed to swing by and pick her up on their way to Chantilly. He was looking forward to learning more about this program, and had to admit he was skeptical about the DARPA Director's claims. He pulled his Toyota Highlander into a visitor's spot in front of her apartment next to her PT Cruiser. Juanita bounded out the door making JT think he was late. He looked at his watch and grinned—just her normal exuberance he decided.

"Hey, you know, I'm really looking forward to this. This program sounds rather exciting. Do you think it's all they've cracked it up to be?"

Even though she grew up in the states and English was her first language, Juanita also spoke excellent Spanish, complements of her mother's tutoring. JT often thought she sounded like a native Californian, guessing that was influenced by her being an Air Force brat. "I hope so, Amiga. Think about all the possibilities here."

"Yeah, both good and bad. I mean did you ever read any of those *Babylon V* novels?"

"Are you kidding? Did you forget about my Dad? He has all those TV episodes on VHS tapes and I know he's watched them several times. In fact, my brother gave Mom and Dad a Netflix subscription so now he's watching them on his computer. But I know what you're leading up to—PSI Cops."

JT was referring to a fictional police force, called the Psi Corps—a feature of the old science fiction TV show *Babylon V*. In this particular future scenario, any person with telepathy or any other psychic ability was required to either join the Corps or submit to drug treatments to suppress their abilities. Although seldom chosen, life-time imprisonment was a third possibility. The Corps was universally maligned, much like the internal affairs departments of police forces are portrayed in most detective novels and crime shows. Corps members were given a numerical rating, based on the strength of their psychic abilities. Alfred Bester, named for a famous science fiction author and played by Walter Koenig of earlier Star Trek fame, was one of the top Psi cops at level twelve. Telepaths not of the Corps were rogues and hunted down—an interesting side plot in the series.

"Well unless everyone has psychic abilities it could lead to that," said Juanita. "These people could really be a help to the government. I don't think the show did them justice—they were just made bad guys to make the show more interesting. Think about it, they could let you know if someone was planning terrorist activities, or had robbed a bank, or committed *any* felony. . . ."

JT interrupted with, "Or not included income on their tax return, or fudged a resume, or watered their grass on odd *and* even days, or looked at their neighbor's wife with lust in their hearts?"

"I'm not saying it would be perfect. There'd have to be some ground rules laid down for the transition period until everyone had the capability."

"You really are a science fiction fan aren't you, Juanita? But I think you hit it on the head with your ground rules comment: we'd have to figure out how people with the 'gift' get treated by the government. Can we force them to use it for only good purposes? How do we tell which individuals have it? Do we look at every successful person and say, 'Hey, you must be psychic—how else could you have made such a success of your life?' Why should people want to help out? After all this is just a natural attribute like brains, or athletic ability, or good looks, or common sense, or whatever else people use to get ahead in life."

"This is different. It lets them get into the minds of their neighbors, and potentially steal their ideas. In any competitive activity half the battle is figuring out what your opponents are going to do. Think of the advantage they'd have in business deals, or playing poker, or taking a test."

"I think you just made my point for me."

"Damn. I think I did."

"Let's keep an open mind—or maybe not—while we talk to these people."

"Now you *are* creeping me out, Amigo."

"I'm just saying we need to stay objective and try to see what's really going on here. We don't have to solve these problems. That's way above our pay grade. We just need to figure out whether or not a murder has been committed, who did it, and if this program has been compromised. And we'll do that like we always do: with good police work."

"Yeah, you're right," Juanita conceded.

"Not to change the subject, but I've got to tell you what Andy said last night. As I was putting him to bed he asks, 'Dada, Osama Bin-Laden is a really bad man isn't he?' I agreed with him not knowing where this was going. Then, 'He's so bad he's going to hell isn't he?' I agreed again. "I'll bet if the devil ever got married he'd be his best man wouldn't he?' I couldn't disagree with that either."

"Where do they get that kind of stuff?" Juanita chuckled.

"School I guess. Isn't that the building over there?"

"It's the right address. The entrance is on the west side and it looks like there is parking over there."

JT pulled up into one of the open spaces and shut the engine off. They gathered their stuff and JT locked the car. The two of them headed toward the secure door located on the far right side of the building. The sign over the door read *Chantilly Acoustical Engineering*. JT pointed to his head and mouthed the words "open mind." Juanita punched him in the arm and reached for the buzzer. The door buzzed open before she pushed it and they gave each other an eerie look.

CHAPTER SEVEN

Friday, Washington, DC

Frances Kalani arrived first and stood for several minutes with her head tilted upward admiring the ceiling of the great hall. She enjoyed visiting the monuments and the museums in the city, and usually spent more time admiring the buildings than their contents.

"Good afternoon," Stan Rodriguez said as he walked up behind her.

"And the same to you," she said without turning around. "I love this place. In addition to being awesome, it reminds me of better, less tense times, or something like that," she sighed.

"I can tell. Let's get some lunch and talk."

They decided on Uno's and walked to the upper level. They both ordered salads, while Rodriguez got some iced tea and Kalani opted for a diet coke. Rodriguez was tall for a Latino, standing just a hair short of six even, and was somewhat heavy set with a full head of dark black hair including a moderate sized mustache. His smooth countenance was marred only slightly by the nearly faded three inch scar down his right cheek and the cleft chin. He was dressed in a brown suit with a white shirt but no tie, and she had a dark pants suit on. They made quite an attractive couple.

When their drinks arrived they ordered and then Rodriguez began with, "So what happened to Toshi?"

Kalani related what she knew and expressed some concern over the circumstances of Doctor Lee's death. She explained that the possibility of a program participant being advanced enough to effect what appeared to be a stroke, was not completely beyond the realm of possibility.

"I'm sure you are right, Frances. I have not kept up with the program progress since I discussed it with Toshi about four months ago, although he was very optimistic at that point. I've had minimal contact with him since then—just some quick phone calls here and there. We've both been so busy."

"I'm sure you would have no problem catching up, and you know we really need someone in there to keep track of things. I've just not had the time to keep up either."

"Nor would we expect you to. I was, after all, on the selection committee, and it is right up my alley. Unfortunately, I've had an unexpected increase in the number of surgeries these last few months, such that I had to cut down to one class and curtail some of my research. Actually, now is not a bad time given the latter two, and the fact that I have only two surgeries scheduled for the rest of this month. I believe I could spend the next couple of days down here getting acquainted and up to speed, work as need be at each place for the next week or so, and then establish a fairly regular schedule between here and Hopkins."

"Oh, thank you, Stan, thank you. I thought I'd have to be more convincing. You probably should have gotten the job in the first place, but I know the timing was not right for that."

"So are we talking about one of those IPA positions like Toshi occupied?"

"I talked to Robin Dornan and she not only agreed to offer you the position, but also said she'd handle it however you wanted. The IPA would be the most beneficial for you we think, unless you actually wanted to become a permanent government employee."

"No. The IPA is best I think. What about salary?"

"You and Miss Dornan can work that out, but you need to make sure you have whatever time is required for you to keep your practice alive. No pun intended."

Rodriguez smiled. "I'm sure we can come to some mutually agreeable position," he said.

"We greased this as much as we could, which took a phone call from the Boss to the SecDef by the way, so all you need to do is settle on the salary and then sign the IPA agreement. Sam Donaldson out at the facility will fax it up to Hopkins, and they only need to sign it and fax it back. I know you'll need to talk to them first. If they give you any push back, have them call the White House. Sam will take care of everything else."

"Since I'm down here, can I go out there this afternoon and get started?"

"Absolutely. I just need to call Robin at DARPA to tell her you accepted so she can get this ball rolling." She dialed her cell phone and asked to speak to the Director when the phone was answered. Shortly into the conversation she gave Rodriguez a thumbs up, and finished the call just as their lunch arrived. "Robin is delighted and wanted to know when you could start."

"I gather that was when you said immediately?"

Kalani nodded. "She said that would be her next call and they would be expecting you. You should probably call her from there, and then I guess you need to call Maureen and Sid soon and let them know. I suspect they'll want to call a meeting to discuss the ramifications of this development."

"Indeed," replied Rodriguez. They spent the next forty-five minutes eating and discussing the program in general, some mutual friends, and the President's chances in the next election.

When they were finished Rodriguez offered, "Can I give you a ride back to the office?"

"That would be great—I'll check that out with my detail."

"I forgot all about that." Rodriguez looked around. "Those guys are good—I don't see anyone who doesn't look like he or she belongs here. You sure it will be okay?"

"I suspect they'll just follow us back in the SUV we came in. Then we could discuss a few things I'd rather not talk about when they're within earshot."

While Rodriguez paid the bill, Kalani spoke to one of the agents, and then the two of them headed out to Rodriguez's car followed by three Secret Service agents.

CHAPTER EIGHT

Friday, Chantilly, Virginia

Sam Donaldson was expecting the two agents and had been monitoring the feed from the inconspicuous video camera located in the sign above the entrance. Once inside, JT and Juanita found themselves on a narrow landing at the top of a staircase leading down one flight to another landing. The lower area opened to the left, and from where they stood, they could see nothing but sterile gray walls and stairs and a black wrought iron railing. When they reached the bottom Donaldson was there to greet them.

"Welcome to the CTF. I hope you'll excuse me if I ask for some ID," he said.

"I'd be disappointed if you didn't," responded JT. He and Juanita showed their creds to Donaldson, who examined them carefully before handing them back.

He then shook both their hands and introduced himself. "I'm Sam Donaldson, no relation, and I'm temporarily in charge until they get another program manager." Donaldson was casually dressed in some cotton slacks, a short sleeve shirt and loafers. His short dark hair and prominent nose supporting horn rim glasses above his clean shaven, narrow face shouted "nerd" to JT and Juanita.

JT and Juanita introduced themselves, even though Donaldson had just seen their badges.

"We're going down the corridor here to a conference room where I'll be glad to answer all your questions." With that said, Donaldson turned around and headed down a hallway which resembled one you might find in a nice suburban house: an oriental rug partially covered a light hardwood floor, and the walls were a beige color and hung with pictures of various nature scenes and Washington, DC monuments. As they passed by each

46

of the doors, Donaldson indicated what was in that particular room, and JT made a mental note of where Doctor Lee's office was.

As they neared the conference room JT asked, "Did you hear the one about the two old men?"

Donaldson shook his head while Juanita rolled her eyes.

"Two old men are sitting in the park, and one looks at the other and asks, 'How's your wife doing?'

"The other says, 'I think she's dead.'

"The first old man says, 'What do you mean by you "think" she's dead?'

"The other says, 'Well, the sex is the same, but the dishes are starting to pile up.'"

To change the subject quickly Juanita asked, "How long has this place been here?"

"I really don't know," replied Donaldson still shaking his head and smirking. "I know it isn't a new building, but not that old I think. Given that our four stories are below ground, I suspect it was built for some government program which was subsequently cancelled, so who knows. We moved in about a year and a half ago when they christened this the Cybernetics Technology Facility, and I think they took about six months before that outfitting it for us. They did an excellent job too," Donaldson said as he ushered them into a medium size conference room with a twelve by four foot table surrounded by straight back but comfortably cushioned chairs on castors.

JT figured the plasma screen TV adorning the far wall was at least a seventy-two inch model. Several pieces of electronic equipment were housed in cabinets below the screen, and a mobile electronic white board stood in the one corner, while a podium sat in the other. Art work was hung on the right side wall as you entered from the hallway, and the left side wall contained a long white board. The recessed side lighting, which was on when they entered, provided a cozy atmosphere.

"You've seen what's on this floor, or what we call the living level," Donaldson continued. "Level two is the dorm; the third level contains the lab, Doctor Lee's suite, and some admin space; and the fourth level is the recreation area. Make yourselves comfortable," he said pointing to the chairs. "Can I get you something to drink before we start?"

They both declined.

"We were hoping to get an overall briefing on the program, as we've not been privy to very much documentation on it," Juanita explained. "Then perhaps we could get into particulars on the personnel and what happened Wednesday night. Sound okay by you?"

Donaldson nodded and removed some folders from a small valise he had been carrying and handed them to Juanita. "That's a copy of each of the staffs' and the participants' personnel records. They include information on each person's background, and the participants' scores on the various admission tests, and their progress in the program up to a week ago. Dr. Lee kept notes on each subject on his iPad and usually recorded them in their file each weekend, usually on Friday. Your guys were here yesterday and took damn near everything from his office and our files. I did get to copy the personnel files before they left. I assume they are making copies of everything else like I asked, since we really need to have it all back for the new program manager. You can go back to his office later and look around. Any questions before I start the briefing?"

"What kind of files are we talking about?" asked Juanita.

"Paper-wise, there were files on the selection process, the personnel records I just gave you, monthly status reports and reference material, and probably some other stuff I can't remember. Electronic-wise, there are probably copies of a lot of the same stuff, communications between the staff and participants, Toshi's notes, relevant material we downloaded from various libraries and journals, the results of various protocols we tried, and again, other stuff I'm sure I have forgotten about. Will you need the hard drives from the participants themselves? Your guys took Toshi's and all the DARPA ones, but didn't take or even ask about the personal ones."

Juanita looked over at JT and then back at Donaldson and then nodded. "If they let us have them I promise to get them back by Monday; otherwise we'll have to get a warrant and take them Monday. Can you tell us how the participants were selected?" she asked. "Sounds like they went through a lot of tests to get here."

"To begin with, it was mostly a record-based selection Johns Hopkins did for us. They used CIA and FBI personnel files, university transcripts, applications for Mensa and some other high IQ organizations, mental institute and other hospital admissions, and . . . I guess that's it. We narrowed the group of forty-seven original candidates down to fifteen finalists. They underwent a three week battery of tests that included physical, medical, mental and psychological exams, and who knows how many interviews. All of them showed some indication of psychic ability as well. Ten were accepted into the program. Eight of them are still here, as are all the staff, except for Doctor Lee of course."

"Two left the program?" asked Juanita.

"Julie Stafford had a death in the family and she left after three months, and Bill Willis was diagnosed with pancreatic cancer after he'd been here almost a year."

"So these were both self-initiated, with no hard feelings?"

"Correct. If anything, they felt remorse at having to leave. Julie did call us and ask if she could get back in the program. We told her she'd be the first one selected if and when we start with another group. Unfortunately Bill died a few months ago."

"I have a general idea of what Mensa is: a group of people with high IQs, but what does it stand for?"

"*Their* name is comprised of two Latin words: *mens*, which means 'mind'; and *mensa* which means 'table,' indicating that it is a round-table society of minds. The program we are working on *here* is also called MENSA, but this being the DoD it's an acronym standing for 'Mental Enhancement by Neuronal Spatial Alignment.' In general the theory is the more neurons you have lined up and connected, the smarter you are, and the more control you have over your mental capacities. What we have determined so far is that some chemicals help this process, as does some radiation. Your DNA makeup is what gets you started in the right direction, and then the above factors take over. There are some other factors we are looking at as well, and we believe once you get far enough along in this process, you can 'think' yourself smarter."

Donaldson took a pause here, and looked at JT and Juanita who were staring back at him in what he read as disbelief. "You're not buying the program, huh?"

"Oh, I am," said Juanita who looked over at JT and then back to Donaldson. "We are. It's just incredible to think this ESP stuff is actually real. I mean, I thought it was always a trick, you know, reading facial tics and other body language like in the program *Lie To Me*, doing background checks on your subjects, using logic, stuff like that."

"I've been a skeptic myself," piped in JT, "but I'm keeping an open mind. Is this the only program of this kind DARPA is working on? "

"Of this specific kind, yes. There are some other prominent neuroscience-related projects they are currently working on including Accelerated Learning, Neurotechnology for

Intelligence Analysts, and Cognitive Technology Threat Warning System. But those are done at other places, mostly at contractor sites. I can briefly describe those if you'd like."

"No, thanks. We had better stay on point here. So what can your participants actually do?" asked Juanita.

"So far they can communicate telepathically to some extent, move objects with telekinesis, albeit lightweight, near-by ones, and consistently manipulate their polygraph tests."

"Well that latter one has some implications, doesn't it?" Juanita offered enthusiastically. "So what do you actually do here every day?"

"We test the participants almost daily and try out different protocols. One of the first things we did with the participants was subject them to transcranial direct current stimulation, or tDCS: a small nine volt battery would run a couple of milliamps through their brains allowing them to concentrate better by lessening the influence of extraneous thoughts. Fairly soon they learned to do this themselves without the current. They then graduated to electromagnetic stimulation that strengthens the neuronal links between their brain cells. We measure the effects of all these different approaches, keep their minds as active as we can by playing what we call mind-expanding games, do research on other similar programs: anything we can think of to figure out how this all works and how we can improve it. As I mentioned before, Doctor Lee kept very good notes and you will learn a lot from them. He was always very explicit about what he was trying to learn, why he thought the method he was using was the right one, and what the results were. I've never worked with anyone so thorough and articulate."

Juanita changed the pace with, "Can you think of any reason why someone would want to get rid of Doctor Lee? Professional reasons, personal ones, even nonsensical ones?"

"I can't think of anyone specifically who would gain from his death, including me—I do not have the credentials and will not be chosen as his successor. I don't believe he had any professional peers who were jealous or anything like that. He was somewhat private, so I can't speak to his personal life, although I know he had a daughter, Chrissie. She lives up north, in Jersey I think. His wife passed away when Chrissie was a young teenager, and he never remarried. He has had a couple of girlfriends though, but he was married to his work and didn't have much of a social life we knew of. It was like we were his family. He treated us all with great respect and dignity—the staff, the participants, the few visitors we've had. I've actually thought about this, and it may sound paranoid, but I think if he was murdered than there may be enemy spies involved."

"What are you basing that on?" asked Juanita.

"Nothing definitive: this program has such potential for learning your enemies' secrets that they'd have to be interested even to the point of sabotage if they couldn't steal it from us."

"You mentioned visitors. Would they be listed on the clearance sheet?"

"We do have a visitor log listing everybody who has been here, but most of them were tradesmen and vendors and were escorted at all times, and had no idea what we do here. Official visitors most often had the appropriate tickets and are also listed on the clearance sheet. One or two people did come by just to check out the facility."

"Can you get us a copy of the log?

Donaldson nodded.

"And now the obligatory investigative question is," began Juanita, "where were you between eight-fifteen and eleven-fifteen Wednesday night?"

"Part of the time I was talking to Jorge on the phone to check on some supplies we had ordered, say nine to nine-thirty, and then I was talking with Tom Parsons about an equipment problem until maybe ten-twenty or so, and the rest of the time I was in my room tending to my emails and reading. Jorge and Tom are both on staff here."

"Do you think one of the participants is advanced enough to 'think' Lee into a stroke?"

"I don't know, but I think it very unlikely. No one is that advanced that I am aware of. And besides, Doctor Lee was exceptionally intelligent. Perhaps you'll get a better feeling for that from his notes."

"I presume Doctor Lee didn't spend all his time here—did he have a place somewhere?"

"Yes, he had a townhouse in Fairfax. The address is in his file."

"What can you tell us about the security around here," Juanita inquired, "and what about the surveillance tapes for Wednesday night, did our guys get those?"

"Well, in addition to the surveillance tapes, which we keep for a week, we have a card-key entry system. You need to have a card with a magnetic strip and you have to enter a PIN number to get in and out. Of course people can tailgate but we try to enforce everyone keying in and out. We keep that data for a week also. And yes, your guys got all of it."

"That's a pretty narrow entrance way we came in," Juanita commented. "How do you get large items in here?"

"Just around the corner from the entrance you came in is the service elevator. It's one that's even with the parking lot surface when not open. The metal doors open up and the elevator comes to the surface. It goes all the way down to the fourth level. To answer your next question, we are confident it was not utilized on the night in question. It is also covered by the cameras, it's quite noisy when in use, and it can only be activated from the inside."

"Is there anything else you want to tell us before we look at Lee's office and his suite?"

Donaldson shook his head. "I do have a question though. I presumed you'd want to talk to everybody so I told them that would likely take place over the next few days. But can I tell the couple of folks who want to go home or someplace else for the weekend that it's okay?"

"Sure," said Juanita. "We'll catch whoever's here today and tomorrow, and the rest on Monday. Here's my card," she said as she handed one to him.

JT followed suit.

"Call us anytime with anything you think is relevant. Can you show us where he was found and then to his office and room?"

"How about a little tour? As you know his office is on this level, and his suite is on level three on the way, and we can end up down in the gym on level four. Then you should be able to navigate on your own."

"Sounds good. Let's get to it."

By the end of the day they had toured the whole facility and interviewed three of the eight program participants and two of the six staff. One of the latter was Donaldson, and the other Jorge Delgado, a combination guard, receptionist and handy man. They had also made appointments with the remaining staff and participants for the next day and Monday. All the participants were amenable to having their personal hard drives copied along with their other electronic information. JT knew the FBI had secured Lee's car, but decided to call the office and find out whether or not the FBI or the FCPD had secured Lee's townhouse. Upon learning they hadn't, he got a Fusion Team contingent to go over and do that.

As they pulled into traffic and headed east along Route 50, JT smiled and asked, "So what do you think about these guys, did you feel like they were getting into your head?"

"I admit I thought about it, but no, not really. They seemed fairly normal to me—smart maybe, but regular folks. Of course we didn't ask them to do anything special. What do you think?"

"In general I agree, but I sorta felt like they were hiding something."

"All of them?"

"Yeah, but then I feel like that about all the people we interview. Probably just my normal cop sense. Apparently we have a lot of material to review."

"Yeah. I think it's going to be a short weekend for us Amigo," she remarked.

CHAPTER NINE

Sunday, Washington, DC

Even though it wasn't as impressive as the standard European version, The Castle stood out among the surrounding buildings due to its distinctive design. It favored the Gothic Revival style with Romanesque motifs, and the façade was built with red sandstone from Seneca, Maryland, in contrast to the marble and granite used for most of the other major buildings in Washington. The Smithsonian Castle, comprised of a central section, two extensions, and two wings, had four towers containing occupiable space, and five smaller towers which were primarily decorative. Serving as the headquarters building for the Smithsonian Institute, the main visitor center was located there, contained interactive displays and maps, and housed most of the administrative offices for the Institute. Unknown to most of its thousands of yearly visitors, was a good size room on the fourth floor of the east wing. The huge wooden table in the center of this room contained sixteen built-in teleconferencing stations, each with its own padded, wooden, swivel conference chair. This was where The Galactic Society held its periodic meetings.

"This emergency meeting of the Board of Directors of The Galactic Society is hereby called to order," intoned Sidney Ellis, their Chairman of the Board. The Galactic Society was an independent, educational, not-for-profit organization dedicated to providing for the long term development and preservation of mankind. In particular they concentrated on the enhancement of human mental capability, neurocybernetics, planetary defense against near-Earth objects, and the development of a galactic transportation system. The former two were not part of their public persona, but were just as important if not more so than the latter two. In fact, they considered mental improvement and the associated neurocybernetics were facilitators, and maybe even prerequisites for the accomplishment of the other two missions.

Ellis' commanding presence made him the perfect spokesperson for the organization: he was a tall, well-built black man with graying hair that belied his tender age of forty, and a veteran of the International Space Station. He had a PhD in astronautical engineering, was very articulate and had, probably, the second most well developed mind of the group—all the members of which had an off scale IQ, not to mention their considerable paranormal abilities.

"All members are present, with Professor Fields, Senator Hemingway and Chief of Staff Kalani connected via secure teleconference," he continued, "so all conversations will be oral. As I am sure you have heard by now, we are here to discuss the unfortunate demise of Doctor Toshi Lee, a candidate for membership who was the manager of the DARPA MENSA program. Before we start however," Ellis said as he looked over at Harry Lisbon, "I want to offer my deepest condolences on the loss of your good friend. I know you two were close."

Lisbon acknowledged everyone's feelings and thanked them for their concern. "I know it's probably not germane, but I do feel like it was partially my fault he's gone since I got him the job. I hope it didn't have anything to do with his passing. I will let everyone know about his arrangements as soon as they are firmed up."

"Thanks, Harry," said Ellis. He then turned toward Charlie Moffett. "Members of the Fusion Team of the Department of Homeland Security are investigating the circumstances of Toshi's death. Charlie, could you bring us up to date on that?"

Charlie Moffett was the Assistant Secretary for Counterterrorism for DHS, and as such the Fusion Team was under his purview. Moffett was an ex-astronaut as well, but grayer than Ellis and a veteran of the older Skylab program. His active life and strict exercise regimen enabled him to keep his slim but nonetheless solid physique. "The death was originally considered to be a result of natural causes, but the US Marshall Service got an anonymous tip claiming it was actually a homicide. They passed this on to the FBI who opted out of the investigation because several program participants are FBI employees. The CIA requested they be given the case to investigate, but really have no jurisdiction, and one of the participants is a CIA employee. Furthermore, the DARPA Director thought the Agency had an ax to grind, given their predilection for polygraphs, and got the DNI to agree with her." The DNI, or Director of National Intelligence, was the nation's top intelligence officer, with all the secret three letter organizations reporting to him, at least in theory.

Moffett nodded at Kalani's screen and continued, "The DNI raised the issue with the Chief of Staff who referred the matter to yours truly. I have two of my best agents on the case. They had both been cleared at that level by virtue of solving another case, involving, coincidentally I hope, a murder of another DARPA program manager. They have already interviewed many of the members and staff, and will complete the process tomorrow. Depending on the conduct of their investigation, I believe we may have to consider reading them into the Society."

Some eyebrows were raised at that statement, and eyes darted back and forth, but no sentiments were voiced.

After a pregnant pause Director Shobha Vipashyin asked, "Is there an autopsy report?" Vipashyin was a Supreme Court Justice and the twin sister of another Board member.

"The preliminary autopsy report suggested a stroke, and a subsequent one was inconclusive. Our ME will do a more thorough examination tomorrow," replied Moffett.

"Are there any more questions for Charlie?" the Chairman asked.

"What about a replacement for Doctor Lee?" asked Shobha Vipashyin's sister Deepika, a Senior VP for The MITRE Corporation. Except for the fact that Deepika kept her hair strait as opposed to her sister's braided style, it was difficult to tell them apart. To the keen observer, however, she was slightly slimmer with a light yellowish-brown circular birth mark just visible above her collar on the left side of her neck. Although both ladies had definite Indian features, their British mother endowed them with a light cocoa complexion.

"I believe I'll let Doctor Rodriguez answer that. Stan . . ."

"I am pleased to announce, thanks to a recommendation from Frances, the President has asked me to assume the leadership of the DARPA MENSA program, and I have accepted." The group all gave him various signs of approval as the hear-hears, bravos and other tidings of support echoed throughout the room. "I start tomorrow and believe I can be up to speed within a week or two."

"Stan, we haven't had an update on Doctor Lee's work in several weeks, are you able at this time to recap his latest findings?" asked Director Christopher Ling. Ling, the CEO of Aston Aerospace, a company heavily involved with the development of NASA's new heavy lift launch vehicle and the crew compartment, also used to work for the space agency as an astronaut. He had a doctorate in computer science and was the first Chinese-American to command a Shuttle mission. He also performed a record-breaking ten hour EVA on his last mission.

"I did summarize his last report, which he submitted three weeks ago and I'm sure you all have read, so I won't go into it," Stan replied. "I could not immediately locate his subsequent notes, but from talking to Sam Donaldson over at the CTF, I know six of the eight participants have shown improvement over the last period, and Toshi was very encouraged by the latest DNA analysis. It appears he finally hit upon a chemical regimen/low dose radiation treatment that effects a just noticeable difference on the neuronal alignment, with no deleterious side effects. Ladies and gentlemen, we are on the way, thanks to Toshi's brilliance and persistence. We are going to miss him."

"Any questions for Stan?" asked the Chairman.

Maureen Fields asked, "Stan, do you plan on changing any of Toshi's protocols?" Fields was a professor of astrophysics at MIT. Although disabled and confined to a wheel chair, she taught several courses in theoretical physics, and was one of the foremost proponents of string theory and the multiverse. A stunning black woman, she would no doubt be gracing the covers of several popular magazines if she were a more outgoing person. Although not at all the candidate one would consider for the next Einstein, this was nonetheless the sobriquet most often used in describing her. "I presume you have already considered the addition of ten new program participants, including yourself?"

"The thought had crossed my mind, Maureen, but to tell you the truth I don't know yet. Toshi and I had different opinions on the most efficacious approaches, but as you have heard, he was successful to an extent. I will need some time to go over all his findings, talk with the participants, and review the extant literature. I may want to involve a colleague as a sounding board," he said as he looked around the room. "I will keep this group apprised of any significant changes in proposed avenues of research or practical applications."

"And will you have the time to devote to this?" Fields queried.

"I recently cut down to only one class, and will curtail some of my research that doesn't dovetail with the MENSA program. I do have two surgeries scheduled this month, and will probably have one or two over each of the next few months.

These activities should take up no more than two days each week, and in fact some of the research I can accomplish at the CTF."

"Anything else for Stan?" asked Ellis. Seeing there wasn't, he turned toward the Chief of Staff and offered, "Frances, I know you nominated Stan and presume you have no objections to his new position or proposed direction."

Kalani nodded.

"Nancy, do you agree with the proceedings so far?"

Nancy Hemingway was the senator from Ohio and chairperson of the SAC, or Senate Appropriations Committee. She was in her late forties, medium height, and presented a very attractive figure in her Versace pants suit. One would not expect that she was also an ex-astronaut. As everyone turned their attention to her on their monitor, she pushed a wisp of her light brown hair away from her face and nodded enthusiastically. "I agree wholeheartedly."

"I sense agreement from all those present," continued Ellis. "Maureen, we await only your approval."

"I agree, Sid, but would very much like an interim report from Stan as soon as he feels ready."

As all eyes turned toward Rodriguez he gave a thumbs up and a big smile.

"Are there other items we should cover now and thereby cancel our next regular meeting?" asked Fields. "Chris, would you want to give us an update on the revived Constellation program?"

"Actually I would prefer to wait until the next regular meeting or perhaps the one after that. I believe I'll be able to make a more definitive report then, as a number of things are coming to fruition over the next week or so."

Fields nodded.

"Since we have some time, I thought maybe we could get Dee's report on our recruitment initiative. Everyone okay with that?" Ellis asked.

Up to this point the Society's Board membership had grown only by personal invitation to individuals those already in the group had met, mostly coincidentally. They had offered membership to Toshi Lee, but of course that wouldn't happen now. Since the group currently consisted of only ten members, four of who were the former astronauts who founded the organization, and since achieving their lofty goals would undoubtedly require a larger group of advocates, Doctor Deepika Vipashyin had volunteered to draft a recruitment program for the organization.

Hearing no disagreement, Ellis continued, "Dee, the floor is yours."

"Thanks, Sid. I have to admit I decided to look at, and perhaps borrow, the methodology used by the DARPA MENSA selection committee. It was somewhat helpful, but it seems as though they started with the premise that the ESP capabilities were paramount, and took a back door route to get there. Given their goals that is understandable. From our perspective however, the intellectual capabilities are more important, but having ESP capabilities may be indicative of the former, especially given the way our group has formed so far. Thus I looked at the extant high IQ societies, and decided we should concentrate on five of them: Mensa, Intertel, Chromium, The Triple Nine Society, and the Mega Society. Two of these, Intertel and The Triple Nine Society, already have representation on our Board. I will describe all five briefly, and provide my reasons for using them in particular.

"Mensa is the largest and best known. They have, as do all the ones I have chosen, administered admission tests, and have in effect done some of our work for us. While Mensa's 98th percentile requirement is not exceptionally selective, many of their members are beyond that, and for quantity reasons alone they should be included. In particular I like their special interest groups and their service programs for obvious reasons.

"Intertel has a libertarian flavor and a 99th percentile entrance requirement. From reading dozens of their members' blogs, I believe they contain a subgroup of like-minded people, and they do have a significant international presence. And we have a current member among us and therefore an in with the organization.

"The Chromium Society, which was not considered by the MENSA selection committee, is a group of high IQ musicians. They have a 99th percentile requirement as well. In reviewing the backgrounds of our current members, I noticed all but one of us have exhibited substantial musical abilities. The MENSA program has determined this ability to be indicative of potential ESP proclivities. Although they have less than 100 members, I believe one or more of them will qualify for membership in our group.

"The Triple Nine Society gets their name from their admission requirement: test scores in the 99.9th percentile. I was very impressed with the insights evident in many of their journal articles. They seem to be the most open to innovation and evolution. They have over 1000 members internationally, and, as with Intertel, we have a current member among us.

"And the last of the high IQ groups is The Mega Society, which has less than fifty members, several of them very well known. Using the 99.9999th percentile as an entrance requirement, they like to call them themselves the one-in-a-million club. I simply believe we cannot afford to overlook these individuals."

"Excellent, Dee. I have reviewed these groups myself and agree completely with your assessment," Fields said excitedly.

Praise from the MIT professor was high praise indeed. "I'm sorry I interrupted you, please continue."

"Finally, I would add the DARPA MENSA group themselves, and any additional astronauts our esteemed erstwhile astros might recommend. As to the procedure for incorporating them into the organization, I would use the same plan that got us to where we are today—personal involvement. I know this is labor intensive, but I will ask for help from the current 'insiders' of which we have three, counting Stan for the DARPA group. Depending upon Stan's recommendation and the Board's approval, we may get some of the DARPA MENSA participants to join us, and then have them work with the four high IQ groups that they have covered. This would result in some overlap, and leave only one of the selected groups without representation—Chromium. I was hoping to get a volunteer to join them. And I will try to vet as many as I can remotely from these groups. But unless we get a personal read from each candidate, we cannot be sure of their mental stability nor of their intentions."

"I agree with Maureen, Dee, excellent plan," stated Ellis. "I had intended to apply for Chromium membership, and will do so forthwith." He quickly surveyed the room for any questioning looks, and seeing none concluded, "Very well then. If there is nothing further, we stand adjourned until a week from Wednesday."

CHAPTER TEN

Monday, Crystal City, Virginia

In contrast to the buildings across the river in The District, which were limited to 130 feet in height, except for a fourteen block section of Pennsylvania Avenue in northwest DC, the buildings on the Virginia side of the Potomac were not so constrained. Juanita was reminded of this every time she took the elevator to her office on the seventeenth floor of the Crystal City headquarters for the Fusion Team: the view was outstanding and included not only good portions of DC but also Reagan National Airport. She and JT had just gotten back from the CTF where they had interviewed the rest of the MENSA participants and staff. "So how many suspects do we have now?" Juanita asked.

"I just started a list," replied JT. "Help me flesh it out." He walked over to a small whiteboard and began writing. "We have eight program participants and two dropouts; and there were five folks who were strong candidates but didn't make the cut. Sam said only the final fifteen were apprised of the general program goals, and only the ten selected were actually cleared; however, the other thirty-two who were considered, but not in the final cut, were obviously pretty smart and must have had a good idea of what was going on; however, we'll discount them for the time being. There were six staff members at the CTF, and five folks on the selection committee at Johns Hopkins. Not counting Doctor Lee in those groups leaves five and four, respectively."

At this point he had jotted down the following:

Original	Final	Position
47	15/10	program participants
6	5	staff (less Lee)
5	4	selection committee (less Lee)
	24/19	

"So how many people are on the clearance list?" JT asked.

"Let's see. If I take out all the ones who would be on your list," Juanita said slowly as she checked off names on the clearance list, "that leaves another ten: the Director of DARPA; the President and Chief of Staff at the White House; the chairpersons of the Senate and House Intelligence Committees; the Director of National Intelligence; two people at the FBI—the Deputy Director and the head of their polygraphy section; and finally, the same two or similar positions at the CIA. Quite a who's who list if you ask me."

"Yeah, I can just see us getting personal information of some of those dudes. Guess we should start with some of the lesser strata folks and work our way up. So now we have thirty-four suspects. Except for those last ten, are there any we didn't run through our data base yet?" asked JT.

"I've got printouts on everyone but the five candidates who didn't make the final cut. I've requested those and should have 'em by day's end. Where do you want to start?"

Before JT could answer, his cell phone rang. "How interesting," he mused, "the caller ID says DARPA. This is agent Dunkirk," he answered. "Yes, Robin," he said as he reached for his pad and a pen.

As he was scribbling some notes, Juanita's phone rang. They ended their conversations within seconds of each other.

"What did she have for us?" asked Juanita.

"The name and phone number of the new MENSA program manager—it's Doctor Stanley Rodriguez from Johns Hopkins, one of the guys on the selection committee. At least we don't have to add another name to our list. I think we can get what we need from him, and won't have to talk to the other guy on the selection committee, Ron Cummings I think Robin said. By the way, who was on your line?"

"It was Sam Donaldson at the CTF about Lee's iPad. When we got back here last Friday, I checked the stuff our guys brought in from the CTF, and it wasn't there. I called Sam back and left a message asking him to check for it again. I went back this morning and double-checked the CTF material, and then looked for it in what we recovered from Lee's townhouse, and it's not there either. Sam said it's not there anywhere, and he assumed our guys took it. I'm afraid we may have a security issue as well now."

"Only if the thief is not on our clearance list," JT kidded. He then put his elbow on his desk and rested his head in his hand. Juanita knew this was his pensive position and didn't interrupt. After a few minutes JT said, "Call Sam back and ask him if he can estimate the likelihood of anyone making enough sense of Lee's notes to compromise anything. We need to talk to the new PM to learn more about the program, and ask him to do the same thing, maybe after he's been on board a while. We also need to talk to Lee's buddy Harry Lisbon over at the Smithsonian to find out more about Lee's private life, and go through Lee's townhouse to see if there's a personal angle we can pick up on. And there's still the notes and DVDs we have to go through and the background on all our suspects."

"You still didn't answer my earlier question."

"Which was?"

"Where do you want to start?"

JT thought for another minute then offered, "How about if I call Rodriguez and you call Lisbon to check on their availability, and we go from there?"

Juanita nodded, checked her notes and started dialing about the time JT was finished dialing.

After their respective conversations JT said, "Rodriguez begged off for a couple of days: maybe Wednesday. He said he wants to talk to everyone first and review all the program material. Naturally he wants all the CTF stuff back, so I'll have to check and see if we made copies of everything yet. What'd your guy say?"

"He's available now and all evening if we want. Want to hit him now over at the Smithsonian, and save this research for tomorrow?"

"Sounds like a plan, Amiga," JT responded as he grabbed his things. "I'll go check with our guys and see if they can't hustle and get the material back to the CTF, while you go tell Hanson what we're doing, okay?"

Juanita nodded.

"Can you drive this time?"

Another nod.

"Okay then, I'll meet you in the garage."

Once in the car, Juanita's phone rang and she handed it to JT. "It's from the office," he said after looking at the caller ID. "Agent Dunkirk here. . . . Yeah, Doc, we're driving to an interview." JT listened for the next few minutes, shook his head now and again, asked a few questions, and responded with an occasional "I see." When he closed the phone he looked at Juanita and said, "That was interesting. Doc said there was definite evidence of a severe stroke, but that was probably NOT the cause of death."

Juanita's eyes opened wide but she never took them off the road.

After a pregnant pause, when JT was convinced she wasn't going to ask the obvious, he continued: "He was burked."

"Burked? Isn't that where the victim's chest is compressed and his airway is blocked?"

"Yes. Doc said this was the most likely cause, but he could only be eighty percent certain based on a *very* comprehensive autopsy."

"I thought you couldn't tell if a person was burked," said Juanita.

"The Doc did say Lee was asphyxiated, and although it was a massive hemorrhagic stroke, given its location, it was unlikely to cause his breathing problems. And he believes there is some evidence of chest compression, so his conclusion is death by burking."

"Wait a minute, I heard you mention the bar bell. Couldn't all that weight have done it?"

"According to our good Doctor Anderson there is no evidence the weights, per se, had anything to do with it: the 210 pounds he had on the bar, distributed as it would be across his chest, wouldn't have hacked it. A person sitting on top of him however, especially if he was holding the bar as well, would have done the job easily. If the bar had crushed his windpipe he'd have been done in also—but there was no evidence of that."

"So Doctor Lee had a stroke and was burked at the same time?" Juanita asked incredulously.

"He said the stroke could have been simultaneous with the burking, or more likely brought on by it, but they were in very close proximity—he said Lee would not have been able to function with such a severe stroke. He also said, given Lee's health and the apparent lack of damage to his heart, he was surprised the CPR and defib didn't revive him, depending on how soon after it was administered."

"So it would appear we do have a murder—makes our efforts seem more . . . I don't know . . . needed I guess."

"It does. Now we're not just solving some mystery. We are, as they say, speaking for the dead."

"Well aren't you waxing philosophic."

"Speaking of which, don't you have just one philosophy class left for your masters?"

"Yes! And I take that this coming semester, which starts next week by the way. I have my thesis finished and accepted, and so far I'm carrying a three-point-eight GPA. This should put the icing on my next promotion. I'm going places, Amigo. How's your schooling coming?"

Rather than answer her question, he asked her another one: "The only place you can go from here is management, if I know OSI. Do you really want to leave field work behind?"

"I do enjoy it and I know I'll miss it, but I really don't want to do this forever. You do though, don't you?"

"Yeah, I do. I love this job. And being a team leader is about as high as I want to go in management. And so far I really haven't done much supervision. Thank goodness the team pretty much manages itself. To answer your other question, I've only got four classes left before I graduate, and so far I've got a three-point-five. I'm quite sure I won't go on for a master's like you though. I know you're learning a lot. And I'm sure I would, but I don't think it would help my retirement income. Besides, it takes so much time."

"Tell me about it. At least you have a family to go home to."

"Little Andy does make it worthwhile and interesting. Which reminds me, he wants to know when you are coming over for dinner and games again."

"Seeing as how it's a Monday night, and my other three offers fell through, how about tonight?"

"Right. I'll call Carmen and let her know."

When he finished talking to Carmen they were passing the Pentagon.

"I love driving into DC," Juanita said. As they crossed over the 14th Street Bridge she pointed out the Jefferson Memorial and the Tidal Basin, then the DC Wharves and the fish markets, the Bureau of Engraving and Printing, and the hard to miss Washington Monument. As if JT had never seen them before.

JT commented, "Yes, Amiga, I know. I've been to all of them."

"And what was your favorite?"

"I was definitely impressed by the five-hundred-million dollar bank note hanging in the Mint."

"Wow," Juanita said as they turned onto Jefferson Drive. And then she called out, "Castle ahead. Let's see what Doctor Lisbon has to say for himself."

CHAPTER ELEVEN

Monday, Washington, DC

Harry Lisbon occupied a medium sized office on the third floor of the west wing of the Smithsonian Castle. His admin assistant sat just outside her boss' office, and occupied a cubicle made from modular plastic and felt boards which must have come from the low bidder. Her name tag, propped atop the front panel, read "Mary." Her head popped up from behind one of the panels just as JT and Juanita approached. "Hi! Are you the guys from DHS?" she gushed.

Juanita flashed her badge as she replied in the affirmative.

"He's been expecting you. Please just go right in."

Juanita thought it must be nice to have such an enthusiastic assistant, so she thanked her as she and JT rounded the cubicle and approached Lisbon's office. The sign on the door read:

Doctor Harold Lisbon
Undersecretary
for
Finance and Administration

Juanita thought everything in Lisbon's office looked antique, in keeping with the building itself. His desk, chairs and bookcases must have been originals left over from when the building opened in 1881. The only piece of modern looking furniture was the PC monitor on his desk. Even the phone was an older rotary dial model. It was not a corner office, and Juanita noticed the view out the old fashioned sash windows was mostly north, across The Mall and towards several of the Smithsonian museums.

After examining their credentials Lisbon addressed Juanita, "I noticed your interest in my phone. It's a bit of nostalgia since it belonged to my grandfather. Still works fine though." He made sure they were comfortable and asked if he could get them something to drink. They declined so he began, "How can I help you?"

Juanita started off with, "Our purpose here is twofold: we're trying to learn more about Doctor Lee and about his program. We understand you were on the selection committee for the MENSA program with him, and that you two were also schoolmates and friends. In particular we're trying to find a motive for his murder."

"Then it was determined to be a murder?" asked Lisbon.

"Our ME says the likely cause of death was burking."

Lisbon nodded his head as if he had heard of burking before, and at the same time squinted his eyes as if he hadn't, or couldn't figure out why that particular method was used.

Juanita paused, expecting another question, but then continued when none materialized. "So can you think of any reason why anybody would want to harm Doctor Lee?"

"Was anything missing from the CTF, or from Toshi himself?"

"Not that any of the staff have determined." Juanita did not mention that they were unable to find his iPad with his notes for the last week.

"Hmmm. If it wasn't a robbery gone bad, which seems unlikely within the confines of the CTF, then I doubt I can think of a motive. Toshi got along with everyone there and in fact was very well thought of. He wasn't married, but he was seeing someone—Trisha Carpenter—who works for one of the national real estate brokers. I'd say he was going with her for three or four months. Before Trisha he was dating a lady from Verizon by the name of Colleen Foster, if memory serves. They broke up about a year ago, but it was amicable according to Toshi. His wife died about fifteen years ago and he does have a daughter. I met Chrissie a few times years ago, but I feel like I know her well since Toshi always talked about her. I called her over the weekend and she is flying in tomorrow afternoon to take care of things and staying at his place in Fairfax. I know he had a few guys he hung around with at Princeton, but I'm pretty sure he hasn't been back there since he's been working on the program. All told, I doubt anyone had a beef with him."

"How about money problems, either him or his daughter?"

"No. He lived for his work and had a simple life style. Chrissie has a good job, with school loans paid off and doing okay according to Toshi."

"Bad habits?"

"He didn't smoke or drink, never did. Actually he was pretty adamant about how bad they were for you. He didn't sleep around that I know of, and didn't believe in gambling either." Lisbon noticed Juanita shaking her head. "I know, this guy seems too good to be true, and this isn't helping motive wise."

"Well you're half right: he does seem too good to be true, but this does narrow our search for a motive. Anything else about his private life you can think of—drugs, kinky sex . . . anything?" Juanita noticed a reaction and glanced at JT, and could tell he picked up on it as well.

"We need to go up into another room before we continue this," Lisbon said.

With that they all got up, and JT and Juanita followed Lisbon out the door.

As they stepped into the hallway JT asked, "Did you hear the one about Forrest Gump?"

"Er, no," responded Lisbon figuring JT was talking to him, not Juanita.

"Well he dies, goes to Heaven, and is met at the Pearly Gates by Saint Peter himself. However, the gates are closed, and as Forrest approaches the gatekeeper Saint Peter says, 'Well, Forrest, it is certainly good to see you. We have heard a lot about you. I must tell you, though, the place is filling up fast, and we have been administering an entrance examination for everyone. The test is short, but you have to pass it before you can get into Heaven.'

"Forrest responds, 'It sure is good to be here, Saint Peter, Sir. But nobody ever told me about any entrance exam. I sure hope the test ain't too hard. Life was a big enough test as it was.'

"Saint Peter continued, 'Yes, I know, Forrest, but the test is only three questions: first, what two days of the week begin with the letter T; second, how many seconds are there in a year; and third, what is God's first name?'

"Forrest leaves to think the questions over. He returns the next day and sees Saint Peter, who waves him up and asks, 'So Forrest, now that you have had a chance to think the questions over, can you tell me the answers?'

"Forrest replied, 'Well, the first one, which two days in the week begin with the letter "T"? Shucks, that one's easy. Those would be Today and Tomorrow.'

"The Saint's eyes opened wide and he exclaimed, 'Forrest, that is not what I was thinking, but you do have a point, and I guess I did not specify, so I will give you credit for your answer. How about the next one?' asked Saint Peter. 'How many seconds in a year?'

"'Now that one is harder,' replied Forrest, 'but I thunk and thunk about it, and I guess the only answer can be twelve.'

"Astounded, Saint Peter said, 'Twelve? Twelve? Forrest, how in Heaven's name could you come up with twelve seconds in a year?'

"Forrest replied, 'Shucks, there's got to be twelve: January second, February second, March second . . .'

"'Hold it,' interrupts Saint Peter. 'I see where you are going with this, and I see your point, although, once again, not quite what I had in mind, but I will have to give you credit for that answer as well. Let us go on with the third and final question. Can you tell me God's first name?'

"'Sure,' Forrest replied, 'it's Andy.'

"'Andy?' exclaimed an exasperated and frustrated Saint Peter. 'Ok, I can understand how you came up with your answers to the first two questions, but just how in the world did you come up with the name Andy as the first name of God?'

"'Shucks, that was the easiest one of all,' Forrest replied. 'I learnt it from my Sunday school song, Andy walks with me, Andy talks with me, Andy tells me I am his own.' Saint Peter opened the Pearly Gates, and said . . ."

"Run, Forrest, run!" interjects Lisbon. By this time he had led them across to the other side of the building and up one level to a corner office on the fourth floor.

"You heard this before," JT moaned.

"No. It just seemed like a good ending." As he unlocked the door they noticed the sign on it sported only three initials: TGS. It was obviously a conference room, and JT and Juanita took the first two chairs near the door at the end of a long table. Lisbon closed the door, and reached over to a control panel located at eye level just inside the door. He flipped a couple of switches and took a seat next to them.

"This room is a SCIF and I can talk a little more freely in here."

JT looked around and wondered if this room was really a sensitive compartmented information facility, and if so, what it was doing in the Smithsonian.

"To answer your last question the only drug Toshi took, other than prescribed medicine I suppose, was one associated with his work. When I was on assignment for the Institute in Tanzania, I came across some natives who were using what appeared to be hallucinogenic drugs. At first I thought it was ayahuasca, which is supposedly found only in South America. There, they gather ayahuasca from a native vine called caapi which they then mix with the leaves from the psychotria viridis plant. This decoction allows the primary psychoactive compound, DMT, to be orally active. How Native Americans managed to figure that out is a testament to human ingenuity."

Both JT and Juanita nodded in agreement.

"Back to Tanzania: I also noticed the Bon-cha, or tribal elder and spiritual leader, took another substance which appeared to give him psychic abilities: telekinesis and telepathy. If I hadn't seen it with my own eyes while I was stone cold sober I wouldn't have believed it. Turns out the native African plant called iboga can be used to distill a naturally occurring psychoactive substance called ibogaine. Ibogaine itself is known to have anti-addictive properties, but, when mixed with another ingredient they haven't named yet, a substance similar to ayahuasca is created which is not hallucinogenic, but does indeed produce ESP type effects. I brought this to Toshi's attention, and he convinced DARPA to look into its possibilities. Hence the MENSA program was born."

JT couldn't help himself and asked, "So the whole MENSA program is all about juicing people up to give 'em psychic abilities?"

"No. There are a host of factors involved," Lisbon said, only somewhat defensively. "Genetics has a good deal to do with it, so-called brain foods help as do mental exercises, and some other more esoteric factors are involved. Trying to figure out all of this is what the program is about. How successful they've been, and any other program details, you'll have to get from them, as you've reached the extent of my knowledge on the subject."

"So Doctor Lee was taking this drug?" inquired Juanita.

"He told me he was, in carefully monitored minute doses, so he could have firsthand knowledge of what he was requiring of his participants. I believe he started taking it shortly after he started with the program about a year and a half ago. He said that, as of about two weeks ago, he had noticed no adverse effects, and indeed it seemed to enhance his abilities."

"So he was psychic too?"

"Yes. But that is not known by anyone but me and Robin Dornan at DARPA. The participants were not aware of this, nor were the staff or anyone else on the selection committee. And we would prefer to keep it that way, not to mention the classification issue. I presumed that would not be a problem, which is why I offered it up in the spirit of full disclosure." He looked expectantly at his two interviewers.

"Not unless it's relevant to closing this case, and only then to the minimum number of people necessary. Fair enough?" asked Juanita.

Lisbon nodded.

"I do have to ask if you think the drug had anything to do with his death."

"I think that highly unlikely. Did it come up in the tox screen?"

"Our ME did not mention any drugs."

"In the small doses he was taking it I doubt it would show, unless you really knew what to look for, and even then I'm not sure."

"So is there anything else you'd like to add that might help us in this case?"

"Have you talked to the new program manager yet?" Lisbon asked.

"No. We only found out who he was earlier today. You know him from the selection committee, right?"

"Yes. And we're both members of The Galactic Society. This is their meeting room we are using."

"That's the 'TGS' on the door?" guessed Juanita.

Lisbon nodded.

"And what do they do?"

"We are an educational organization dedicated to the preservation of mankind. We feel the principle way to accomplish that is to develop a planetary defense against near-Earth objects and a galactic transportation system."

"Isn't that NASA's job?" asked Juanita.

"Yes, especially the former; however, they are also working on a more near-term space transportation system. But we can help a great deal in several ways: bypass some of the politics so often involved in any government agency and get them pointed in the right direction; assist with scientific personnel searches; lobby on their behalf; and even supplement their funding in certain critical areas."

"I have one last question to ask: where were you last Wednesday about nine in the evening?"

"I was here with two of my staff preparing for an audit we suffered through last Friday."

"I guess I'm through then. JT, do you have anything to add?"

"No, I'm good. Thanks, Doc. Here are our cards," he said as both he and Juanita handed one to Lisbon. "Please call us if you think of anything."

"I do have a question of a more personal nature if you don't mind," said Juanita. Sensing he didn't, she continued, "So you got 'bumped up' to this undersecretary position? Isn't that a real letdown from playing out in the field?"

"That's actually two questions and the answers are yes and no. It's really more of an honorary position, although I do have to sign off on a lot of administrivia. Thank goodness I have a great staff here. I have raised a lot of money for the Institute, probably because a few of those field trips you mentioned were quite successful, and fund raising continues to be one of my main functions. As to your second question, I still get to do some field trips," he finished with a smile.

"Oh, I almost forgot," said JT. "Did anyone contact Lee's girlfriend?"

"Chrissie said she called Trisha shortly after the FBI called her."

"Okay, thanks."

They said their goodbyes again and headed back to the car where Juanita commented, "This case just keeps getting weirder and weirder: burking, psychedelic drugs, intergalactic transportation, secret psychics. And tell me, didn't you get a funny feeling when he finished your joke back there? Think maybe he was reading your mind?"

"Come on. He probably just heard it before. And it's a natural ending for the joke if you've seen the movie. Besides he's not one of the guinea pigs over at the CTF."

"Those sound like rationalizations to me, Partner. He may not be a program participant, but he is involved. He was on the selection committee and best friends with the program manager. And, by his own admission, is the person who got him started on this program. What have we gotten ourselves into, Amigo?"

"This *is* going to be an interesting case, Nita. No doubt about it. Speaking of which, we need to check out Toshi's townhouse ourselves tomorrow morning, and get it released so his daughter can stay there. I know the FBI already took care of

Lee's car, so she should be able to drive that back if she wants to. How about we head back to the shop now so I can pick up my car, and then we head on home to dinner?"

"Let's do it," she said as she headed south over the Fourteenth Street Bridge.

CHAPTER TWELVE

Tuesday, Fairfax, Virginia

As Juanita turned onto Government Center Parkway from Waples Mill Road she remarked, "There's certainly no lack of fancy *shoppes* here—trendy place." But JT paid her no mind. Shortly after heading north on Ridge Top Road she turned onto Abner Lane and started checking addresses. When she pulled up in the driveway she asked, "Did our guys do anything besides seal the place off?" The place she was referring to was Toshi Lee's home away from the office. It was just west of Fairfax City in an area called Charleston Square. She could tell it was a fair-sized brick townhouse, probably three bedrooms, with a nice little front yard and a one car garage, and wondered why a bachelor needed such a big place where he spent only weekends.

"Oh yeah. Hence the four boxes of stuff labeled 'Lee, Toshi, Case #1747L' sitting beside my desk."

Juanita nodded. "And we're here because . . ." She was startled by the presence of someone standing right beside her car door, and turned to find a cherubic face staring at her.

As she rolled down her window JT said, "Juanita, meet Melissa Barnes, search agent extraordinaire."

"Hey, Melissa. Don't mind me if I look a little surprised, but JT didn't mention we'd have company."

"Yes, I know. It's a little thing we do. Hi, good looking," she said as JT stepped out of the car and she went around to meet him. "How are ya?"

They met at the back of the car and shared a quick hug. Barnes was a Fairfax County police officer who specialized in search warrants. Her smooth, round face, sparkling brown eyes and short, pleasingly plump figure made Juanita think of a Christmas elf, albeit a pretty one with long brown hair. Her FCPD uniform tended to ruin the effect though. She certainly seemed easy going and, according to JT, she was very good at her job. Barnes worked for JT's old sergeant, now Lieutenant Reynolds, who was noted for his ability to elicit interagency cooperation, and thus often let her gain experience on federal cases. The fact that Reynolds and JT went back a ways didn't hurt either.

"Sweet Melissa, how's Loo-ten-ant Dan treating you?"

Barnes laughed. "Ever since you called him that at his promotion party he's never lived it down. We're always putting little Forrest Gump reminders all over the office, and he's always going around taking them down. Last week we left a box of chocolates on his desk with little messages under each piece."

"That's too funny," chuckled JT.

"So tell me, what do we have here?" the ace search executer asked.

As he ascended the steps and unlocked the front door JT gave her an unclassified overview of the case. "I'm just hoping this guy took his work home with him, even though most of what he did was classified, and maybe our guys missed it. He was really brilliant so I wouldn't put it past him. We're looking for notes or any other case related data. Of course we checked the PC he kept here and his work computers, phone records, and all his financials, but we're hoping for something more that he maybe wouldn't have put in plain sight. Juanita and I will just wander around checking out the place while you do your thing."

"You got it," Barnes said as she started checking everything out.

"This does *not* remind me of your typical bachelor pad," stated Juanita after quickly surveying the first floor rooms. "There is only a bare minimum of furniture, but everything is so neat and ordered. This place must have come furnished—there's not even a TV in the living room, if you can call it such with only a couch, two chairs and two end tables with lamps."

"Kinda like your place," JT offered.

"No it's not," Juanita retorted. "At least I have a TV and some books and magazines in my living room. I'm going upstairs," she huffed declaring victory as JT fell in behind her.

They didn't find things much different in the upper floor rooms. One was used as a bedroom, another for storage, and the third as an office. The latter contained a large, gray metal desk that smacked of government surplus, bookshelves, and hookups for internet access on the wall with the window. Another desk, apparently used as a work area as it was filled with drawing instruments and paper and reference works, was against a second wall, along with several bookcases stacked neatly with more reference works. Two lateral filing cabinets and a closet decorated the third wall. Located on the wall with the door were another lateral cabinet and a bookcase. They poked around in everything, but found nothing out of the ordinary. There were no pictures on the walls, but JT remembered one of the guys who cleared the place mentioning that several charts were tacked up here and there in the office. There was no TV up here either, even in the bedroom, but then a lot of people don't watch TV in bed. The DHS guys also mentioned that the only media they found, besides about 350 jazz CDs, were apparently work related. JT figured Lee must have used his computer to listen to the CDs, or perhaps his car player, as he had no other player in the house. JT made a mental note to have the team check out all the CDs to make sure they were as advertised on the outside, and likewise with all the books. In Lee's bathroom cabinet they found the normal toiletries and linens, and his bedroom closet and chest of drawers contained the usual household items and clothing.

Barnes was coming up the stairs, so they decided to go back down to stay out of her way. In the kitchen they found one small wooden table, four chairs, and some small kitchen appliances and an AM/FM clock radio on the counters. JT made another note to ask his guys if they had thoroughly checked out the radio. In the cabinets were a minimum of dishes, glasses and cutlery, along with a few canned foods and dry goods, including coffee. The freezer contained ice cubes and a pint of ice cream, and the refrigerator had remnants of a fairly decent assortment of fruits and vegetables and cheeses, along with two bottles of blue cheese dressing, a half filled two liter bottle of Diet Rite Pure Zero cola, and some low fat Half and Half. JT noticed a few decanters of various colored liquids which could have been anything from orange juice to lemonade, or perhaps some vitamin drinks—or perhaps some of the stuff Lisbon had mentioned. JT decided to start writing the notes down. Apparently Lee was a healthy eater at home, and they found no evidence he had ordered in. According to his credit card receipts, he usually ate out once a weekend in the medium to high scale restaurants, often with someone. When questioned by JT and Juanita, the staff at the CTF had mentioned Lee's good eating habits. As they poked around the garage they found only a few tools and partially filled trash and recycling bins. He was pretty sure his guys had gone through the little bit of trash stuffed in there, but he made another note to verify that back at the office.

"I realize this guy only lived here on the weekends, but this place is really sparse. Didn't he have a place up in Jersey?" asked Juanita.

"Still does," responded JT, "at least according to the data I was reading on him over the weekend. Not renting it out or anything, though. Guess he figured this was only a temporary gig."

"Hey, I'm sorry I wasn't there this past weekend looking over all Lee's stuff with you."

"You don't need to apologize to me, Nita. Family comes first, and it was your dad who went into the hospital. I'm just glad everything turned out okay." Juanita's father was admitted after complaining of chest pains, but luckily it turned out to be nothing more than some serious indigestion.

"Hey guys! Come on up here," came a shout from the upper floor.

"Oh, oh, I like the sounds of that," cried JT as he headed up the stairs followed closely by Juanita. "Sweet Melissa, what do you have for me?" crooned JT.

"This molding above the window felt a little irregular so I checked it out. Looks like your guy carved out a little niche in it and the wall behind it, and covered it with another thin piece of wood to conceal it: not that you could see it anyway unless you climbed up on the desk here. I flipped out the piece on top and look what I found—" she said as she waved a plastic bag in the air, "a sixty-four gig flash drive smaller than a Bic lighter. Bet you could store some data on this sucker. I'm sure I didn't mess up any prints on it, and I'd be real surprised if it wasn't your guy. Anybody who went to that much trouble had to have some secrets to hide. I've got a few more places to check out, but I think this is the mother lode."

Barnes spent another thirty minutes checking out the last of the upstairs before she headed for the garage, which she always saved for last. She said she usually found the best stuff hidden there. After another forty minutes she called it quits and told JT, "By the way, as usual I didn't check out all the books and CDs—figured your guys had already done that."

"Melissa, Babe, I'm gonna make sure you get another letter in your file for this one," said JT.

"Don't worry about it. Lieutenant Dan doesn't mind and neither do I."

"Well I'm doing it anyway because it doesn't hurt and may actually help," promised JT. Tell the Lieutenant hi for me and thanks a bunch, Melissa," JT said as she gathered her stuff and headed out the door. And then to Juanita, "I think we can leave this place to Chrissie now. Let's head on back to the farm to see what's on this little gem."

"Maybe we could stop for lunch. We passed by some nice restaurants on the way here."

"Did looking in his fridge make you hungry?" asked JT.

"No, you know me, I'm always hungry," Juanita said as she backed out onto the street.

CHAPTER THIRTEEN

Tuesday, Crystal City, Virginia

Back in the office JT and Juanita took the flash drive down to the forensics lab. "Hey, Sam, got a minute?" asked JT. Sam Kenilworth, the resident geek, looked up from his monitor and greeted the pair with a nod. He had on a Hawaiian shirt and cargo shorts and would have worn flip-flops if the boss didn't give him a dirty look the first time he did. "We were hoping you could get this thing open and let us know what's on it," JT said as he handed Sam the bag with the drive in it. "After you check it for prints," he chided.

"I got a rush job for the Boss," Sam replied. "But if you leave it I can get to it in about twenty or thirty minutes. I can also let you know what we found on the hard drives we got from the CTF people."

"Great. Can you buzz us upstairs when you're ready?"

Sam shook his head, said "You got it," and went back to his monitor.

"Might as well get back to our lists," JT conceded as he and Juanita headed back upstairs.

"Who do you want to look at first?" she asked.

"How about you start with the CTF staff and the two program dropouts, and I take the eight program participants," offered JT.

"Sure, sounds like a plan. Of course you think the killer is one of the participants, don't you?"

"The odds are it's one of them and I'm the lead, right?"

"I know, RHIP. Okay, I'm on it." Juanita gathered up the personnel records on the staff they got from Sam Donaldson, and the criminal and other record runs on them her guys had completed. Half way through compiling her two lists she realized she was missing an important piece of data, so she looked up and asked, "By the way, did Doc give us a TOD yet?"

"Yeah," replied JT. "Nine-fifteen give or take fifteen minutes, and he was fairly confident about that."

"Okay," she said as she continued to work up her list. An hour later it looked like this:

DAPRA MENSA Program Staff

Name	Employer	Position	Criminal record	Other	Educ/ origin	Alibi/ motive
Delgado, Jorge	Shurcor	Guard, recep, etc.	Traffic tickets	Married, 2 kids,	CC/ local	Yes (absent)/ money
Donaldson, Sam	DARPA, GS-15	Asst. PM, librarian	none	Married, Triple Nine Society	MBA/ local	Iffy/ takeover
Farthington, George	Shurcor	Maint, cook	Domestic dropped	Divorced, no alimony	HS/ local	No (absent)/ money
Parsons, Tom	Johns Hopkins loaner	Lab asst.	none	Single, some school debt	PhD/ Balt	Iffy/??
Pullman, Robert	DARPA, GS-13	Techie, records	none	Single, gambling	BS/ local	No (absent)/ money

Ex-MENSA Program Participants

Name	Employer	Position	Criminal record	Other	Educ/ origin	Alibi/ motive
Stafford, Julie	DOI, GS-14	Financial analyst	none	Single, left due to death in family	BS/ Boston	No/ program reentry
Willis, Bill	Self-employed	Stock-broker	Traffic tickets, DUI	Married, 3 kids, left due to cancer, MENSA	MBA/ NYC	Yes/??

89

She would not have arranged the tables like this herself, but from past experience knew this was how JT would do it, and thought they may as well be consistent. She figured JT would take longer with his list, so opted to review the information she had on the suspects one more time to see if anything else relevant to the case popped up. After another forty-five minutes of review she hadn't added anything else to her matrix, but had thought twice about her weak potential motives, deciding ultimately to leave them in. When she looked over at JT she saw he had done likewise with his first eight suspects, and was apparently at a stopping point.

"Before we swap lists, what's with this Shurcor company?" Juanita asked.

"It's a manpower shop that specializes in supplying people with top secret and above security clearances. I think it stands for 'Specialized Human Resources Corporation.' DoD uses them to get already cleared people on board in a hurry, but as a contractor. You'll notice a lot of the participants were detailed from their parent agencies, just as you were from OSI to DHS, but some of them were civilians. If their parent company wouldn't agree to keep them on the books, or they didn't have one like Krumski, then they could work for this company and not go through all the hassle of being hired by the government."

"Okay, got it. So what's yours look like?" she asked as they swapped lists. After reviewing her list for a few minutes JT asked, "So does anything pop out at you on this thing?"

"Not really. I don't see any strong motives. I think the two drop outs are nonstarters, Willis for obvious reasons. Perhaps Stafford offing him to stop the program and allowing her to get back in sooner than the next group would work, but I'm not buying that. Although she had no alibi as such, I've got no indication she left Boston at that time. If I know DARPA, Donaldson was not a likely candidate to take over the program and he had to know that. And Lee being done in for money by any of these guys just doesn't ring true: not with the access to his room that they apparently all had. Farthington had a domestic violence beef his wife dropped, but he seems pretty straight now, and he did get the clearance. Time wise, Farthington and Pullman have no alibi, but of course they were not in the building at the time as best we can tell. Neither was Delgado and he has a good alibi. He was at home, which was verified by neighbors, and remembers talking to Donaldson about nine-fifteen or so but is not sure of the exact time. Because of the TV show his wife was watching, he knows it was between nine and nine-thirty. Donaldson and Parsons were in the building, but would have had to act really fast to pull it off, unless they were in it together. I'm afraid I don't see any candidates here unless there is something personal we haven't hit upon."

"Makes sense," agreed JT. "As far as my list goes we have Pennington, Simmons and Thompson claiming they were watching a movie together from eight-forty-five to ten-thirty. The problem I have with that is the theater room is on the same level as the gym, and it would have been very easy for one of them to slip out unnoticed for the few minutes required to do the deed. Brosard was on the phone with his boss part of the time, but not enough I think to eliminate him. The others don't have an alibi for the time frame Doc gave us, and of course none of this considers any help from the outside."

JT's list looked like this:

DARPA MENSA Participants

Name	Employer	Position	Rap sheet	Other data	Educa-tion	Alibi, motive
Brosard William (Bill)	CIA loaner	Psionics research-er	Traffic tickets	Single, Mega Society, gambles	PhD/ local	Partial/ $$, prof
Cutler Paul	SYRAE loaner	Systems Analyst	none	Divorced, alimony, MENSA, womanizer, twin	MS/ Colorado Springs	No/ $$
Krumski Ralph	Shurcor (was self-employed on sabbatical)	Psychia-trist	DUI, traffic tickets	Divorced, 2 kids, TNS, no alimony, gambles, wealthy	MD/ Atlanta	No/ prof
Pacquin Thomas (Tommy)	FBI detailee	Polyg-rapher	none	Married, no kids	MS/ Quantico	No/ dscvd body, prof
Pennington Gayle	Library of Congress detailee	Archivist	none	Single, Intertel, credit debt	MA/ local	Yes/ $$
Rydell Sharon	Shurcor (was Fairfax Gen Hosp)	Register-ed nurse	DUI, juvi record	Engaged, quit job, twin	BS+RN/ local	No/
Simmons Brandy	Shurcor (was US Congress)	Congress. staffer	none	Single, quit job, MENSA (appld)	BA/ Palo Alto	Yes/ last to see TL
Thompson Randall (Randy)	FBI detailee	Data analyst	Traffic tickets	Married, no kids, big mortgage	BS, Chicago	Yes/ $$

JT reviewed what he had written then admitted, "I'm having real trouble with motive on my list too. Rydell has one DUI and a juvenile record, but certainly seems to have turned her life around. Likewise Krumski has a DUI and some traffic tickets. Perhaps our CIA guy, or the FBI guy, the polygrapher one, or the psychiatrist, could have a professional motive, but I think that's weak. None of them have any serious money problems. Brosard gambles and Cutler has alimony and a few girlfriends, but neither has any serious debt. Simmons and Rydell both quit their job, but neither are in debt. Pennington has some credit card debt, but she's making payments and seems to have cut down on her spending since joining the program. Thompson's got a big mortgage but two incomes to meet it, and Krumski's rich, but he's a gambler. Basically nobody has a good motive I can see unless, as you say, there is something personal we haven't discovered yet."

"I guess . . ." Juanita's phone rang. "Yeah, Sam. . . . Okay, thanks. . . . Yeah, we'll get back to you."

JT raised his eyebrows and his palms went up in supplication.

"Sam says he can't get into Lee's flash drive: it's password protected and he tried all the usual easy ones. He said Lee must have put some kind of routine on it which won't allow him to bypass the entry algorithm, like he usually can, without potentially destroying the data, so he wants some password suggestions from us. Oh, and no prints but Lee's."

"Great," moaned JT. "Let's worry about it later."

"I see Cutler and Rydell are twins but have different last names even though Rydell is not married," noted Juanita.

"Cutler's whole family, his twin sister and both his parents, were killed in an auto accident. He had no other close family so he was shuffled around between several foster homes.

Rydell said her twin sister ran away from home as a teenager, and she doesn't know where she is now."

Juanita nodded.

"Do you know if our guys finished reviewing the surveillance data or the card-key entry information?" JT continued.

"I'll walk on down and see. I'm going to get a soda on the way. You want something?"

"No thanks. I'm going to work on these lists," JT said as he spread his and hers out on the table beside his desk. He'd been at it about ten minutes when Juanita called him. "JT," he said into the phone as he recognized the number as an in-house one.

"You need to come down to the lab," Juanita said.

"On my way," he replied.

Once there JT spotted Juanita over by Tommy Philbert's work station. "So what's up?"

"There is nothing from the surveillance or the card-key entry system from eight-forty-four to nine-forty-seven." Tommy showed them some data on his PC monitor that apparently made his point.

"So no one came in or out between those times?" lamented JT.

"No," explained Tommy, "there's *nothing* on the hard drive for those times—they've been wiped. Irretrievably, I'm afraid."

"Could this have been a malfunction," asked Juanita, "like a power loss or something?"

"No, they were definitely erased, no doubt about it. And by somebody who knew what he was doing. I'm afraid I can't tell you if anyone came in or out during that period. I guess you already knew there was no backup either."

JT nodded.

"Sorry, JT."

"Actually that's good information, Tommy. Thanks. Nita, let's head over to Sam's desk and see if he's come up with anything yet."

Sam still hadn't been able to get into Lee's flash drive. "His daughter's name is Chrissie and I'll send you the name of his last two girlfriends," offered JT.

"Tried 'Chrissie' already because Juanita mentioned her name," said Sam, "but I didn't have his girlfriends' names, so yeah, shoot them to me," he agreed, "and anything else you can think of."

"Soon as we get upstairs," said JT. "You mentioned the hard drives earlier—anything there?"

"Not that looked interesting. I'll have print outs for you by tomorrow, but I didn't see anything even remotely case related."

"All, right, thanks."

On the way back to the office he told Juanita, "That means our killer probably had help. I'm still convinced someone inside is involved, now more than ever."

"Could be he just erased the data to make us think someone else was involved."

JT raised his eyebrows at Juanita's statement.

"Okay, that shows inside involvement." She paused for a minute. "Unless our killer didn't think we'd pick up on that, but instead would figure someone got in during that time, only had time to pinch Lee's iPad before he got caught in the process, struggled and got the better hand, and then got out with no one seeing or hearing anything because the surveillance gear malfunctioned or the killer managed to disable it remotely."

JT remained silent.

"Quite a fairy tale, huh?"

He consoled her with, "It's good to consider all possibilities. I think it would make a lot of sense if one of the participants with a good alibi had outside help. What we need to do is see if we can't find some connection between Lee and these folks other than work. And we need to put together the lists of our other candidates. Guess it wouldn't be any fun if it was easy, huh?"

CHAPTER FOURTEEN

Wednesday, Chantilly, Virginia

Doctor Stanley Horatio Rodriguez had only been on the job a few days, but he was a quick study. DHS had returned all the documents and other data media on Monday afternoon, and Sam was a big help in getting him onboard as well. He knew Tom Parsons, the CTF's lab assistant, from Hopkins, and in fact had made some suggestions on his doctoral thesis. He had also interviewed all of the candidates, although that was almost two years ago, but they had made some lasting impressions. He was already considering how to limit his time back at Hopkins as he learned more and more about how far the program had come. The problem was that he was one of the few neurosurgeons who operated on certain portions of the brain, and his reputation was building with more and more patients being referred to him. *Well, I'll just have to work something out*, he thought. He was deep into Doctor Lee's notes when Sam interrupted with a knock on the door.

"Doctor Rodriguez, the DHS agents are here to see you."

"Oh, yes. Please have them come in," Rodriguez said as he got up to greet them.

JT and Juanita introduced themselves and passed their credentials over to him. Donaldson asked if he could get anyone something and they all declined. Juanita took a second glance at the assistant program manager as he left the room, and stifled a comment on his Hawaiian shirt, cargo pants and high-top sneakers.

Rodriguez handed their creds back and offered them the two visitor chairs in the room. He rolled his chair out in front of his desk so he could be closer to them. As soon as he was seated, JT asked him if he heard what happened at the local Senior Citizens' Center.

Rodriguez shook his head, wondering what this had to do with anything, and Juanita just rolled her eyes.

JT continued: "Well it was entertainment night there and Claude the Hypnotist was the night's entertainment. Claude explained: 'I'm here to put you into a trance; I intend to hypnotize each and every member of the audience.' The excitement was almost electric as Claude withdrew a beautiful antique pocket-watch from his coat. 'I want each of you to keep your eyes on this antique watch. It's a very special watch. It's been in my family for six generations.' He began to swing the watch gently back and forth while quietly chanting, 'Watch the watch, watch the watch, watch the watch. . . .' The crowd became mesmerized as the watch swayed back and forth, light gleaming off its silvery polished surface. A hundred pairs of eyes followed the swaying watch until, suddenly, the chain broke and the watch slipped from the hypnotist's fingers and fell to the floor, breaking into a hundred pieces. 'Shit!' said the hypnotist. It took three days to clean up the Senior Citizens' Center. Claude was never invited back."

Rodriguez chuckled and, keeping true to form, Juanita took the lead on this interview and hurriedly began, "Doctor Rodriguez . . ."

"Please call me Stan," he interrupted still chuckling.

Juanita changed the mood quickly. "Stan, we are certainly sorry about Doctor Lee. I understand you didn't know him that well, and neither did we of course, but by all accounts he was an exceptional individual."

"We did have a good professional relationship. We were both on the MENSA selection committee, and over the last couple of years we talked occasionally about various aspects of the program. Actually, he was more of a help to me than I was to him. I have some huge shoes to fill."

"We have two purposes here: the first is trying to make some sense out of his murder; and the second is learning more about the MENSA program, hoping familiarity with it will aid us in our investigation. Can you offer up any possible motives for his murder?"

"If it wasn't a robbery gone south, then I can only suggest someone was not happy with the way the program was going, or perhaps the program in general, but I cannot offer any specifics along those lines. I do know only a small number of people are read in on it, so your list of suspects should be relatively small. Barring that, it must have been personal, and I'm sorry but I have no clue there."

"Well, you're not alone there. Why are there only ten folks in the program?"

"We thought ten gave us enough variety in personality types, but not too many participants to give personal attention to; in fact, if we didn't get at least seven or eight good solid candidates from our group of fifteen, then we would have gone back to the list and picked up the next best candidates to try to get up to ten."

"Did the candidates who didn't make the final cut of fifteen know what was going on here? Did you use the Ganzfeld procedure on them?"

"I see you have done your homework. To answer your last question first, no, we did not use Ganzfeld because it's rather old hat and they would have known or strongly suspected we were looking for ESP abilities. To answer your first question, it's hard to say. They were *not* read into the program. They *were* told we were looking for ways to improve analytical reasoning and memory retention, and in fact, since they all were all quite intelligent people, we also told them we were particularly interested in their detailed backgrounds for indications of any factors that might have enhanced these abilities. I do not believe they knew we were looking into any psionic abilities; however, we had some, we thought, cleverly worded questions hinting at those. In retrospect, I believe we were not as clever as we suspected."

"Well that clears that up," stated JT.

"Sorry. Does that make them suspects? I would say possibly, but not strong ones. But you guys are the detectives."

"Yes, they are suspects. Did you have any inkling you might be recommended for Doctor Lee's replacement?" asked Juanita.

"When Frannie called me I was flabbergasted—initially, by learning Toshi was gone, and secondly, by being asked to replace him. Those were truly a couple of bolts from the blue."

"Frannie," Juanita said with raised eyebrows.

"Frances Kalani, the White House Chief-of-Staff. We are both members of The Galactic Society and she knew of my practice, my participation on the selection committee, and my general interest in the subject, so she recommended me to the President and then to Robin Dornan. To get back to your question, I had not even given it a thought when I was on the selection committee, and after she called me I spent a very restless night considering whether or not to accept the position."

"So you are giving up your practice at Hopkins then?"

"No. I'm going to scale down and accept fewer patients and transfer my research to another Hopkins staff member. I already cut back to one class and will finish that up this semester, and only serve as a guest lecturer on occasion. I can't in good conscience stop conducting surgeries, either for my own benefit or that of my patients."

"Three last items before we get into the program itself: (1) I will have to admit we checked into your whereabouts on the night in question and know you were on the Johns Hopkins campus until at least eight-thirty; (2) do you think one of your subjects could have induced a stroke in Doctor Lee; and (3) could you assess the security risk of Doctor Lee's missing iPad?"

"I appreciate that I have an alibi, but that doesn't clear me as I could have had an accomplice. To your last point, Sam mentioned he couldn't find Lee's iPad. It's definitely gone?" he asked while squinting his eyes and shaking his head.

"We've looked every likely place, including his townhouse. We know he transferred his notes to his PC and put them in report form at the end of each week. What we don't know is if he erased them and started anew, or kept a week or two worth of data or even more. Obviously, the more he kept, the more risk involved."

"I'll look at all the data and talk with Sam and the others and see what I can come up with. I understand Lee never took it from the premises so it could very well contain classified data. My gut feel is that there was a considerable amount of raw data on it, but not much in the way of reports. Sam said he did those on the PC in his office. Therefore I don't believe it would be of much value to someone not thoroughly familiar with what we are doing, but I guess we won't really know until it's recovered. As for your second point, inducing a stroke, I don't know. From what I learned in reading the material I have been able to so far, and from what I have seen, no. Could one of the participants have progressed far enough to cause a stroke and us not be aware of it? Perhaps, but I think that unlikely. Lee knew his team and left no indication in his notes that any were capable of such . . . medical telekinesis. Although, I'll have to admit anyone with medical training, such as Krumski or Rydell, would be suspect as far as I was concerned."

Juanita looked over at JT and he nodded. "I guess we're in receive mode now, Doc. We got a very brief program outline from Robin, somewhat more from Sam, a short history from Harry

Lisbon, and did minimal research on our own. We really are babes in the woods here."

"Okay. I hope I'm not too repetitive. The basic purpose of the program is to learn how to develop and enhance psychic abilities in individuals so they can determine if subjects are lying—very much like a polygraph, but more accurate. In other words we want to be able to read peoples' minds to get at the truth of a matter, or more specifically what they believe to be the truth. Procedurally, we would ask them a question and see what pops into their mind—literally. Or more surreptitiously, 'read' what's on the forefront of their minds, that is, what they are thinking about at the moment. A corollary ability is mind-to-mind communication or mental telepathy—talking to each other by thought transference. As you can imagine, this would be a significant advantage for our clandestine agents. They would be able to communicate what they were seeing and hearing to outside agents with no threat of detection."

"They would be the ultimate moles," offered Juanita.

"Exactly."

CHAPTER FIFTEEN

Wednesday, Chantilly, Virginia

"While the mind reading and the mental telepathy are the basic program thrust," Rodriguez continued, "there are some related ones we are also developing. These include telekinesis and thought implantation. Obviously you know what the former is, and the latter is just what it implies—putting an idea into a person's mind so they think it originated there. Some potentially beneficial side effects of the program include: the ability to enhance a person's native intelligence—their ability to reason both inductively and deductively; the capacity to store and recall significantly more information; and the abatement or even reversal of some neurodegenerative disorders, or actually thinking yourself out of various diseases such as Alzheimer's and Parkinson's. What we have not seen any indications of, are remote viewing, mind control, precognition or retrocognition, empathy or mediumship. I can explain these if you like."

Juanita shook her head but JT said, "I'm not sure what empathy is and I thought you said mind control was an ability you were working towards."

"In the usual sense empathy means taking on others' feelings—having their emotional state transferred to yourself, often involuntarily. It can also mean picking up on their emotions by mental telepathy, but we have had no more success at that then you could determine by a person's outward demeanor. Most people have broadened the use of the term to mean picking up thoughts from inanimate objects or animals as well. Once again, this is something we have not seen, nor done any research on. As for your second comment, we have implanted ideas, such that a person has a thought we put in their head they believe is their own, but by no means are we in control of their thoughts or their minds. We cannot make them do anything they wouldn't want to do. Any other questions so far?"

JT commented, "I'm not sure how you could use telekinesis."

"We weren't either at first. It became a goal subsequent to the other three mainly because it manifested itself and it does seem to strengthen one's ability in the other areas. Of course a sufficiently strong ability could be useful in self-defense or in other areas."

Juanita took JT's nod to mean she should continue. "Okay, so we know where you are going now. I guess the next step is how the program works to get you there."

Rodriguez continued, "As you know, we enlisted the help of ten, now eight, people who exhibited two of the abilities we are looking for to a greater extent than the average individual—high intelligence and superior memory—and some psychic ability. I understand Sam mentioned the latter was difficult to determine before we actually cleared the subjects for the program, and caused some initial consternation among the selection committee members. We finally came up with what we thought were a few clever indicators that pointed us in the right direction, based on the original abilities exhibited by our potential participants. These individuals have been thoroughly tested and examined to determine what factors, if any, they had in common which allowed them to develop their abilities. Some of these were genetic, such as both parents having superior mental abilities or being a twin. Others appear to have been environmental, such as playing a musical instrument, practicing some form of altered state like yoga or Zen, having to overcome very difficult life circumstances, speaking two or more languages, especially if learned at an early age, or significantly participating in challenging mind games such as chess."

"Have you found any one factor overwhelmingly important?" asked Juanita.

"Not really. At first our research showed the genetic ones had the more important roll, with being a twin the leading indicator there, but the more we look into it, the environmental ones are gaining ground, with language ability having a slight edge at this point."

Juanita nodded and asked him to continue.

"We also tried to find commonalities in their diet which may have affected their abilities, but had insufficient data to determine that. We are relying on the scientific findings that various foods and supplements can enhance brain activity, and think we are seeing positive results there. I know you talked to Harry Lisbon, and I'm sure he mentioned that certain chemical ingredients used by a group of native Africans produced altered states and apparent psychic abilities, so we have included a chemical protocol as well. Finally, there has been considerable research indicating certain electromagnetic radiation can have an enhancing effect on neuronal development, and hence mental capacity and ability."

"So what you do here at the CTF," offered Juanita, "is have these people, who were predisposed to be intelligent folks by nature and/or nurture, practice these various methods of increasing their mental capacity to see if they work? In other words they are human guinea pigs."

"Succinctly put, but somewhat misleading. Most of the protocols are not inherently dangerous—brain food, mind games, yoga, etc. The only possible harm we can envision is from the exposure to the gamma radiation and the use of the AJ."

"Excuse me," said JT. "What's AJ?"

"Oh, I thought Harry would have mentioned that. AJ is a pseudonym for the active chemical ingredient in the decoction the natives he saw demonstrate psychic abilities were imbibing.

It's a psychotropic drug derived from the reproductive juices of the male aardvark. Hence the term 'AJ' for aardvark juice."

"How in the world do you get that?" asked an astounded Juanita.

"As Harry says, *very* carefully. Seriously, he observed the natives capturing the animals, milking them after a fashion, and then releasing them unharmed. How they originally figured out the benefits of doing that I doubt we'll ever know, but there it is. We did the same thing for our initial supply, but after a good deal of initial difficulty in obtaining the natural goods, we put forth a considerable concentrated analysis and finally managed to synthesize the active ingredients. We did, to the best of our ability, given the dislike of the natives for medical exams, manage to determine there were no deleterious effects from its use. We have proceeded very slowly and carefully with its introduction to our participants, with their full awareness and consent by the way, and continually monitor for any indication of adverse reactions."

"You mentioned drugs that produced altered states as well."

"I did, but they were used by the chiefs to make the rank and file more susceptible to their suggestions, and generally to feel good I suppose. We do not use any of those; only the AJ derivative, which is what the chief used to produce his psychic ability. Harry said he never saw the chief partake of the other drugs."

"So the AJ is the only drug used here?" asked Juanita.

"Yes, in our experiments. We do have a small pharmacy with over the counter drugs we use for common medicinal purposes. They are not a regular part of our program. The 'brain food' we use here is of two types—general brain health food, and dietary supplements that enhance specific brain activity. The former includes your everyday cuisine like fish, blueberries, spinach, almonds, etc. The latter includes items you may not suspect like caffeine, glucose, guarana and L-theanine, and some things you may have heard of, and we think are promising, such as ginkgo biloba, Chinese ginseng and cocoa flavanois. To answer what I am sure is your other concern, the radiation we use is likewise applied in very small doses, again with constant monitoring and participant knowledge and consent. I have to admit we have not had much success with that as yet."

"Are you psychic, Doc?" asked JT.

"I knew you would ask that," he said as he smiled. "I like your style, Agent. No, I am not. I am a student of the brain and feel very privileged to be able to study this mind expanding program. I am jealous of the participants' abilities, but will not begin any self-administered regimen until this program is over and very well documented as totally safe and effective. I do feel as though there is some risk here, minimal though it may be, and cannot afford to do anything to cloud my professional administration of the program, not to mention my responsibility to my patients at Hopkins."

"What's been accomplished so far?" asked Juanita.

"I thought you'd never ask. How about a demonstration by a couple of our participants?"

Both JT and Juanita responded enthusiastically. Rodriguez made a call to Donaldson and asked him to tell Paul and Sharon they were ready, and then invited JT and Juanita to follow him out to the elevator. They got out on level three and turned into the lab where the two program participants met them. JT and Juanita had interviewed both of them, along with almost everyone else connected with the program, not to mention reviewing their records. Thus they knew Sharon Rydell was engaged and had quit her job as a registered nurse at Fairfax General Hospital to join the program, and Paul Cutler was a divorced systems analyst on loan from SYRAE.

Cutler had impressed Juanita during the interview, and she remembered he was a handsome young man who was well aware of it. Although he came on a little strong, he had a mysterious aura about him which was emphasized by his penetrating deep brown eyes that seemed to look right through you. His haircut was perfect, his clothes tailored, and his grin pasted on and artificial. Rydell, on the other hand, seemed just the opposite—vulnerable and shy. Her short brown hair, undistinguishing features and reserved attire made you want to hug her and say everything would be alright. Probably not a bad persona for a nurse—unless you wanted reassurance rather than a tug at your mothering instincts.

At Rodriguez's behest, Cutler handed JT a sealed envelope and Rydell handed Juanita one. They were told to keep the envelopes in their pockets for the time being. He then put the two of them through some paces, having Rydell "read" Juanita's mind and Cutler JT's. They were not successful at first, and it was not until Rodriguez convinced them to relax, let down their mental barriers, and concentrate on a general class of objects, that they were able to succeed. He would mention fruit and Cutler would tell JT what kind he was thinking of. Rodriguez tried animals with Juanita and Rydell knew which species she "had in mind." He then explained that reading the minds of subjects who knew they were being probed was sometimes difficult, because of the mental resistance the activity naturally introduced in them. Reading the minds of those who didn't know they were being probed was easier. All of the participants could read passive minds to some extent, but some, like Paul and Sharon, were better at it; that is they could probe further and deeper into the subjects' minds and could do it at distances approaching ten or fifteen meters. The others were not there yet but were getting better week by week.

"Obviously the passive reading can be used in situations where the reader is unknown to the subject, such as in clandestine spy scenarios, and the active reading would be used very much like a polygraph exam," Rodriguez offered. "Now I'd like you each to tell me if you have had any odd thoughts in the last fifteen minutes or so."

Juanita considered that for a few moments, and then mentioned an image of a pink bunny rabbit wearing a dunce cap did flash through her mind. JT described a scene with an elephant balancing itself on its trunk with its four legs off the ground. Rodriguez then told them to open their envelopes.

"Oh my god!" exclaimed Juanita. "You planted that thought." She showed JT the enclosed drawing of more or less what she had described. She looked at JT with raised eyebrows.

JT showed her the elephant picture in his envelope. "Absolutely amazing," he conceded. "I had no idea where that idea came from, until now. Is it really so easy to do?"

"As you probably figured out, Paul and Sharon planted these ideas shortly after you let down your defenses. Since these were extraordinary things that you don't normally encounter," Rodriguez continued, "the ideas popped up rather quickly into your forethoughts. When we plant less conspicuous ideas, they generally take longer to register in the subjects' minds. If we planted the picture of you blowing your head off, on the other hand, it probably would have surfaced relatively quickly, but you would have had no compunction to act upon it. You might think that was odd and wonder what your brain was trying to tell you, or may dismiss it altogether as just a random thought. Is there anything else we can demonstrate for you?" he asked.

"I'm good," said Juanita as she glanced at JT.

"One question has been bothering me," JT said. "Isn't this facility misnamed given what you're doing here? I thought cybernetics had more to do with the man-machine interface—robotics—than intelligence or ESP."

"That's not really true," responded Rodriguez. "A lot of people also confuse it with artificial intelligence. The word *cybernetics* stems from the Greek work for 'the art of steering.' The practitioners of cybernetics use a system and organizational approach to study the object or concept in question, and try to build a workable model of it by combining goals, inputs, feedback, and even conversation, in the hope of achieving an understanding of how it works or how 'to steer it.' That's really all we're trying to do here with the human brain. We're just putting a little more emphasis on the extrasensory capabilities of that system."

Rodriguez looked expectantly at JT. "Did that help?"

"Yes, thank you."

"Then I guess we're done her," said Juanita. "Thank you for this very enlightening demonstration. If you can think of anything that might help us in our investigation please don't hesitate to call us," she said as she handed him one of her cards.

JT did the same.

Back in the car JT said, "The whole time I was trying not to think of Paul and Sharon as suspects, but I know it popped into my head a few times. I really wonder if they picked up on it."

"What does it matter if it did? They have to know we would think of them as such. It's what we do."

"Yeah, that's true. But tell me, do you have this strong feeling neither of them could possibly be the murderers?"

"Oh, no. You don't think they . . . Quit messing with me!"

JT laughed and then said, "We both need to constantly remind each other that the facts are what matter in this case, and stay focused on them. We've had contact with all of the participants, and for all I know any of them could have messed with our perceptions of the case. What did you think of Rodriguez?"

"I like him. He's obviously a very smart man, yet he didn't talk down to us. He reminds me of Arati, except his speech isn't quite as stilted. It's going to be hard to think of him as one of our prime suspects. I mean he does have Lee's job now."

"Yes. But I feel more like he's doing the government a favor by taking the job, given the lucrative practice he's giving up or downsizing to come here."

"Which may be a thought he planted."

"I'll tell you what other thought came to mind during the Doc's explanation of the process—AJ, or some of the other things he talked about could be the password Lee used on his flash drive. I'm going to compile a list and send them off to Sam. Maybe he'll have something for us when we get back."

"Good idea. Can we get some lunch now?"

"You're driving, Amiga."

CHAPTER SIXTEEN

Wednesday, Crystal City, Virginia

JT decided they needed to develop the rest of the suspect lists. They had already looked at the MENSA participants including the two who had to drop out. They looked at the financials, criminal records, employment histories, the rather substantial file compiled on them during the interview process, and their time in the program. They had also done due diligence on the staff, including Doctor Lee and the new program manager, Doctor Rodriguez, as well as Lee's friend Doctor Lisbon. Since JT had convinced the boss they needed Arati's help, she had already spent a couple of days looking into whatever other data bases she could access, and did the background checks on Lee's two girlfriends and his daughter. He and Juanita wanted to see what Arati had come up with so far, and had invited her up to the office this afternoon. Then they needed to decide which of the remaining possible suspects they should look into, and wanted Arati's input on that as well.

JT was waiting for Arati and realized she was fifteen minutes overdue. He walked over to Juanita's cubical and found her and Arati chatting away. Arati, who pronounced her name "arth'ee", had helped them out with a previous case while a Naval Research Laboratory employee working on a DARPA project, and then came on board as a member of the Fusion Team. Since she and Juanita were both single with very little family in the area, they had hit it off together, and Juanita's "Americanisms" were rubbing off on Arati, not to mention some of JT's colloquialisms.

"Ladies, if we can get started," suggested JT.

"Hey, JT. We were just catching up with things. How have you been?" Dr. Arati Jabornae earned her PhD in information technology at Caltech, and then worked for the Navy at China Lake. After a few years there, she came to Washington to join the

Naval Research Laboratory's Information Technology Division. She had been promoted to Director of their Center for Computational Science when she met JT and Juanita, and eventually came over to the dark side to join them. Although she was born and raised in India, her parents emigrated to the U.S. just after she finished high school, and she became a naturalized citizen when she was twenty-three. She was as tall as JT, and he figured she probably matched his 145 pounds as well. Her medium brown skin, dark brown eyes, full face, and jet black hair she kept in a pony tail that reached down to her waist, definitely gave her a South Asian look. She normally wore a light colored blouse, medium to dark pants suits and comfortable flats, and today was no different.

"Excellent. Thanks. It's nice to be working closely with you again. We'd like to see what you have for us so far, and then maybe you could help us decide how to get info on our remaining suspects. Let's go over to the conference room."

Arati grabbed her files, JT and Juanita went back and got theirs, and the three of them met in the conference room around the corner.

After she laid out all her documents on the large table Arati began, "I ran his girlfriend, Trisha Carpenter, and his ex-girlfriend, Colleen Foster. They are both well off and, by all accounts, model citizens. I could not find any jealous exes, money problems, or any other deleterious items on either of them. Miss Foster has a new boyfriend and Lee has not been in contact with her in over three months. Lee and Miss Carpenter had dinner the Sunday before his murder, and talked on the phone the night before his death. You have not interviewed his daughter or Miss Carpenter yet, have you?"

"No," responded JT. "We thought we'd catch Chrissie Friday after Lee's memorial service. She said she'd probably be here for another week after that settling up his affairs. You probably didn't hear he donated his brain to the program, no doubt so the new PM could examine it for any sign of the program's effects on it," he offered somewhat snidely. "We'll schedule Carpenter soon as well. How about the data on the rest of the troops?"

"I uncovered some interesting facts on two of the CTF staff. I know Jorge Delgado has significant debt. It appears that braces for his youngest child precipitated this. He is also in the process of refinancing his house; however, I believe he will be able to manage the new payments if he keeps his future debt level down. The other item I uncovered on the CTF staff is that Robert Pullman, their IT person, has a number of gambling markers, I believe they are called, from his horse race betting at Charlestown, West Virginia. He has not made a serious effort to pay these back as far as I was able to determine."

"The rest of the staff checked out okay?" asked Juanita.

"I could find nothing more than what you already uncovered."

Juanita nodded.

"However, I did find out several interesting items regarding the participants," Arati continued. "William Brosard, the CIA loaner, has reported significant gambling winnings on his tax returns, apparently from visits to Las Vegas and Reno, where he was a regular customer before he joined the program. He continues to win reasonable amounts at various casinos in Atlantic City, where he spends many weekends.

"Paul Cutler, the loaner from The SYRAE Corporation, is currently being sued by his ex-wife for more alimony. She claimed he had several affairs during their marriage. He was also the subject of two harassment suits at SYRAE, both dropped with no action taken. He has been banned from several casinos in Atlantic City. Finally, his twin brother and parents were killed in an auto accident and he has resided in several foster homes.

"Doctor Ralph Krumski also has quite a storied career. He has settled two malpractice suits out of court. Both were brought by patients claiming the use of 'unconventional methods' that referenced consensual sex. His wife claimed 'mental cruelty' on her divorce petition. Nonetheless, his clientele include several individuals who would occupy prominent places on a 'Who's Who' list of Washingtonians.

"Lastly, Sharon Rydell is engaged to a doctor at Fairfax General Hospital who had a malpractice suit 'recanted' by a patient. Other than these items, I found nothing unusual."

"Arati, why didn't this stuff come out during the selection process the participants all went through, or the clearance process they and the staff went through?" asked Juanita.

"Some of this data is more recent. And a number of the items were in 'difficult to access' data bases."

"I guess that's a euphemism for restricted," offered Juanita.

Arati grinned and responded, "I followed the most recent DHS protocols in the acquisition of this data. By the way, you never mentioned whether or not the forensics team obtained any information from the crime scene."

"Seems to me as though it was unusually clean for a common area. They did get Pacquin's fingerprints on the weight bar, but of course he's the guy who found Lee and pulled the bar off him. Naturally they got Lee's as well, but other than that the bar was just a smear. They did find some of Rydell's hair at the scene, but she was one of the individuals giving him CPR. They also found Simmons' hair at the scene, but she's who Lee was with just prior to going to the gym. The only other identifiable stuff was from the EMTs. So in other words, nothing," lamented Juanita.

"Our job here becomes all the more important then," offered Arati. "Would you like the information on the selection committee members now?"

"Bring it on, Lady," blurted out JT, but before Arati could say anything else they were interrupted by JT's cell phone.

JT held up his hand to pause Arati and answered, "Agent Dunkirk. . . . Yeah, Sam. . . . Ha! I knew it. . . . I'll be down to pick it up shortly, and hey, thanks a million. . . . More than one, Buddy." JT turned to an expectant Juanita and Arati. "Sam got into Lee's flash drive. The password was 'aardvark' just like I guessed after talking to Rodriguez. I'll drop down and get it and we can go over it together."

Juanita and Arati decided to lay out the remaining suspect lists while JT went downstairs. As far as the selection committee went, JT and Juanita had already checked out Lisbon and Rodriguez, and of course Lee was the victim. The only two who had not already been vetted by them were Ronald Cummings and Alfred Westinghouse. The former was the committee chair and the head of the Neurology Department at Johns Hopkins University, as well as one of its vice presidents, and the latter was a research assistant and doctoral student at the University. Arati determined they were both in San Francisco at the time of the murder attending a neurology seminar. She had found no adverse data on Cummings, but Westinghouse had one drunk and disorderly charge for which he paid a fine but did no jail time, and he was barely scraping by on his research assistant salary, a situation that would likely improve once he finished paying off his student loan in twelve or thirteen months.

"I'm not big on motive for either of these guys," commented Juanita.

"I would have to agree with that," said Arati.

JT walked back into the room just then and asked, "Did you all decide anything?"

They told him what they had discussed so far.

"Let's talk about the rest of the potential suspects before we delve into this flash drive," he suggested. "Arati, the only folks we haven't discussed are some of the ones on the clearance list, and the five non-selected candidates. As for the latter, we did do data searches on them and found nothing unusual. Did you uncover anything?"

"Nothing I would consider relevant," she replied.

"Okay, then, let's get to the hard part—the clearance list individuals that are not participants, staff or on the selection committee. Juanita and I made a stab at who we should look at, but we'd like your take on them. What do you think?"

"I think we should start with anyone who either had a personal connection with Doctor Lee, or had something to gain from the demise or disruption of the MENSA program. Right now, the only one left on that list we are sure had some connection with Lee, besides his friend Lisbon and his girlfriends, is the Director of DARPA. We need to establish whether or not there are any other connections and go from there. I can do this, but I suggest it be accomplished by a thorough investigation of Lee's activities, rather than looking into the activities of anyone on the list, unless of course we make a connection. My concern here is for the political sensitivity of any inquiry into some of these individuals. As far as motive is concerned, we know Lee's replacement, Doctor Rodriguez, is a friend of the Chief of Staff, but I can't see either of them having a strong reason for killing him. A motive could be suggested for the Head of the Polygraph Division at the CIA and his counterpart at the FBI, although I personally consider that to be weak as well. I believe my time would be better spent looking deeper into our more likely suspects."

"Nita, do you agree with Arati's assessment?"

"We should definitely continue to look for connections by checking out Lee. I would also look into the DARPA Director and the Chief of Staff—either may have wanted Rodriguez closer at hand—and the two polygraph guys. I'm not sure the Boss will agree with us, but I'd push for it. Then we check out anything that pops from that. And we certainly need to delve deeper into the suspects we have already looked into."

"In other words you partially agree with her, but not about the part where she has more work to do," he said with only a faint trace of a smile on his face.

"I can help with that—she gets me into the various data bases and I can do the grunt work. You know we can't leave any stone unturned. Besides, you're closer to retirement than I am, right?"

"That's why I'm checking it out with the Boss," JT countered. "And I really think we should interview the CIA and FBI guys for 'background information' if nothing else. The Chief of Staff is a no brainer: she's too involved and has to realize we're only doing what she requested."

"That she requested?" asked Arati.

"This was originally supposed to go to the FBI or the CIA, and she nixed their involvement due to a potential conflict of interest."

Juanita interjected with, "Or because she thought they might uncover something we wouldn't."

"Well we can test her commitment then, can't we," JT suggested.

CHAPTER SEVENTEEN

Wednesday, Crystal City, Virginia

"Let's change directions for a minute," said JT. We are pretty sure this is an inside job, although with a possible outside connection. I've been wondering about our deep throat. Who wants us to solve this murder, or at least wants us to consider it as a murder, and why?"

"Someone who wants the program terminated might think a murder would do the job," said Juanita. "The only people in my estimation who would fit into that category are polygraph manufacturers, or anyone who can fool the machines, but is afraid they couldn't fool a 'tester' with ESP capability."

"So who gets added to our suspect list," asked JT, "remembering that an insider is most likely involved?"

"Well," Juanita pondered, "perhaps the two polygraph folks we just mentioned, and anyone with a significant investment in the manufacture or sale of polygraph machines. And to me that potentially implicates the deputies of the CIA and the FBI, and the DNI, all of whom were aware of the program. And it suggests either our CIA or FBI polygrapher as the potential insider. This assumes the only ones who know about the program are the ones with a clearance, or know someone with a clearance who is less than trustworthy."

"Arati, what do you think?"

"I agree. I can set up Juanita so she can help. I do think we need to get the Boss' approval before I start looking into our FBI and CIA personnel, as well as the DNI. I might not be able to do this without raising a few flags, in which case we will need some cover. Juanita should probably concentrate on the program participants. I will compose a list of polygraph manufacturers, stock holders or retailers and show it to you before we proceed. Does this sound okay to you?"

"Excellent," said JT.

"You know," said Juanita, "one of the participants could just have had some suspicions about one or more of the others—not enough to point a finger though—so they decided to have the Federal Marshalls look into it, and really weren't thinking about what it would do to the program."

"Good thought, Partner. To me that points back to an inside job, and we have those folks lined up already."

"I am curious," Arati began, "as to how you managed to get around the password protection on Lee's flash drive. I thought Sam determined it had a subroutine to destroy the data if a bypass was attempted. He did not use brute force on the password did he?" she asked incredulously.

"Well, I wouldn't call it brute forced exactly. After Nita and I talked to Doctor Rodriguez, we found out the MENSA program was using 'aardvark juice' to help facilitate their ESP capabilities. I'll explain later," JT offered a skeptical Arati. "So I thought aardvark would be a likely password and forwarded it to Sam, along with a few other words I came up with after our talk with the good doctor. Sam said most people would suspect a word beginning with a 'double a' to be tried very early on in a brute force program, so they would try something like putting a symbol in front of it or spelling it backwards. Turns out Doctor Lee did both, and used '#kravdraa' as the password. And now we're in."

"I am impressed," said Arati.

"Me too, Partner," chimed in Juanita. "Let's hope it points us in a fruitful direction."

"Yeah. Why don't you two start on your searches, and I'll look into this flash drive to see what I can find." JT looked at his watch and said, "Let's meet back here at four-thirty and see where we are and what we have to take to the Boss."

At half past four JT was already in the conference room and looked none the worse for the wear, when two bleary eyed ladies arrived there. "I gather from your demeanor you didn't find anything significant so far," offered JT.

Arati mentioned they had only just begun, while Juanita shrugged her shoulders and said, "There's a lot to look at. Did you have any luck?"

"I think we can narrow our search, at least for now," JT beamed. "In his notes Lee mentioned he had suspicions about four of the program participants. He kept a record of his personal, apparently unsubstantiated, feelings about the participants. I can't tell from the entries if Lee was using any ESP ability of his own to arrive at his reservations, or if they were merely based on the keen observations of a person who was very well versed in the vagaries of human feelings and relationships."

Arati raised her eyebrows at that remark, not having been privy to the fact that Lee was capable of and using ESP himself. Juanita had a similar physical reaction, but because she was impressed with JT's erudite remark.

JT smiled and went on. "Lee felt quite strongly about Brosard, the CIA detailee, and considered him a borderline megalomaniac who was using his ability to win at gambling. Something you may have just substantiated for us," he said glancing at Arati. "He had obviously been very clever at it, never winning too big or too much in one place, and reporting all the income. Lee felt Brosard's position as a psionics researcher, and his considerable intellectual talents, made him think he was much too clever for discovery by either polygraph or any other normal investigative procedures. Not that he had any indication of wrong doing, other than his gambling, if indeed those activities were less than honest. Lee also felt Brosard was underplaying his abilities, and using the program to enhance them for his own personal gratification."

"Just your typical PhD-CIA weirdo," offered Juanita.

"Oh, it gets better. He felt Cutler was also underplaying his abilities, and he was using his psychic ability to 'impress' women with his 'irresistible' charms. Lee thought Cutler was merely coasting and his real intent was to get what he could out of the program for his own personal gain. He mentioned Cutler very often seemed to have trouble concentrating, like his mind was a million miles away. Lee figured this guy would quit the program in the near future to go out and 'make a million' using his enhanced psychic abilities."

Juanita and Arati sat wide eyed and slack-jawed.

Realizing he had a captive audience, JT continued. "Krumski, on the other hand, was apparently an enigma to Lee. Lee had respect for him as a psychiatrist, and felt he contributed a good deal to the program and how it was affecting the participants. He did mention his first impression was that the guy was amoral, but then he later recanted and said he seemed to follow some internal set of principles, but Lee wasn't sure what those were. He did think Krumski was the smartest person he had ever run across." JT paused.

"Had some definite opinions, didn't he," Juanita commented. "You said four participants. Who's the last one?"

"Miss Rydell, the erstwhile nurse and recent fiancée. Lee thought she was a very conflicted lady. He considered her to be very principled, but hiding something deep down causing her grief. I'm thinking it might be whatever's in her juvie record. He also mentioned her superior intelligence, but apparent feelings of inadequacy and even gullibility. How about them apples?"

"Wow!" said Arati, which was quite a statement for someone who didn't usually express surprise. "You mentioned Lee might have been using ESP himself. And you say this because . . ."

"Because Doctor Lisbon told us as much, and asked that it not become a well-known fact if we can help it," responded Juanita.

"After reading his notes and given everything else you have learned about him thus far, do you think his observations were based on ESP?" Arati asked JT.

"Lisbon gave me the impression Lee had only just started to use it, and he wasn't very far along or advanced, but I could certainly be wrong. And so could Lisbon for that matter. While I haven't read every word of Lee's notes, I don't recall him specifically mentioning he used ESP. I'll go back and carefully reread them, and you two obviously need to read them as well, but my opinion is he tried to 'read' the participants without them knowing it. Given his subjects that might have been very difficult. In any event, this gives us reason to concentrate on these folks I think. But we still need to interview the other people we mentioned earlier. I'll go talk to the Boss and see what he can do for us in setting those up. You guys want to knock off for the day?"

"Yes," replied Juanita. "But I'd like to come in early and read Lee's notes. You gonna put them in the safe?"

JT nodded.

They said their goodbyes and JT went off to see Hanson.

CHAPTER EIGHTEEN

Thursday, Springfield, Virginia

"Come on, Andy, we gotta go." JT was trying to get his son off to school before he went into work today. "Carmen, can you pick him up after school as usual?" he asked his live-in housekeeper, cook, sister-in-law of his ex-boss and, more and more lately, his good friend. She came from a fairly well to do family in Panama, and had an upper-class education. She spoke English with only the slightest accent, and JT was convinced she would have no trouble landing a good paying job in the DC area. Even though he paid her a little above scale, and she certainly had no expenses she didn't want, and even then they were often things for Andy, JT still felt guilty about all the work she did for him and Andy. Naturally he paid her social security and she did seem to be saving money, but he could not convince her she was not building a big enough nest egg for her retirement. He kidded her about finding a sugar daddy and/or mooching off her sister, and she would just respond that things would work out for the best.

Andy was finally ready with homework, books and lunch in his backpack, so they piled into the Highlander and headed off for Andy's school, which was only a half mile away. After dropping Andy off JT headed for work. The whole way to Crystal City he kept wondering what strings Hanson would have to pull to get interviews with the CIA and FBI chief polygraphers. It wasn't like he thought either of these guys had anything to do with the murder, but he couldn't leave any stone unturned. *Well, that's why the Boss gets the big bucks*, he thought.

Crystal City, Virginia

Forty minutes later he pulled into the parking lot. After exiting the elevator and heading toward his office he went by Juanita's desk. He saw she was still reviewing Lee's notes. It was 9:00 now so he wondered just how "early" she got in. "Find anything interesting other than what we talked about yesterday?" he asked as he plopped down in her visitor chair.

"A few things," she replied. "We'll talk about them later. How'd it go with the Boss?"

"I told him what we wanted to do. Said he'd think about it overnight, and make whatever phone calls he needed to today. I'll go see him shortly, after a cup of coffee."

She could see his thoughts were elsewhere so she asked, "What's bugging you? Other than the fact we don't have any idea what's going on here."

"I've been wondering about our Deep Throat. Since there was actually a murder, either he or she knew there was one, and very possibly who did it, or had a strong suspicion about one or more persons. If they knew, then why didn't they just come forward?"

"Being afraid of a murderer is not necessarily a bad thing. Or maybe they were a part of it and then changed their mind."

"If they were a part of it, then tipping us off would be tantamount to turning themselves in, in which case they may as well come forward. And I can't believe any of these folks would be afraid to come forward for fear of retaliation. It's not like we're dealing with the Mafia here."

"Just because they're really smart doesn't mean they can't be emotional basket cases, or just do things you and I would consider dumb. But let's say you're right—someone there had a strong suspicion, but no proof. So they either had a strong sense of ethics, and wanted to do the right thing, just in case it was a crime, or they had reasons for wanting to end the program and thought Lee's murder might accomplish that. I can see a number of the participants in the former role. They would want to report it, but maybe not want to be questioned about their suspicions or put themselves under the microscope, or be embarrassed if it turned out not to be true. The more I think about it, the more this scenario makes sense."

"I have to agree with you there. And if it's someone wanting to end the program we've already put together that list," said JT. After a few moments he continued, "All I saw in Lee's notes were suspicions, what about you?"

"So far."

"His last posting to the flash drive was over the weekend— Sunday. And he died on Wednesday. He could have come up with something definitive in that time frame which he confronted the guilty party with, and entered in his iPad, but didn't mention to anyone else. He gives the guy some time to think about taking the honorable way out of the program, but instead the guy does him in, steals the iPad, and deletes the surveillance and entry data just to throw us off track. He thinks he's home free because of his clever COD, but then we get a tip, and voila, we're here."

"Now all we have to do is figure out who *he* is," laments Juanita, hinting by her emphasis it could also be a woman. "Seems to me," she continued, "if Lee talked to him or her, then it couldn't be anything really serious; otherwise he would have called the authorities. I mean you don't kill a guy for revealing your gambling or womanizing proclivities which everyone knows about anyway."

"Yeah," said JT. "I'm going to see the Boss."

A half hour later JT returned. "Well we have our marching orders," he announced to Juanita.

"So what's the plan?"

"We talk to Brosard and Pacquin, and explain how we'd like to talk to their bosses to get background material and ask them to set it up for us."

"Oh, I like that idea. Was it yours?"

"No. Gotta admit it was the Boss's. Should work, and hopefully won't seem like an interrogation and get the CIA and FBI's panties in a twist. However, he thinks we should just pop in unannounced to see the CEO of SYRAE, Cutler's boss, and Rydell's boss, the head nurse at Fairfax General Hospital. I'm afraid he didn't have any suggestions for who to talk to about Krumski."

"Shouldn't that be 'whom'?" chided Juanita.

"Please allow me the forbearance of an occasional linguistic inaccuracy."

Juanita laughed. JT was trying to break some of the bad speaking habits he picked up in dealing with criminals when he worked as a street cop, not to mention the cops themselves, and had asked her to correct any improper language she caught him using.

"Well Krumski had to work with somebody—I mean he couldn't run the sort of practice he had without some help. Why don't we get Arati on his case and see what she comes up with?"

"Good idea. Why don't you do that, and also talk our two boys into setting us up with their Boss. I'll call the SYRAE guy and the head nurse at Fairfax, and tell them we're OPM investigators doing a periodic background check on someone who listed them as a reference."

A few minutes later Juanita looked over at JT, who was on the phone, and gave him a thumbs up. When he hung up he looked over at her and did likewise.

"Arati's on it, and our boys both said they'd try to set us up for tomorrow. How'd you do?"

"We can go see the SYRAE guy now, and the hospital said the head nurse would be in around eleven. I told them we'd be there about then. So you ready to hit the road?"

"Let's go."

CHAPTER NINETEEN

Thursday, Arlington, Virginia

JT was driving this time so Juanita looked up what she could on Dr. Charles Langford, the CEO of SYRAE, the organization Cutler was on loan from. SYRAE used to be an FFRDC, a Federally Funded Research and Development Center, but was now a not-for-profit public service institute. It was located in Arlington, just a short hop from their office down I-395, which was also called Shirley Highway, so Juanita didn't have much time to look up anything personal on Langford on the organization's website other than his bio. Langford was instrumental in establishing SYRAE, which was an acronym for SYstems Research And Engineering, as an FFRDC in 2004, and Juanita was familiar with some of their programs. They specialized in rapidly incorporating research results into existing military systems. Langford received his PhD in electrical engineering from Penn State and had worked for the DoD and CIA in intelligence and counterintelligence positions. Juanita knew Cutler had worked directly for him for the last two years, and before that for a division director under Langford.

As they approached, JT commented that the building looked more like a government one than a private one, then corrected himself by calling it a semi-public building. Langford's office was on the eighth floor and his secretary said he was expecting them. As they walked in the SYRAE CEO commented, "They send two of you on background investigations now?"

Langford looked like a college professor: average height, a little stocky, smug disinterest, thick eyebrows, and, yes, a cardigan sweater. JT expected him to light up a pipe any second. He and Juanita showed the man their credentials as they introduced themselves. Langford looked at them with interest and asked, "And how can I help the Department of Homeland Security?"

Juanita apologized for their slight deception, explained in general what had happened at the CTF, and said they were primarily interested in background on Cutler. JT looked around the room and observed several pictures and plaques on the walls: a photograph of Langford shaking hands with the Secretary of Defense; two certificates denoting his membership in two honor societies; a family picture of Langford with three teenage children and a plain but healthy looking wife; his PhD sheepskin from Columbia University; his MENSA membership plaque; and several awards. JT disliked "I love me" walls, except when they helped him get a bead on someone.

"Paul is a brilliant integrator and has a great knack for combining diverse systems," Langford began. "He is a bit rambunctious and sometimes goes off on a tangent. If you can keep him focused, then he does great work. We brought him here from Colorado Springs when we opened this office in two thousand four. I can get you a copy of his personnel record if you'd like."

"That would be great."

"Let me make a quick call and we'll get that in the works."

When he hung up Juanita asked, "What can you tell us about the two harassment suits brought against him?"

"Wow. You guys did your homework didn't you? I would not have thought those records were available since the suits were both dropped."

"We do have our sources," commented Juanita.

"Hmm," Langford muttered as he raised his bushy eyebrows. "To answer your question, most of that is annotated in his personnel record. Are we off the record here?"

"Unless you say something directly incriminating him, than nothing has to come back to you," offered Juanita.

"I personally feel he was guilty on both counts, just knowing his personality and his opinion of himself. Why these ladies dropped their suits I don't know, other than the fact that there was no smoking gun in either case. I'm sure they were both delighted to see him leave. In fact, I'm not unhappy about his departure myself."

"Were these ladies given promotions or bonuses?"

"Fair question, but we don't play those games. The answer is no. We did offer them transfers to another division, and I looked for 'other opportunities' for Paul. The DARPA program just happened to come along at that point, so he left and the ladies stayed. I hope you won't need to talk to them. It could bring back some bad memories for them."

"Actually we will need to, but we've done this before and I don't think it will be traumatic for them."

Juanita asked several more questions, but got little additional information. They picked up the folder on Cutler, the names of the two ladies and directions to their offices. In the hallway Juanita asked, "How come no corny joke for Mr. Langford?"

"You know, he just didn't seem like the type to appreciate it."

"Yeah, I got the same impression."

Both ladies were in and, given the nature of the questions they were going to be asked, JT thought it best if Juanita did the talking. The two SYRAE employees recited pretty much the same story, relating how Cutler was "creepy" and overbearing, thought he was god's gift to women, and couldn't understand why they wouldn't go out with him. That said, they both admitted they were tempted and almost agreed on his third or fourth attempt—after all, he was single, good looking and smart. When asked why they recanted, they again had the same story: Cutler apologized, seemingly very sincerely, said his divorce hit him hard, asked for their forgiveness, told them he was in the process of looking for another position, and it would be "best" for the organization if they considered not pursuing the complaint. Neither of the ladies admitted to being pressured by him, nor anyone else in the company, to drop their complaint.

After they had cleared the building and were headed toward the parking lot Juanita asked, "Do you believe those two?"

"Those were two remarkably similar statements, weren't they?"

"You think?" Juanita commented. "I find it difficult to believe those weren't prepared answers, but I also find it difficult to believe that anyone in an organization as together as SYRAE would have prepped them both to respond so similarly."

"Apparently Cutler was quite persuasive."

"Yeah. Makes you wonder doesn't it? You know I don't usually come on so strong about suspects, one way or the other, at least not this early in a case. But I have really strong feelings about most of them, the program participants anyway. Some I'd swear were guilty right now, but with others even strong evidence wouldn't convince me they did anything wrong."

"Well don't tell me who you think are who. I'm still trying to keep an open mind here," JT chided.

"Yeah, yeah. You want to stop for some coffee on the way to the hospital?"

"Thought you'd never ask."

CHAPTER TWENTY

Thursday, Falls Church, Virginia

Fairfax General Hospital presented itself like most hospitals—pastoral pictures and murals, clean, orderly, but still a place you didn't want to be. Shirley Pascal had been the head nurse there for over four years and was very good at her job. After a few inquiries JT and Juanita found her checking her nurses' schedules at the main station on the second floor. While she did look a lot like Nurse Ratched, her personality was far more pleasant. When they showed their creds and explained what they wanted to talk to her about, she directed them to a nearby office and begged off for five minutes while she took care of something. Four and a half minutes later she entered the office.

"I've asked personnel to make a copy of Sharon's file. It should be here shortly. How else can I help you?"

JT asked, "In general was she a good employee? I assume she was a good nurse or she wouldn't have been working here."

"She was both. She was a fast learner and I could count on her to pick up a new procedure before anyone else, and then help teach it to the ones who needed a little help with it. If anything, I'd say she tried too hard sometimes—like she was trying to prove something."

"Do you have anything negative to say about her?"

"The only thing I can think of is that she was perhaps too quick to implement something. She'd plow headlong into something and then maybe a week later mention it might work better if we did it the new way."

"And that's bad?"

"Well, I always felt she knew how to improve it upfront, but didn't want to say anything without some data to back her up. I guess she was afraid she'd be criticized if something went wrong."

"What do you think about her engagement?"

"She's rushing into something she's not prepared for in my opinion. Doctor Samson hasn't been her very long so I don't know much about him, but then I don't think she does either. And you probably don't know he narrowly got out of a malpractice suit just recently."

"Actually, we do. But what do you mean by narrowly?"

"The patient had a good case—I'm sure it would have stuck. Not that he's a bad doctor mind you, but I believe the circumstances were stacked against him. In any event, I can't believe the patient withdrew the suit."

"I don't suppose you know why?"

"No. I have no idea."

"Did Sharon talk to this patient at all?"

"Not that I know of. She would have no reason to before the suit, since she was not involved with the patient's care, and after would have been improper since Samson was her fiancé."

"Do you want to add anything else?"

"Only that I feel she's a very good person, and I can't believe she would have anything to do with a murder."

JT thanked her and handed her one of his cards, and Juanita did the same. Juanita grabbed Rydell's personnel record, which had been delivered while they were talking, and the two of them took their leave of head nurse Pascal. They were both lost in their own thoughts as they headed out to retrieve JT's car. Their silence was interrupted by JT's cell phone. He could tell the call was coming from the CTF so he answered, "Agent Dunkirk here."

A few nods and a few okays later he pressed mute and looked over at Juanita. "This is Brosard, and he says if we could get over to Langley before three we could talk to his boss. The guy's taking off tomorrow and won't be back until next week."

She gave him a thumbs up.

JT hit mute and said, "Tell him we are on the way. I presume he'll clear us with the front gate? Okay thanks, Bill. This should help. We appreciate it."

He hung up and turned to Juanita. "Guess we're off to the fairy-land on the Potomac."

"What do you mean by that remark?"

"It's the land of make believe. In my experience, hardly anything these guys say can be taken at face value."

"Well then let's not even go—it will be a wasted trip," offered Juanita only half-jokingly.

"No. That's the point—it's the lies and half-truths, what they leave out and what they imply, that tells you what you want to know."

"You've got a twisted mind, Partner." She paused for a minute then asked, "So what do you think about Langford? Was he straight with us? After all he's not CIA."

"He used to be, but I don't think he or anyone else put those two ladies up to it. Nobody but Cutler himself that is. I think he planted those thoughts and that's why they were so similar. Lee said Cutler was coasting and underplaying his abilities. I bet he was capable of 'convincing' those two ladies without their knowing it, which got him out of any legal action. Unfortunately for him, that still left the stink of two suits being filed against him, so he looked for another job in order to leave the whole mess behind him."

"Whoa! I was thinking the same thing but really didn't want to suggest it. But it worked with us back at the CTF didn't it?"

JT just nodded.

CHAPTER TWENTY-ONE

Thursday, Langley, Virginia

JT figured the quickest way to Langley was up the Capital Beltway almost to the American Legion Bridge, and then down the George Washington Memorial Parkway. His GPS didn't agree, but then he was driving. The beautiful scenery along the Parkway made for a pleasant drive, short as it was, to CIA Headquarters. At a couple of the viewing spots it was even more so, and he thought maybe they would stop at one of those on the way back to the office. For now it was through the checkpoints to the main building of the nation's spy center. JT was thankful Brosard's boss, Randal Cunningham, had let the gatekeepers know they were coming. Unlike the last time they were here working a case, their time at the reception desk was short, and in nothing flat they were escorted up two floors and down three sterile hallways and were in Cunningham's office. Apparently this guy had some juice around here. The escort knocked on Cunningham's door and was told to come in. He announced the two visitors from DHS and closed the door after they entered.

"Good afternoon," said Cunningham as he introduced himself. "If I could see some ID, then we can get down to business."

JT and Juanita walked over to his desk and passed their creds to him. After Cunningham examined them he passed them back and indicated they should draw up two of the chairs against the wall. The CIA division chief was a big man who obviously didn't miss too many meals. His round face presented a pleasant, almost smiling, countenance that belied his sharp and sometimes gruff behavior. He was not well liked by his employees, but the management thought a great deal of him.

"I checked with Robin Dornan and she informed me you two were cleared and asked for my cooperation. So, I am all yours for the next . . ." he glanced at his wall clock, "hour and a half if need be."

"Thank you," said Juanita.

JT interrupted with: "Did you hear the one about the CIA, FBI and Secret Service agents stranded on a desert isle?"

"Yes," he replied. "Next question."

Juanita stifled a laugh and continued. "We just need to clear up one detail regarding our case, and then we were hoping you could help us understand a little better what the DARPA program is trying to accomplish—from a non-DARPA viewpoint."

"Fire away."

"We understand Dr. Brosard called you the evening of Dr. Lee's murder, is that right?" asked Juanita.

"Yes, that's correct—apparently right about the time it happened."

"And what was this call about?"

"Well, I'm not sure I remember. Bill called me periodically to discuss some of his ongoing work which others were continuing in his absence, and he usually gave me an update on the progress of the program over there. As much as he could on an unclassified line, although he did occasionally communicate via the SIPRNet."

Both JT and Juanita were aware that the SIPRNet, or Secret Internet Protocol Router Network, was the government's system of interconnected computer networks used to transmit classified information.

"And he mentioned Dr. Lee's demise then?"

"No; however he did call me back later the same night when he found out about it. He wanted to let me know what had happened. He was concerned, I think, the program would end and he wanted to make sure he still had a job back here in that event."

"And that was in question?"

"Not as far as I was concerned. He is a valuable employee and I really hated to detail him over there, but it was an excellent chance to learn about what DARPA was working on, a good deal of which may be applicable to what we do here, so I just couldn't pass up the opportunity. And they agreed he could continue to keep his hand in here, rather like a consultant."

"I suppose you already know the program will continue with a new program manager, and I assume Brosard will continue his participation."

"Indeed."

"Okay. What is your job here?"

"I'm the Chief of the Cognitive Sciences Division. I have four branches under me: Polygraphy, Neurolinguistics, Psionics Research and Cognitive Forensics."

"I'm sorry, but based on the MENSA program clearance list I thought you were the Head Polygrapher," said Juanita.

"Actually I am. I was the Chief of the Polygraphy Branch for years. About two years ago I was promoted to Division Chief. We haven't really found anyone qualified to take my old job, at least no one who wanted it. So I'm really double-hatted and handle both jobs. No one who works for me, except Bill, is cleared for the MENSA program."

"Got it. Speaking of Brosard, what did he do here?"

"Bill runs our Psionics Research Branch where we look into various paranormal activities that could potentially be of value to the Agency, such as remote viewing, psychokinesis, telepathy, clairvoyance, precognition, psychometry, and extrasensory perception."

"What are clairvoyance and psychometry?"

"The former involves the transmittal of information without the use of the normal five senses. It differs from telepathy in that there is no exchange of data between two persons. Clairvoyants usually say their source of information is the 'spirit world.' Psychometry is the ability to 'read' information from objects which people have handled."

"And have you had any success with these?"

"We've had modest success with remote viewing. We were actually very big into it during the cold war, when various Soviet locations were well described by our viewers. The trouble was they were not consistent, nor could we determine how to make them consistent. We think we have developed a testing method that identifies potential viewers, but there are no readily identifiable indications of these abilities, and you can't test everybody. We have not been able to enhance the abilities of the ones we have identified, nor improve their hit or miss percentage. One big 'success,' if you can call it such, is that we've debunked every clairvoyant and psychic reader who has volunteered to be tested by us. And believe me, we've tested dozens of them over the years. We have actually noticed similar brain wave patterns being exhibited by these folks, but to no avail."

Cunningham took a moment here, like he was trying to remember what he hadn't covered, or perhaps what he could tell his listeners about. Or maybe he was just catching his breath.

"Surely you have more success stories to offer," coaxed Juanita.

"We've had spotty success with telepathy and telekinesis—nothing to brag about however. I understand the DARPA program *has* had success in those areas, somewhat to our chagrin I must admit. I think they had a more scientific approach and therefore were more likely to succeed. Ours was tainted with too much politics I suppose, and not enough science."

"Any success in the precognition area?" asked Juanita.

"We had two individuals who showed some promise in early tests with 75 and 80 percent success rates, but in later tests they both dropped to 50 percent in equal probability tests and less than 15 percent in random probability tests. So no, we don't have a good track record. That's why we were interested in the DARPA program."

"What is neurolinguistics?"

"It's the study of how the brain processes language. In particular, we are interested in learning how to develop better interpreters for obvious reasons. Different parts of the brain are used in speaking various languages, and which part you use depends upon the first, or primal, language you develop a facility with. This is generally the same part of the brain you continue to use when you later learn another language, even though native speakers, those for whom this new language for you is their primal language, may use a different part. We're trying different learning techniques to rewire the language learning ability. So far we've attained a fifteen to twenty percent increase in language acquisition skills."

"And what is cognitive forensics?"

"CF is the branch which studies the physiological methods for telling whether or not a person is telling the truth: eye movements, muscle tics, voice inflection, body positioning and the like—the functions not monitored by a polygraph. This is referred to as kinesics."

"Thank you. That was very helpful. I need to ask you now about Brosard himself. What kind of employee is he?"

"He is one of the most brilliant persons I've ever met. He honestly believes there is a portion of our brains we are not using, or not using fully. He believes we can use this part to enhance our understanding of ourselves and our fellow beings by what he calls direct communication, or mental telepathy. That's why he was so tickled to join the DARPA program."

"We rather assumed as much. I was referring more to his personal traits."

"I do know he gambles; in fact everybody does since he brags about how well he does."

"Well he was telling the truth there. Why do you suppose he's so successful?"

"I'm really not much of a gambler myself, but I imagine it's because he counts cards. He's obviously not an idiot savant, but he does have an eidetic memory."

"Do you believe he has any ESP abilities he uses to do that?"

"As you know, that is something we study here, and I did not believe he had any ESP ability himself; however, he was selected for the DARPA program. I thought if he did have ESP abilities, his ego would not have let him keep it a secret. Seriously, I myself never saw any indication he could read minds or had any of the paranormal abilities we study here, but he is apparently doing some of that now."

"Have you had any complaints about him, any disciplinary actions in his file, anything indicating any criminal or immoral activity on his part?"

"The complaints we had were not actionable: he's not reasonable; he's a braggart; he doesn't allocate work fairly; he expects too much of me; etc. It's the kind of stuff many good supervisors get. As far as any criminal activity, he wouldn't be here if that were the case. We have a very good vetting process at the Agency."

"Okay, then. I guess I'm out of questions. JT, do you have anything?"

"Actually I do have one question—what is Noetics?"

"Excellent, Agent. I thought you would never ask."

"I have to admit when I was reviewing the case last night and thinking about what I wanted to ask you, I remembered reading about it in Dan Brown's *The Lost Symbol*. It occurred to me there is some connection between Noetics and what the MENSA program is trying to accomplish."

Cunningham nodded. "Noetic theory claims that just as gravity affects all matter, thoughts do as well, although to a lesser degree; that is, thought processes are not immaterial—there is actually a physical particle, something like a photon or some subatomic particle, which travels between your neural synapses and is the basis for thinking. This happens in all thinking processes, but the actual physical effect is extremely minute. Some ESP proponents contend this particle could be made to travel even further, into another person's mind, to implant an idea there, or even to move an object. Perhaps you've heard of atomic entanglement or spin reversal."

"I have read about that," proffered Juanita. "So this Noetics is a real scientific discipline?"

"Well . . . others consider it less grounded in the physics of the matter, and contend there is a cosmic or ethereal connection between an individual and the collective consciousness of the universe. If you recall, in *The Lost Symbol* they postulated that the human soul was actually the collection of these particles in your body. The Institute of Noetic Sciences was founded by Apollo 14 astronaut Edgar Mitchell, the sixth man to walk on the moon. On his way back from the moon, he claims to have experienced this sense of universal connectedness, like knowledge was 'coming to him directly.' The idea of group prayer affecting an outcome stems from this idea; that is, a large group of people, each with only an extremely small physical effect, when added together, can actually change a physical condition. To answer your question, there is a field of study called Noetic Sciences, which claims to be an interdisciplinary field using objective scientific techniques, coupled with a 'subjective inner knowing,' to study the whole gamut of human experience."

"Do you have any more questions, JT?"

"No, I'm good. Guess we should take our leave now. I'd like to thank you for your cooperation Mr. Cunningham. Here's my card if you think of anything which might help us."

Juanita also handed him a card and Cunningham called for an escort for them.

"My head is swimming, Partner. What say we call it a day," suggested Juanita once they were back in the car and headed out the gate.

"Okay. But before it swims off completely, what did you think of Mr. Cunningham?"

"He seemed pretty honest to me, especially in the assessment of his program successes. I thought he would be more protective of the Agency and less protective of Brosard, but it seemed just the opposite. I don't think he's very big on jokes. What was your take?"

"Definitely a killjoy, and I have to say he didn't impress me. Not because he didn't like jokes, although you have to wonder about that kind of person, but he just didn't seem up to par with the other folks we've interviewed, intellectually anyway. I admit he did seem to know what he was talking about, but I didn't like the way he paused before he answered any question—as though he had to think hard to remember the answer or perhaps whether or not it would get him in trouble. He certainly did not leave me with the impression that he believed in Noetic Sciences."

"Well he is CIA after all, and apparently a good manager. His bio didn't mention any advanced degrees, whereas a number of his employees do have them. I think perhaps you're right, though, and he just doesn't believe in anything not verifiable. He did write a book on polygraphy, which I noticed was sitting on his desk, but I heard it was criticized in the community as not scientific enough."

"Jeez, where did you get all that and when?"

"The other day after we put him on the suspect list I looked him up on the internet."

"Good for you. Well, what do we have just ahead but one of the scenic overlooks. I'm gonna pull off for a look see. Only take a few minutes and then back to the office for your car."

"Fine with me. We don't do this often enough."

CHAPTER TWENTY-TWO

Friday, Fairfax, Virginia

The Thomas Fowler Funeral Home and Mortuary was located at the end of a treed cul-de-sac behind a shopping center in the Old Town section of Fairfax City. Surrounding the dead-end street were the mortuary itself, the owner's home, a six-car garage and a thirty-two vehicle parking lot, split in two parts on either side of the street. The store backs which weren't blocked by the aforementioned buildings were hidden from view by an eight foot fence and cleverly placed trees and shrubbery. Eight-foot fences also separated both parking lots from the residential neighborhood, and the tops of several two story houses were visible wherever the tall oak and maple trees afforded a view. The Fowler family had done a reasonable job or providing a bucolic setting right in the middle of town.

JT and Juanita had arrived an hour before the service to talk to the current funeral director, the grandson of the founder. Chrissie Lee had told the director she wanted to hold a short memorial service with an open casket, and offer the floor to anyone who wanted to say a word or two. She would conclude with a eulogy, after which Lee's body would be cremated. In accordance with her father's wishes, his remains would be taken back to New Jersey. The two agents wondered who would show for the service, and planned on annotating that as unobtrusively as possible. JT thought Lee didn't look too bad for a dead man with no brain, and caught himself before he verbalized the thought.

Miss Lee arrived not ten minutes after they did. She wore a somber dark gray skirt with matching jacket over a white blouse, and gray open-toe high heels. JT knew she was twenty-nine but thought she looked even younger, even in her conservative attire. Her ebon hair and eyes and slender build accentuated her Japanese ancestry, but her comportment was all American girl. She seemed upbeat under the circumstances, and was certainly an attractive lady, but it was evident from her slightly swollen eyes she had been crying recently.

Doctor Lee's daughter had not met JT and Juanita, so they introduced themselves when she entered the building.

"We are so very sorry for your loss," said Juanita. "The more we learn about your father the more we admire him. I hope you don't mind if we ask you just a few questions, either now, or after the service or even later today or tomorrow if you are up to it."

"Well, if you don't mind let's do it now," she sighed.

Juanita looked over at JT, and since she had started the discussion he indicated she should continue. She asked about his friends and acquaintances, ending with his former girlfriend.

"Dad was quite happy with Trisha," Chrissie said, "and his 'breakup' with Colleen didn't even qualify for the use of that term—it was much more of an amicable parting of the ways. He was excited about his job and almost always told me something about it every time we talked."

Juanita asked a few more questions trying to glean any motive for Lee's murder. As they expected, his daughter was not much help in that department. At this point guests were starting to arrive so they finished up and Chrissie went over to greet the mourners.

Between the two of them, JT and Juanita had met and talked to all of the attendees except for Trisha Carpenter. Chrissie had mentioned she was coming, and they knew the woman she was talking to now had to be Trisha from the way they consoled each other. All eight of the MENSA program participants were there, as were the five CTF staff and Rodriguez. Lee's friend Harry Lisbon and Robin Dornan from DARPA had come to pay their respects as well. Juanita thought his former girlfriend Colleen Foster might show, but wasn't even sure if she knew about it.

Chrissie waited until everyone had walked by the casket to say goodbye in their own way before getting up to speak. She introduced herself and thanked everyone for coming, and quickly mentioned her father's wishes for cremation and for his brain to be donated to the program to help further their research. She suggested that her dad would want the service to be short and not too somber, and on that note invited anyone present to say a few words if they were so inclined.

Sam Donaldson took her up on it and spoke about what a good manager Toshi was, and how he treated everyone like family and was always kidding around with the participants and staff.

Harry Lisbon told the audience about some incidents back in school which nearly got him and Toshi expelled that not only showed his human side, but also emphasized his quick wit. From Chrissie's reaction it was obvious she hadn't heard these stories before now.

Robin Dornan followed Harry and struck a more somber tone: she mentioned he was on the cutting edge of some very important research, which he himself had initiated, and that would greatly benefit the country some day. She said he was the personification of the dedicated scientist, except for the standoffishness many of them displayed.

Chrissie got back up when it was obvious no one else wished to say anything. She began her eulogy by relating a few poignant moments with her dad from her childhood and young adulthood. As a result, she lost it twice and took a few moments to recover each time. It was obvious she loved her dad a great deal and would miss him terribly. In closing she mentioned that she would be taking her father's remains back to New Jersey in accordance with his wishes, and again thanked everyone for coming. As the attendees started slowly filing out, JT and Juanita exchanged greetings with the CTF personnel, Lisbon and Dornan. Finally only Chrissie and Trisha Carpenter remained.

JT walked up to them when there was a break in their conversation, and asked if he and Juanita could have a few words with Miss Carpenter. Chrissie explained to her who they were and she agreed. Carpenter was a few years younger than the late Dr. Lee, in her early forties, but looked younger. She had very light features and accented her eyebrows and lashes and dyed her hair dark brown. Her crimson lipstick and bright blue eyes gave her an intense but attractive look. JT asked essentially the same things of her Juanita had asked of Chrissie earlier, and got pretty much the same answers.

"The last time we talked on the phone, I asked him how work was going and he mentioned some possible trouble with one of the participants," Carpenter said. "Toshi didn't expressly say it, but from something he did say I got the impression he was going to have to let this person go."

They thanked her after offering their condolences once more and walked out to the parking lot.

"I hate funeral services," said Juanita, and before JT could correct her, "and memorial services."

"So do I. At least there were no little kids to worry about. I've been to too many services for officers who left a young family behind. That really sucks. It's the primary reason I quite being a street cop. When I joined the FAM Service I knew it would be a lot less dangerous, but I didn't know how much time flying would actually keep me away from my family—I was missing a good part of Andy's growing up. So when the opportunity became available with DHS, I jumped at it. After Sara died I was pretty well settled into this job, and I cut back a bit so I could spend more time with the little guy."

"I know, Amigo. I remember."

"Yeah. Sorry. Let's change the subject. What did we learn today? Anything new?"

"Not much, I'd say. I have to admit I have even more respect for Toshi now than I did before. I can't believe he left his brain to be dissected to see if he suffered any ill effects from the program—talk about dedication."

"I was actually wondering if we learned anything that would help our case."

"Oh, yeah. Actually, his donating his brain says to me he was experimenting on himself like Lisbon indicated. . . . I think Carpenter pretty much verified what we suspected from Toshi's notes about letting someone go. . . . She's either a consummate actress, or she really was upset over his death. . . . There were no outsiders at the service. . . ." Then, in her best impersonation of Forest Gump's partner Bubba in the shrimp business, she drolled, "Thas's about it."

"Very funny."

"I don't want to get too focused at this point, but I'm thinking we need to concentrate on the guys Toshi indicated problems with."

"I agree, but we do need to get this interview with Pacquin's boss over with since we already have it in the works. Then we can see if Arati has come up with anything else on our list of suspects before we decide where to go next. In the mean time, it's off to Quantico."

CHAPTER TWENTY-THREE

Friday, Quantico, Virginia

Quantico is thirty-five miles south of DC straight down Interstate 95. The Marine Corps base sprawls on either side of the highway in a rural area with the small towns of Triangle and Dumfries nearby, although the good sized town of Fredericksburg is only twenty miles south. The base houses not only a host of Marine Corps schools and training facilities, but also the FBI Training Academy. Both JT and Juanita had been to the Fullbore/Highpower Facility, which was collocated with the Academy, just last year at the invite of the then DARPA Director Tommy Townsend. They witnessed the test firing of a new gun the Agency was developing—the H&K MP3000. JT wondered if this awesome weapon was in the hands of the troops yet. Unfortunately this trip would not be nearly as exciting or entertaining, but at least it was nice to get away from the city for a change.

JT and Juanita spent a good two hours with Roger Barrister, Tommy Pacquin's boss, but didn't glean any information about Pacquin they hadn't already uncovered themselves. "Tommy is a model employee and he has contributed a great deal to the mission," Barrister told them. "I wish I had more guys like him. I hated to let him go for this long, but I thought it was good for him, and would make him better at his job here in the long run. I just didn't know how long this run would be." They did learn a little more about polygraphy and were now more convinced than ever it was a good, reliable tool for investigations, especially when used by a highly skilled operator who had familiarity with the subject and what they were trying to learn about him or her.

While JT and Juanita didn't write Pacquin off after their interview with his boss, they did place him fairly low on their suspect list. As they exited the Quantico gate and headed toward the ramp to I-95N, JT asked, "So what did you think of the guy, Nita? Was he straight with us, or was he hiding something?"

"I know he was cleared for the MENSA program, but he seemed to know very little about their actual goals. Either that, or he was just not being cooperative. I felt like he was hiding something, but I don't know if it was case related or not. How do you figure him?"

"I think he was being honest," said JT, "but just didn't have much to offer. He certainly does know his trade. I did feel like he was trying to get rid of us after we stopped talking about polygraphy—not because he was trying to hide something, but just because we were not interesting anymore."

"Well that's two totally different reads. I do admit I can't really ascribe much of a motive to him. He thinks polygraphy is here to stay."

"Yeah, I agree with that," commented JT. "I keep going back to our prime suspects; at least the ones I consider prime."

"Let me guess: Cutler, Krumski and Brosard—the same three Lee had concerns about."

"Certainly those three," agreed JT, "but I would also add Rydell. Cutler is totally in it for himself; Krumski is amoral, and according to Lee, the smartest person he ever knew; Brosard is a megalomaniac; and Rydell has something to hide. And none of them have an alibi. Problem is none of them have any strong motive we can uncover either."

"They all have their little quirks, probably because of their high intellects I suppose, but I don't see any of them having a reason to murder Lee."

"Not that we've found yet," cautioned JT. "If you subscribe to the 'I did it because I was mistreated as a kid theory,' then Cutler, who had some bad breaks growing up, and Rydell, who apparently did also, based on her juvie record, would move to the top of the list. And both Krumski and Rydell have medical backgrounds."

"But these guys are brilliant. You think they'd be able to think of a way to accomplish the murder without casting suspicion on themselves and provide themselves with an alibi. Besides, they are all smart enough to carry out the burking scenario."

"Okay. Put yourself in the perpetrator's shoes: Lee's got something on you, something he just found out, and he's about to kick you out of the program, or worse, turn you into the police. You are all holed up together in a semi-fortress, and good opportunities are slim. You keep an eye on Lee until you can get him alone. The opportunity presents itself when he goes to the gym late one evening. You've already thought of the burking thing, and know where he keeps his iPad, which is not under lock and key. You do your thing, grab the iPad, and then delete the surveillance and keycard data to divert suspicion to a potential outsider. See any holes in that?"

"Well, a couple of things," offered Juanita. "One, how does the apparent stroke play into this? Two, what happened to the iPad? We searched the place and it wasn't found. Three, if you wanted to make it seem like a natural death, then why bother to delete the surveillance data since that would indicate it being a murder?"

"Good points," JT concedes. "Let's talk about 'em. No one we talked to really believed the stroke was caused by any ESP ability of the participants. And the Doc says the stroke could have been a byproduct of the burking. So you plan all along to kill him by sitting on his chest, which in most cases is not detectable. But then, after the deed is done, you have second thoughts and want another plausible explanation for murder, just in case we figure out the burking." JT paused at this point, and looked at Juanita to see if she was buying this.

"In the heat of the battle, after committing a heinous crime for maybe the first time, he or she may have gotten worried and changed his or her plans," Juanita conceded. "We've seen a lot worse. But how did whoever it was manage to overpower a person as fit as Lee? I mean there were no wounds, either defensive or disabling: no knock to the head, no indication he was bound, and absolutely no trace of any drug in his system. You can't just jump on a guy's chest and not have him try to knock you off or otherwise defend himself."

"That's a tough one. We'll have to work on it."

"And what about the iPad?" she asked.

"It's not too difficult to believe we missed it in that place. It's four stories and we let folks go home for the weekend after a cursory search."

"Whoa!" exclaimed Juanita. "I just thought of something. What if our guy disabled the surveillance so he could get the iPad outside someplace safe until he could pick it up later?"

"That would work. And another thing— two guys could overcome Lee."

"I don't figure this as a conspiracy, at least not among two insiders. On the other hand, disabling the surveillance to let in a cohort-in-crime makes sense."

"Yeah, but the timing troubles me. Unless the guy was sitting outside waiting for who knows how long for the right moment to be invited in, that's not too feasible."

"But plausible," offered Juanita.

"I'll grant you that. So our prime suspects have the means and the opportunity, but I'm still struggling with the motive. We need to do more digging there. Maybe Arati has come up with something."

"By the way, did our guys ever interview Krumski's cohorts?" Juanita asked.

"Oh yeah. I forgot to mention that. They talked to his only employee—his chief-accountant-and-scheduler—and she was none too happy. She kept his records, did his billings, set up his appointments, and apparently did everything else but actually counsel the patients. He gave her a severance pay of six months' salary and a great recommendation, but she has not been able to get another job. At least not one to her liking—the guys say she's selling perfume at Macy's. Anyway, they got nothing out of her we didn't already have. While she didn't actually call him a slime ball, about the best thing she could say was that he was a 'smart Southerner.'"

"Interesting. How much notice did he give her?"

"Apparently very little, but he did give her six months' pay," said JT.

"Seems reasonable to me. I think she needs to blame her troubles on the economy, not Krumski."

"Let's hope Arati's got something for us back at the ranch."

CHAPTER TWENTY-FOUR

Saturday, Manassas, Virginia

Paul Cutler liked the movies almost as much as he liked gambling, but not as much as he liked women. When his mom and dad and sister were still alive, they went to the movies several times a year, and those were some of the best memories he had. After their deaths in an auto accident, he was shuffled around between several foster homes—never anything permanent, probably because he was a teenager. His two surviving grandparents were in nursing homes, and his one estranged uncle lived out in Seattle and claimed he just couldn't raise another kid at his age. So now Cutler went to the movies often. He especially liked the stadium seating and the smell of popcorn, but the whole experience was wonderful. There was a good movie showing in Manassas this weekend, and he really didn't feel like driving out to Charlestown, West Virginia to gamble. Besides, it wasn't as much fun there as Atlantic City, but they banned him from the New Jersey Mecca after accusing him of counting cards. Little did they know. He was being much more careful at Charlestown, and was also finding out about and starting to frequent the poker clubs in the area. But this was a movie weekend.

The first show was an action flick that let out at 5:30. Then he only had to wait fifteen minutes for the second show, a comedy, to start. At 8:45 Cutler was in his car and decided to stop for a bite before heading back to the CTF. His favorite cuisine was Mexican, and Anita's Restaurant, which served "New Mexico Style" Mexican, was on the way and just too tempting to pass up. He had nursed one medium container of popcorn and a small drink through the two shows, and could now use a good meal.

Chantilly, Virginia

The place was not very crowded for a Saturday night, perhaps because of the late hour. In any event it was quiet and he had time to think about his situation. His quandary was whether to stay with the program longer and probably learn more about increasing his ESP ability, or to leave now and be unfettered in his earning potential. Partial evenings and weekends just weren't enough time to cut it. From everything he had seen and learned so far, his capabilities, which hadn't really increased that much until the last few months, now seemed to have reached an apex. He was often tempted to reveal his significant real talent, but every time something held him back. He just felt like he needed to keep an ace in the whole. Maybe the new guy would take a different tact and speed things up, and, who knows, he might actually get stronger still. He guessed he could hang around a little while longer to see how Rodriguez handled the pace of the program. Besides, if he left now it might draw suspicion on him for Lee's murder. That's it: he'd made his decision. Now he could head on back and catch a good night's sleep. He left a nice tip and said goodnight to the waitress.

On the drive back Cutler thought about how lucky he was to "convince" those two broads at SYRAE to drop their complaints. *I was obviously not as careful with them as I should have been. I know they both liked the attention I paid to them, in fact asked for it, but I didn't consider beforehand their reaction to my public display of it. I am slipping—it took me twice to figure that out. Damn, they were both hot too, but messing around in your own sandbox is just too risky.*

As he pulled his Ford Mustang into the CTF parking lot, he noticed it seemed darker than usual. He looked around after exiting the car and saw that all of the parking lot lights were lit, but the spot light on this side of the building wasn't. He'd check the switch when he got inside, and turn it on if it wasn't already.

If it was on, he'd make a mental note to have George or Jorge replace the bulb. As he started to slide his ID into the card-key entry device, he thought he heard something behind him and looked around. Someone was standing not ten feet away. He appeared to be dressed all in black, but it was difficult to tell with the guy silhouetted against the background. And, holy shit, there was a gun pointed at him! Cutler started to say something then heard a noise somewhere between a soft thud and a hiss. At that point his attacker turned and hightailed it out of there. As the assailant rounded the corner and disappeared, Cutler just stood there for a moment, too stunned to move. He quickly came to his senses however, turned, and swiped his ID through the card-key slot. But then he couldn't think of his PIN code! He stopped, took a deep breath and slowly exhaled. The PIN code came to him and he entered it. After rushing inside he slammed the door shut.

Cutler didn't feel any pain so figured the bullet missed him. Or perhaps with all the adrenaline pumping he didn't realize yet he'd been shot. He ripped his shirt open and examined his chest, and then the rest of his body. Based on the lack of any blood and the absence of any physical discomfort, he decided the shooter either missed or perhaps the gun misfired. He sunk down on the landing and heaved a huge sigh of relief. "What to do? What to do?" he thought out loud.

After what seemed like a long time he collected his wits and realized he needed to call the police. The nearest phone was only a few feet down the hall from the bottom of the stairs, so he got up and bounded down them three at a time. He was intent on dialing 9-1-1, but when he got to the phone he paused. *The cops aren't going to do anything*, he thought. *I need to call that DHS agent and let him know what's going on.* Back in his room he found his phone and JT's card, and punched in the cell phone number listed on the bottom. *It's after eleven o'clock, but the man said to call him anytime.*

JT picked up on the third ring. "Agent Dunkirk."

"Hey. This is Paul Cutler over at the CTF."

"Yeah. What's up Paul?" It was obvious Cutler was either upset or pretty excited about something.

There was a pause and JT was about to say something when Cutler came out with, "Someone just tried to kill me."

"Whoa! Where are you? Are you hurt?"

"I'm in the CTF and I'm okay. I think maybe his gun misfired or something. He took off and I came in here and called you."

"Are you sure you are okay, sometimes people get shot and don't even realize it what with all the adrenalin?"

"I checked myself and I'm sure I didn't get shot, but can you get over here right away?"

"Yes, as soon as I can. You're inside and safe now, right?"

"Yes. I'll watch for you on the monitors and won't open the door til you get here."

"Good. Get yourself a drink and write down what you remember. I'll be there in twenty minutes max."

JT had called Juanita and arrived at the CTF only two minutes ahead of her. Although JT had further to come he did so with lights and siren when necessary. Juanita took a minute more to get out the door and didn't drive quite as fast. JT was anxious, and about to enter the building, when he saw Juanita drive up. "Okay Partner, let's go in and see what the hell is going on."

Juanita nodded and was about to ring the buzzer when the door lock disengaged. They walked down the steps and Cutler and Gayle Pennington were waiting for them in the hallway. Cutler looked calmer than he had sounded on the phone, and they could tell Pennington had been comforting him.

"How you doing, Paul?" asked JT.

"I'm better now. Calmed down a lot I guess. Gayle heard me on the phone with you, and after I hung up I told her what happened and what you said, and she wrote down what I could remember. She was one of the few people here this evening when I got in."

"Okay, great. Thanks, Gayle. Paul, how about if you go over it with us. Nice and slow and easy—we got all night. Oh crap. I forgot my recorder."

"Not to worry, Amigo," Juanita said as she pulled a recorder out of her bag. "Be ready to go momentarily."

When Juanita gave him the go ahead, Cutler recounted his harrowing experience, every now and then referring to the notes Pennington had written down. Neither JT nor Juanita interrupted until he was through. He finished with, "And then I called you and Gayle came in and I told her. Then I had a drink and started dictating to Gayle."

"I know this will be a little redundant," said JT, "but I'm gonna ask a few very specific questions you more or less already answered. First, other than his approximate height and weight, you really couldn't identify this guy, in fact you're not even sure if it was a guy, right?"

"Wow. I guess that's right. But my impression was that it was a man, and like I said he was dressed in black clothing."

"Okay. And he didn't say anything to you at all—not stick 'em up, hand over your wallet, or anything?"

"Right. No, wait. When the gun misfired I'm pretty sure he said 'Oh shit!' or something like that before he turned and ran."

"Excellent. Now you're sure he had a gun."

"No doubt about it, Agent. Dark as it was, I could see the outline of a gun very plainly against the background lighting. I couldn't tell you what kind, but I know it was a gun."

"Did you see a flash when he fired the gun?"

"Most definitely. And I remember thinking that light travels faster than sound, and the next thing to hit me would be the bullet, and I'd never hear the sound of the explosion. I can't believe I thought of all that in an instant."

"But of course you did hear a sound. Can you describe it for us?"

Cutler made several attempts before he mimicked what he thought it sounded like.

"Paul, did you piss off anybody tonight? Did anybody follow you back here?"

"No. I didn't really interact with anybody other than the ticket taker and the girl behind the snack counter."

"How about at the restaurant?"

"Just the maitre d' and the waitress. I even left her a nice tip."

"Did you cut anybody off, or piss off any drivers some other way?"

Cutler thought about it for a minute then answered in the negative. He started shaking his head. "Someone tried to kill me tonight, Agent. This wasn't a robbery attempt or some random act of violence. Someone is out to get me: maybe my ex-wife."

"She is your ex, right? You are divorced?"

"Yes."

"Well then there's no reason for her to do you, other than just pure spite I guess. I mean, her alimony issue would die with you, right?"

"Yeah. Just a thought, Agent. I guess I would *rather* it be her. At least then I'd know my enemy."

"Did you hear any vehicle start up or pull off before you got inside?"

Cutler shook his head. "Oh, Gayle and I checked the surveillance system and, as usual, it turned off automatically right at eleven o'clock. We looked, and it obviously didn't record my arrival since the cardkey system has me coming in at ten after."

"Just missed it. But I'm not sure it would have told us much that you didn't already. By the way, the outside light wasn't working when we came in."

"Yeah. I noticed it was out and was going to mention it to Jorge. Think that's a coincidence?"

"We'll check it out when we leave and also look at the surveillance tapes to see if we can catch anyone fooling with it earlier, but I wouldn't hold my breath on turning up anything. Is there anything else you want to add?"

"No, but I do have a question. Do you think I need protection?"

"Do *you*?"

"Hell yeah! Someone tried to kill me tonight. Isn't that reason enough?"

"We'll bring this up with the right people. In the mean time stay here. I think you'll be safe enough inside this facility. That probably just kills your Sunday, which is actually today," JT said glancing at his watch, not realizing until too late he hadn't made the best choice of words in this situation. "We should be able to get a decision by Monday afternoon, Tuesday morning at the latest. Okay?"

"Fine. Can we tell the rest of the folks here what happened?"

"No reason not to," said Juanita.

They asked Pennington a few questions, then said their goodbyes. Once outside, JT asked Juanita to wait by the entrance while he went to get his car. He parked next to the building with his rear bumper underneath the nonworking spot light. He got a latex glove and a plastic evidence bag from his kit, handed the bag to Juanita, put the glove on, and climbed up on the back of his car. He reached for the light and twisted the bulb. After a few turns the light came on. "How about them apples!" he exclaimed. He unscrewed it and placed it in the bag Juanita was holding open.

"What a coincidence," his partner said. "Doubt we'll find any prints on it though." They both got into JT's car and she asked, "So what do make of this?"

"This sounds like someone trying to intimidate or send a message—I mean no verbal communication and only an attempt to shoot him. It's easy enough to believe he heard a squib firing, and saw a small flash under those conveniently dark conditions—enough to give him a good scare. The chances of having a bad commercial round are pretty slim, and a pro could certainly doctor a self-load to misfire. Your average street thug would have said something, and I think a hit man really intent on killing him would have cleared the squib, fired again, not worried about the lighting conditions, and got the job done."

"What about the 'Oh shit!' comment?"

"Just an attempt to mislead us into thinking it was a real hit."

"But would a pro really think he was going to fool us?"

"Maybe they were only worried about scaring Cutler."

"They certainly accomplished that." They both sat thinking about the situation for a few minutes before Juanita broke the reverie with, "Let's do a quick reconnoiter and see if we find anything."

"Good idea. I'll take the north and east sides and you take this side and the south side."

Fifteen minutes later they met on the opposite side of the building from the CTF entrance and compared notes. They both agreed there was no evidence left behind, and the chances of there being a witness were miniscule. With only night lighting in most of the windows they could see, there appeared to be no one in the CTF building's upper floors, or any of the adjacent buildings at this hour, not even any cleanup crews. They'd have to send a team over to canvass Monday morning, but weren't very hopeful about getting anything. JT was about to suggest they head back to the cars and call it a night when he heard . . .

"All right you two, I want to see four hands in the air now."

They looked up and saw a Fairfax County police officer with his gun pointed at them. Now they were aware of another officer behind them.

"Good evening officer. We're federal agents. I'm going to reach very carefully into my jacket and get my creds."

The officer nodded but didn't lower his pistol. JT pulled his credential case out, placed it on the ground and slide it over to the officer.

"I got 'em covered Tom," they heard from behind them.

"Now my partner's going to do the same," advised JT. Master Police Officer Tom Reidy reached down to retrieve their badges, all the while keeping a bead on JT. He looked at the badges and asked, "So what's going on here? We got a report of two people shining flashlights around this parking lot."

JT quickly explained what had happened, and what they were doing in the parking lot. The officer relaxed and reholstered his gun. His partner did not.

"I'm gonna call my supervisor, Agent."

"Are you guys out of the Sully Station?"

Officer Reidy said they were.

"Have your sergeant call Lieutenant Dan from the day shift."

Officer Reidy called the station and talked to his supervisor. He nodded a few times and said yes as he looked at JT and then Juanita. He finished with, "Got it, Sarge."

"Well?" JT queried.

"Sarge didn't need to call Lieutenant Dan—said he knew you and agent Singletary, and described you both. I will need some info for my AOA report."

JT had filled out his share of Assistance to Other Police Jurisdiction reports. It was almost a given if you were a law enforcement officer in the Washington Metropolitan area. It used to be called an Assist Other Agency report and the troops still called it an AOA. Now at least, if everything checked out, you just made a computer entry and marked it closed. They both handed him a card as JT asked, "What's your sergeant's name?"

"Rafferty, Greg Rafferty."

"Yeah. I remember him from Dan's promotion party."

"Can you fill us in a little more on this case?"

"Let's walk around this way to where this is a little more lighting," JT said as he led the little troop around to the main building entrance, the three of them in the front with the second officer, now visibly relieved, trailing behind.

When they got to the front of the building Officer Reidy asked, "Say, wasn't there a death in this place about a week, a week and a half ago?"

"Turns out it was a murder, Officer," said Juanita. She went on to explain the basic facts of the case.

"Looks like you guys have your work cut out for you. Can we do anything to help you out?"

"We could use the name of the person who reported this," said Juanita. "Maybe they saw something else that will help."

"I'll email her contact info to you," he said, waving their cards in the air.

"Tell Lieutenant Dan and Sergeant Rafferty we said hi. By the way, is your buddy a rookie?" asked JT nodding in the direction of the other officer.

"He's not that new. Actually he helped sharpen my technique when he rode with me. We'll probably keep him. You guys have a good night."

"Goodnight, Officers. I'm glad you guys are on our side," JT said as the two officers headed off to their respective cars.

Juanita turned to JT. "Well that was fun. I gotta admit those guys were really on the ball. But what did you mean by the rookie crack?"

"The guy was a little over cautious. There aren't many fake credentials out there, but it doesn't hurt to be on the safe side. I'm going home and sleep on this. Tomorrow we'll have to ask the Boss about Cutler's protection request. I'm sure he'll kick that up to Charlie Moffett. I think this one is really a fence sitter, but when you look at the big picture, who knows. I'll call you in the morning. Is nine o'clock all right?"

"Yeah, nine's fine," responded Juanita. "I'll be up by then."

They got in their cars and headed home.

CHAPTER TWENTY-FIVE

Sunday, Springfield, Virginia

JT rolled out of bed at seven and found Andy constructing his latest Lego contraption. Andy had over a dozen of them and managed to put the last two together almost completely by himself, which was good because JT was starting to have difficulty with them—apparently his brain just wasn't put together like his son's. JT usually fixed breakfast on Sunday and it was always Andy's choice, which probably meant pancakes, sometimes with little chocolate chips mixed in. Today was no different. After breakfast he gave Andy the choice of going into the office with him, or going with Miss Carmen over to her sister's house for a barbeque. They were both invited and would have gone anyway, but now Carmen would take Andy and JT would join them when he could. There would be a number of kids there his age so he would enjoy himself.

He rang up Juanita right at nine. "I'm thinking we need to go in to take care of all this: we need to contact the Boss; we need to get our thoughts around what happened last night; we gotta set up a canvas."

"You don't need to convince me, Partner," Juanita intoned.

"Just convincing myself I need to ruin a Sunday, I guess. You want me to pick you up?"

"How about if you come by and I'll drive? About eleven?"

"Great. That'll give me time to run first. I'll see you then." JT got into his running gear and let Carmen know what he was doing. He donned his ear buds and fastened his iPod to his arm. Shortly after his wife Sara died he realized he hadn't been reading as much, what with everything going on at home and at work, so the last year or so he had been downloading books and listening to them while he was running. He tried listening in the car, but his traveling time was usually consumed with thoughts about the cases he was working on. Since he was usually "on the clock" while he was driving, he figured that was only fair.

He was currently listening to Michael Connelly's *The Drop*, and thought about how the main character had been named after a famous person, just as JT had—well maybe a character in JT's case. Connelly's protagonist, Harry Bosch, was named Hieronymus "Harry" Bosch by his mother, after the famous fifteenth century painter; JT was named James Tiberius Dunkirk by his father, after the twenty-third century character James Tiberius Kirk, captain of the starship *Enterprise*. He assumed Harry's mother was impressed with Bosch's paintings; he knew for a fact his father was a huge *Star Trek* fan. JT knew Tiberius was one of the Roman emperors, but didn't really know what that had to do with anything. Maybe it was because Kirk ran his starship like an emperor.

JT looked around and for a moment didn't know where he was. Then he recognized the intersection and knew his body had been on autopilot. As he continued along his regular path he thought about how much he missed Maryjo. Maryjo Myers was an interpreter for DHS whom JT had started dating last year. She was the first person he had gone out with since his wife died. She was currently out in California teaching a class, and wouldn't be back for another two months. He had talked to her a couple of nights ago, and she thought she might have to come back to DC for a meeting in a couple of weeks.

JT suddenly realized he was back home already. Apparently almost his entire run was on autopilot. And he couldn't even remember what had happened in Harry's case in the meantime. He'd have to listen to those parts again: he probably missed a good clue. He had just enough time left to get cleaned up and head off to the office.

CHAPTER TWENTY-SIX

Sunday, Crystal City, Virginia

By 2:30 they had documented Cutler's close call, reviewed everything Arati had left for them on Friday, got the Boss to commit three men to do a canvas of the buildings around the CTF on Monday morning, documented their interview with Trisha Carpenter, and set up a meeting with the witness to their parking lot search the night before. Now their "murder book" was as up to date as they could make it. What they didn't have was a decision on Cutler's request for witness protection. Hanson said he'd have to get his boss, Charlie Moffett, to weigh in on that, but he wasn't hopeful under the circumstances as JT had described them.

"What say we close up shop for the day," offered JT. "Do you want to come over to Lieutenant Dan's place this afternoon and goof off? There'll be some damn good grub there, and maybe an edible, I mean eligible young member of Fairfax's finest."

Juanita laughed and wondered if the slip was intentional or not. "Sounds like fun. I got nothing else to do, but don't play matchmaker for me. The last thing I need is to be hooked up with a county police officer."

"I'm just saying . . ."

"By the way, how's it going with you and Maryjo?"

"Now who's playing matchmaker?"

"I'm just saying . . . I only ask because you haven't mentioned her in a while."

"She's TDY to Monterey to teach a Navy class how to speak Urdu. Been out there two months now and scheduled back in two more. She and Andy get along great and Carmen likes her too. And yeah, I do miss her. I talked to her Friday night and she was going hiking in the national forest out there this weekend."

"Alone?"

"I hope not. That's probably more dangerous than our job."

"Doesn't she have relatives out there?"

"Yes, a brother. He's only about forty minutes from the school and she's been staying with him and his family."

Just then JT's desk phone rang. "Agent Dunkirk," he answered. After a few seconds he motioned Juanita to run a trace on the call. She got to it while JT took notes. When he hung up he saw Juanita shaking her head. "You didn't get anything?"

"I did get the number but didn't have time to do anything else. Let me look it up in the reverse directory." She got nothing. "Maybe the guys can do better tomorrow."

"Don't' bet on it. It's probably another throw away cell."

"Why do you say that?"

"Because I think it was our Deep Throat. But this time he called direct instead of going through the Marshalls. If so, he obviously figured out we were working the case."

"So what did he say?"

"He, and I'm pretty sure it was a he, said, and I quote, 'You were lucky the intended hit on Cutler went south. You had better keep him under wraps if you think you can, because the person who set him up was Randall Thompson.'"

"Holy shit! That's the other FBI guy in the program, not the one who found the body. Guess you better call Hanson back."

JT did, and was instructed to call the Assistant Secretary himself. After the new development was explained to Charlie Moffett, he authorized an around the clock guard for Cutler.

"It sounded like he asked about every detail of the case. I thought he was a big picture man. The budget must really be getting tight if you have to go through all that with an Assistant Secretary," bemoaned Juanita.

"I could be wrong but it sounded like personal interest to me. In any event I have to call some of the team and see who wants some overtime. Then we need to see Cutler and explain what's going on. He's going to hit the roof. Probably need to do that in person and right away. We can talk to our parking lot witness later."

"Right. I'll call her and let her know. But what do we do about Thompson?"

"*That* we're going to keep to ourselves, at least for now. We can keep an eye on him and see what kind of a reaction he has to the protection detail, if any. You want to help with the calls—I'll take Alpha and Baker Units, you take Charlie and Delta?"

Juanita agreed and within twenty minutes they had agents lined up through Monday. She cautioned the first guy not to get there for another hour. "You ready to head out there?"

"Yeah, we can talk in the car."

Once under way Juanita said, "We were thinking this was an inside job and it's looking more and more like that. But you were also thinking they were just trying to scare Cutler. You still think so?"

"Somebody killed Lee, and I think it was intentional and personal. I haven't figured out the motive yet, but I'm pretty sure it wasn't to kill the program. That would be overkill, so to speak, but if we have a nut in the program, I guess he or she could have reacted that way."

"Actually I agree with you. But we do need to work on motive. What about the 'fake' hit on Cutler? How does that figure in?"

"Let's assume for a minute we have the same Deep Throat making both phone calls," JT proposed. "I think it's also reasonable to assume his motive hasn't changed between the two events. So what would someone accomplish by letting us know Lee's death was no accident, but not naming a suspect, and that

Cutler's near miss was really an attempted murder, but naming the suspect?"

Juanita thought for a moment then offered, "Could be he didn't know who the guilty person was in the first instance, and couldn't take a chance on guessing just in case he was wrong—he'd lose all credibility. Seems to me if he knew he'd tell us as that would better suit his purpose."

"Which is?"

"Either turn in the guy because he was afraid of him, or had something against him, or put the program on the skids for his own personal reasons."

"What if our Deep Throat is the guilty party?"

"That would bring Lee's death to light as a murder, which *would* accomplish his purpose if he was trying to kill the program, but would also throw suspicion on himself."

"He may have thought he covered his tracks too well to get caught," said JT. "So why would this same person now set up a fake hit on one of the participants?"

"The same two reasons: get rid of the guy—and he's figured out who it is in the meantime—or kill the program."

"But this guy believes, or wants us to believe, that this was an actual hit. I guess either way it puts the program in jeopardy. Our Deep Throat could be thinking this was a golden opportunity to accomplish what the first incident didn't—stop the program."

"So you're saying he isn't the murderer," said Juanita, "but took advantage of the misdeed. However, since it didn't produce the desired result and, since he didn't actually want to kill anybody, he fakes a second murder attempt and implicates another participant."

"If at first you don't succeed . . ." JT chimed in. "Obviously we need to check out Thompson's activities Saturday night. I was thinking though, what if Cutler is the perp?"

"That makes sense. You set up a fake hit to draw attention away from yourself, but unfortunately you play right into someone else's hand who's trying to scuttle the program."

"We have two good scenarios for last night's action," summarized JT. Then added, "I can tell you one thing for sure: Cutler was either really scared or he deserves two academy awards."

"Oh he was scared, Partner," said Juanita. "Gayle confided in me that he shit himself, but made her promise not to mention it."

"*Now* you tell me. Well, we still have one good scenario. Let's go give the good news to Cutler."

CHAPTER TWENTY-SEVEN

Sunday, Chantilly, Virginia

Sam Donaldson was a little surprised to see them, but not unhappy. He mentioned Cutler was a bit agitated after his near miss, and hadn't come out of his room all day. As assistant program manager, Donaldson was hoping they could talk to Cutler and calm the man down; as an individual he was getting a little tired of the complaining. JT confided that wasn't a likely outcome, but didn't give him any details. He did ask Donaldson if he could verify Gayle Pennington's account of where everybody was on Saturday night. Donaldson handed JT a piece of paper. "Here's the total roster—first column is where I'm reasonably certain everyone was based on surveillance and card-key data, if they were here; second column is where they said they were."

"Nice work," complimented Juanita. "Thanks. I can't remember, which room is Cutler's?"

Donaldson told her the number and then she and JT took the elevator down to the dorm level. Juanita knocked on the door and announced herself and JT.

Cutler responded with, "Just a second." They heard the door unlock before it opened. "So do I get some protection here, Agents?"

"Well, Paul, it's complicated. Why don't we all sit down and I'll explain it," said JT. He proceeded to explain they had a witness to their activity in the parking lot, and would talk to them to see if they saw anything else. In addition they'd canvass for other witnesses tomorrow. He then gave Cutler his take on the hit, explaining the reasons he thought it was not the real McCoy.

"Easy for you to say—you're not the one in danger," Cutler said.

"Paul, we really don't think this is credible; nonetheless, the Assistant Secretary of DHS has authorized around-the-clock protection for you, which will start as soon as the first man gets here, probably within the hour. An agent will accompany you in all the open areas here, except when you're in the lab with Doctor Rodriguez, and everywhere on the outside."

"Man, I'm out of here! I'm leaving the program. I can't hang around waiting for someone to punch my ticket. You need to give me a new identity and put me in the witness protection program."

"Paul, I got you protection based on your staying in the program. We *are* going to look into this and get to the bottom of it. We *don't* believe it's the same person who killed Doctor Lee, but rather someone who wants the program ended. Like I said, that's why he didn't really try to harm you—just scare you and make the program look bad."

Cutler took a deep breath, held it for a few seconds, then exhaled. "Okay," he said. "I guess I can hang on for a while. Especially if you have someone here. But you guys gotta promise me you'll keep working this, just in case you're wrong about the attempt being a fake."

"That's our job, Paul, and we have a lot of high level attention and thus a lot of resources on this. Juanita, why don't you see if our first man is here yet."

Juanita used her cell to call Ronnie Hamilton, a member of their Alpha Unit, who was the first person up for guard duty. "She's waiting upstairs for us with Sam. Why don't I go brief her why you finish up with Paul?"

JT decided to shoot a few jokes at Cutler to get his mind off the case. "Do you know what an Australian kiss is?" he asked.

Cutler gave him a funny look and shook his head.

"It's the same as a French kiss, but 'down under.'"

Cutler let a small laugh escape.

JT decided to go nonstop. "What do you do with 365 used condoms? You melt them down, make a tire, and call it a good year. Why were hurricanes normally named after women? Because when they come, they're wild and wet, and when they go, they take your house and car with them. What did the psychiatrist say to the man who showed up for his session wearing only saran wrap? I can clearly see you're nuts. Say Paul, did you hear the one about Forest Gump going to heaven? . . ."

Fifteen minutes later, which was apparently none too soon for Cutler, Juanita came in with Hamilton and introduced her. "Perhaps you could give her the nickel tour so she knows her way around."

Ronnell (Ronnie) Gloria Hamilton cut an imposing figure. Her five-nine slender frame, short red hair and emerald eyes gave her a healthy, youthful appearance. In spite of her attractiveness, she really didn't need the gun on her hip to give the impression she could take care of herself. One look at her and Cutler gladly agreed, so JT and Juanita took their leave of them.

"Think we have time to talk to our witness before we head out to Sarge's house?" asked JT as they headed toward the car.

"Yeah. She lives in a condo only a mile or so away from here, so let's get it over with. And by the way, you've got to quit calling him Sarge. But I have to tell you, I'm really working up an appetite, Partner."

"The better to enjoy the fruits of *Lieutenant Dan's* grilling expertise, Amiga."

"And Maria's culinary expertise. Are your Mom and Dad going to be there?"

"You know they wouldn't miss a chance to be with little Andy," he said as Juanita pulled out of the parking lot.

The witness was a middle aged patent attorney who lived in a condominium development within walking distance of her workplace. She told JT and Juanita she was working late Saturday night, preparing a case for a client who was going to court on Monday. Somewhere around 11:00 she decided to take a smoke break on the patio of her building since it was a nonsmoking facility. From her fifth floor perch she noticed the wandering flashlight beams in the parking lot of the building next door and called 9-1-1. She had only been there a few minutes and saw nothing else out of the ordinary. She was totally involved with her work for several hours before her smoke break, and would not have noticed any activity that occurred during that time. In fact, she said she did not even see the police arrive or what happened when they did, and assumed all that went on after she had gone back inside.

"Oh, well," moaned Juanita on the way back to the car. "At least we are leaving no stone unturned. Let's get over to the Lieutenant's place before all the food is gone."

"You're driving," said JT, "so I'll punch Summer Hollow Court into the GPS."

CHAPTER TWENTY-EIGHT

Sunday, Chantilly, Virginia

Dan Reynolds and his wife Maria had moved to Chantilly shortly after his promotion to Lieutenant. Due to the housing slump they practically stole a not-too-old, foreclosed, midsized house on a heavily treed half acre lot on a quiet cul-de-sac. Black Gum Court was situated in a quiet neighborhood, yet all the amenities were close by in Chantilly. Plus, it was only a few miles to the Sully Police Station Reynolds worked out of. They rented their place in Annandale, figuring if it was occupied just half the time they could afford to keep it until the market improved.

Although twenty-five hundred square feet only qualified as midsized these days, it was more than enough space for four bedrooms and two and a half baths. New vinyl siding covered the upper façade, with spider plants and small perennials backed by five-foot boxwoods hiding most of the reddish-brown brick lower half. The front of the house was situated toward the small side of the trapezoidal shaped lot, and the narrow front yard was anchored by two large tupelo trees, each surrounded by a small stacked slate wall. This left barely enough room for a two car driveway, but that made for a good sized back yard which was one of its main selling points.

This afternoon's get-together served not only as one of Reynolds' semiannual parties for the station officers on his shift, but also a housewarming of sorts. JT was invited as well since he used to work for the lieutenant, and partners are always welcome; besides, who wouldn't want Juanita at one of their parties. Reynolds had also invited JT's mom and dad, as he and Maria had met them at some of JT's parties and had become friends. Ten of Fairfax County's finest were there also, most with wives or girlfriends, and three or four with kids. It was a decent group for a party.

Things were well underway by the time JT and Juanita got there. Andy ran up to greet his dad and Juanita when he saw them, but quickly resumed playing with the other kids. JT said hi to his mom and dad, and then was introduced to the officers he didn't know. Juanita was already ahead of him in that department. Luckily there was plenty of food left, so with a beer in one hand and a plate of international food in the other, they both started to unwind.

With the amenities out of the way and their appetites slacked, JT and Juanita walked over to see what Lieutenant Dan and JT's dad were talking about.

"Good night, Lieutenant, your smoker over there looks like it could roast a whole pig," JT opined.

"It can," Reynolds replied. "And next time that's what we're going to do. So how's the job going, JT?"

"Well, one of the latest things cooking is intelligence about al-Qaida's planned Christmas attacks next December, both here and in Europe. So of course DHS sprang into action and told al-Qaida, 'Hey, you can't call them Christmas attacks. You have to call them holiday attacks.'"

After the groaning died down one of the officers commented, "Yeah, I heard Jay Leno tell that on his show."

"I never claimed to use all original material," JT shot back.

"Thank goodness. Then the jokes could be even worse," kidded Reynolds. "Not to change the subject, but it's a good thing I get to see your dad every once in a while," he lamented. "He knows more about what's on the Chief's mind than I do." Hal Dunkirk was a member of the West Springfield Police Station's Citizens' Advisory Committee, and their Principle Representative to the Chief's Advisory Council. This group consisted of representatives from the eight police districts, and was charged with presenting the citizens' concerns to the Chief. In return, the Chief kept them abreast of what was going on in the department.

"Did he tell you about the new helos?" asked JT.

"Yeah—ones with two engines instead of a single point failure. Lord knows we need them, but I would rather have a raise next year for the troops. This is the third year in a row with no salary increase. And they can't make it up nearly as well with the one quarter freeze in overtime pay either. No wonder so many of them go for the off-duty jobs."

"What else did you learn from that font of wisdom?" JT kidded as he smiled at his dad.

"How the County Executive feels about the Citizens' Review Board. We all knew where the Chief stands: he's okay with either one of the first two models in a four model scenario everyone's looking at; that is, the two with the least amount of power to affect the findings. But Felton would only like to see the first one get approved, if any at all."

Simon Felton was the Fairfax County Executive and ran on a tough-on-crime platform. Not that Fairfax was the crime capital of the metropolitan area; in fact, it was better than most of the seven other local jurisdictions, but he claimed he wanted it to stay that way.

"The least intrusive model is basically just an auditor function—someone to make sure all the *i*'s are dotted and the *t*'s crossed," explained Dunkirk. "The next model up, which the Chief said he could go along with as well, is a citizen-police appeal board. After all, all the review procedures are already in place in the department to handle officer shootings."

"Then why do you need one at all?" asked Juanita. "Do the police not follow them? Have there been instances of abuse?"

"Not really. It's just that there is always the possibility of sweeping something under the rug when an agency reviews itself. The public would be more inclined to think justice was done if an outside, independent group without an ax to grind said the shooting was righteous. They usually won't argue if the finding is otherwise. What I found interesting was the experience in San Diego. They have a fairly stringent CRB which agreed with the department's findings in thirty-seven of the thirty-eight cases reviewed. Makes you wonder if it wasn't a waste of taxpayers' money, doesn't it?"

"That's probably why the County Executive doesn't like that model," said JT. "It all comes down to money. What got everybody's shorts in a knot anyway, Pops?"

"This has been kicking around nationally for a while. Do you remember that shooting down in Prince William County last year where the officer looked pretty guilty in the press, but was exonerated by the internal review board? The locals raised a stink and a couple of our supervisors decided to be proactive about it."

"What's Felton's take on the illegal immigrant situation?" Reynolds asked the senior Dunkirk.

"I don't know that. The chief's position, as I'm sure you are aware, is unless they commit a crime, we shouldn't mess with them. In other words, don't stop them for a proof-of-citizenship check."

"Did you hear what Dallas did?" asked JT.

A number of heads shook. At least half of those in ear shot expected another JT joke.

"They passed an ordinance requiring that drivers pulled over by a law enforcement officer, who cannot provide proof of insurance, have their car towed. To retrieve the car from the impound lot they must show proof of insurance. This not only made it easy for the City of Dallas to remove uninsured cars—a good thing—but also just nine days after the 'No Insurance' ordinance was passed, the Dallas impound lots were full and accident rates were going down—an even better thing. Seems over eighty percent of the impounded cars were driven by illegals."

Dunkirk commented with, "Not a bad idea. I know most illegal immigrants contribute a great deal to our society, but getting the ones off the streets who don't have insurance is the right thing to do."

"Yeah, but what about the hospitals they tie up and the other benefits of citizenship they enjoy but don't pay for?" asked one of the officers.

"Make 'em legal and make 'em pay taxes like the rest of us," lamented Reynolds. "Anything else I need to know about the Department, Hal?"

"They are looking hard at some federal grants to get the in-car video capability back. I understand they have one lined up but unless they can get maintenance money put in the budget they probably won't do it—it would die due to lack of maintenance just like last time. And I guess there was one more item he spent some time on: in addition to the pay freeze you mentioned, he's really upset that Fairfax is seventh out of eight in total compensation in the local jurisdictions, and firemen contribute only seven percent of pay rather than your twelve percent towards retirement, but earn the same two-point-eight percent per year on the force. As you know, they started to reduce your contribution by one percent per year, but had to put a hold on it due to the budget crunch. Those were the hot items. The main thing is they don't have to plan for a force reduction."

"This shop talk is depressing," bemoaned one of the officers. "JT, what exciting federal case are you working on?"

"We ran across an interesting group on our current case. Did any of you ever hear of The Galactic Society?" JT asked.

"I'm a member, Son," said his dad.

"Really? I didn't know that. Do you go to any of their meetings?"

"No. I just make a contribution now and then, pay my dues, and add to their member count. But that helps them in lobbying for their main mission, which is developing a galactic transportation capability."

"You gotta be kidding me," said the officer who had asked JT about his case. "I mean like that is way off in the future. How do they influence that?"

"They lobby for the various NASA missions which would contribute to that goal. We believe our influence turned President Simmons around on the NASA budget."

"But that is way down the road. Are we even close?" the officer continued.

"No, which is my point. We either have to have a lot fewer people doing a lot better job of conserving the earth's resources, or we need to find another place to live. We are finding extra-solar planets out there in the goldilocks zone, so we'll have places to go to, it's just a matter of how we get there."

"So what does that have to do with your case, JT?" asked another officer.

"A DARPA program manager was murdered and we interviewed his best friend who was a member."

"You have some suspects?"

"We have no lack of suspects, and plenty of opportunity. What we don't have is a motive."

"Did I understand correctly that a few of our guys rousted you outside a building up at Routes 50 and 28 last night?" Lieutenant Dan asked, affording JT a chance to forestall any further discussion of an open case.

"Wow, news sure travels fast, doesn't it?"

"Well, you did use my name after all," Reynolds commented. "Hal," he continued, "what do you think about what's happening all over the Middle East?"

"As you know, many of those dictatorships have been overturned, and I think the handwriting is on the wall for the rest of them. The question is what has or will replace them. We'd all like to think a more democratic form of government will develop, but they don't have a good history of that happening, and they do have a history of Islamic fundamentalists getting a strong sway on the populace, or the military being reluctant to relinquish their power."

"Maybe democracy isn't for everybody," one of the officers piped in, garnering a number of stares from the assembled group.

"That's probably true to some extent," offered Juanita, "at least not full- blown democracy, and not right away. They probably need to get there in a few small steps as opposed to one giant one. Surely they deserve the right to self-government as much as anyone else."

"That's what I meant," the officer responded somewhat defensively.

Juanita followed up quickly with, "Mister D, did you ever hear of Noetics? We learned from one of the guys at The Galactic Society it was started by astronaut Edgar Mitchell." Juanita asked him that because she knew he used to work at NASA.

"Sure," he replied. "I was working the Apollo 14 mission in 1971when he supposedly experienced his 'profound sense of universal connectedness.' For those of you who don't know, he was the sixth man to walk on the moon, and he was no dummy either—had a doctorate from MIT in astronautics. He founded the Institute of Noetic Sciences a couple of years later, because his experience led him to conclude that life was more complex than he had learned studying conventional science. Science, he said, is grounded in measurement and experimentation, and then objective evaluation of what you find; in Noetics however, or so its advocates claim, you have to consider the subjective, or internal, way of learning as well. That means you take into account hunches, intuition, and other feelings or experiences which may not be rational, but nonetheless feel absolutely real. I

182

think it's interesting that this apparently led him to believe in UFOs and the Roswell cover-up conspiracy."

"Hey, Juanita. Did JT tell you what he did to me after my bike accident?" asked Reynolds trying to get the conversation back on a lighter note.

Juanita shook her head.

"He put training wheels on my office chair."

The crowd laughed as JT offered his protestation: "No one ever proved it was me. And besides, Andy didn't need training wheels anymore."

"As precocious as ever, aren't you, Son? Dan, did he tell you what he asked his mother and me on his eighteenth birthday?"

The lieutenant shook his head and smiled in anticipation.

"He said, 'Hal, Emma, we've known each other for eighteen years now. Don't you think it's time we were on a first name basis?'"

From there the conversations went into JFK, politics, public figures, sports and several other areas, and people broke off into splinter groups depending on their interest. JT couldn't resist playing with some of the younger officers in his group so he posed a problem for them. "Say you are driving down the road in your sleek sports car on a wild, stormy night, when you pass by a bus stop and you see three people waiting for the bus: one, an old lady who looks as if she is about to die; two, an old friend who once saved your life; and three, the perfect partner you have been dreaming about. Which one would you choose to offer a ride to, knowing you could only take one passenger in your car?"

He could tell everyone's wheels were grinding, but only one officer offered a solution: "The old lady," he said, "since she has the greatest need. The other two will understand. Just make sure you get their phone numbers so you can hook up with them later."

"Not bad," JT commented. "This is a moral/ethical dilemma once used as part of a job application. You could pick up the old lady, because she is going to die, and thus you should save her first, like Ken here suggested. Or you could take the old friend because he once saved your life, and this would be the perfect chance to pay him back. However, in that case you may not be able to find your perfect mate again and the old lady might die. The candidate who was hired, out of some 200 applicants by the way, had no trouble coming up with his solution. He proposed giving the car keys to his old friend who could then take the lady to the hospital. He would stay behind and wait for the bus with the partner of his dreams."

"I think the correct answer is to run the old lady over and put her out of her misery, because the president's new health care plan won't pay for her hospital visit anyway, have sex with the perfect partner on the hood of the car, then drive off with your old friend for a few beers," stated Lieutenant Dan. When the laughter died down Reynolds said, "JT, come over here for a second. I want to ask you something."

JT complied as they stepped over to a corner of the yard.

"Did you hear Melissa has a new boyfriend?" he asked.

"Yes, she mentioned him. Seems like a nice guy from what she tells me."

"That's what worries me. You remember what happened last time, right?"

"Of course, but I wouldn't worry about it," said JT. "She's a big girl. Besides, both of you probably already looked him up in your data bases."

"Sure. I don't know about her, but at least I did. No wants, no warrants, nothing out of the ordinary—not even any tickets. But you know that doesn't necessarily tell you a lot about a person. I was wondering if maybe you . . ."

"Why, Lieutenant Dan, you wouldn't be suggesting I use my position to look a little deeper into this person's background would you?"

A sheepish grin crept over JT's former boss' face, and then he noticed JT had the same look about him. "Believe me, this guy doesn't have blot one on his record, any of his records, anywhere. Melissa's a good friend of mine too, you know."

"You da Man, JT. You da Man."

Since most of the officers there didn't have a shift until late the next day, the party carried on until the wee hours of the morning. JT, and a few others with young children, regrettably left before then.

CHAPTER TWENTY-NINE

Monday, Crystal City, Virginia

Arati had collected a good deal of data over the last few days, and JT and Juanita had spent the morning going over it. Some of it wasn't easy to come by, and Arati had to access a number of very sensitive data bases in the process. At least the information on the polygraph manufacturers and stock holders wasn't difficult to obtain, but there was a lot of it. The manufacturers were a highly diverse group located in the states and overseas, and there weren't any retailers, per se—most of the manufacturers sold direct to the customer. Arati determined no one company had a lock on the business, and the biggest one was in the states, but had multiple small investors. She didn't see any one gaining enough to sabotage the DARPA program, and in fact the industry was diversifying into mobile units for private industry and local law enforcement organizations.

They had decided to break for a late lunch, when Hanson came over to where they were working. "Just the three people I needed to see," he said. "Let's go back to my office."

After they were comfortable—as comfortable as you can get when called into the boss' office when he has just a slight hint of irritation in his voice—Hanson began. "I know I approved your gathering of data on the FBI and CIA individuals. And I got that from Charlie Moffett himself. But it seems both organizations are upset with the intrusions into their data bases. I think mostly because they thought it couldn't be done, and are embarrassed by the apparent breach of their security measures. Charlie did say he had approved your actions and he'd figure out a way to make it go away. A worse problem, and one which may require a little more finesse on his part, is the tapping into the private financial and other data on the two employees without a warrant. Interestingly enough, the CIA noticed the same probing of the

DNI's records, informed him of that, and he shrugged it off as part of the job. He did suggest the Company look into the possibility of non-authorized personnel being able to use Arati's techniques. In any event, Charlie wants to see you three, and I am pretty sure he's going to ask if you got what you need and if this activity will cease."

"Wow. Sounds like we may have turned over some rocks," said JT.

"Possibly," offered Hanson. "But I think it's more political than anything to do with trying to derail your case. Although we wouldn't be doing our jobs if we weren't thorough, and we do have White House backing. Just be reasonable and discreet. And remember, I work for Moffett."

"So now what, Boss?" asked Juanita.

"So gather your stuff and go see Charlie downtown at four o'clock this afternoon. Oh, by the way, Bill and two of his guys were doing the canvas for you this morning. They should be done by now so you might want to call him before you go." Bill Hastings was the leader of the Bravo Team. Since his guys had just closed two major cases and their current work load was minimal, Hanson had asked them to do the canvass for JT.

Juanita called Bill's cell.

"I'm afraid it was pretty much a bust, Juanita. Nobody saw anything except the witness who spotted you two in the parking lot," Hastings told her. "There are two employees who were working late who aren't in today. We left cards with their coworkers and asked them to give us a call. We do have to hit the two cleaning crews and we have their schedule, and we should be able to talk to them about five this afternoon. Let you know how it turns out."

"Okay, thanks, Bill. Appreciate it." When she hung up she noticed JT was on the phone. The way he was shaking his head she knew it wasn't a good conversation. When he got off she asked, "What was that all about?"

"You're not going to believe this, but our buddy Paul Cutler is causing problems. That was Rodriguez on the phone, and he said Paul apparently suspects one of his fellow participants is the one who tried to shoot him the other night. He's acting paranoid and irritating everybody. Rodriguez said if Paul doesn't calm down he's going to have to ask him to leave the program. Wants to know if we'll come talk to him again, because he thinks it might pacify him if we update him on our progress."

"Crap. You think he read our minds, because we damn sure didn't tell him?" asked Juanita.

"I don't know, Partner. A few people knew, and maybe he got it from them."

"I know Cutler," interjected Arati, "and all the participants for that matter, are very intelligent, but it is possible he is losing it, as you say. Perhaps his continuing use of the synthetic aardvark extract is having deleterious effects."

"Wouldn't surprise me," said Juanita, "but everyone else is apparently okay with it. We have to leave shortly to see the Assistant Secretary, so I guess we go see him later this afternoon or tomorrow. What do you want to do?"

"Let's clean up here then go talk to Mr. Moffett. After which we can head out to the CTF. Arati, we can drop you off on the way back, if you'd like. Juanita, would you call Rodriguez and see if we can't get in to see him before we talk to Cutler? I think we'll need some background first."

"I'll call him from the car."

The three of them gathered their stuff and headed down to the parking lot.

CHAPTER THIRTY

Monday, Washington, DC

Moffett had not met Arati before so he began by getting up and introducing himself. "Tom Hanson has told me a lot of good things about you. I'm glad he convinced you to come work for us.

"I am thankful for the job, Sir. It is quite challenging and I am enjoying it."

Moffett sat down at this point and looked serious. JT and Juanita figured the niceties were over and the gloves were now off. Much to their surprise the session went far better than they had anticipated. Arati didn't really know what to expect. Surprisingly, both the CIA and FBI agreed that, if Arati explained how she did it, they in turn would agree to drop the matter. Further, they'd explain how she left one little trace behind which enabled them to track her down. Moffett agreed to this and insisted on being present at the debriefing. In fact, he said that due to the classification of this investigation, he was going to personally take it off Hanson's hands, and JT, Juanita and Arati would be reporting to him in the future. As to the financial and other personal data gathering, Moffett explained that the DHS General Counsel believed the four employees in question, five if you count the DNI, had no reasonable expectation of privacy from their respective employers, and this could be extended to the DHS organization under these circumstances. Finally, they were not told to lay off the data gathering, but instead to make sure the report that went to the DoD and the White House, which he would sign off on, was as thorough and professional as they could make it. He then asked them to bring him up to speed on the case.

As soon as the coast was clear and they were headed out to where they had parked the car Juanita gushed, "Man, I thought we were going to get our asses handed to us, and instead we got carte blanche to press on."

"I'm thinking Charlie's got something up his sleeve, like a White House card or maybe something embarrassing to the players," commented JT.

Arati responded with, "Perhaps the Assistant Secretary mentioned the White House would not take kindly to personal information on top level employees being so easy to obtain. After all, there are a significant number of top level employees working in the White House."

"I suspect he reminded them that neither President Simmons nor Chief-of-Staff Kalani had any problem with the procedures we followed. He had to have cleared the idea with them first. Whatever he did, Charlie Moffett is definitely a political animal. I'm glad he's playing in that arena and not me," said JT.

"Well there's political, and then there's political. I find it interesting that, while he knew we looked into the chairmen of the Senate and House Intelligence Committees, he thought it would be a good idea to downplay that as much as possible," Juanita offered.

"Right. By the way, did our guys get anything from the spot light or the Saturday night surveillance tapes?"

"Yes. Tommy sent me a text message. He said the only distinguishable prints on the spotlight were Jorge Delgado's, and he most likely put the thing in originally. There was nothing on the surveillance tapes for the previous week that indicated anybody might have screwed with it, so to speak."

"Another dead end," lamented JT. "What time did you tell Rodriguez we'd be there?"

"Considering we need to drop Arati back at the office, the time that we are going to get there—six-fifteen."

"You're good."

"I know."
Arati just laughed.

CHAPTER THIRTY-ONE

Monday, Chantilly, Virginia

Rodriguez was actually out in the parking lot when they got there. Seems he wasn't used to being "cooped up," as Hopkins was a very open place, and decided they could talk more freely outside. The MENSA program manager felt he didn't have a lot of options with Cutler, and had already talked to the DARPA Director about letting him go from the program. "She was concerned," Rodriguez said, "but indicated it was my decision to make as program manager. If Cutler is at all 'salvageable,' she would not like to lose any more participants, and hopes he'll come around, particularly if you guys solve the current homicide case and apparent fake homicide attempt. If he is indeed losing it, we'll have to consider the potential damage to the program and the world in general if he's cut loose."

"I'm sure you feel like you're between the devil and the deep blue sea," offered Juanita. "I guess the question is, what do you think about Cutler."

"He is hard to read. Outward he seems calm, but he doesn't participate like he used to according to several of the other participants. And he acts, I don't know, suspicious; that is, suspicious of everyone around him. He asks questions of the others which aren't really relevant, and several have reported to me privately they thought he was trying to read them without permission. I guess he is trying to establish if any of them have a motive to harm him."

"Can he do that—read them without their permission or knowledge?"

"Everyone here has said they can pick up on and block any mental intrusions. We have tested that, and ninety-five percent of the time the participants were able to tell when they were being probed, and no information could be obtained from them.

Occasionally, we have surprised one or more of the group and they mentally 'blurted out' a thought which was picked up by those near them. We have noticed that if you are one of the surprised ones, you don't pick up on anyone else's outburst."

"So what do we do about Paul? What should we say to him?"

"I did talk to Ralph Krumski to get his professional opinion on Paul, and he said he was acting better than most folks in his circumstances."

"And that's good, right?" asked JT.

"Not according to Ralph and his admittedly less-than-in-depth psychiatric evaluation. He feels he is internalizing the trauma and his activities are indicative of that."

"Did he mention a prognosis?" asked JT.

"Actually he did. Absent any progress on the case and also any more events, Paul would probably come around in a few weeks or so and get back to some semblance of normality. That could be a shorter period of time if we solve the case. If we have another event, depending on what it is and how it affects him, almost anything could happen."

"Well, that's helpful."

"I do feel it is as accurate as we can get without some actual therapy for Paul."

"What about that? Not with MENSA participant Ralph Krumski I guess, but another professional."

"Ralph and I feel it would be counterproductive at this time. So how is the case coming? That may change what I think should be said to Paul."

"I feel we are narrowing down the outside suspects," replied JT. "We have got no viable motive for anyone outside of Lee's immediate circle. And in there, we are where we were before: we think Lee found out something significant about one of the participants which they didn't want revealed, and that's where we are concentrating our search. Lee's iPad probably would have helped in that regard, but we're sure it's long gone. I'm not sure how to put this to you Doc, but we were thinking you might uncover the same thing Lee did, or the perpetrator thinks you might, and we feel you may be in some danger. The guys 'guarding' Paul are aware of this and are serving a dual purpose here."

JT looked at Juanita and gave her a slight nod.

"Doc, we need to tell you what Lee had written down on the flash drive we found in his townhouse," said Juanita.

Rodriguez gave her a look with "Hello!" written all over it.

"I know, but this information is very relevant to the case and we needed to vet you thoroughly first."

"So now I'm vetted and not a suspect?" he smiled.

"Let's just say we thought we could trust you with this, and it might be helpful not only to your program, but to our investigation." Juanita went on to outline the suspicions the former program manager had recorded on his flash drive. She handed Rodriguez a summary of the notes.

"In my short time here, and in reviewing the data I've seen so far, I can't say I disagree with any of this. I will review it thoroughly and let you know what I think. Sounds like you have, tentatively at least, focused your investigation on these four individuals."

"Oh we're still looking at everyone. We have more than Juanita and I working the case. And yes, we would appreciate your input on Lee's comments. By the way, there was an anonymous tip that Randall Thompson had something to do with the Saturday night incident, but his alibi checked out, although he could have had help. So you should probably keep an eye on him and the other four."

"Is Paul aware of this tip?"

"No way."

"Good. To answer your earlier question, I think we need to reassure him as much as we can. Other than that I have no recommendations. I did suggest to the participants they try to buddy up as much as possible, just as a precautionary feel-good measure."

"Is that working, and who's Paul's buddy?"

"Krumski's his buddy, and except for Paul, I think it is working. At least everyone seems to be calm."

"Alright. I guess we need to get in there and talk to Mr. Cutler. We'll put our best shine on the case, and even offer some extra protection if we need to. Please let us know what you decide after reviewing Lee's notes, or if anything comes to mind which might help."

They all walked in together and JT and Juanita proceeded to find Cutler. After JT's presentation, which wasn't all song and dance, Cutler seemed to settle down, declined the extra protection, and went so far as to express an interest in trying to help them with the case. They agreed to a meeting later on in the evening at an outside location, where he could present them with his take on the participants.

They met at Anita's because Paul loved their standard fare of "New Mexico Style" Mexican food. JT was okay with the choice since it was also one of his favorites and close by. Paul was driven over by Scotty Westfield, the Bravo Unit member who was just finishing up his afternoon MENSA-sitting shift, and decided to join them for dinner. Paul offered his thoughts on all the participants, detailing his observations, thoughts, and "purloined" information from illicit probes. Juanita duly recorded them since she didn't eat much after mentioning this wasn't her style Mexican food. All told, it took almost two hours, during which time Paul barely managed to eat his dinner, taking a mouthful between every thousand words or so.

"Paul, this has been immensely helpful, and we will add this to the other data we have collected," said JT. "I hope you realize we wouldn't be doing our job unless we still considered you a suspect as well."

"Of course. I understand completely. But I'm sure this will get you pointed in the right direction. And don't hesitate to ask for any clarification."

"I've gotta get home now before my little boy forgets he's got a dad."

They settled the bill and headed back to the CTF to drop off Cutler, and Westfield headed home. Since they had left his car at the office, Juanita agreed to drop JT off at his place and come back to pick him up in the morning.

"Wow. I thought Scotty was going to lose it there once or twice. It's obvious this is not the way Cutler acts back in the office. I don't think he noticed Scotty's reaction as he was too involved in his dissertation."

"I noticed his reaction too, but then I was looking for it. Hopefully Paul didn't. So what do you think, Partner?" asked JT.

"I think this guy has lost it. I know he's smart and he's on a different level than us, but he really seemed to be ranting tonight, even considering he's upset and an apparent attempt has been made on his life. I think this guy's a loose cannon, and we can't in good conscience recommend he stay there as a participant. I really think he needs help."

"I agree. We need to pass this on to Rodriguez and see if our impressions make a difference in the way he, and maybe Krumski, think about the guy."

"By the way, why did you tell Paul we still considered him a suspect?"

"I thought he would think that anyway, so if we came right out and said it, it would help relieve any suspicion on his part. If he's guilty, I thought it might push him into doing something which will give him away; if he's not, then I think he'd figure he has nothing to hide or worry about us uncovering."

"Makes sense."

A few minutes later, Juanita's cell phone interrupted their discussion of the case. Juanita could tell it was Bill Hastings calling, and indicated as much to JT. A few nods and okays later she hung up.

"So what did he have to say?" asked JT.

"One of the cleaning crew saw a black SUV leave the parking lot sometime after eleven on Saturday night. Said he thought it looked funny since the guy appeared to be in a hurry. Didn't get a plate but did say he was pretty sure it was a Suburban. That's it for the canvas."

"Well, we covered the bases."

"Yeah. Let's go home."

CHAPTER THIRTY-TWO

Tuesday, Cape May, New Jersey

As he approached the ticket booth at the ferry entrance, Bill Brosard was thinking about the long weekend he'd just spent in Atlantic City. He hadn't had a day off in quite a few weeks so he decided to take a short vacation. The program participants who worked for Shurcor got four weeks of leave a year, and the rest got at least three weeks from their parent organizations. Most of them took ten of those days in early July when the CTF was closed for two weeks for various maintenance tasks, although a few went back to their "regular" jobs just to keep in touch. Brosard, as usual, had done well at the tables, playing mostly Texas Hold'em and other games where he wasn't taking from the House but rather the other players. He particularly liked playing at Bally's and Harrah's, but spent time in most of the casinos, usually three or four a trip. He always stayed at the Trump Taj Mahal Casino Resort where he was a platinum member. Not only did they regularly comp his room, but he also didn't pay for very many of his drinks. If he gambled there he never came away a big winner, and in fact usually made sure they were aware he had dropped half a grand or more. He always made those losses up in spades at the other establishments.

Brosard had lived in Northern Virginia for eight years, and prior to that in California. There he earned his undergraduate degree in Integrative Biology and Physiology from the University of California at Los Angeles, and then obtained a PhD in Psychology at Stanford University. The latter was where he talked to some CIA recruiters who convinced him to come to Langley. He really didn't know what to expect from The Company, but thought it would be fun and interesting. The recruiters talked about the dire need for really smart individuals at the Agency who could make a difference to the country in the post nine-eleven milieu. He had been on a few interviews with local organizations, and was not impressed with what they had to offer, nor the caliber of his interviewers. It wasn't hard to read their unspoken disdain for someone with superior intellectual abilities, and, quite frankly, he was getting tired of proselytizing himself to those who couldn't appreciate his potential. Besides, accepting the CIA position meant he could leave the banality of California behind for some work with national and even international consequences. He didn't have any romantic ties in the area since he liked to play the field, and his parents were considering retiring to Arizona, or maybe Texas, so the timing was perfect.

He had left the CTF Saturday morning and spent three nights at the Trump. His "luck" at the tables had been considerably less than spectacular this trip. Although the cards ran cold for his opponents as well, he could usually play the difference knowing for the most part what they had going for them. His major opponent at one house was quite inscrutable, and became a challenge. Thus Brosard played against him longer than he would have normally. Although the two of them were the winners at their marathon session, he figured he ended up breaking even against the guy. He imagined this was what it was like "playing with a normal deck of cards," and it certainly was more exciting than his usual game.

Brosard was young, only 34, tall with an athletic build, and had blond hair and blue eyes the ladies loved to get lost in. At least he never seemed to have any trouble convincing them of his charms, and since he had come to the east coast he figured he'd averaged close to one "serious relationship" a month; that is until he joined the MENSA program, which he blamed for cramping his style. That was another reason he liked these New Jersey trips: he spent less than half his nights in the Las Vegas of the East Coast alone. But this trip the gambling seemed to consume him, so after four afternoons and three evenings at the tables he'd had enough and didn't mind heading back home.

The Delaware Bay

As was his wont, Brosard took the ferry route up to Atlantic City rather than drive all the way up I-95. He thoroughly enjoyed the trip through rural Delaware and Maryland, as well as the journey up the coast of New Jersey, where he often stopped at the little seaside towns just to putz around. Again, as usual, he played late into his last afternoon there, but still hit the road with plenty of time for the ferry trip to Lewes so he could make it back home before midnight. The cool breeze blowing across the Delaware Bay made the voyage a real pleasure, and he spent most of the seventy minute journey at the outside bar sipping two bay breezes, a specialty of the boat containing vodka, cranberry juice and pineapple juice. He normally quaffed the sea breeze, the same drink but with grapefruit juice rather than pineapple, but was in the mood for something a little sweeter. He hadn't drunk all afternoon, so he figured he could enjoy two of these on the trip back and still be okay to drive. He used to speed regularly, and collected more than a few tickets along the way, but had forced himself to slow down since he hit the "Big-Three-O" a few years back. He certainly didn't want to risk getting pulled over for speeding and have a DUI conviction jeopardize his job. He was nothing if not a careful man.

As he enjoyed the drinks, the sunset, the cool breeze and the lack of any interruptions, he started waxing nostalgic. He recalled growing up in Cerritos, a bucolic neighborhood in the LA area out on the eastern edge of Los Angeles County. His mom was a high school science and math teacher for the county, and his dad was a history professor at UCLA. As an only child, with two teachers for parents, Brosard was continually challenged to improve his mind—something he found exceptionally easy and fulfilling. He was an honor student all through school and took every advanced course offered. Nonetheless, his parents discouraged him from accelerating his education and skipping grades, perhaps for fear of stunting his emotional development. Instead he took each course as it came, learned as much as he could about the subject, and often challenged and tested his parents with his new knowledge.

His mother was somewhat chagrined at his choice for an advanced degree, hoping instead he would use his biology undergraduate to go premed and earn an MD—a not uncommon maternal instinct. But he found the human mind fascinating and an exceptional challenge, and segued easily into psychology. It was while he was at Stanford that he realized he really was smarter than the average bear, and he became interested in psychometrics—the study of educational and psychological measurement—probably to see if he really was as smart as he thought. That introduced him to the work of Ronald K. Hoeflin and the Adaptive IQ Test and he joined the Mega Society. This was right down his alley, and when the CIA offered him the opportunity to keep on learning rather than set up a practice, he just couldn't refuse.

He'd always considered himself an excellent judge of character, due in no small part to his educational pursuits. He tried to put himself in the other person's shoes and guess what they were thinking, and more often than not he was right. It wasn't until he happened to be in the wrong place at the wrong time, and got swept up in a campus drug bust, that he really did know what someone "had in mind." The thoughts of the company he was keeping that evening literally leaped out at him. With patience and practice Brosard learned to use his new tool, and told no one, not even his parents, about it. He was fascinated by the polygraph he took for the CIA, couldn't believe how easy it was to control his physiological responses, and requested a position in that section of the Agency.

Lewes, Delaware

His reverie was interrupted by the call for everyone to head back to their vehicles for debarking. He had been lucky enough to catch a beautiful pink sky painted on scattered clouds at sunset, shortly after they left the dock at Cape May, so as they approached Lewes it was just past dark and the shore lights beckoned the ferry home. Since he was one of the last ones on the ferry, he was one of the last ones to drive off in Lewes. The first time he made the trip, it seemed his GPS was confused in the round-about journey through Delaware, but he had the route down pat now.

Georgetown, Delaware

As Brosard approached the four way stop sign in the small village of Georgetown, he paused to put a different CD in the car stereo system. There was certainly no traffic at this time of night, and this would only take a second. He was into the eighties and nineties music he heard growing up, but he also liked the "oldies" that his parents often played around the house. He'd have to subscribe to XM Radio, as this was probably cheaper in the long run than buying a lot of CDs. As he reached over to get his CD case on the passenger seat, a bullet screamed through his driver side window.

CHAPTER THIRTY-THREE

Tuesday, Georgetown, Delaware

Officer Ramon Delgado of the Georgetown Police Department was the first to respond to the 9-1-1 call. As he pulled up to the intersection, he saw the car sitting on the cross street just as was reported. His headlights illuminated the driver's side of the stopped vehicle, and he saw the bullet hole in the window. The caller said he wasn't hit, and Delgado figured he was damn lucky based on the location of the hole. The man got out of his vehicle and headed toward the police car. Delgado got on his PA and asked for verification again that the victim didn't need any medical assistance. The man seemed okay and was shaking his head so Delgado said, "Stay there and I'll be with you in a minute, Sir." Delgado ran the plate. When the data came back he took a quick look at it and then got out of the car.

"Officer, when I got to the intersection I reached down to get a new CD out of the case on the floor when my window exploded. I didn't know what had happened but I instinctively covered my head and stayed down. Then I heard a car drive off really quickly, or maybe it was a truck because it sounded like a diesel engine, and I'm pretty sure I smelled diesel fuel when I finally got out of the car. After a minute when it was obvious the truck was gone I looked up and saw the holes in both my windows. It had to be a bullet."

Brosard spit this out so fast the officer asked him to repeat it, but more slowly. "Did you see the vehicle at all?" Delgado asked when Brosard was done with the second rendition.

"No, I didn't. He must not have had his lights on because I think I would have noticed him sitting there otherwise."

"Did you hear a gun shot?"

"Honestly, I don't think so; just the sound of my window, windows, breaking."

"One of our guys is going to come out here and take some pictures. As soon as he gets here I'd like to give you a ride down to the station so we can get your statement. Shouldn't take too long, and if you want we'll get someone to drive your car to the garage where you can get those windows replaced in the morning. Or if you want we can tape 'em up and you can get back on the road tonight, and take care of the repairs back home. You going back to Virginia tonight?"

At first Brosard looked confused, but then he figured the officer had run his tags. "Do you think those windows will hold together with tape all the way back to the other side of DC?"

"Hard to say, but if I were you I wouldn't take a chance on flying glass or reduced visibility at highway speeds."

"Good point, Officer. Let's do the garage thing. Is there a hotel around?"

"Got a nice one just down the street from the station. I'm sure they'll have a vacancy on a Tuesday night. Oh, there's Richard now. Let me talk to him for a minute and then we'll head back. Why don't you get in the passenger seat and I'll be right there."

Chief Charles Petrie had come in from home and was dressed in civvies. Brosard didn't think he looked old enough to be the Chief of Police, but it was a small department. He was clean-cut and very courteous, and an image of Sheriff Andy Taylor kept crossing Brosard's mind. He couldn't help trying to see if the Chief had a weapon on. The statement took a lot longer than promised, as the Chief kept trying to get more job related information out of Brosard than he was forthcoming with. "But that relates to why someone would want to shoot at you," Petrie mentioned several times. "We just don't have random shootings in my town, and it's pretty obvious you're not a member of the one 'gang' that we do have here," he intoned.

After two hours Brosard had had enough and said, "Look, I'm connected with a highly classified government program back in Washington. Believe me, very, very few people know about this program so it's extremely unlikely this is job related. As I've said already, I have no enemies I can think of, and just have to assume this was either a case of mistaken identity or just some random act. I seriously doubt anyone followed me over here from Atlantic City, and besides, I didn't rip anybody off or send anybody to the poor house while I was there. Can we call it a night, please?"

The Chief could tell he had gotten all he was going to, so they wrapped it up. They had recovered his overnight bag from the car and brought it to the station before locking the vehicle up in the local garage. They offered to have an officer stand guard outside his room for the night, but Brosard said that wouldn't be necessary. So an officer accompanied him on the short walk down the street to the hotel, and said good night after Brosard checked in.

Brosard figured he'd better call Rodriguez and tell him what had happened and that he'd be late the next day—it depended upon what time the garage opened and how quickly they could get his windows fixed. Rodriguez seemed extremely concerned, and asked him to reconsider the offer of police protection. Brosard declined and said he'd be fine, and he'd see Rodriguez tomorrow. He then called down to the desk, and asked if there was any place he could walk to at this time of the evening to get a six pack. He was told if he hurried the gas station down the street might still be open, and he could accomplish his mission there. A short walk later he had purchased a six pack of Corona and a lime, a bag of Doritos and some salsa, and settled down to a movie on cable TV.

CHAPTER THIRTY-FOUR

Wednesday, Crystal City, Virginia

Arati, accompanied by Charlie Moffett, had spent two hours at Langley early Tuesday morning showing their computer forensic types how she had penetrated their data bases. The Agency had already closed the backdoor which Arati came through, but asked for the briefing anyway just to make sure they didn't miss anything. They didn't have to tell her how they detected her intrusion, as that became obvious to her midway through her explanation. Another two hours before lunch, spent in the J. Edgar Hoover Building on Pennsylvania Avenue in downtown Washington, DC, yielded much the same results. Although the FBI techies weren't positive how she managed to break into their program, as it required a more convoluted route than the CIA entry, they were close. The trapdoor was closed before she left the building. Although both agencies were reluctant, they both kept their word to Charlie Moffett, and allowed Arati a password protected entry into their systems. This gave her access to a select group of data bases, but tracked her comings and goings. It was a reasonable compromise which allowed her the access she needed to accomplish her purpose. She then spent the afternoon and evening collecting and cross-referencing data on all the suspects. As a result she didn't roll in to work Wednesday morning until 9:30, and both JT and Juanita looked at her like "Where in the hell have you been?"

"To quote a lady I know, gimme a break," she said.

JT and Juanita both raised their eyebrows at Arati's unconventional use of such a common phase. Her English was flawless, and she rarely used slang or contractions. Apparently her two cohorts were a bad influence on her.

"I gather you were here late last night," said Juanita.

"I was not that late, and my efforts were fruitful." She paused at this point.

JT gave in first and asked, "Okay, how fruitful?"

"I will start with Brandy Simmons."

"Whoa! You have something on sweet little MENSA participant Brandy Simmons?" exclaimed JT.

"Brandy was homecoming queen of her high school in Palo Alto, California, had a child out of wedlock with the help of her homecoming king, and had married, miscarried and divorced before her eighteenth birthday. She came to Washington to live with an aunt, attended college here and, as you know, has remained single."

"Not too incriminating," offered Juanita. "Where is her former lover now?"

"Still out in California, and settled down with a good job, a wife and two kids."

"Who's next?"

"Gayle Pennington has been downloading pornographic movies in her spare time."

"You are a font of knowledge, Arati. Perhaps we should have spent more time looking at the participants' laptops. Please continue," said JT suppressing a grin.

Arati continued unabashed. "Sam Donaldson has a juvenile record I was unable to access."

"Interesting, but probably has no effect on his ability to run the program. I wonder if that came up when they processed his security clearance?" asked Juanita.

"I see no reason why it should have, unless of course he offered it up, which he apparently did not. Roger Barrister, participant Tommy Pacquin's supervisor, has a security violation on his record for taking home a classified document. He claimed it was a test of a new polygraph procedure he was developing. Interestingly enough it *did* result in a physiological procedural change. This resulted in a one week suspension and a $500 fine, which seemed to enhance his career rather than serve as a detriment."

"Okay to bend the rules I suppose—as long as you're right. Anything else in that magic hat of yours, Arati?" asked JT.

"Doctor Ralph Krumski was implicated in a cheating scandal at Emory University in his home state of Georgia. The University could find no proof and concluded it was a hoax that was played on him. The school newspaper, which he had a connection to, intimated the source was a jilted girlfriend, but nothing was ever proven. However, there was a statistically significant drop in academic scores following this incident."

"I'm loving this, Arati. And it just keeps gets better. Please continue."

"Doctor Charles Samson, Sharon Rydell's fiancé, whom I earlier determined had a malpractice suit 'recanted' by one of his patients at Fairfax General, also lost his house after settling another malpractice suit two years before. And finally, Miss Rydell herself has been sending money to a woman on the west coast, who could be her long, lost sister. I did not notice this earlier because I mistook the transfers for student loan repayments."

"It would seem Miss Rydell has considerably more financial problems than we suspected," said Juanita. "The missing sister angle is interesting. Is she contributing to her fiancé's financial situation?"

"Not that I can determine. He paid the full settlement on the suit, which cost him his savings and the money he made selling his house, which was less than twenty thousand due to the depressed market at the time. He does have a good salary that he seems to be living within, but also has two canceled credit cards and the law suit on his record."

Sensing she was through JT asked, "Anything else for us, Arati?"

"No, but I have not finished examining the voluminous phone records I have. Truthfully, I am not entirely sure what to look for and I was hoping you or Juanita could help me with them."

"Be glad to," responded Juanita.

"So does any of this shed light on potential motives for our suspects?" Arati asked.

"I believe we need to look at Sam Donaldson and Sharon Rydell's juvenile records; however, I doubt there's anything so bad in either one of those that'd be worth killing someone in order to prevent them from bringing them to light. And I can't believe Doctor Lee was the kind of person who would do that in any event. Nonetheless, I feel we need to see them, so I'll talk to Charlie about getting us access. I do believe, Arati, that we need a better look at Miss Rydell's financials and also her doctor friend's. Other than that, I didn't see anything especially incriminating in your findings. What do you think, Juanita?"

"I have to agree. The incident with Barrister doesn't surprise me. He reminded me of someone when we talked to him down at Quantico, and it just now came to me who—Gregory House."

"Doctor House. Yeah, I think that's a reasonable fit, Juanita, but I don't think anybody's that good and that arrogant."

"Sometimes I think I am missing out on life by not watching more television," said Arati, "and movies as well."

"Just don't watch the CSI shows," said JT. "They leave you with the impression all the forensic results are obtained instantly; well, within an hour's time anyway."

"True," said Juanita, "but they have helped me preserve the crime scene a little better than I used to."

"There is that, but . . ." JT's phone interrupted him. He mouthed "CTF" to the ladies as he pushed the speaker button. "Agent Dunkirk," he answered.

"Agent, this is Stan Rodriguez and I'm afraid another disturbing incident has occurred." Doctor Rodriguez explained briefly the near miss experienced by Bill Brosard the night before. "I suspect you're going to want to talk to him. He said he'd be here around eleven since he left Georgetown at nine."

"Yeah, Doc, we will. We'll see you about eleven," he said and then disconnected. He relayed the info to Juanita and Arati. "How about them apples," Juanita said as the three of them looked at each other in disbelief. "This just gets curiouser and curiouser."

"I know that one—it is from Alice in Wonderland," said Arati.

"Good. There's hope for you yet. Do you want to come with us?"

"I think I should stay here as I have additional data to gather. Hopefully I will have more information for you when you return."

"Sounds like a plan. Let's hit the road, Amiga."

"Let me guess: I'm driving and we're stopping at Dunkin' Donuts on the way."

"You are such a good detective," complemented JT.

CHAPTER THIRTY-FIVE

Wednesday, Chantilly, Virginia

Stan Rodriguez had overcome a particularly rough upbringing in a barrio of Los Angeles, due in no small part to his exceptional intelligence and the unending devotion and persistence of his mother. When she wasn't working to provide for herself and her two progeny, she was helping them with their school work. After her oldest was killed in the crossfire of a local gang war, she redoubled her efforts for her youngest, Stan, and literally worked herself to death. Rodriguez's fondest memory was the look on her face when she learned he had been awarded a premed scholarship to USC. If only his mother could see him now, he thought, as he waited for JT and Juanita in front of the entrance to the CTF. He knew she would approve of his work at Johns Hopkins, but wondered what she would think of the MENSA program. His reverie was cut short by the arrival of the two DHS agents.

"Hi, Stan," said JT as he greeted them at the car. "Has Bill made it back yet?"

Rodriguez shook his head. "I expect him at any moment."

"How did he sound when you talked to him?"

"Last night he sounded a little shook up, but this morning when we talked he sounded almost philosophical. I expect he'll be joking about it when he gets here. In spite of his ego he's fairly easy going. I'm rather certain he won't react the way Paul did after his incident. Speaking of which, we now have a double header here—I'm sorry, a triple header with Toshi's death. What are we doing wrong?"

"I wish I knew," bemoaned JT. "In spite of the program's classification, we still have quite a few people who are aware of it, at least to some extent, and thus a potentially large suspect list. I do think we have it narrowed down to a few likely culprits, who,

211

unfortunately, seemed to have covered their, or his or her, tracks rather well. We have not uncovered any viable personal motive as of yet, and the professional ones are not playing out like we'd hoped either. Not yet, anyway. We are digging deeper into Lee and all the suspects, and we'll connect the dots eventually. Is that Bill pulling up now?"

"Yes. So how do you want to proceed?"

"Let's get a debrief from him and then continue our discussion after that."

A half hour later they had the story in what little detail existed, and had determined Brosard did indeed seem to be taking the incident in stride. He declined any protection and offered the opinion that his incident and Cutler's were attempts to derail the program, not actually to kill anyone. Further, he felt the death of Lee was not related. He offered no reason for this other than the severity of the one compared to the other two. Nor did he have any suggestions as to any motive for the murder.

"Besides the Georgetown Police and us, did you tell anyone else about this incident?" Juanita asked.

"I did call my boss before I settled in last night."

"And...?"

"He was pretty upset at first, but after we talked about it I think he calmed down. I wouldn't be surprised if he runs it up the flag pole though."

"And the consequences of that would be? . . ."

"Honestly, I don't know. He, the Agency actually, were originally unhappy with my coming over here, but then thought they may learn something useful and were apparently okay with it. I think they may be fast approaching the point where they think my progress thus far has barely merited what the Agency has gotten out of it. Nor does the likelihood of any potential advances merit my continued involvement. I'd like to stay, but

I'm effectively working two jobs here, and I wouldn't mind going back to the Company full time again."

JT decided to wrap it up. "Okay, Bill. We appreciate what you've been through and your assessment of the situation. I sincerely hope you are right about not being a target, but we are going to ask our guys here to be extra vigilant. And you should be too. Thanks."

After Brosard left Rodriguez's office the three of them continued their parking lot conversation.

"He does seem rather cavalier about it, doesn't he," offered Juanita.

"I think he believes what he's telling us. Don't you Stan?" asked JT.

"I think with his ego, he has convinced himself he has enough 'facts' to be quite confident in his assessment. I really don't think he's concerned. However, shouldn't we be?"

"I think we should err on the conservative side," said JT. "However, we are not likely to get any more manpower assigned here. We can ask the guys when they are here to keep an eye out for Brosard as well as Cutler. We do have to brief the Assistant Secretary and he may have a different idea. I'll let you know what he says. I also need to let Moffett know he may be hearing from the CIA. Have you got anything else for us today, Doctor Rodriguez?" JT kidded.

Rodriguez mentioned he'd had a chance to review all of Lee's notes, and didn't feel like they offered any information JT and friends hadn't already garnered. He did have a suggestion, however: "I was thinking," he said slowly and with obvious reflection aforethought, "that it might be useful to invite the MENSA participants to join The Galactic Society."

"And you think this because?" JT asked.

"They are all obviously quite intelligent; the society could use some new blood; and, as I'm sure you are aware, one of our goals is the enhancement of human intelligence. Seems like a natural to me. And . . ." he added quickly as he saw JT about to make a comment, "I don't think it compromises or complicates your investigation." The last he said with an ear to ear grin.

JT paused for a moment, then said, "You're probably right, but let me run it by Moffett, first, alright?"

Rodriguez nodded enthusiastically.

"Juanita, would you call and see if we can get to him this afternoon?"

"Yeah. I need to make another call too. I'll go out to the car and meet you there in a few minutes, alright?"

"Okay. I've just got two more questions for the Doc."

Juanita put her notes away, nodded at Rodriguez and said, "See you later, Doc."

JT had a hunch and now was the time to test it. He had seen many a violent crime scene, most of course after the fact, and some were truly gruesome. One in particular he recalled, more often than he cared to and usually in his sleep, was that of a young man with a bullet hole through his forehead and the back of his head gone. His brains were scattered all over the wall and ceiling behind him. When he and Rodriguez were alone, JT mustered up as much emotion as he could and burst this violent image into his head, but with Rodriguez' face on the dead body of the young man. Rodriguez turned his head only slightly, but very quickly, towards JT, and at the same time raised his eyebrows and widened his eyes, also only slightly. He knew instantly he'd been had.

"You got me agent. When did you know?"

"I didn't until just now, but I suspected soon after I met you. I'm pretty good at reading people, and I was more convinced when I asked and you denied it. It just made sense. Lee had the ability, and I think his buddy Harry Lisbon does to. What I don't know is how strong you are, and if the other folks in The Galactic Society have it as well."

"Why do you suspect them?"

"Well, you and Harry are psychic and are members; Lee was, and he was going to be a member. Your Board of Directors is a real 'Who's Who' list, and I'm thinking that ability helped them to get there. Not that you can't be successful without it, but it's gotta help. Plus four of your ten members are ex-astronauts and veterans of long exposure space flights. The capper for me is Charlie Moffett. Every meeting I've ever been in with him, he seemed to anticipate what folks were going to say. I used to think he was just well-prepared, but now I think I know the real reason. What say, Doc?"

"I'd say you're a damn good detective. I hope you can appreciate our reluctance to make this public, which is why I was less than honest about it before."

"No problem. But let me ask you this: why can't you tell me if any of our participants are involved in this?"

"One of the first things you learn is how to tell if other people are reading you. The next thing you try to learn is how to block them. It's difficult and it takes control, but it's a lot easier if you have someone of comparable ability to help. All the participants have had training in this. Lee had the inherent ability, but it was weak, and he developed it only after he was onboard for a while. Thus he only had strong suspicions about some of the participants. I'm in the same boat; that is, I can't get through the mental blocks our team members have developed."

"Can you give me anything on our suspects that will help me?"

"Not that I haven't already, JT. I verified Lee's impressions of the group, and have told you how I feel about each of them. As you know, it's pretty much the same vibes you got from them. I was hoping that mingling our participants with the Society members might prove useful, which is why I suggested it."

"You want to elaborate on that?"

"Not yet," Rodriguez admitted.

"Are you going to call Moffett?" JT asked.

"No. At least not until you talk to him. That's all on you."

"We'll keep you informed, Doc."

On the way back JT informed Juanita his plan had worked, and filled her in on the details. Then she told him they couldn't get an appointment to see Charlie Moffett until the next morning.

CHAPTER THIRTY-SIX

Thursday, Washington, DC

Charles Theodore Moffett never wanted to be anything but an astronaut. He grew up reading science fiction, and when Sputnik was launched he had attained the very impressionable age of fifteen. The space race was on and like his fellow future astronaut, Buzz Aldrin, he was driven to be a part of it. Unlike Buzz, he didn't necessarily have a burning desire to walk on the moon, although that would be okay if it happened: he just wanted to be out there among the stars. He was brilliant, excelled in math and physics, and played the piano exceptionally well, due in no small part to his unparalleled muscular coordination— or maybe it was the other way around. Taking advantage of his college's ROTC program, he earned his private pilot's license, enabling him to become a test pilot in the Air Force. There, during his spare time, he earned dual masters in aeronautical and electrical engineering. Selected into the astronaut program in 1971, he flew the last Skylab mission in 1973-4, working in space for 84 days. He saw the handwriting on the wall and knew NASA was in for some hard times, so he requested a position in their long range planning department. While stationed at Goddard he earned a masters in business administration on his own. Parleying the contacts he made there into a position in a major aerospace company, and worked his way up to senior vice president. When the Department of Homeland Security was formed in November of 2002, he was motivated to join, became a division chief, and then assistant secretary for counterterrorism. His regular visits to the racquetball court and the weight benches kept him slim and taunt—only his graying hair and accomplished manner hinted at his age. In other words, Charlie had been there and done that—he was one cool character—which is probably why JT was so impressed with him, and always a little apprehensive when he went to see him.

This time was no different. Juanita had given him a heads up yesterday when she called for the appointment: it would not be the best thing for their careers if the CIA contacted Moffett cold about an attempt on the life of one of their employees, especially if the CIA man was involved in a case which his agents were investigating before he heard it from his own guys. And here it was just two days ago that Juanita, along with Arati and JT, were in to see Moffett about other CIA problems with the very same investigation. She hadn't gotten any reaction from him on the phone, so they didn't know what to expect. Once again, however, they were surprised at his response to the "near miss" on Brosard, the potential CIA interference, and the Rodriquez suggestion.

After they had laid out the details, Moffett said, "Interesting, but I'm inclined to agree with Brosard on his assessment of the situation. And don't worry about the Agency—I can handle any problems those guys try to deal us. I must admit though, I do like Stan's suggestion to offer the MENSA participants membership in The Galactic Society. That will give me a chance to meet these folks without raising any suspicions. It's not often I get to be involved in a case like this. I look forward to it. In fact I'll call Stan and get a meeting set up. Have you got anything else for me today, Agents?"

They answered negatively and took their leave of DHS Headquarters. It wasn't until Juanita's PT Cruiser was headed back across the Fourteenth Street Bridge that she finally broke the silence she thought JT's contemplative mood suggested she maintain. "So why do you think he wants to get the MENSA troops into The Galactic Society?" she asked.

218

"I think he just wants to be more involved in the case. Sitting behind a desk is probably a little boring for an ex-astronaut."

"You think?" she kidded. As an afterthought she added, "Yeah, that could be it. But I bet his current job gets pretty exciting at times."

"If you can call dealing with bureaucrats exciting. He may make some important decisions, but nothing rises to the level of exciting I'm sure."

"That's your law enforcement bias coming out. No wait, you're trying to dissuade me from going for a promotion so you can continue to have me serve as your lackey out here on the streets."

"Like I said before, you're such a good detective. Be a shame to waste all your talent elsewhere." Changing the subject he asked, "What do you think of the memorial over there on the right?"

"The Air Force Memorial? I like it. I think the Marine Corps Memorial down near Quantico is pretty neat too. They are both very symbolic."

"I knew you'd say that. But I prefer the Iwo Jima Memorial—much more meaningful. I also like the Navy Memorial downtown—also more meaningful and practical."

"What's that one look like?"

"It's a statue of a lone sailor overlooking a map of the seven seas etched into the large circular concrete sidewalk in front of him. There are also a number of bronze plaques around the outside commemorating historical naval events."

"Do the Army and Coast Guard have a memorial?"

"The Coast Guard has one in Arlington Cemetery I'm sure you'd like: very symbolic. To tell the truth I'm not sure if the Army has a memorial per se. They have lots of memorials to various battles and groups. I'll have to look that up. You think there's more to Moffett wanting to get The Galactic Society involved?"

"So you do think there's more than meets the eye here, don't you?"

JT shrugged.

"He is a member; there are a lot of smart persons in the Society, I suppose, if he, Lisbon and Rodriguez are members. And I think you're right about him wanting to take a more hands-on approach for a change. So you don't like the idea?"

"No, it's not that. I just don't like my bosses involved in my investigations. Hanson always gave me free reign and seldom got down to the nitty-gritty level. Just not used to it, I guess. Hell, maybe Moffett will have some good investigative suggestions. Let's get back to the shop and see if Arati has come up with anything."

CHAPTER THIRTY-SEVEN

Thursday, Crystal City, Virginia

Arati was munching on a salad she brought back from The Underground when JT and Juanita walked in. She told them she had spent the morning rummaging data base after data base, and most of the relevant ones two or even three times. Then she started searching far afield: Facebook accounts, Amazon accounts, you name it. So far nothing was popping out at her, but she was at least as persistent as she was brilliant—an awesome combination. She was happy for the company though, as she hadn't talked to anyone all day other than the person who sold her the salad. "How did it go with Secretary Moffett?" she inquired.

Juanita hit the highlights of their meeting with the assistant secretary, and answered the few questions Arati asked about it.

"I can't get over how cool and collected Moffett is," said JT. "I always heard that about him, and now that I've seen it a few times I certainly believe it. Would you believe he wants to meet with the MENSA group to 'become more involved with the case'?"

"Really? JT, I would love to be there. Do you think you could get me an invitation?"

"Arati, we haven't been invited yet, and I don't know if Moffett intends to ask us or not. If he does I'll put in a plug for you to come along. How's your data gathering coming?"

"Only one of our participants, Pennington, has a Facebook account, but everyone, other than Krumski, has purchased something from Amazon at one time or another. None of them tweet that I have been able to determine, but many send text messages, some of them quite regularly, and all have active email accounts. The staff are a bit more active, but I have found nothing significant in any of their transactions we did not already know about. I have not started on the other suspects as of yet—I hope to get to that this afternoon. Unless you have something else for me," she said expectantly.

Juanita smiled and asked "What about their communication patterns?"

"I would like to have you look at those with me. I am not sure I would be able to detect anything subtle. Other than family and what I suspect are a few friends, I could find no unusual pattern among their non-work communications. I do find it strange that only Pennington and Brosard communicate regularly with their former office or other work place."

"That is interesting. I guess the others are glad to be away. We already knew Brosard was keeping his foot in the door at the Agency according to both him and his boss."

"Yes, but there is something else going on here I think. He spends, what seems to me, an inordinate amount of time on the phone with his boss. From snatches I have managed to get, I believe he is keeping him informed about everything going on in the program. They talk often—three or four times a week."

"Okay. What about Pennington? Did you get a feel for what she's doing?"

"It appears as though she is mixing business with pleasure. She is continually answering questions from one of her office mates about file dispositions and other work activities. There is also a lot of banter back and forth between them, including arrangements for meetings I believe you would call girls' nights out. It seems fairly normal but, again, I would like you to go over them with me," she said looking at Juanita.

"You mentioned earlier she was into internet porn. Can you tell from that or her relationships if she is gay?"

"Oh, my. I never thought of that. I mean, I did not examine her pornographic activity that closely. Perhaps if Juanita looked at it with me."

JT cast a surprised look at Arati, and then glanced over at Juanita.

"Oh, I did not mean to imply . . ."

JT and Juanita both started laughing, causing Arati to breathe a sigh of relief. "I still have a lot to learn about the American sense of humor," she complained, probably for the tenth time.

"We know what you meant, Arati. Do you want to get to that now?" Juanita asked.

"Yes, but, I do want to mention one other thing I noticed."

JT and Juanita knew her habit of saving the best for last, so they both looked at her with anticipation.

"Well, have either of you ever heard of steganography?"

"Sure," JT replied. "Andy is in to that at school."

Juanita looked amused, not so much at JT's answer but at Arati's reaction to it—amazement. She also had an inkling of what was coming.

"It's the drawing of dinosaurs, isn't it?"

Arati started laughing, and then stopped abruptly when she saw the grin on JT's face. "You are pulling my leg again," she scolded him. "Seriously, do you know what steganography is?"

"Arati, it sounds familiar, but no, I don't have a clue."

"Me neither," added Juanita.

"It's the art of hiding messages in plain sight," she began. "There are various types; for instance, invisible ink or microdots, or even knitting yarn. I just finished John Sandford's *Invisible Prey* novel, where curses were concealed in quilt patterns. These are examples of physical steganography."

"I guess that's pretty popular," said JT. "In the movie Wanted, Morgan Freeman leads a group of assassins who hide instructions for their next hit in quilts."

"You only remember that movie because Angelina Jolie is in it," offered Juanita."

"Not to contradict anyone," interjected Arati, "but today the digital forms are more prevalent."

"I remember now," Juanita piped in. "In one of my courses they explained how a message could be hidden in a jpeg file by altering some of the bits."

"Indeed. The most popular methods in use today, we think, are digitized photographs, which are stored as an array of colored dots, or pixels. Each pixel's color is determined by how much red, green, and blue it has in it, which is the basic idea behind color TV. The intensity of each color has a value from 0-255, which is stored in eight computer bits. If you change just the least four bits of intensity, the difference in the color will hardly be noticeable. Since text is usually stored using eight bits per character, you can conceal one and a half characters in each pixel of the photograph. So a standard 640x480 pixel image, which would be about the size of a five by seven photograph, can hold over 450,000 characters. That is a considerable amount of data!"

"I suppose you could hide a picture in a picture as well," offered JT.

"Yes, you could."

"So you either compare the doctored picture to the untouched one, or you know which pixels are the ones with the information ahead of time."

"Exactly."

"But wouldn't a good agent, one trained to look for these things, be able to pick out the hidden data?" asked Juanita.

"That is a good possibility. So most people do not use the former picture comparison technique, but rather encrypt the data before they put it in the picture. Or, they scatter it across the picture randomly. Of course the recipient has to know the decryption algorithm or the pattern to retrieve the information. If you use both methods, then retrieving the information becomes considerably more difficult."

"A great tutorial, Arati, but now are you going to tell us where this is leading?"

"I noticed Mister Cunningham, Chief of the Cognitive Sciences Division at the CIA, has been sending pictures of baseball trading cards to another individual."

"From his personal computer?"

"Yes."

"And did they have hidden information in them?"

"Maybe. I really have no indication they do, but that seems odd to me, and I am pursuing it."

"Is there anything suspicious about this other individual?"

"Not that I have discovered as of yet. But then, so far I have checked him out in only a few data bases."

"Aren't any of the others passing pictures via email, or posting them on their Facebook accounts?" asked Juanita.

"Yes, many of them are. But all of those incidents seem normal to me."

"Which is how it would be with a good spy, which is not what we are investigating here."

"I know, but . . ."

JT held his hands up and interrupted her with, "I have no problem with you looking into that, Arati, as long as it doesn't interfere with our investigation." He was smiling so she knew he was not upset. "Why don't you ladies do as Arati suggested, while I add all this new data to our board. If you find anything significant then I'll add it as well. Sound like a plan?"

"Let's do it."

CHAPTER THIRTY-EIGHT

Friday, Crystal City, Virginia

They'd been in the office for several hours working on their SOC, or state of the case, boards when JT's phone rang. He didn't recognize the number, but thought it was a New York or New Jersey area code. "This is Agent Dunkirk," he intoned.

"This is Chrissie Lee, Agent Dunkirk. I'm glad I caught you at the office. I guess you know I'm back home now."

"Please call me JT, and yes, I knew you'd finished up here and returned. What can I do for you?"

"Actually I think I have something which might help you. I finally got around to all my unopened mail last night and there was a note from my dad."

"Really? I hope that wasn't too traumatic for you."

"It brought a few tears, I have to admit. I had to wait until today before I could call you. From the post mark, my guess is it remained in the out-going mail at his work facility for a day or two, or perhaps at the post office, and got here the day I left to come down there. I think it will be relevant to your investigation, so I've scanned the note and the envelope, and I'm emailing them to the address on your card as we speak. I'll drop the real things in the mail to you if you want."

"Can you hang on a minute will I check my mail?" JT reached over to his computer and was about to click on the send/receive icon when the message arrived. He opened the attachment and gave it a quick read. "Holy Christmas!" he exclaimed. "Would you mind sending the originals FedEx?" he practically begged.

"It would be my pleasure," she replied. "I will want these back when you are through with them. And JT, you will keep me informed?"

"As promised, Chrissie, as promised. And thank you. Talk to you later."

"Glad I could help. Take care."

JT printed out the note and walked over to where Juanita and Arati were working. "Ladies," he beamed, "you are not going to believe this."

Juanita and Arati had not been paying much attention to JT, considering they were deep into phone call and email deciphering. They were aware he was on the phone, and did look up when they heard "Holy Christmas!" But they figured it was just his normal exuberance and continued working. They missed his "Chrissie" comment, so had no idea what was coming. Their curiosity was piqued however, when he walked toward them looking like a smug Garfield the Cat, from the Jim Davis comic strip, after he had pulled another fast one on his fall-dog, Odie.

"I know we often speak for the dead as part of our job," JT said, "but there are times when the dead speak to us. Chrissie Lee has sent me a note her dad sent to her just before his death. It was apparently delayed in the mail and she didn't open it until last night. Listen to this," JT said as he read the printed out email attachment.

Dearest Chrissie,

I'm sorry that we haven't talked much recently but I have been extremely busy. Our rate of progress has increased as of late, and I am more and more excited about the potential for what we are accomplishing. I wish I could tell you more about it, and I will some day; but for now, you already have the general idea from our previous conversations, and you are a smart lady. Unfortunately this is not just a friendly note, but instead I need to relay information to you for safe keeping in the event something happens to me. Do not worry, this is very unlikely, but I'd be negligent if I didn't inform someone of my suspicions—make that knowledge. One of the participants in the program, Paul Cutler, is guilty of several rapes. I am pretty sure these were committed when he was in his late teens or early twenties in San Francisco. This is where he grew up and first started working. I am confident that he is not aware of my knowledge, and I have no definitive proof of his guilt. Thus I can only bide my time, until I can devise a plan to remove him from the program, if not have him prosecuted. Although, as I understand it, depending upon the circumstances, the statute of limitations may apply. I am working on something, and hope to have this resolved within the next few weeks; however, that may not come to fruition and I will have to learn how to deal with it. My biggest fear now is similar circumstances with other current or future participants will arise as the program proceeds, and will present a serious challenge to the eventual program implementation. I will call you in a few days, and try to get up there for a short visit in a few weeks or so. Once again, please do not worry, as deleterious consequences are highly unlikely; but you know what a stickler I am for taking precautionary actions, as was so hilariously demonstrated by the infamous fire extinguisher incident. Love you.

> *Dad*

"Wow!" Juanita exclaimed. "We just got our motive."

"Probably. But we'd have to prove that: (1) Cutler did indeed commit those crimes; (2) he thought there was no statute of limitations on one or the other of those particular transgressions; and (3) he knew or suspected Lee was on to him," said JT.

"That is a lot of 'ifs' to contend with," offered Arati. "From the way the note is worded, I believe we can conclude that Lee was sure of Cutler's guilt, but had no proof. I suspect therefore, it was through his ESP abilities he learned of this, probably unintentionally."

Both JT and Juanita pondered this for a minute or two.

Juanita finally broke the silence with, "That's the only way it makes sense to me. I can't see him pursuing this kind of information intentionally. He wasn't that kind of person."

"I agree for the most part," said JT. "But it is possible he was trying to protect the program, and did probe for potential spoilers. So what are we going to do with this information?"

"I could search for unsolved rape cases during the times and places Cutler has lived, and review my extant information on him," offered Arati.

"Good. Juanita and I will do the same. I'm beginning to think the attempt on his life was something he set up to throw us off track. We've got nothing but his word on that whole incident—other than the departing SUV."

"Perhaps," said Juanita. "But he was really convincing."

"He was," JT agreed nodding his head. "He was indeed."

Several hours and one lunch later, JT and Juanita were deep into re-reviewing everything, and Arati was researching Cutler's life history, when JT got a call from Charlie Moffett. "Yes, Sir," he said, wondering if somehow Moffett had already found out about Lee's note to his daughter. That was not what the Boss had to tell him. In fact, it wasn't even close. JT hung up and walked over to where Juanita was working. "Can you get Arati and meet me in the conference room?" he asked.

Juanita thought he looked worried, but figured she wouldn't make him go through it twice, so she stifled her questions for now, except for one: "Do we need to bring anything?"

JT shook his head.

"Arati will meet us there in a few," she said after hanging up.

"You look worried, JT," Arati said after he had shut the door and they were settled in the conference room.

"I just got off the phone with Mr. Moffett. Seems Senator Birmingham of South Carolina has somehow gotten wind of the MENSA program, and is threatening hearings on this 'potential invasion of the basic human right to individual privacy.' I don't think Charlie believes there is a leak in the department, but he did ask us to consider where the Senator might have gotten his information from. He wants to meet with us tomorrow morning at nine, to discuss where we are on the case. Thank goodness it's a Saturday, or we'd be there at six in the morning."

"Did he say anything else?" asked Juanita.

"Yeah. He believes there might be an item in tomorrow's paper regarding the Senator's concerns."

"Wow. That might blow the lid off the whole thing," said Juanita.

"Does this Saturday morning meeting include me?" asked Arati.

"All three of us. And yes, this may have some serious consequences. Did either of you get anything additional on Cutler?"

"Not I," stated Juanita.

"Nor do I have anything definitive," said Arati.

"Then I'm not inclined to work on this anymore until we get some direction from Moffett. I'm ready to brief him on what we've got. At least we have some new information for him. What about you guys? You ready?"

Juanita looked over at Arati and then back to JT. "Yeah, we're ready and I guess we've had it too. Arati and I are going out for some dinner. You want to join us?"

"No, I'm going home. Want me to pick you two up in the morning, say eight-twenty or so," he said as he looked at Juanita then Arati.

They both nodded and JT headed back to his work place, gathered his stuff and headed home.

CHAPTER THIRTY-NINE

Saturday, Springfield, Virginia

JT was up early and had checked his inbox periodically for Washington Post news items which were emailed to subscribers throughout the day. *Either it's not that newsworthy or the senator thought twice about releasing anything*, he thought. He decided to go jogging and refrained from picking up the hardcopy of the Post on his driveway as he stepped over it. On the weekends he usually jogged around Burke Lake, with Andy following him on his bike. Since he had to go into town later he decided instead to take another tour of the Daventry neighborhood, hilly as it was in some places. He often thought about the cases he was working on during his runs, or was lost in the music from his iPod, or some combination thereof, sometimes to the exclusion of his surroundings. Occasionally he'd find himself looking at the seemingly unfamiliar streets and taking a few moments to realize where he was. Today was no different, and he couldn't help but turn over in his head what he was going to say to Charlie Moffett in a few hours. *This is dumb— I just tell it like it is.*

When he got back to his driveway, he reached down and pulled the newspaper out of the plastic bag and shoved the crumpled container into his back pocket. He scanned the front page and felt mildly relieved. The second and third pages contained no articles on the program either. Back inside at his kitchen table he looked through the Metro section and again found nothing. Although this was a classified program, he'd seen this game played before, with politicos trying to gain points with the public for "keeping them informed" of the manner in which their tax money was being spent. Like these guys really cared— more likely they were just keeping their name in the public eye. Of course they would only "reveal" unclassified information and hint at the rest. *No sense crying over milk that isn't even spilled yet,* he thought. *But, how would Average Joe Citizen react to finding out about the MENSA program? The press would probably have a heyday, but would the guy on the street really care? DoD could probably down play it to a point where it wasn't so threatening, the 1984 connotations notwithstanding. I wonder how Charlie Moffett will see this.*

Andy usually slept in on the weekends, and JT didn't have the heart to wake him. After his shower he found Carmen in the kitchen. "I'm afraid I'm going to miss breakfast with you guys this morning," he said. "The big boss wants to see us downtown, but I should be back home by eleven. Please tell me you didn't have anything planned before then."

"I'm good," replied Carmen. "I do want to go see Maria this afternoon and maybe spend the night. I think she wants to take me shopping to 'update' my wardrobe."

"Sounds like an excuse to me."

"No, she doesn't need one. She'll probably end up buying some clothes for herself or something for the house and I won't buy anything, but it will be a fun time. I might talk her into a movie too."

"Alright, I'm outta here. I'll call if I'm going to be late," he said as he shoved the paper in his backpack and headed out to the car.

Annandale, Virginia

Soon after Arati started working for DHS and hanging with Juanita, she moved out of Southwest Washington to Annandale. Juanita mentioned there was an apartment going vacant in her building, and Arati snapped it up the same day. So JT was on his way to Annandale to pick up his two cohorts in anti-crime. Lost in his thoughts about the case, he reached Annandale in what seemed like no time at all. The ladies were waiting for him at Juanita's place.

"What are you two so up about?" he asked as they got in his car.

Juanita answered: "Why not? From what you said Mr. Moffett is not mad at us. He may be unhappy with the progress of the case, but honestly, what more could we have done? I'm thinking this is just a strategy session."

"Arati, what's your take on this?" asked JT.

"I do not know. I never have understood American politics, and from what I have seen, I do not want to. I hope we get to continue on the case, because I think no murder should go unsolved, nor unpunished. Additionally, I hope the MENSA program continues, because I think it is good for the human race in general; however, I do have a concern for whether or not we are capable of handling the consequences of a successful program. But if any country can do it, we can."

"So you think the Senator should bring the program out into the sunshine?" JT asked.

"I must conclude, from all of my reading, that is usually a good thing. What do you think?" she asked.

"I guess I have been dealing with the criminal element so long I am a dyed-in-the-wool pessimist. I think the case will go on, with us working it, but as for the program going public—not a good idea. I'm thinking if this Senator really believes what he is preaching, or thinks this will play in Peoria, he may try to end it. I really don't know if DoD wants to play in that ball game."

"And you, Juanita," JT asked.

"I think I'm somewhere in between. I certainly believe the program is a good thing, and letting the sunshine in, as you say, is usually a good practice. But you never know how the public will react. If Birmingham raises enough stink, and rallies a vocal minority, then the program may be toast. The Guantanamo thing still lingers, what with the way Simmons waffled on it; the immigration issue is getting hotter everyday it seems; and look at the ruckus TSA raised with the airport inspection procedures. All these are rights issues which affect everybody when you look at the big picture, but they don't have a daily effect on every John Q. How is he gonna react when he realizes the person next to him could be a government agent, who is probing his psyche for potential criminal activity? I guess I've just talked myself into the idea that the program is not yet ready for prime time."

They were all lost in their own thoughts for the rest of the trip into town.

CHAPTER FORTY

Saturday, Washington, DC

Since its inception shortly after the events of Nine Eleven, the Department of Homeland Security has been headquartered in a former naval facility just off Nebraska Avenue in northwest Washington. The thirty-eight acre site is across from American University, and has thirty-two buildings in various states of repair, or more often, disrepair. The Department planned to consolidate its sixty-plus Washington area offices into a single headquarters complex at the former Saint Elizabeth's Hospital campus in the Anacostia area of Southeast Washington, but that was likely still a few years off. Moffett's current fifth floor office afforded a reasonable view of Rock Creek Park, and the Assistant Secretary appeared to be taking it in when JT and company were shown in. After everyone was settled in their seats, Moffett thanked them for coming and then laid out his agenda for the meeting: "(1) I realize we just talked two days ago, but I'd like a progress update; (2) I'd like to discuss how Senator Birmingham got wind of the MENSA program; (3) I want to know your opinion about program promulgation; and (4) I'd like your thoughts on how the troops would react to an invitation to join The Galactic Society."

In spite of the businesslike manner in which his agenda was presented, JT thought Moffett seemed more friendly than usual. And he was asking for their thoughts and opinions. *I'm really starting to like this guy*, he thought. He didn't let Moffett's pause after mentioning his last agenda item become a pregnant one. He brought the Assistant Secretary up to speed on the items they'd uncovered since their last meeting with him. He included Arati's suggestion that Cunningham's use of baseball trading card pictures could be a steganographic communication, and their belief that Pennington might be gay. He saved the best for last and handed Moffett a copy of Toshi Lee's note to his daughter.

It wasn't hard to know when he got to the rape part. A few moments later Moffett looked up at the assembled group: "You got this from Miss Lee yesterday?"

Before JT could respond Arati piped up with: "Yes, Sir. I spent the afternoon looking for unsolved rape cases in the times and areas where Cutler lived, but could find nothing definitive. Several were promising, but I could not connect them with any confidence. This was quite time consuming, and I have more places to check. We may be able to build a strong enough circumstantial case to at least convince Cutler we were on to something."

"Excellent, Arati. This would certainly afford him a motive. Please continue to pursue that. Is Rodriguez aware of this?"

JT responded with, "No, Sir. We knew we were coming here this morning so we thought we'd wait on that."

"What is Stan's take on Cutler?"

"He's more hopeful than I, but then I'm not hopeful at all. Krumski thinks he might be salvageable with therapy, but I doubt Cutler would sit for it. I think the program should write him off, except his reaction to that could very possibly be damaging. If we can get him on the rapes or Doctor Lee's murder, his departure would be a moot point."

"Tell us what you really think, JT," Moffett said with a smile. "I'm inclined to agree with you, so let's solve this case and be done with it. Arati, I presume you were the one working the trading card issue."

"Yes, but without a key, I do not believe we have enough computing power to determine if they are being used in that manner."

"Okay. So what about Pennington? Do we have a motive there?"

Juanita fielded this one: "Although she's not exactly out of the closet, the door is wide open. Turns out most of the people she knows are aware of her sexual proclivities, so we have discounted that as a motive."

"All right then. Is that it for the case update?"

JT looked at his cohorts and then nodded at Moffett.

"Continue what you have been doing except for one thing—hold off on the trading card part of the investigation until I check something out. How about if we take a short break and head down to the cafeteria for some coffee? When we get back I'll fill you in on my end of this case. JT, there is another matter I need to discuss with you first. Would you ladies mind going on ahead? We'll be right behind you."

Juanita and Arati headed out to the cafeteria, and closed the door behind them. JT was pretty sure he knew what was coming, but also knew enough not to volunteer.

"So Stan tells me you're on to us," Moffett said.

"Well, I wouldn't put it that way, Sir. And I did have to use a little subterfuge to find out for sure."

"So I heard. I only have three questions for you, and I suspect you know what they are, but I'll ask them anyway. Who else knows, are you and they okay with the program and where it's going, and can you keep this to yourselves?"

"Both Juanita and Arati know: Juanita's my partner, and I imagine Arati figured it out on her own, or would have in short order. She didn't act very surprised when I told her. We have discussed this among ourselves, Sir, and none of us have a problem with the program or keeping it to ourselves."

"That's what I wanted to hear. Let's join the ladies."

When they returned, Moffett gave them each a copy of the letter of inquiry from Senator Birmingham's office. "So what are we going to do about this, Sir?" asked JT when everyone had finished reading.

"As you can see from his letter," Moffett began, "Birmingham has asked for a program brief. Since he's the Chairman of the Judiciary Subcommittee on Privacy, Technology and the Law, it's likely he'll be cleared and a briefing scheduled. I've talked with the Senator's staff and they're letting on like they don't know what he'll do. I think they're being cagey, so there's a possibility he wants something in trade for his silence. Our fear is he actually wants to make an issue of the privacy concerns he purports could be inherent in a program of this sort. We may or may not be able to handle the publicity in that case, but probably not, if he is as persistent and public on this as he was on the DoD internet privacy issues last year. I guess we'll just have to cross that bridge if and when we come to it. Right now I'd really like to know how he got wind of it, but I strongly suspect it was from one of our Agency friends. What's your take on this?"

"I strongly believe it was from the same person or persons who gave us the tip on the murder, 'shot at' Cutler in the parking lot of the CTF, and 'ambushed' Brosard in Georgetown. Our feeling is it's either a program participant, albeit with outside help, or someone aware of the program, and you've seen our list of those folks."

Moffett looked at Juanita and Arati and saw they were in agreement. "Now for the next bit of bad news: the CIA Director and the DepSecDef are questioning program continuance based on Birmingham's possible meddling and potential political fallout, and the possible danger to the participants based on Doctor Lee's murder and the two incidents you mentioned, particularly the one with Brosard. As you know, we have had strong White House backing, but both of these individuals are close to Simmons. Basically the program is on hold until Robin Dornan and I give the two of them a program update at the White House and propose a course of action. Any suggestions?"

The trio was caught quite off guard with that last question and a pregnant pause followed. Arati looked over at JT after a few moments and asked, "May I?"

"Please, by all means."

She turned to Moffett and said, "Solving the case would alleviate many misgivings about the situation; although, depending upon the identity of the guilty party or parties, it could raise other concerns. In any event, we are proceeding in that direction, as we must, and I do not see how we could be doing more at this point. We have discussed among ourselves the idea of going public with the program, and decided that was not in our best interest at this time. As to the Senator's concerns, are they more about privacy issues or monetary concerns, or perhaps even a personal motive? Depending upon the answer to this we may be able to chart a different course."

"And I thought you said you didn't understand politics," JT commented.

"Well, that is the rub, Doctor Jabornae," said Moffett. "The Senator has been consistent on the privacy issues, and if that is truly his concern, he'll probably settle for nothing less than the program's demise. I don't think it's a monetary issue because the program is not expensive—a small part of DARPA's budget, which is a small part of the DoD budget. As far as a personal motive, the only one connected with the program who he has knocked heads with is the Secretary of Defense, and he is not pushing the program. Other than the DARPA Director, I don't think he'd connect it with anybody else."

"How about President Simmons?" asked JT.

"I doubt he makes that connection, per se, although I wouldn't put it past Birmingham to use this in general as an embarrassment for the Administration. Or he might withdraw his objections in trade for support for some program he's interested in."

"Maybe we should find out what his problem is and just submit to the blackmail if we need to," said Juanita, "but I guess that wouldn't satisfy the CIA or DoD."

"That is an option, but I was hoping for some more proactive, out-of-the-box thinking on this."

"Another option would be to hide the program in another large government organization. However, in that case, you'd probably have to have the CIA and DoD participants leave the program. A third option is to just kill it for a time, and then resurrect it under another name."

"I see you've been around the government a while, JT. Both would work to some extent. The former generally has too much negative fallout potential, whereas the latter tends to lose a lot of program momentum."

"What if this wasn't a government program?" asked Juanita.

"Interesting. And what would you suggest?" Moffett queried.

"Maybe one of the universities, or a non-profit, or possibly even a public-minded commercial organization," she offered in response.

"I know I said this was a small part of DARPA's budget, but a small part of three billion can still be a lot of money. I doubt these entities would be interested without the six mil a year of government funding."

"Perhaps one of the high IQ societies would like to take this on," JT suggested.

"They are funded primarily by member dues," said Arati. "An organization funded by endowments and contributions may be able to afford it, if they had an interest. The Smithsonian might be a good candidate, although it's not exactly in their bailiwick."

"I like the way you think, Arati. I was leaning in a similar direction myself. What do you think of The Galactic Society taking over the program?" Moffett asked smiling.

"Awesome!" both JT and Juanita exclaimed simultaneously. Arati was equally impressed, but less vocal about it.

"What do you think, Arati?"

"Sir, I think the two are an excellent fit. TGS definitely has the interest, there is already a connection there with Doctor Rodriguez, they have no association with the government, and I suspect they could afford it."

"We would have to get buy-in from the participants and their employers," said JT.

"Which would include whom?" asked Moffett.

"Staff-wise that would be three DARPA people: Sam Donaldson, Robert Pullman and Doctor Rodriquez. The doc is an IPA so it would be easy transition for him; Pullman is just a techie and easily replaceable if he didn't want to transfer; but Sam Donaldson's got a lot of government time and would be a real loss to the program. Government-wise, for participants we've got two FBI types, and one CIA and one Library of Congress employee. Of those four, I think the only questionable one is the CIA guy, Brosard. The non-government participants work for Shurcor, except for Cutler, who's on loan from SYRAE; but I think his continued participation is iffy. Oh, there's the loaner from Johns Hopkins on staff as well. That doesn't address the program sponsors though," JT concluded.

"And those would be?"

"Well, DARPA and thus DoD since it's their program, and indirectly the organizations which are loaning or detailing the staff or participants. I think DARPA would be glad to get rid of this now controversial program, and the rest of the organizations probably don't really care, except for maybe the CIA; and they can just withdraw their guy who Lee thought was going to leave anyway. There may be some personnel details to work out, but I'm sure they're doable."

Moffett leaned back in his chair, interlocked his fingers and leaned his chin on his extended thumbs. His squinted eyes and pursed lips seemed to indicate he was checking off items in his mind. After a few moments he said, more to himself than to the assembled agents, "I'm going to recommend a switch to TGS sponsorship, which should alleviate the CIA and DoD concerns. It should also take the wind out of Birmingham's sails. The CIA can withdraw their man or not, their choice; and you're right, the rest probably won't care. We'll work out the HR details, and make the government personnel DHS employees if we need to and if they're willing." As he came out of his reverie he asked, "You guys see any problems with that?"

"If you don't mind my asking, Sir, who will you 'recommend' this switch to?"

"Good question, JT. I'll run the idea by the Secretary, but since at most it will cost us a few salaries, I know she won't have a problem with the transfer. I've hinted at this in the past. The White House will make the decision, I suppose when I brief them, so it will be a moot point for her and for the DepSecDef. And I am confident of Simmons' support. I've already talked this up among several Directors of the TGS, and they would be delighted. I think the only person who might be upset would be Robin at DARPA, but I'm sure she'll see the efficacy of this. That leaves the participants, and, as you know, I've already talked to Rodriguez about an introductory session for them with the Society. That is set up for this coming Tuesday morning. We'll enamor them with what we're doing and then ease them right in."

"May we attend?"

"I don't think that's a good idea. I also don't want a word of this to leave this room. Any other details?"

Arati asked, "What about the program classification?"
"Good point. I'll have to think on that for a while. Any other questions?"

JT looked at his cohorts and then responded, "Just two, Sir: When do you brief the White House, and what does a program hold mean?"

"To answer the second question, all Rodriquez told the participants was that he and Sam Donaldson have to attend some briefings up at Hopkins on Monday, so they don't need to show up until the TGS session at the Smithsonian on Tuesday. Hopefully, by that time we'll have some resolution as to the program disposition and we can go from there. As for the White House soiree, right now we are scheduled for some time Monday afternoon, probably around lunch. I'd like you three back here for a case update Tuesday afternoon, and I'll let you know how that and the session with the MENSA group went."

"I guess we're out of here. Thank you and we'll see you next Tuesday. If anything breaks I'll be in touch sooner."

"Thanks. You all enjoy the rest of your Saturday."

CHAPTER FORTY-ONE

Monday, Crystal City, Virginia

Arati had spent all morning and a good portion of the midday searching the UCR and NIBRS data bases. The former was the Uniform Crime Reporting system—a part of law enforcement since its establishment by the International Association of Chiefs of Police in 1927. Eventually all law enforcement agencies throughout the country were using this system to report crimes to a central data base, managed by the FBI, which enabled them to gather meaningful crime statistics and analyze them. While very useful, the UCR was a summary system that described a limited number of offenses, reported only the most serious crime in any one multiple-crime incident using a hierarchy rule, and didn't differentiate between completed and attempted crimes. Further, it had only two crime categories—crimes against persons and crimes against property—and participating agencies submitted UCR data in written documents, which then had to be hand entered into a computer system. In 1988 the National Incident-Based Reporting System was established to enhance the usefulness of the UCR: it expanded the number of crimes that could be entered into the system; allowed multiple crimes to be entered for an incident; added the major category of "crimes against society" such as drug offenses, terrorism and child pornography; and allowed data to be entered electronically. There were other enhancements as well, all together making it a much better tool for crime detection, analysis and prevention.

The only problem was not every jurisdiction was completely up to speed in implementing NIBRS. Even Fairfax County, Virginia, had to wait until the implementation of their I/LEADS system in 2010 before they could adequately interface with NIBRS. In trying to correlate crime data with Cutler's whereabouts, Arati found the San Francisco data quite useful, and uncovered five incidents of reported rapes that looked promising. The Colorado Springs data was spotty; nonetheless, she found two incidents there that Cutler could possibly have participated in. She contacted the reporting police departments, and managed to find and talk to the detectives who investigated four of the seven cases. She was beside herself when she heard what one San Francisco and one Colorado Springs detective had to say: Cutler was a person of interest in their cases. In either case there was not enough evidence for an arrest, but in the Denver case the victim identified Cutler but almost immediately recanted. The detective remembered it because the victim was so sure it was Cutler early on in the investigation, and then was just as sure it wasn't him in the end. The officer was convinced that Cutler had threatened the witness into keeping quiet.

Arati found Juanita in the canteen, and said she had some news they needed to get to JT and probably Mr. Moffett. When they got to JT's desk, they found him on the phone and in a very good mood. He motioned for them to sit down and indicated he'd only be a minute.

"So what are you all smiles about, Partner?" asked Juanita.

"Maryjo's coming back to DC for a meeting a week from Friday. She'll be able to spend the weekend. And what are you two smiling about?"

Arati explained what she had found out from the UCR and NIBRS systems, and from her conversations with the two detectives. "I was thinking it would be a good idea to get this information to Mr. Moffett before his meeting with the President."

"True, but too late," replied JT. "His secretary called just before I talked to Maryjo, and said the meeting was over and he wanted to meet with us here about two o'clock."

"Did she say anything else?"

"Of course not. I am glad we'll have some new info for him at least. We've got about an hour and a half before then, so I'm going to pop down to the food court real quick. Anybody want to come along?"

They both agreed to join him.

"I need to let Hanson know Moffett's on his way here, and ask if he wants to join us for lunch. Be right back."

Hanson declined, so as the three of them got into the elevator Juanita asked, "Do you suppose his coming here is good news or bad news?"

"I suspect he was coming anyway just so he wouldn't have to go back to his office today. As for how the meeting turned out, your guess is as good as mine. I think this program is too, I don't know, immaterial for DoD and they'll be glad to get rid of it. Especially with it raising some questions on the Hill. On the other hand, I think the Agency feels it's right up their alley, and they'll put in a bid for it. Remember the CIA Director was there, but DoD was represented by the Deputy Secretary, and Charlie is only an Assistant Secretary. He did seem pretty confident when we talked to him Saturday, so I wouldn't be too surprised if he got what he asked for. I also wouldn't be surprised if no decision was reached, and the group was asked to put together a briefing to take back to the White House in a week or two."

"Well that clears that up," chided Juanita. "In any event I guess we'll find out shortly."

When they got back from lunch Moffett was already there chatting with Tom Hanson. They both seemed in a pretty good mood, as they were laughing and joking. When Hanson saw JT in the outer office he motioned for him to join them. "The Boss tells me you're not making very good progress on this case, JT."

JT shot back with, "We're doing the best we can with the resources we get from headquarters, Boss."

All three of them laughed.

"You still haven't forgiven us for the trick we played on you, have you?" commented Moffett. One afternoon last year, before JT knew the Assistant Secretary very well, Hanson had insisted JT forward a colorful joke to Moffett's cell phone. Moffett called back a few minutes later saying he had given his phone to his preteen girl, and feigned righteous indignation. "Are you and your troops ready to find out where the program is going?" asked Moffett.

"Waiting with baited breath, Sir. You want to use the conference room?"

"Yes. I'll be there shortly."

When they were sequestered in the room, JT relayed to Moffett how Arati had correlated Cutler's whereabouts with at least two rape incidents. He seemed pleased and said, "We'll discuss him after I tell you about the meeting with the President."

JT asked, "Was anyone else there besides the CIA and DARPA Directors and the DepSecDef?"

"Just the Chief of Staff, who as you know is also a member of The Galactic Society, so we were playing with a stacked deck. I believe Miss Dornan had basically been told that DoD wanted out of it, so she didn't raise any issues. When Simmons said he'd decided to get the program out of the government to negate Senator Birmingham's criticisms, the CIA Director offered to take it over and keep it under the radar. But Simmons took the wind right out of his sails when he said the Agency and DARPA had both had their chance, and he was switching this to DHS, but only in the sense we'd be monitoring it. The actual program implementation would be carried out by TGS. It was a short meeting."

"When will this transfer take place, and is there anything we need to do to help?" asked JT.

"I'm shooting for the end of this week. The Secretary agreed to take it on if President Simmons directed it, which he did. If the government employees want to stay with the program, but their organization is uncomfortable with the new arrangement, we'll give them a chance to transfer to DHS. We'll pick up Rodriquez's IPA from DARPA, which has agreed to transfer the assets, the Shurcor contract, the prepaid rent, the CTF equipment, etc. to us. Robin said we could have Sam Donaldson also if he wanted to come over. I think the only thing remaining is for us to sell the participants, and we'll take our best shot at that tomorrow. The President and the Secretary are concerned with the potential danger to the troops, and I assured them we were making progress on that front. Did I forget anything?"

"What about Senator Birmingham and the program classification?" asked Arati.

"I'm going to inform the Senator of the program's transfer out of the government when we are done here, and also tell him Simmons will be in touch with him regarding this. I think the President plans on offering him something, but he was rather cagey about what. As for the classification, we are going to declare the MENSA program complete, but leave the classification in place. Hopefully that'll circumvent any FOIA inquiries, and dissuade Birmingham from doing anything foolish. We'll restart the program under another name as a TGS proprietary program requiring confidentiality agreements. It should be transparent to the participants. Now, what about Cutler?"

JT sat up in his chair and steeled his resolve. He didn't like jumping to conclusions, and felt like what they had against Cutler didn't even measure up to circumstantial, but he figured Moffett would take it for what it was if he couched it like he saw it. "He certainly appears to have a motive, and I believe if we worked with the two victims we discovered, we could build a strong case against him depending upon the details and the statute of limitations in those jurisdictions. We believe his 'botched' shooting was strictly a figment concocted by him to allay suspicion. However, we aren't sure how the attempt on Brosard fits in, as it seems a little far-fetched for Cutler to pull that off without some help. There's no doubt he had opportunity, as of course did a number of others. As for the method of Doctor Lee's demise, Doctor Rodriguez feels Cutler, or possibly any of the participants, could have accomplished the murder. Given what we know, it almost certainly had to be an inside job, and we really don't have a stronger contender. We could confront him with all this, and maybe get a confession, but I doubt it: we don't have a smoking gun by any means. As you probably know, Doctor Rodriguez believes Cutler's continued participation in the program is disruptive, but that he wouldn't voluntarily leave, in spite of his threat to do so."

Moffett concluded with, "In other words we need to get a conviction or convince him to leave?"

"We could always work on the latter if the former doesn't pan out," offered Juanita.

"Okay, but don't do anything along those lines until you hear from me. I need to talk to Rodriguez and maybe Krumski about him first. Perhaps I can get a sense of his resolve at tomorrow's meeting. Speaking of which, I've asked Cunningham and Barrister to attend, figuring the CIA and the FBI guys might be hard sells, and Brosard and the two FBI participants might be more inclined to transfer if it was okay with their respective bosses. Anything else?"

"Where and when do you want to meet tomorrow?"

"Can you all come over to Lisbon's office about noon?"

"We'll be there."

"Well, alright then. I'm going to call Birmingham's office, and then I'm going home early for a change. See you tomorrow."

"Good afternoon, Sir," they responded in unison.

CHAPTER FORTY-TWO

Tuesday, Washington, DC

All sixteen of the teleconferencing positions around the room's center table were occupied this morning. Seated at nine of the positions were CTF personnel: seven of the MENSA participants, with Brosard remaining at the CTF due to an intestinal malady, and staff members Stan Rodriguez and Sam Donaldson. Also accepting the TGS invitations were Randall Cunningham from the CIA and Roger Barrister from the FBI, supervisors of two of the participants. Finally, there were five TGS members there in addition to Rodriguez: Sid Ellis, Charlie Moffett, Harry Lisbon, Chris Ling and Dee Vipashyin. Harry Lisbon had met the non-TGS members at the front door and given them the fifty cent tour on the way to the Castle's fourth floor conference room—The Galactic Society meeting place.

Ellis began the meeting with brief introductions of the Society directors, with each raising his or her hand as he mentioned them. "Mr. Charlie Moffett is the Assistant Secretary for Counterterrorism for the Department of Homeland Security. He is an ex-astronaut and a veteran of the Skylab program. Dee Vipashyin is a Senior Vice President for the MITRE Corporation, and a computer scientist. Doctor Stan Rodriguez, whom most of you already know, is the MENSA program manager, and a neurosurgeon at Johns Hopkins University Hospital. Doctor Harry Lisbon is a linguistic anthropologist with the Smithsonian Institute, and also serves as their Undersecretary for Finance & Administration. Doctor Chris Ling is the CEO of Aston Aerospace, and also used to work for NASA as a Shuttle astronaut. I used to be an astronaut too, but now I don't do anything more complicated than run this place." His last remark garnered a few chuckles, so he shuffled a bit before going on. "Board members not in attendance are Professor Maureen Fields of MIT, Senator Nancy Hemingway of Ohio, Frances Kalani, the White House Chief of Staff, and Shobha Vipashyin, a Supreme Court Justice and twin sister of Dee."

Ellis could see the participants were impressed, as was his intent, so he let the aforementioned pedigrees sink in a bit before he continued. "As most of you know, Stan has been a member of the Society for some time, as has Harry Lisbon. Harry made the original discovery which instigated his friend Toshi Lee to approach DARPA and begin the MENSA program. Thus, we have been keeping abreast of your progress and decided, since we are pursuing concomitant goals, it was time we had some cross-pollination. I'm sure most of you checked us out on the web and know we are an independent, educational, not-for-profit organization dedicated to providing for the long term development and preservation of mankind. Phew. But you're probably wondering what our well-publicized goals of the development of a galactic transportation system and a planetary defense against near-Earth objects has to do with the MENSA program. One of our not-so-public goals is the enhancement of human mental capability via neurocybernetics—something you troops have been making progress on over the last year or so. In fact, to paraphrase somewhat, 'There has never been a greater concentration of intellectual power in one place since Thomas Jefferson dined alone.' With apologies to President Kennedy, I may be exaggerating a bit, but not a great deal."

The non-TGS folks looked pleased with his comparison, but Ellis could tell they were skeptical about a collaboration with them. "I know you all have questions," Ellis continued, "but let us first describe our Society's composition and organization, our accomplishments and the contributions of our members, our mission and goals, and finally, how we would mutually benefit by joining forces." With that, he and the other members present took turns covering their agenda, attempting to emphasize the potential enhancement of their knowledge base and intellectual prowess, and referring only obliquely to the Society members' paranormal abilities.

The MENSA group was attentive, and asked several pertinent questions during the presentation. When the TGS Directors concluded their presentations, it was Sharon Rydell who spoke up first: "I thought, as I think we all did, this was going to be an invitation to join the Society as regular or maybe supporting members. Now it seems there is more to it than that, and we'll be working together. Could you be a little more specific?" There was a general nodding of heads around the table.

"An invitation to join was our original intention," admitted Ellis. "We felt each of you could contribute greatly to our knowledge, and hopefully vice versa. Thus, we'd offer you positions on the Board of Governors, and, depending upon your suitability, participation and desire, you would eventually be eligible for Directorships. However, as you know, the program has suffered some difficulties of late with Doctor Lee's demise, and the apparent attempts on Paul Cutler's and Bill Brosard's lives. What you are most likely not aware of, is that Senator Birmingham has raised privacy issues with the program, and the CIA Director and the Deputy Secretary of Defense have questioned the program's continuance under these unfortunate circumstances. Consequently, Charlie Moffett met with those two gentlemen, Miss Dornan from DARPA, and the President and Chief of Staff yesterday, and the President directed that the program transfer to The Galactic Society."

The group was taken aback, if not stunned, and several posed questions at the same time.

"I know this is a significant change, and you all have a lot more questions, and we'll answer each one in time. Basically, the program will go on under TGS aegis, with potentially few if any of your employment conditions changed. You could still work for whomever you do now, the CTF will continue to be the base of your operations, Stan will still be the program manager, and I suspect there will be little change to your daily activities. Those of you working for government organizations will be detailed to the Department of Homeland Security, Mr. Moffett's organization, instead of DARPA. If your organization is uncomfortable with this arrangement, we can transfer you to DHS, same grade, pay, etc. This of course is all pending your approval and desire to remain with the program. We asked Mr. Cunningham and Mr. Barrister here, thinking that if they were aware of the President's desire, they could advocate for their employee's continuance in the program if their respective agencies had a problem with the transfer. We don't think any of the others will mind. Now, let's take a short break. We have some coffee and some other refreshments in the outer room. In ten or fifteen minutes we'll reconvene in here and answer any specific questions you'd like to ask."

CHAPTER FORTY-THREE

Tuesday, Crystal City, Virginia

Arati was frustrated at not being able to uncover any further information to help the case. She'd perused every data base she could think of, but nothing additional had popped out that was pertinent. So JT tried to cheer her up by relating one of the jokes JT's partner pulled on him his first day as a rookie cop for Fairfax. It wasn't that they picked on JT because he was shorter than most of them, although that did open up another whole avenue for pranks, but rather because he gave as good as he got. He had a genuine talent for making the obvious, but not so socially correct, comment. Not only did he have a good memory for jokes (of which he had a vast supply, which he supplemented by reading joke books and watching the comedy channel), but he also knew how to adapt them to his current situation. Sometimes they were on the corny side, but you expected and accepted it because it was JT. In fact, the team had come to rely on his knack for lightening up a tense situation when tempers flared. It was usually beyond human capability to remain mad or upset when he came out with one of his off-center remarks. Just before he was finished, Tom Hanson walked in, laughed when JT delivered the punch line, and then told them about a prank JT had pulled on him. JT was about to break into another story when Charlie Moffett walked in.

"Good afternoon, Troops. JT wasn't regaling you with more of his cop stories, was he?"

"Yes, unfortunately," replied Juanita, "but at least I'd only heard his last story one other time."

"Well, there is that. Let's go over to the conference room and I'll fill you in on this morning's get together."

JT was no less impressed with Moffett than he had been before, but he had become more comfortable around him, and felt he could read him better now. This man who had flown in space, earned a slew of degrees, been a senior vice president of a major company, and was currently an assistant secretary in the third biggest executive department, was excited. He knew Moffett had something for them.

When they were situated comfortably in the conference room, Moffett began: "Overall, I believe the prospective TGS members were impressed. The MENSA participants are obviously brilliant and asked penetrating questions, some of which I had difficulty skirting around, if indeed I did. By the way, Brosard was not there—something about the flu. With that exception, I feel strongly they will all opt to join, including Sam Donaldson. We'll have to invite Brosard separately, which we will do tomorrow at his place. Cunningham and Barrister were there, and they were less enthused; and I have to admit I was not impressed with either one of them. I'm sure they will bend to the political will at their agencies, and frankly I don't have a read on that. All but the two FBI guys had no problem with the transfer to DHS, and in fact thought it would be better career-wise. I volunteered to contact all of their employers to explain the program change and request their transfers." Moffett paused here and took a sip of the drink he brought in with him.

They all looked at him expectantly.

"We at the TGS know you are aware of our capabilities. What you don't know is their extent, which, with one, maybe two exceptions, exceeds that of the MENSA folks; in some cases, notably Sid and Maureen, we are considerably beyond them. Thus we can tell you Paul Cutler is one weird puppy. His mind was essentially unreadable, either because he is so confused— mentally unstable—or he has immense control. All indications are it is the former. It would be in all our interests to remove him from the program. Sharon Rydell has more control than most and may be one of the exceptions; nonetheless, we feel she has nothing to hide but a minor incident in her youth. Ralph Krumski, on the other hand, was playing with us and may be the other exception. He knew what we were doing and invited us in. However, what we all saw was benign, although very self-centered, and even Sid was comfortable with eliminating him as a suspect. The rest of the MENSA crew we feel we got a good read on, most likely without their awareness, including Sam Donaldson. Remember, this is by no means an exact science, nor is it anything which would hold up in court or should be taken as proof positive at this point. However, it does on occasion provide us with another avenue of investigation, doesn't it?"

"Wow. That more or less agrees with what we were able to determine, but I'm sure you know that from reading our reports," said JT.

"Yes, and while it may have colored my impressions, the other members who were not privy to your reports got the same impressions. As to where we go from here: we press on with trying to get something definitive on Cutler. I have talked to Stan about him but no longer feel the need to discuss him with Krumski."

"What about the two visitors?" asked JT. "Did you pick up anything on Cunningham and Barrister?"

"The MENSA participants and staff agreed to mind probes as part of being in the program. Now I admit we may have taken advantage of that in this case, but I'm comfortable with it under the circumstances. We did not probe the two non-MENSA attendees. Roger Barrister hardly paid attention to us, and we feel he is quite removed from the whole thing. However, Sid got an interesting vibe from Cunningham: the CIA man was thinking of something so intensely it 'leaked out' to the point Sid picked up on it. Arati, I want you to pursue what we discussed about him earlier. I also want you to check on financial transfers from this overseas institution to see what you come up with," he said as he handed her a piece of paper. "And finally, JT, I want Mr. Cunningham under surveillance on the weekends as much as we can. Work it out with Hanson and use other team members if you need to."

"Anything on the rest of the prime suspects?"

"I may have further direction after Sid and Harry visit the CTF tomorrow. If they can, they're going to get a read on Brosard and the other staff members not there this morning. To close on a happy note, I'm excited about having new members for the Society—I think the new blood will bring in some new ideas. Now, go forth and do good things."

"Yes, Sir."

CHAPTER FORTY-FOUR

Wednesday, Chantilly, Virginia

"Agent Dunkirk, this is Stan Rodriguez and I hate to bother you at home, but Paul Cutler has disappeared. . . . It looks like he took all his stuff and cleared out for good. . . . We checked the security system, and the door was opened at four-eleven this morning. . . . No, just that once. . . . We searched stem-to-stern and your agent is checking outside now and asked me to call you. . . . He really didn't seem any more agitated than the rest of the folks were with the transition to the Society and DHS. . . . We didn't do anything when we got back—we gave everyone the afternoon off so they could think about the change and decide what they wanted to do. Hang on—your guy is back. . . . He says the car is gone as well. . . . Yeah, I'll pass that on. See you then." Rodriguez hung up the phone and passed on JT's instructions to the onsite agent.

JT got there about thirty seconds before Juanita. "So our boy flew the coop," she said as the door buzzed open for them. "Whose turn was it to watch him anyway?"

"Randy Pascal from Charlie Unit," replied JT as they descended the steps and turned into the main corridor. "There he is. Let's talk to him before we see Stan."

Agent Pascal didn't have a whole lot to add: "He seemed fine to me. He watched a movie with the troops, then said he was going to his room to read a while before turning in."

"Not agitated, upset, nervous?"

"No. Like I said, Man, he seemed fine. In fact, he was a lot calmer than most of them. They all seemed excited about some change in the program. They're moving to another sponsoring organization, like this week I think."

"Brosard?"

"He missed the meeting the rest of them went to yesterday, and he was asking a whole lot of questions. That's how I learned what was going on. Is there anything I can do?"

"You put out the BOLO on him and his car?"

"No: wouldn't know how to word it."

"Yeah, I guess you're right. Well then you're done here. Why don't you call and cancel your relief. Then you can check with your Unit leader and go back to your regular schedule."

"Okay. Hey, I'm sorry he skipped on my watch, Man. I have no idea how he got past me—I was wide awake the whole time, honest."

"Not your fault. You were asked to watch over him at his request, not detain him, since we didn't expect him to bolt. Thanks for your help. Is Doctor Rodriguez in his office?"

Pascal nodded, gathered his stuff up and left.

They found Rodriguez on the phone. When he hung up he said, "I took the liberty of calling Paul's boss at SYRAE just in case he might show up there. He said he'd call us if he shows. I'm worried he might do something drastic. He didn't seem that upset, but it's hard to tell with him sometimes."

"We need to think about where he might go," said JT.

"It's not going to be business as usual with him," offered Rodriguez as he walked over to a small dry erase board on an easel. "He could just disappear," he said as he annotated the board to that effect."

Juanita contributed: "I suppose he might be inclined to go after someone he's got a beef with. That could include the two ladies at SYRAE, perhaps his boss, some of the ladies he allegedly attacked in either Colorado or California, or maybe some we don't know about yet, someone on our team . . ." She waited until Rodriguez caught up with her. "Or someone here?" The last was more of a question than a comment.

Rodriguez addressed her last statement with, "He didn't get along great with anyone here, but he didn't seem to have any great dislike for them either. Except for a short time right after the apparent shooting attempt when he was bugging everybody, equally I might add, he hasn't really been belligerent or even anti-social. And everyone is here and he did leave."

"Let's assume he's rational enough to put some thought behind his craziness," said JT. "That should help us prioritize the list as far as whom we first need to check with, or perhaps warn. As you say, Doc, the folks here are probably low on our list. Can we remove his badge from the security system?"

"Even better, we can get an alarm to go off if he enters his PIN number. Let me make a phone call and get that done now."

"Next on the list would be the two local ladies. How did you leave it with Cutler's boss?" asked Juanita when Rodriguez was off the phone.

"He doesn't want him back there so he'll call us if he shows. He also said he'd call both women and give them a heads up, and call us if he can't get a hold of them or if either of them does not report to work today."

"Okay, great. Next would be our team. I thought Juanita and I got along well with him, so I don't think he harbors any resentment there. He knows we suspected him along with everyone else here, but maybe he read more into it. In any event we'll be careful—it's part of the job. Did he have any words with the agents who have been here lately?"

Rodriguez shook his head. "Not that I'm aware of."

JT continued, "He's never met Arati, but he did meet Charlie Moffett yesterday, who said Cutler was one confused puppy, by the way. Think I'll give him a call with an update and see if he has anything to add."

From his body language and his side of the conversation with Moffett, Juanita could tell JT was becoming increasingly agitated. When he finished she asked him, "What's the problem, Partner?"

"Charlie thinks he may have underestimated Cutler. At the time he was pretty sure, but not positive, that Cutler didn't get a read on him. Now he thinks he may have spooked him. He said Cutler's apparently jumbled-up mind may not have been as bad as it seemed, or that could have been a cover by him. If he did get any info from Charlie, then he probably knows we're checking into those rapes, which means he knows about Arati as well. Juanita, call her house and I'll call the office."

"Her phone went to voicemail," said Juanita a few moments later. "Did you have any luck?"

"The Boss was in and said she told him yesterday she was going to the NCTC today to check a few data bases we don't have access to at our place. She couldn't take her cell phone up there, so I'll call their switchboard."

Both Juanita and Stan kept looking for a good tell when JT was on the phone, but didn't get one.

"The guy she usually works with said she was supposed to be in about an hour ago. "Let's head over to her place. We'll phone again from the car," JT said as they both headed for the door.

"Good luck, Guys," Rodriguez yelled after them.

Juanita drove so JT could work the phone.

His next call was Lieutenant Dan. "Dan, I need you to get a nearby unit to swing by an Annandale address and check on two vehicles for me." JT gave him the address and Cutler's car description and plates as well as Arati's.

Several minutes later JT's cell rang and he damn near broke the answer button. "Yeah, Dan."

Turning to Juanita JT said, "Dan says her car is out front but there's no sign of Cutler's. . . . Dan, ask him if he can go knock on the door, it's unit 109. . . . No, we'll be there in a few minutes and Juanita's got a key. Ask him to hang on til we get there, and thanks, Dan. I'll get back to you."

JT reiterated the last part of the conversation to Juanita: "The officer didn't get any answer and said the door would need a battering ram, and he'd have to take the whole window out to get in that way. I don't like this."

"Me neither. That's not like Arati. If her car is there then she's got to be inside and should be answering the phone and the door. I'm hitting it, Partner. Hold on," Juanita yelled as she switched on the blue lights.

CHAPTER FORTY-FIVE

Wednesday, Annandale, Virginia

Although they were catching the tail end of the rush hour and going with the traffic, Juanita got them there inside of eleven minutes. The lights and siren helped. She pulled into an open space right in front of Arati's place and right next to the police car. Juanita jumped out and addressed the officer, "Anything new?"

He shook his head.

"Okay, I've got a key and I'm going in. You with me?" she asked the officer as she tried not to run up the steps to the apartment.

"Right behind you, Ma'am."

JT had checked Arati's car and, finding nothing, fell in behind Juanita and the police officer.

"Arati, it's Juanita, are you here?" she called as she entered.

They noticed a robe strewn on the living room floor and a coffee table turned over.

"I'm going to the bedroom, you guys check over there and out back," Juanita yelled pointing in the direction of the kitchen."

JT looked in the kitchen while the officer glanced out the back door at the small deck. Then they heard Juanita.

"Aw shit! Partner, call 9-1-1!"

Arati was lying naked on her bed, alive, but obviously out of it. Juanita thought her face may have been a little bruised, but didn't see any blood or any other apparent injuries. She saw sheets and a comforter on the floor beside the bed. She picked up the comforter from the heap and covered Arati with it. "Talk to me sweetheart, come on, come on." But Arati just stared vacantly at her bedroom wall.

"Her pulse and breathing are okay, but this doesn't look good," said Juanita.

"The EMTs are on the way. You keep talking to her while I call Rodriguez," said JT. When he got off the phone he addressed the officer, "MPO Tipton, this is now a federal case and we got it from here. Tell Lieutenant Dan we'll keep him informed as best we can. Can you direct the EMTs in here when they arrive?"

"Yes, Sir. I hope she's alright."

"Thanks. We appreciate it." When the officer exited JT got Juanita's attention. "Listen, we let the EMTs check her out, but we keep her here until Ellis and Lisbon get here."

"Ellis and Lisbon? From the TGS?" Juanita asked incredulously.

"Yeah. They were on their way to the CTF and Stan rerouted them while I was on the phone with him. They should be here in less than ten minutes. He said if she doesn't have life-threatening injuries, it is paramount they get to work with her." JT heard the approaching emergency vehicle and looked at Juanita.

"Are you sure, Partner?"

"How does she look to you?"

Juanita took another look at Arati laying there, curled in the fetal position, not moaning or even moving—just staring at her bedroom wall, or more likely something far beyond it. "Okay, but let's see what the EMTs have to say."

JT quickly up-righted the coffee table and hung the robe up in the bedroom. JT met the ambulance attendants at the front door and ushered them to the bedroom.

"So what happened here?" the lead EMT asked.

"Our friend here didn't report to work and we were worried about her, so we came by and found her like this."

"Was she raped or was there some other sort of foul play here, and that's why the cop is out front?"

"There's no evidence of rape or of anybody being here. The cop's a friend also and was in the neighborhood. We're federal agents and we got in using Agent Singletary's key." JT showed his creds to the guy.

It didn't look like he was buying JT's explanation, but he didn't say any more about it. "She on any medications or have any medical history we need to know about?"

"That's very unlikely—she's a good friend and I know her very well," Juanita explained.

When they were through with their preliminary examination the lead EMT said, "All her vitals are okay and I don't see any physical problems, other than her non-responsiveness. It's hard to tell, but her face may be bruised. We need to take her in and get her checked out."

"Hey, Doc!" JT said as the others turned around to see who had entered. "This is Doctor Ellis and Doctor Lisbon. They've been working with Arati for a few months now. I called them when we couldn't get a hold of her."

Ellis addressed the EMTs, "What do you have?"

They explained what they'd done and the readings they had taken. Ellis asked a few questions of them and then turned to Lisbon.

Lisbon nodded his head.

"This is not a physical problem, Gentlemen. I'm afraid she's had a relapse, and we need to get her out to our facility in Chantilly for a few sessions. We'll check her out thoroughly. I think we can snap her out of this in a day or two."

"What's the matter with her?"

"She has occasional bouts of catatonia, usually brought on by a drastic change in her routine. But this is the first one in some time—she was doing so well."

"Hey, I'm really sorry guys," JT said apologizing to the EMTs. "When we couldn't get anything out of her we thought maybe she fell and hit her head or something. I mean we didn't see anything amiss but you never know."

"No problem. It's better safe than sorry. We'll head on back now. I hope everything works out for her."

"Thanks again guys," JT said as he helped them carry their stuff out to their vehicle.

"So what do you think happened?" Lisbon asked Juanita. "That asshole Cutler raped her than fucked up her mind," blurted out Juanita. Neither Ellis nor Lisbon responded, but rather waited for her to calm down. She took a deep breath, then, "I'm sorry—just had to get that out I guess."

"Was she definitely raped, and did you find her in this position when you got here?"

"She was like this when we got here. When the cop left I rolled her over and checked, and yeah I'd say she'd been raped. Then I rolled her back on her side cuz it seemed more comfortable for her."

"And did she respond at all during any of that?"

"No."

"But she apparently turned on her side by herself."

"Ah, probably, yeah."

JT had returned by this time so Ellis addressed both of them. "I think we know what Cutler did—basically mind rape her then physically rape her. I'm hoping we can go in, undo Cutler's damage, and bring her back to reality. If we can, then we'll most likely be able to repair the psychic damage of the rape as well. Can we do that for her?"

Juanita's fists and teeth were clenched as she looked at Arati. JT walked over and put his arm around his partner. "I think this is the right thing to do, Nita. I trust these guys and I think Arati would want them to try. Alright?"

After a short pause, "Okay. Do we need to do anything to help?"

"You need to go out in the hallway and be quiet. You can watch if you want, but it's safer for you to have some physical distance from us."

JT and Juanita walked into the hallway and turned around to watch. Ellis pulled the comforter up, lifted Arati's arm out, replaced the comforter and laid her arm on top of it. Both men knelt on the floor beside her and placed both their hands on her arm. They lowered their heads and closed their eyes and remained like that for what seemed an eternity to Juanita.

Juanita looked at JT and whispered, "How long?"

"It's been fourteen minutes now. Hang in there."

In another two minutes they heard a rustling and thought they saw Arati moving beneath the comforter. The two men raised their heads and Ellis turned and motioned Juanita over to them.

"She's coming around and she needs to see a friendly face. Reassure her and answer any questions she has in a calm voice, and be truthful." They backed off and Juanita knelt down and faced Arati.

"Hey . . . Juanita . . . what's going on?"

"Oh, Arati, you're going to be okay, but we think you have been . . . assaulted."

"You are right—something is definitely wrong. I was in this dark place fighting to stay conscious. How long have I been like this . . . and how did you get here?"

"When you didn't report to work this morning we got worried, and JT and I came to check on you."

"JT is here?"

"Yes, and so are the two gentlemen who helped revive you." Juanita moved aside so Arati could see the three men standing behind her in the room.

"And here I am lying . . . naked on my bed?"

Juanita started laughing and crying at the same time and threw her arms around Arati as best she could. When she regained her composure she said, "We thought we lost you but it sounds like you'll be okay. Do you remember anything?"

"Only vaguely, and it is not good. Can you enlighten me?"

Juanita turned to the audience behind her and asked, "Can we have some time to get her together?"

"Why don't you take a few minutes so Arati can make herself more presentable. But it's *really* important for us to hear *everything* she has to say so we can determine the proper course of action," said Lisbon.

"Got it. We'll just be a minute."

When Arati was ready Juanita called them back into the room. Arati was dressed, and she and Juanita were sitting on the edge of the bed. JT outlined the events of the morning and what they think happened, but not mentioning her likely attacker's name. Lisbon explained who they were, and what they did to bring Arati around, and how they thought it best to not leave things as they were.

"I am quite sure what you describe is what happened, but I have no cognizance of it. Are you saying you want to 'enter' my mind again and bring those apparently suppressed memories to the surface, and if so, how do you suppose my state of mind will be affected?"

"Yes—we want to do exactly that. Because it is our fervent belief these events will resurface eventually, and it is better to have that happen sooner rather than later, especially in the presence of ones who can confirm or deny your recollections. Also, since you are fairly positive there is something you are repressing, it is better to face it than to worry about it. We have done this before, albeit only once, but, believe it or not, under less desirable circumstances, and that worked out well. Doctor

Ellis and I are confident we can control any adverse reaction which may develop."

"Will my mental faculties be diminished in any way?"

"We earnestly do not believe so."

"Enhanced?" she asked smiling.

"Probably not."

Arati looked at Juanita who pursed her lips and nodded her head.

"Let us begin."

Juanita and JT went out into the hallway again, and Ellis and Lisbon knelt and grabbed Arati's arm as before. The three of them closed their eyes and a second period of silence commenced. The pair in the hallway could not see the face of the two men, but Arati's face seemed to say it all. She grimaced, twitched, gritted her teeth and jerked her head from side to side, all the while with her eyes closed tight, but with the rest of her body surprisingly relaxed. This session took only thirteen minutes by JT's account, which was about fifteen minutes too long for Juanita.

When the three of them opened their eyes and Ellis and Lisbon stood up, Juanita rushed in and sat beside Arati, grabbed her hand and squeezed. "Are you okay?"

"Well, I was raped, and we may have to attend to the physical consequences of that, but I think these two gentlemen have ameliorated the psychological ones. In fact, I feel surprisingly calm under the circumstances. My sincere thanks to you for that," she said addressing Lisbon and Ellis. And to Juanita and JT: "And to you two for finding me and for being my friends. I suspect you saved my sanity, if not my life."

"Arati, I hate to ask so soon but do you think you can talk about it now?" asked JT.

"Oh yes. I awoke sometime early this morning because I thought I heard someone at the front door. Indeed, the doorbell rang, so I got out of bed and wrapped myself in my robe and went to see who was there. As I got close I experienced a severe head pain, similar, I believe, to what I have heard people describe as a migraine. I felt an uncontrollable urge to unlock the door, and when I did, it burst open and a man rushed me and knocked me over. I apparently blacked out, perhaps because I hit my head—I am not sure. When I regained consciousness, I was on my bed with a man kneeling over top of me, and he had his hands on my cheeks and was squeezing me, shaking my head. I wanted to scream but was unable. Then I realized it was Paul Cutler because, I think, he wanted me to know it was him getting even with me for exposing him. I tried to push him away but was unable to coordinate my movements. My head was swimming and then I seemed to enter an anoetic state and all I could think of was—pardon the language—fuck me, fuck me. And he did. I do not think I wanted to enjoy it, but then I wanted it and did not want it at the same time, if that makes any sense. When he was through, the head pains got worse and worse until I blacked out again. Then I heard people calling to me from afar. As they got closer and closer, I seemed to regain consciousness, and then awoke and saw you looking at me."

"Oh my god, Arati, I'm so sorry. We're going to get him and make this all right, I promise," Juanita said hugging her again.

"Getting better, as I have already, is wonderful and more than sufficient; catching him and rendering justice would be better, but not necessary."

"How can you say that?" asked Juanita.

"I believe these two gentlemen can answer that better than I."

Juanita looked at Ellis and Lisbon.

"Part of the healing process," remarked Lisbon. "Better all around."

"Well we'll be no less vigilant in apprehending the son of a bitch."

"That's your job and I would expect no less," said Ellis. "I believe we are done here, but if you want to talk about any of this, Arati, it would be my honor and privilege to do so. Call anytime if you have doubts or questions, either one of us, okay?"

Arati agreed and they each gave her a business card, and then took their leave. When they were out front Lisbon said, "An excellent job, Doctor Ellis, excellent indeed. But then we had a marvelous specimen to work with didn't we?"

"Indeed, Doctor Lisbon. That woman has a splendid mind: so organized, so self-assured, so . . . beautiful. I look forward to seeing her again. I am drained, however. How about if we postpone our CTF visit until tomorrow?"

"Capital idea, my good Sir. We'll phone Doctor Rodriguez from the car," Lisbon responded as they got into his late model Cadillac."

Back inside, Arati and Juanita discussed the physical consequences of her rape. She was not concerned about conceiving, but thought she should get tested for HIV. Her face and genitals, although bruised, would heal. JT was on the phone with Moffett who said he'd set up a trace on the fugitive, and told JT to put out a BOLO on Cutler and his Mustang and how to word it.

CHAPTER FORTY-SIX

Wednesday, Richmond, Virginia

Cutler thought they'd start looking for him as soon as they decided he wasn't coming back to the CTF. He just wasn't sure when that would be. He knew his car would be hot once they discovered Arati. Not that they'd be able to prove anything, after what he did to her; but there were those other two ladies who could figure into this, and they might put it all together. Most likely that wouldn't happen until at least after he made Richmond, but he didn't want to chance it any further. He hoped finding his car and/or noticing his account activity here would lead them to think he was headed south. Since the Richmond BOA branch opened at nine, the timing was right and he would have no trouble getting the last of his money. He had already closed out his other accounts over the last month, and a substantial amount of cash was in his backpack. He thought about buying a cheap clunker in some shady used car lot, but didn't want to take that chance, so he opted for the less risky method of grand theft auto. On the way into town he noticed a parking garage about two and a half miles from the bank, about a thirty-five minute walk, and he figured no one would report a missing vehicle until quitting time. It took him a while to find an unlocked one, and longer than he anticipated to hot wire it. But it all worked out and now he was on I-64W headed toward Charlottesville.

Crystal City, Virginia

Doctor Rodriguez agreed to test Arati, so Juanita drove her to the CTF, while JT returned to the office. He wanted to keep track of the search for Cutler, and they had given his office as the point of contact on the BOLO. Tommy Philbert was manning the incoming line they had given out, and JT stopped by to tell him he was back in the office and to call if anything turned up. Sam Kenilworth was monitoring Cutler's bank accounts and credit cards. "Hey, JT," he called over to Philbert's station, "is that you? I've been trying to reach you. I got something on Cutler."

JT hurried over to Kenilworth's cubicle. "Whatcha got, Sam?"

"About twenty minutes ago Cutler withdrew most of the money he had in his BOA account—eight thousand bucks and change. He did it in person at a branch in Richmond."

"Did you call the Richmond police?"

"I did and they said they'd send a car over there. I sent them a copy of the BOLO and we should hear from them any time now."

JT started pacing back and forth. "You'd think I've been on enough of these surveillance gigs to get used to the damn waiting," he remarked to Kenilworth, who just nodded. Twenty minutes later JT's phone rang.

"DHS, Agent Dunkirk speaking. . . . Yes, that's my BOLO." JT listened for several minutes, nodding his head while jotting down some notes, and then finished the conversation with, "Okay, thanks a bunch. Call me on this number if you find out anything else."

"So what's up?" asked Kenilworth.

"It was definitely Cutler—two tellers identified him from our photo. They found his car in the parking lot, abandoned and empty. They figure they missed him by thirty minutes or so and have cars in the neighborhood. There are a couple of bus lines that go reasonably close by there, and one place he could have grabbed a taxi. They are checking on those, but he could have hitched a ride. They asked us if we could check on the rental agencies, so can you work that angle?"

"You got it."

Akron, Ohio

An uneventful ride so far, but then he was very careful—no more than five miles an hour over the limit, and he didn't use his credit card to buy gas. Cutler figured there was no hurry as long as he got to the border by this evening. It was unlikely in the extreme that they'd have his picture at all the border crossings the same day, or that they'd have an alert there on a car stolen in Virginia. Once in Canada he'd ditch the car where it wouldn't be found for a while, and hitch his way to Nova Scotia. From there, the right amount of money in the right place would buy him a passage to the Caribbean, and eventually to South America. He stopped for dinner at a quaint looking place just off the highway, and backed into a spot against the back fence. Since the front plate was now missing he doubted the car would be spotted even if the Ohio State Highway Patrol was looking for it.

The restaurant was homey and the menu American: roast beef, mashed potatoes, string beans and apple sauce, with coffee and then peach cobbler for desert. Here he was on the run and yet calmer than he'd been in a long time. It was like he finally had a purpose in life, although at this point that was escape; but there was the exciting prospect of a new beginning in a new place—somewhere the past wouldn't haunt him. He figured he'd have enough cash left over to buy a small business which could support him until he figured things out for the long run. It could be a long evening, so he decided on one more cup of coffee. *Damn, that waitress looks nice. I'll bet she really wouldn't need much convincing; in fact, maybe none at all. But no time for that now. Gotta hit the head and then the road if I want to make it to the border before it gets too late.* He paid the bill in cash and left a normal tip. *Nondescript is the key now*, he thought as he headed out to the car.

Back out on I-77 it was less than fifteen miles to I-80. That would take him to Toledo where he would pick up I-75 for the remainder of the journey. *God bless the Interstate system—it makes getting around America so easy.* Odd, but he just remembered for every five mile stretch or so of every Interstate, there had to be a one mile straight section for aircraft to land in the event of an emergency. *So close to Lake Erie and no time to appreciate it,* he thought as the miles clicked off. *But then there were so many places in the U.S. I wanted to see but never got around to. At least I've seen a good part of California, Colorado and the DC area. The trip to Puerto Rico and the weekends in Las Vegas were nice, too. I guess there's a lot of things I'll miss in this country, but then I hear Bolivia is a good place for bank robbers.* He laughed out loud at his mind's reference to the old Newman/Redford movie. *Ah, look at that sign—TOLEDO 105.*

CHAPTER FORTY-SEVEN

Wednesday, Crystal City, Virginia

"Nothing? We've got nothing yet?" moaned JT. "He could be out of the country by now."

"We know he didn't pick up any flight out of Richmond, or any airport within five hundred miles, and that includes commercial and private passenger airlines and any transport flights as well," said Tommy Philbert. "My guess is he went to one of those truck stops and hitched a ride. He's still here and he's gonna make a mistake—they all do."

"This guy is smart; desperate, but smart. We know he's got at least forty-three thousand counting the eight he withdrew this morning. And who knows how much more. Why didn't we catch that earlier?"

"We can't monitor for everything," offered Juanita. She got into the office about an hour ago. She had Arati in tow after spending the rest of the morning and all afternoon with her. Juanita tried to get the recent victim to crash at her place for the next few days, thinking she wouldn't want to return to the scene of the crime, or anyplace that reminded her of it; but Arati insisted on coming into the office—work therapy she called it.

"He's either hiding out in Richmond some place, or he's hit the road, probably via a trucker like Tommy suggested. He didn't take anything commercial, including a rental car."

"Did you guys ask if his car was operable?" Juanita asked Philbert. "Maybe he had to abandon it."

"Yes. It was working and our search of it didn't provide us with anything.

We checked dealerships and used car lots, trains, buses and cabs, and had the locals show his picture around at most of the nearby motels. He doesn't have any connection to anyone in Richmond we can come up with."

"Sounds like you covered it, Tommy. What about the port of Richmond? Or maybe Richmond is a red herring and he's doubled back to take a ship out of Baltimore," commented Juanita.

"We got the ports covered," replied Philbert.

"Red herring or not, are we sure he was the individual at the bank this morning?" asked Arati.

JT and Philbert both nodded.

"Maybe after he left me, his only thought was to get out of town fast and the closest freeway was 95. Since northbound had to be crowded at that time of the day, he went south, and it was not intentional."

"So he's headed south, leaving before he really planned to because he realizes we're on to him, has to stop in the BOA branch closest to wherever he is when they open at nine to get the last of his money, and that turns out to be Richmond. Now he figures we'll know where he is fairly soon, if not right away, so the question is what does he do now," poses Juanita.

"What about stolen car reports?" asked Arati.

They all turned to Philbert who answered, "We got two reports, both within the last hour, and they already found the one car abandoned a few miles away, and they've got a BOLO out on the second one and will let us know."

"If I were him," pondered JT, "I'd double back up 95 to New York via a friendly trucker, cross over to Canada at one of the minor check points, and then take the Trans Canada Line to the west coast and buy my way out of the country on a steamer."

"Have we got his picture at all the crossings and did we check the Richmond truck stops?" asked Juanita.

"Yeah, we asked the Richmond police to show his picture at the local stops, but we haven't heard anything back yet—not sure they got to it what with all we asked them to do. And we have got his picture at all the crossings from Maine to

Washington and Texas to California. But that doesn't mean he won't slip through or that he doesn't have a fake passport. You know, those guys don't always take a good look at the photo, and he may have disguised himself as well."

"That's what I like about you, Tommy, you're so encouraging" said JT.

"Just telling it like it is, Boss."

"I think it's going to be a long night."

CHAPTER FORTY-EIGHT

Wednesday, Detroit, Michigan

Guess this is the first and only time I'll get to see Detroit, but I can't say as I'll be missing much from the looks of it. Ah, there's the sign: next right for the Ambassador Bridge border crossing. This is really easy—right off of 75. Not much traffic this late at night so this should be quick. Oh, oh—a little bit of a backup at the check point.

"Good evening, Sir. May I see your passport, please?"

"Sure, Officer, is there some holdup here this evening?"

"We're under a special terrorist alert, Sir, and quite frankly, we don't know if it's an exercise or the real thing. We have to run everyone's name through the FBI terrorist screening data base, and it's talking us a little extra time. I should have you and the person in front of you through here in less than ten minutes."

"Okay, I'm in no hurry." *She certainly believes what she's saying. Just need to stay cool for a few more minutes then I'm home free.*

The duty officer in charge got a hit on Cutler's name and he read the BOLO. "They gotta be kidding me. I have to call them on this," he said to no one in particular as he picked up the phone. "Hi, is Special Agent Dunkirk there? . . . This is Agent Willis Bradbury at the Ambassador Bridge border crossing in Detroit. I have your fugitive Paul Cutler trying to get through my check point and I wanted to verify the BOLO instructions. . . . No, I'm in the control center. The guy out front is just following the terrorist alert protocol and is not aware of the BOLO. . . . Yeah, we have the equipment. Do we really need that many men? . . . Alright, Agent, I'll call you back."

As instructed, Agent Bradbury kept what was going on to himself, and made up a good story for delaying the suspect. He got on the intercom to the stations: "Guys, I'm afraid the data base is down, but the FBI said they'd have it back up in a few minutes. Greg and George, I checked the names of your leading customers, and Saunders and Conway are cleared, but the rest are on hold. Sheila, I didn't get to your names yet so you're on hold. Ralph's on the phone with the feds now. He said if we're not back up in ten minutes we can wave them through with normal procedures. Stand by."

Agent Sheila Hollings stopped at the car in front of Cutler and said something to the occupant, then approached Cutler's vehicle. "Sir, it's going to be a few more minutes. There's been a data base glitch. They said if they don't have it fixed in ten minutes we can let you through."

"Okay, thanks." *No reason to panic. I heard most of what they said and it sounds legit. This gal certainly believes it. These things happen all the time.*

Cutler noticed a few more cars lining up behind him. *Good thing it wasn't earlier or they'd have an insurrection on their hands*, he thought. He had started to fool with the radio to pass the time when he noticed some shadows pass in front of him. He looked up and saw two men approaching the check point. *No, they are coming towards me. I'm not getting a good feeling here. They've got fucking tasers—gotta stop them.*

As the two border patrol agents came around the front of the car and approached Cutler, one of them let out a yell, dropped to his knees, dropped something then grabbed his head with both hands. The other agent stopped dead in his tracks, with his hands in his pockets and a confused look on his face. At the same time Agent Bradbury approached from the back of the car, and zapped Cutler with five hundred thousand volts.

The car engine raced as Cutler's foot hit the accelerator when he jerked back into the seat. If the car was in gear it would have slammed into the car in front of it. Bradbury tried the door handle and found it locked. He reached through the window and opened the door from the inside. The suspect's body was still trembling when Bradbury pulled him out of the car, and he landed face up on the pavement before the agent could catch him. He flipped Cutler over, pulled his hands behind his back and slapped cuffs on him. The standing agent had apparently snapped out of his spell so Bradbury asked, "Roger, you okay?"

The guard shook his head to clear it and said, "Yeah, okay now, Boss."

"Sheila, see if Stanley's alright. Roger, help me carry this guy over to the holding cell. If you start feeling funny again yell at me, and then just let go of him and I'll zap him again. If you see me let go of him, then you drop him and zap him again, and be damn quick about it."

Agents Roger Finster and Bradbury hauled Cutler across the parking lot, his toes dragging and his head dangling. He felt like a vibrating dead weight. Fortunately they got him into the cell before he recovered from the shock. Bradbury told everyone to give the prisoner a ten foot minimum breadth at all times. Then he went out to check on the disabled agent. When Stanley Pommice came around a few minutes later, apparently none the worse for the wear, Bradbury called JT.

"Agent Dunkirk, we got your man in lock up. The taser did it, but he got two of us first—one only momentarily stunned, but the other was out for a few minutes. . . . Hell, we don't have any guns, only the up close and personal contact units. . . . I saw what he did, Man. We are *not* going near him. . . . I'll mention it to 'em. . . . No, I'll be gone by then but I'll brief my relief. If you guys don't get here tomorrow, we may have to transfer him to Detroit Metro. We only have the one cell here. . . . He's got a john, a sink and privacy. He'll get fed breakfast about eight in the morning. . . . We'll use a ten foot pole. How are you gonna transport him back? . . . Sounds like fun. What do you want us to do with the car? . . . Does this mean the FBI exercise is called off? . . . Aw nuts. I thought you guys did that just for him. . . . You're welcome, it was fun. . . . See ya."

Bradbury got back on the intercom and addressed the troops. "Okay, Folks, we're back in business. Ralph will be checking on your customers for a spell." He then walked over to Pommice and Finster. "They say this guy does some kind of mind thing, but I guess you figured that out already. They'll have a couple of doctors down here tomorrow, and the DHS agent said they could check you out and see if this guy did any damage."

"How they gonna do that?" questioned Pommice.

"I don't know. Maybe some *Star Trek* mind meld kind of thing. He said he really wasn't worried about you, Roger, but he thinks you might want to talk to these guys, Stan. It's up to you, and if you feel all right you can probably skip it, but they'll be here about eight-thirty or nine."

"I'm fine," said Finster.

Pommice said, "I'll see how I feel in the morning, Boss, if that's okay."

"Totally your call, Man. You okay to drive?"

"Yeah, sure."

"Okay then. Why don't you two knock it off for the night. I'll see you next shift."

CHAPTER FORTY-NINE

Wednesday, Crystal City, Virginia

The troops were still discussing likely scenarios at 9:30, and thinking about assigning shifts to man the phone, when JT got the first incoming call from Detroit. Twenty minutes later he had a second conversation with Agent Bradbury. The troops knew from his end of the conversation, and from his ear to ear smile, that things went well.

"Looks like I'm going to Detroit tomorrow. I've got to call Moffett to see whom he wants to accompany me and set up transportation. Damn good thing we jumped on this. Good work everybody—he hasn't even been gone a full day yet. Hot shit— that's the way things are supposed to work."

"If you don't need us, Partner, I'm gonna take Arati home. I'm guessing you won't need me for the Detroit trip, so I'll see you when you get back. Tomorrow we'll work on the other two cases. Knowing he's in custody may encourage his victims to come forth. Sound good?"

"Great. Arati, how you doing?"

"I am quite fine. Apparently Doctors Ellis and Lisbon are very good therapists. I do not believe I have felt this relaxed in some time. Perhaps I have been working too hard," she said with a smile.

"Yeah, maybe so," said JT. "So why don't you two take the rest of the night off," he said, barely suppressing a grin.

With that the ladies left and JT proceeded to call Moffett, who answered his cell before the second ring. He told JT to give him some good news.

"My pleasure, Boss—we got him. One of our Detroit guys saw the flag on the name and called me. He said he wanted to verify the BOLO instructions. Can you imagine that?" he asked rhetorically while barely suppressing a chuckle. "Three of them approached him with hand held tasers and the one guy got him, but two of them got stopped in their tracks. They seemed okay, but I offered to have one of your troops check them out if they wanted. . . . They have him in a holding cell and said they'd maintain their distance. . . . Well, Sir, it brings to mind one of those old Superman episodes where a crook discovers the hero's secret Clark Kent identity. So the Man of Steel puts the guy on a mountain top until he can decide what to do with him. The guy tries to climb down the mountain but slips and falls to his death. . . . That's probably a better idea, Sir. Will an hour be enough time for you to contact them? . . . I'll call the three of them with the flight information in an hour or so, and tell them where to meet me. . . . I'll call you when we're on the way back. . . . Thank you, Sir, it does feel good. Good night."

CHAPTER FIFTY

Thursday, Quantico, Virginia

Doctor Harold Lisbon picked up his good friend and cohort Doctor Sidney Ellis, and the two of them swung by the Cybernetics Technology Facility in Chantilly. There they picked up a third member of The Galactic Society—Doctor Stanley Rodriguez. The night before they had conferred with a fourth member, Assistant Secretary Charles Moffett, regarding the disposition of Paul Cutler, a participant in a Defense Department mind-expanding program termed MENSA. Cutler was also a suspect in several rapes and one murder, and two other less serious felonies. As they cruised south on I-95 toward Quantico Marine Corps Base in Lisbon's Cadillac, they discussed the pros and cons of various forms of detention for Cutler. The problem was his apparent unprecedented ability to control the thoughts of those in close proximity to him. The three distinguished gentlemen ensconced in the comfortable vehicle were no strangers to extrasensory ability, each one a practitioner of various forms of it himself. Two of them together were able to undo the psychic damage Cutler had visited upon a brilliant scientist, but none of them were able to penetrate the psychic wall the MENSA participant had thus far maintained. They were not sure, even acting collectively, that they would be able to counter his ability in a mental showdown, or worse, that they wouldn't suffer psychic damage themselves. It was a lively discussion.

"Stan, can you relate again what contraindications Toshi had regarding Cutler?" asked Ellis.

"His notes regarding that were not definitive, at least not substantiated as to cause and effect. He *felt* Cutler was stronger than he let on; that is, he would intentionally show no more, or only slightly more, improvement in ability than his cohorts in the program did. Toshi thought he was self-centered and in fact narcissist to the extreme, although he controlled it in most situations, and could be very affable if it suited his purpose. He apparently never tried to read Cutler, nor any of the participants, as he thought that unprofessional. I could find no data to support his postulations, although Toshi felt quite strongly about them. He was also convinced Cutler believed he was benefitting only minimally from the program, and would quit when he was sure of that."

"And your impressions?" Lisbon asked Rodriguez.

"I was actually leaning in those same directions before I read Toshi's hidden notes. After Paul's experience in the parking lot he acted upset, as though he was throwing psychic barbs at the other participants; but, in retrospect, they really only complained about him on a physical level. This would, however, not be an unnatural consequence of his experience. Some of his cohorts did voice concerns about working with him on a professional level, indicating he wasn't as forthcoming in his interactions with them as the others were. I never tried reading him, or any other participant, for the same reasons I believe Toshi didn't, so I cannot testify as to his resistance."

"And what do you think his current actions indicate?" asked Ellis.

"There is little doubt of his culpability in Arati's rape, and given her 'liability' in connecting him with other rapes, I believe he would do anything to protect himself. Given his history—the loss of his family, including a twin sister, his living in several foster homes, his erratic behavior— I think we have to consider that he is paranoid and acting totally defensively. I know I did not put these in the same terms Krumski, for instance, would have, but I'm sure you get the drift."

"Well, Harry and I can testify as to his ability to project— he reached down quite far into Arati's mind. Granted she was stunned and sleepy, but even with full mental alertness, I doubt she could have resisted him—casting doubt, therefore, on our ability to resist. What we have here is a powerful rogue psychopath with extraordinary mental abilities. So how do we detain him?"

"Gentlemen, we'll have to continue this discussion on the plane," said Lisbon. "Right now I need an ID from each of you for the guard here."

After the ID check, the guard asked Lisbon if he knew how to get to the airfield. He didn't, so the guard handed him a map with the parking lot circled, described a landmark located at a pertinent turn, and bid them a good day. Lisbon handed the map to Ellis so he could navigate. When they got to the parking lot, they found JT waiting for them.

Although probably not unique, there could not have been too many runways with the same numbers painted on both ends. Since the winds were from the north the Hawker Beechcraft aircraft took off from runway 02, with a twenty degree heading on the compass. If the winds were from the south the plane would be taking off from runway 20, with a two hundred degree heading on the compass. They were actually borrowing a Customs and Border Protection King Air 350 temporarily stationed at Quantico for U.S. Coast Guard familiarization flights. The twin engine multi-role enforcement aircraft was designed for ground interdiction operations, air-to-air intercept operations, and medium-range maritime patrols. It was equipped with a sophisticated array of active and passive sensors, satellite communications capabilities, a wide area marine search radar, a ground moving target indicator, and various other technical collection equipments. Few of these would be needed on this flight, but then the plane was available. CBP was about half way to their proposed end fleet of fifty aircraft, and the plane had thus far received many kudos from the troops.

The King Air 350 was normally manned by a crew of four, but two of those were sensor operators who employed the mission equipment and coordinated the flow of information to the ground. Only the pilot and copilot were needed for this trip. The six vacant seats meant the three TGS members and the DHS agent were quite comfortable. And there was still room for the passenger they were picking up in Detroit. JT had flown an inordinate amount as a Federal Air Marshall, more than pilots some weeks. Although he tired of the routine fairly quickly, which was one of the major reasons he left the job, he never tired of seeing large metropolitan areas from the air. He loved to pick out the monuments, the bridges, the major highways and anything else identifiable from the air. As they flew north up the Potomac, he sighted Fort Washington, then the Wilson Bridge and National Harbor, and finally Reagan National Airport before the plane took a more easterly heading as it gained altitude.

"Gentlemen, we need to discuss our plan of attack," said Sid Ellis once they had all settled in.

JT tore his attention away from the window. "Well, I've got a warrant and I plan on arresting him for rape. I've got cuffs and will probably use them to keep him in that back seat right there. I do have a taser gun I'm accurate with up to twenty feet. The rest is up to you guys."

"I think we need to play it by ear," said Lisbon. "We discussed this in the car on the way to Quantico. If he cooperates, we think we can leave him conscious, but be prepared to subdue him with the taser gun if need be. Charley did mention you'd be bringing one. Then we can use the sedatives we've got to put him out for the rest of the trip. Unfortunately, that's the easy part. We obviously need to keep him in isolation, and will have to figure out how best to handle his arraignment and trial. We may need to keep him sedated more often than not. If convicted, we really didn't see any option other than isolation and special handling."

"Can you guys disable him like he did Arati?" asked JT. "I know this must present a moral dilemma, but I'd just like to know all our available options."

Rodriquez fielded JT's question: "We don't know; presumably yes, but we're in uncharted territory here. Not only did he seriously disrupt Arati's cognitive abilities, but we're thinking he may have done the same with Doctor Lee. And they were both highly intelligent, with Toshi possessing an apparently respectable degree of ESP. None of us have ever done this, but Sid and Harry more or less did it in reverse with Arati. We just don't know the extent of his abilities, and whether or not any one of us can match them. We don't even know if our abilities are cumulative for that particular application—although we believe they are, since they are for other applications—or if they are, if that would be sufficient. He is an anomaly."

"Not exactly encouraging."

"It's definitely not a rosy scenario."

"Did Moffett tell you my Superman solution?"

"Yes, he did," said Harry laughing, "and it's not a bad idea. It would be nice if he cooperated, but given his flight and the dismal possibilities of his likely incarceration, which he has no doubt considered now since he has been apprehended, we doubt it. We are hoping we can communicate with him on a level which allows us to determine his capabilities, and they are not too much for us. If so, we can handle him; however, two or more of us will probably have to accompany him to any legal proceeding or other activity where he can't be sedated—not a pleasant prospect."

"Well, technically, it's not your problem; but morally, I guess it is."

"Yes, it is. Not only did we get DARPA started in this direction, but who else but us could accomplish what needs to be done?"

"You're right. Like you said, we just play it by ear."

JT sat back in his seat and thought how nice it was to be able to relax on a plane. This was something he could never do as a FAM, except for some of the longer international flights where he did drift off now and again, but even then his body seemed to know he was still working. He vaguely heard the others talking shop, and with the aid of their sing-song conversation and the droning of the aircraft engines, he actually got some sleep.

CHAPTER FIFTY-ONE

Thursday, Detroit, Michigan

As the crow flies the trip to Detroit was only 400 miles—at a cruising speed of 350 mph the trip was almost over before it began. JT awoke a short time later when he heard the "prepare for landing" announcement. They were landing at Coleman Young airport, which was closer to their destination than Detroit Metropolitan.

There was a Customs and Border Protection converted Tahoe driven by CBP Agent Tamika Watson waiting for them at the airport. Watson was very out-going, but knew very little about what went on the previous night. She did know these were high level folks from headquarters who had come to take charge of a very unusual prisoner. In less than half an hour they were at the Ambassador Bridge border crossing, but JT figured she had talked at least forty-five minutes worth.

The plan was for Ellis to ask Cutler if he was willing to cooperate with them, without any attempt to play mind games. If he tried anything, then Rodriguez and Lisbon would jump in and the three of them would try to control him. If they couldn't, then JT would zap him. The trick for JT was determining if that was the case or not. None of the three TGS members could be sure of being able to give JT a definitive sign, short of the three of them sprawled out on the floor or otherwise obviously disabled. Like Lisbon had said earlier, he'd have to play it by ear. If Cutler decided to cooperate, then JT would place him under arrest for the rape of Doctor Arati Jabornae, inform him of his rights, and then ask if he would be willing to talk to Doctor Rodriguez and company. If he agreed, they would make him aware of their capabilities in an attempt to have a very forthright communication. If he invoked his rights, they'd take him back to

DC, and question him with his lawyer present. It was all up to Cutler.

Agent Watson parked the vehicle right in front of the main entrance to the administration building. As they were getting out of the Tahoe, Agent Bradbury surprised JT by coming up and introducing himself. "I thought you said you'd be off duty this morning," commented JT.

"Are you kidding me? This is the coolest thing that ever happened on this job; maybe in my whole life. I wouldn't miss it."

JT introduced his cohorts, emphasizing the "doctor" part. Bradbury was obviously impressed with Rodriguez's DARPA pedigree. He didn't find it difficult at all to believe this highly secretive agency was involved with something akin to mind control. He had never heard of The Galactic Society, but knew if they were involved with DARPA they were special as well. And besides, he told himself, all three of these guys had doctorates, probably in psychology and/or in neuro-something-or-other.

"Has he given you any trouble other than last night?" JT asked Bradbury.

"Took your advice and didn't give him a chance. We made him stand in the back of the holding cell and we pushed his breakfast tray up to it with a pole and let him reach through the bars for it. I don't think we came within twenty feet of him. And two of us had the tasers at ready just in case."

"Has he said anything to you?"

"Not a word, and according to the night crew, not to anybody else either."

JT handed him a small canvas tote bag.

"What's this?"

JT just smiled.

"Three taser guns! Hey thanks, Man."

"They're fully charged, and I want you to be obvious about having one pointed at Cutler when I talk to him. Speaking of whom, let's go see him."

Bradbury fastened two of the tasers on his belt and said, "I'll hold on to these two, but let's put this other gun and your sidearm in the office and then go see the man."

"Good morning, Paul. How have they been treating you?" asked Ellis. He had met Cutler just two days ago, although it probably seemed more like a week to both of them. Cutler hadn't slept well and looked tired and resigned, almost lethargic. He was still dressed in the clothes they apprehended him in, which were dirty and partially torn from his encounter with the parking lot. His shoes had scrape marks on the toes from where he was dragged across the pavement to the holding cell. Ellis addressed him again.

Cutler took a deep breath and exhaled slowly. He stood up and walked to the front of the cell and looked past Ellis straight at JT. Bradbury was ready with the taser gun and had situated himself where he would have a clear shot. Cutler, however, didn't appear to notice him as he was fixated on JT. "I know why you're here, Agent, and I see you brought the Psi-Corps with you. Let's just get this over with."

"Have it your way." He nodded at Bradbury who said something into his collar transceiver and the holding cell door opened. JT walked in and closed the door behind him. He read the prisoner his rights and placed the cuffs on him.

Cutler refused counsel.

JT asked him to verify his refusal and got the same response, so he asked Cutler if he would answer some questions then.

"Oh, I'll tell you whatever you want to know, since I'm sure you figured it all out anyway. But I was thinking I might have something to trade here."

"Paul, I'm not empowered to make a deal. That's something for the U.S. Attorney back home. In which case you probably shouldn't answer any questions, and you should definitely think twice about getting an attorney."

"I'm not worried about anything I admit to having any effect on my deal, and I don't need an intermediary to make one."

"Paul, it doesn't sound to me like you're making an informed decision. I gotta tell ya . . ."

Cutler interrupted JT with, "I did what I did and there are no extenuating circumstances—I'm guilty. What I have to trade is my apparently unique mind. I'm willing to be a guinea pig for the program—and really participate this time—for a pardon when they've exhausted my usefulness. What do you think, Doctor Rodriguez?"

"Like JT said, we can't answer for the U.S. Attorney, but I do think you have something to trade. We'd certainly like to help you: maybe figure out if this was something you had no control over, and that might affect the other participants. If so, then you might be a great help to us in learning how to prevent it, if that's possible. It could be something we did in the program caused this anomaly, and we should certainly look into that possibility. Sid, would TGS be willing to work with Paul under those circumstances?"

Ellis addressed Cutler, "We would have to be assured of your continued cooperation, and the safety of the people you would be working with. I'm not sure how you could guarantee that to our satisfaction, but we would certainly be open to the idea."

"Okay, here's how this is going to work, then," said JT. "We're going up to the interrogation room and make a video record of you declining counsel, and then answering my questions regarding your culpability in Doctor Jabornae's rape.

Then my colleagues will interview you to determine whether or not we feel safe allowing you on the plane with us. If so, we take you back to Virginia, and detain you in isolation until we can get a meeting with the USA. Then, depending upon the case you, and I guess Doctor Rodriguez, make, we go from there. Is that how you want to play this, Paul?"

"I'm good. Let's go."

The "interrogation room" turned out to be a mid-sized conference room located on the second floor of the administration building. Agent Bradbury led the prisoner into the building, up the stairs and down the hall to the conference room, with the TGS contingent following them. JT brought up the rear keeping one of the taser guns at the ready. The room did not have two-way glass, but was set up for sound and video recording, and Bradbury gave JT a quick tutorial. It did have a large plasma screen hanging on one wall, so JT figured it must have doubled as a meeting room. Once in the room, JT asked Cutler to sit near one end of the center table with Ellis and Lisbon on either side of him. He stationed Rodriguez at another small table at the other end of the room, and a sufficient distance from Cutler. He thanked Bradbury and told him he really couldn't be here for this confession/interrogation. The CBP agent was disappointed but understood. He indicated he would hang around and see the group off when they were finished. As Bradbury left, JT handed the taser off to Rodriguez, and then grabbed the chair across from Cutler and started the recorder.

JT did the standard introduction mentioning the time, place, individuals present and the purpose of the meeting. He again read Cutler his rights, and verified he had refused counsel, was ready to discuss his involvement with the rape of Doctor Jabornae, and had been promised no deals for his confession. JT asked him to relate the circumstances in his own words.

"I found out from Moffett that she had information concerning a few rape cases I was a person of interest in."

JT interrupted to clarify who Moffett was, and the "she" he referred to was Doctor Jabornae. He asked Cutler to be as specific as he could, so the statement would stand on its own.

"Okay. When we met with The Galactic Society, I intercepted the thought from Charlie Moffett that Jabornae had been delving into my past, and had connected me with some unsolved rape cases. I decided to pay the good doctor a visit and determine the extent of her knowledge regarding those incidents, and to 'adjust' her understanding of them. I used my ESP ability to influence her to open her door, and intended to physically restrain her until I could get a reading on her. However, she continually struggled against me, and in my attempt to physically overpower her we somehow ended up in her bedroom. She put up a strong mental barrier, plus she kept fighting me physically, so I finally had to 'blast her mind' into submission. At this point she became pretty passive and, since I hadn't had any sexual relations with anybody for weeks, and this practically nude woman was right underneath me, I lost control and raped her. That was not my intent when I went to her place. After I was through, I tried to delve into her consciousness. I guess I pushed her too far into her subconscious, and I couldn't get anything. Or maybe I was just too overcome to concentrate. At any rate, I just left her lying there and decided to head for the border."

"Why did you go to Richmond?" asked JT.

"I don't know, actually. I just wanted to get away and started driving. First thing I knew I was on 95 South. I had pretty much decided to leave the program and the area the night before I went over to her place, and had most of what I wanted in the car with me, included all but one last bit of my available funds. I decided to get them out of the BOA branch in Richmond, and leave you guys with a false trail. That's when I decided on Detroit and headed out 64 West to get over to 81 North. I was sure my car would be hot in short order, so I borrowed one from a nearby parking garage before I left, thinking it wouldn't be missed until quitting time. I hadn't considered leaving the country until after the incident with Jabornae, so I didn't have time to get a fake passport. Besides, I was pretty sure she wouldn't be able to identify me. I figured if I got to an out-of-the-way border crossing that same day you wouldn't have an alert out for me yet, and I could get across on my own passport. Once in Canada, I'd head toward Nova Scotia and try to buy my way onto a ship to South America. That was pretty tricky having three guys with tasers attack me. If not for that, I would've made it."

"That's good, Paul. Just a couple of questions and then we're done. Were you involved with, or do you know anything about, the murder of Doctor Lee?"

"No. That was a complete surprise to me."

"Do you have any idea who was behind the attempt on your life or the one on Bill Brosard?"

"Not a clue, Agent."

"Okay then. Paul, if you'll wait here for a few minutes, I need to talk to these gentlemen out in the hall. The windows don't have bars but it would be a tough twelve foot jump down to the pavement with those cuffs on. And besides, I'll be watching you through the window in the door."

With that the four of them got up and headed out into the hall.

"So what do you guys think? Was he telling the truth in there?"

Lisbon looked over at Ellis who placed his palms up and smirked.

"I don't know either," said Lisbon. "He either totally believes what he's saying, or his mental processes are better than ours. I didn't detect any hesitation or equivocation—not on any of it. What do you think, Sid?"

"I agree. He seemed straight forward to me. From what he said, I believe there can be no doubt about his guilt in the most recent rape, but I'm not so sure about the others, or his answers to your last questions."

"Do you think you can control him on the trip back?"

Ellis fielded this one: "Yes, I think we can. Given his difficulty with Arati, and the fact that there are three of us with apparently stronger abilities than hers, his seeming resignation to his circumstances, and his expressed belief he can make a deal for himself, then yes, I believe he won't give us any trouble, or if he does, we'll be able to handle it. Nevertheless, I'd keep a taser handy. What about you, Stan?"

"I agree. But I thought this might be a better solution," he said as he reached into his briefcase and removed a vial of propofol.

"Works for me," said JT. "Let's go home."

Before getting back in the DHS transport, JT thanked Bradbury for all his help and, much to the agent's chagrin, emphasized the confidential nature of what he had been a witness to.

"I'll make sure an appropriate letter of commendation makes it into your file," JT promised as they bid their goodbyes.

They decided to keep Cutler alert until they got him on the plane, and had an uneventful trip to the airport in spite of that.

CHAPTER FIFTY-TWO

Friday, Chantilly, Virginia

Doctors Ellis and Lisbon finally got around to visiting the CTF. It's not like they didn't have good excuses for their delay: Wednesday they helped bring a beautiful mind back from the abyss, and Thursday they helped confine a dangerous one. Speaking of which, they had discussed in great detail the pros and cons of accepting Cutler's "deal" of trading his cooperation with the program for his eventual acquittal, or exoneration, or pardon, or whatever the U.S. Attorney wanted to agree to, if anything. The problem was that it would take a great deal of convincing of the right people to bring such a deal about, and part of the convincing would be assuring Cutler could be trusted to cooperate, and not try to escape or inflict any other damage. Right now they just didn't know enough to assure anybody of anything, and did not think even a "mind probe" would produce a reasonably definitive answer to that question. And there in lie the dilemma—how could they learn anything from this situation if they didn't trust him?

Ellis was hopeful Cutler himself may have a suggestion as to how he could be "controlled" which would present an acceptable level of risk. In order to investigate that possibility, he asked JT to look into the feasibility of an exploratory session between Cutler and the Ellis-Lisbon-Rodriguez trio. JT's boss, Charlie Moffett, agreed this "meeting of the minds" was critical for the proper adjudication of the case, and was meeting with the DHS Secretary and the Attorney General to explain the situation and the reason behind this very unusual request. It was looking like this wouldn't happen until Monday at the earliest, but since Cutler had agreed to waive his right to an arraignment, that didn't present a problem. Keeping Cutler on ice until then was a different matter.

In the meantime, Doctors Ellis and Lisbon were at the CTF to present the case for the MENSA program transferring to The Galactic Society to Brosard, the one MENSA participant who missed the session at the Smithsonian. Rodriguez, as the program manager, thought he should be there as well, so Brosard wouldn't feel outnumbered. Besides, he harbored a feeling that Brosard was reluctant to attend the previous session and had faked his illness. They met in one of the smaller Level I conference rooms, with Brosard and Rodriguez on one side of the table, and Ellis and Lisbon on the other. After introductions, Ellis gave a brief overview of the Society and then asked for questions.

"Actually I don't have any," said Brosard. "As you know, the program's on hold, so we haven't had much to do around here this past week. As a result, I've talked to most of the others about their visit, and, just for curiosity's sake, got answers to what questions I had. I've also spent some time back in my office at the Agency, and in general thinking about my situation. All of which has led me to the conclusion to quit the program."

This was news to all three folks in the room with him, but not unexpected, at least not by Rodriguez. He had noticed Brosard becoming increasingly withdrawn during the past week, and visibly nervous about this meeting, or perhaps about announcing his withdrawal. But Rodriguez thought there was more to it than that, and decided to pursue it.

"But Bill, we've come so far. Are you concerned about potential changes in the program due to our move, or is there something we've done you are not comfortable with?"

Brosard answered Rodriguez, but looked at Ellis and Lisbon who were staring at him with an intensity that he thought was indicative of attempted mind reading. "I just think I've grown about as much as I could here, and any additional time spent in the program would be wasted."

"How can you say that? I admit we have proceeded with caution, for your own safety, but there are so many things we could accomplish yet; so many avenues of research we haven't travelled down. Don't you think that's a very parochial view?" Rodriguez asked with what he hoped was just the right amount of irritation.

Brosard hesitated so Rodriguez continued with, "There's got to be something else behind this decision, Bill. Is there a personal reason you really don't want to mention? Is everything okay with your family?" Rodriguez knew Brosard was not married, had no siblings, and was not on the best of terms with his parents. He had earlier confided to Rodriguez that his mother was unhappy with her thirty-four year old son who had a new girlfriend every month, and hadn't even thought about getting married, let alone producing her a grandchild to dote over.

Brosard stood up abruptly. "Look, my reasons are mine, and I don't have to explain them to you."

"Bill, come on, sit back down and let's talk. Actually, given all the time we've invested in each other, I think you do owe us an explanation."

Brosard turned around and headed for the door. "I'm outta here."

"Could it be because you know who killed Doctor Lee?" asked Ellis.

Brosard stopped dead in his tracks. For ten or fifteen seconds you could have heard a pin drop on the carpet. Brosard turned slowly to face Ellis and said calmly, "You've been reading me all along."

"No," replied Ellis just as calmly. "You've got to be aware that you just blurted that out so strongly it would be loud and clear to any receptive mind."

"Yep, I can believe that," he said resignedly. "That's what got me in trouble in the first place."

"What do you mean, Bill?" asked Rodriguez.

Brosard sat back down, breathed a sigh of relief and sunk into his chair. "The night of Toshi's murder, I was in my room on the second level watching one of those CSI shows, New York, I think. I got this blast about a murder and at first I thought my mind was playing tricks on me. I really get into the shows, and I can usually guess who the killer is, and even visualize the scenario; but then I realized the murder that flashed through my mind had nothing to do with the show. So I thought someone must have been out in the hall and I picked up on their thinking, so I went over and opened my door. I heard, but did not see, a door close, in the general vicinity of Paul's room, and maybe that's why I had an 'inkling' he had done something. I was ready to dismiss the whole thing until I heard Toshi was dead."

"And you did nothing," lamented Lisbon.

"I didn't say anything because I really didn't know anything, not for sure. And that would not be any kind of proof in an investigation anyway. I did mention it to my boss and he agreed with me."

Ellis and Lisbon both raised their eyebrows at Brosard's statement, and Rodriguez jerked his head back.

"Shit! I just did it again didn't I?" Brosard yelled.

Ellis waited a moment then calmly asked, "Would you care to elaborate on your and your boss' involvement in the shooting attempt on Cutler?"

"Humph," he snorted as his whole body shrugged. "I might as well, since it seems you'll get it out of me anyway. But I've got to ask you a question first: Who are you guys? I know Stan has ESP ability, as do all of the folks here. But none of them, to the best of my knowledge, could read me if I didn't want them to. You two don't seem to have any trouble at all."

"As I mentioned earlier, one of our major goals is the enhancement of human intelligence and the concomitant mental abilities. I'm sure you already knew that from questioning your cohorts, and I suspect they also mentioned that we subtly hinted at the ESP abilities of our members. Well, what we didn't tell them is our abilities are substantial: not because they were developed in a program like MENSA, but rather naturally via methods we are not fully knowledgeable of—hence our interest in your program. So, let's go back to your involvement in the Cutler shooting incident."

"Are we being recorded?"

"A little late to ask," offered Rodriguez, "but no, we are not."

"Okay. I don't think I've done anything wrong here, and I know this will all be hearsay, and not admissible in court, but I want it understood I'm offering this all up freely in a spirit of cooperation."

"Acknowledged," said Rodriguez.

"I called Randal, my boss, right after I got that blast from someone in the hallway. I was a little upset about it, but after discussing it with him I felt better, thinking it was just an anomaly. When I heard about Toshi, I called him back and we agreed it was best not to mention it to anyone. I mean, it was nothing definitive, certainly not provable, and it might make me look like an agitator, or worse, crazy. Then later I hear someone called the FBI, or some such agency, and reported a murder. I *suspect* it was Randal, because he was becoming less and less a fan of the program, and had even mentioned that if it ever did work we'd be out of a job. I thought that was pretty flimsy, since such a substantial change wasn't going to happen on our watch. He was, is, always bugging me about the progress of the program, and whether or not I thought we'd ever be able to replace polygraphers with mind-readers."

"So how does this relate to the attempt on Cutler?" asked Ellis.

"A few days later, Randal says he can't believe the program hasn't been shut down because of Toshi's death, and starts hinting that another incident might just do the job. Then about a week later, I hear someone took a shot at Cutler. From talking to Paul himself about it, I got the impression it was a professional job, which I wouldn't put past Randal given his previous connections with the black ops guys in the Agency. I didn't *really* suspect his involvement until I went back to Langley and saw him in his office a few days after the incident. I got a definite vibe from him: didn't read his mind—just got a feeling."

"And again you did or said nothing because you only had feelings—no proof," said Lisbon.

Brosard nodded. "Even if I knew it was him, it's no harm, no foul, right? I mean, what would be illegal about that anyway?"

Ellis avoided answering and instead asked, "What about the 'attempt' on your life?"

"Strictly a coincidence."

Everyone but Brosard smiled at his gratuitous remark.

"That's where it gets a little sticky," he relented.

"I'm sorry, but I have to take a short break. Go on without me," said Lisbon as he left the room rather hurriedly with one hand on his stomach. Once out in the hall he popped into another room and made a call, then proceeded to the nearest restroom.

Inside the conference room Rodriguez tried convincing Brosard to change his mind and stay with the program, outlining some of the upcoming protocols which hadn't been revealed to the participants yet. Ellis touted the achievements of The Galactic Society, and hinted at the power the organization wielded given its luminary membership. Rodriguez was indicating how this might accelerate some of the new methods they wanted to try, when Lisbon walked back into the room.

"I apologize for taking so long, but I had to find one of the staff to get me something for my stomach. I called my wife, who's exhibiting the same symptoms, so we believe we may have gotten some tainted food at the restaurant we ate at last night. The staff here asked if we wanted some coffee and, although I'm certainly going to decline, they'll be here with some for the rest of you shortly."

Before he could get another word out the door opened behind him and the coffee service arrived.

"Ah, very shortly it would seem."

They had just finished fixing their drinks and sitting down to resume, when the door opened again and in walked JT. "I heard you guys were here having fun without me," he said.

Brosard jumped up and blurted out, "You guys set me up! I'm not saying another thing until I get a lawyer."

"Okay, Bill, a lawyer is an option, but I thought you might want to sit down and listen to what I have to say first—don't talk, just listen," JT said as he calmly sat in the chair next to the one Brosard had vacated.

"Hell no. I'm leaving and calling my lawyer."

"I said the latter was an option, but leaving is not."

"You can't hold me here," Brosard said his voice rising noticeably.

"Actually, you're right—I can't hold you here. But I can arrest you and take you to our detention center and hold you there. And then you can call your lawyer."

"On what charges?" he asked, his voice going up another notch.

"Well, for starters, there's withholding information in a federal investigation, conspiracy to commit assault, providing false information to a law enforcement officer, and probably one or two others I could come up with if I wanted to be thorough."

"What assault?" he asked, his voice yet another notch or two higher.

"The one on Cutler. Did you think you could just threaten someone with a gun with no consequences? And before you ask, you filed a false police report on the fake hit up in Georgetown."

"You guys may think you know what happened, but you can't prove it."

"You're certainly right about our knowing it, thanks to these gentlemen here. So with that certain knowledge, how hard do you think it would be to get the proof? After all, you weren't the only one involved here, and from what I understand, we already know who that is."

Brosard was crestfallen. "I do admit, two botched professional hits on two participants in the program is hard to swallow as circumstantial. And besides, I'm not lucky enough for them to have missed if they were trying. Naturally Cunningham is my prime suspect in those, but I really don't know if he's guilty for a fact." He sat back down, shook his head and let out a long, slow breath. After a minute he turned to JT and said, "Look, I can tell you what I know and what I strongly suspect, but I don't think you're going to be happy with that. So, under those circumstances, what's in it for me if I cooperate now, versus getting a lawyer and 'cooperating' through him later?" he asked, pausing to put air quotes around the cooperating word.

"The key word is *cooperate*. Doing it openly and above board, in a timely fashion, without some manipulating defense lawyer delaying and obfuscating things, is how the U.S. Attorney defines cooperation. I have not talked to him about this specific circumstance, since I didn't have time, but I've dealt with him a lot, and I know how he operates. You help us out now, and I'm there for you one hundred percent when it comes to getting your sentence reduced—likely no jail time at all. And you are welcome to 'read' me for verification if you want."

"I don't think that will be necessary," Brosard conceded.

"But . . ." JT added as Brosard looked at him expectantly, "if you had anything to do with Doctor Lee's death, or any other felony we don't know about now, then everything is off the table."

"I didn't and I don't, but I do have some suspicions about others."

"You willing to talk under those circumstances?" asked JT.

"Let's do it."

CHAPTER FIFTY-THREE

Saturday, Loudoun County, Virginia

The Loudoun County detention facility of DHS was hard to find, difficult to get to, and impossible to get out of if you weren't supposed to. Cutler was there in one of four 15x15 foot cells in the A block of the building. The other cells were empty and the guards were well aware of his capabilities. There was one other prisoner in cell block B, but he was not "isolated" as was Cutler. They kept the erstwhile MENSA participant under constant surveillance, and made him stand in the back of the cell when they brought him his meals. The guards were under strict orders to never approach him any closer than the fifteen feet of his cell length, and to keep one person in the control room when the other guard delivered his meals. They were not taking any chances with him, and were told that even if Cutler managed to disable one guard, the other was not to approach under any circumstances, and to call and wait for backup. They made sure Cutler was aware of these protocols.

George Mavens was making the 11:30 check, the last round before the change of shift at midnight. He looked through the window in the door to cell block A, where he had a good view of the two front cells, but not the back two. "Charlie, I'm going in. Is the prisoner in position?" he called on his voice activated personal intercom. Charlie Hastings was the other guard on duty.

"All clear, George. I've got eyes on him and I'm opening the door."

The door lock buzzed and Mavens pushed it open. He thought Hastings sounded a little odd, but then he usually got sleepy toward the end of the shift, at least since that little bundle of joy had arrived at the Hastings household. As he approached Cutler's cell, Mavens experienced a wave of nausea. He became disoriented and fell to the floor in front of the cell.

Cutler said, "Open the door, Charlie," into Mavens' mike, and his cell door buzzed. He pushed it and propped it open with a book. He pulled Mavens inside and swapped clothes with him. When done, he laid Mavens out on the bunk, which was located against the back wall, and covered him with the blanket. Now looking like a DHS guard, he put the book on the table and let the cell door close as he exited.

As he approached the corridor door he called out, "Coming out, Charlie." The door buzzed open and Cutler hurried up to the control room. He checked the time, then looked around for weapons. He figured they wouldn't carry inside, so there must be a weapons locker here somewhere. It was 11:45 and the shift change could show at any time, so he'd have to forget the gun for now. He ran over to the front door and waited.

Four minutes later a car drove up and the first relief guard got out. He grabbed some stuff from the back seat and headed toward the building when he noticed another car approaching. No doubt it was his partner so he waited for him. After the second car parked, he walked over to it and greeted his partner as he exited the vehicle. "Did you bring the tape of the game?" he asked.

"Yeah, I did," the man replied as they headed toward the door. "Let's go do some perpsitting."

Cutler went back to the control room. "Charlie, go to the bathroom and wait there for me to come get you. Wave to the relief team coming in the door just before you enter the bathroom."

Hastings got up and headed down the hall, waved at the guys coming in the front door just before he entered the john, and once in, sat down right in the middle of the tile floor.

The first relief guard, Tom Wilshire, saw Cutler and asked, "What's with Charlie? He looked a little under the weather."

"He said something about some bad sushi late this afternoon. Hi, I'm Greg Bemis. And you guys are? . . ."

"I'm Tom Wilshire and this is my partner Harry Brookings. Where's George tonight?"

"They told me at headquarters that one of the regular swing shift was sick, and pulled me from sitting on some guy at the safe house in Arlington. Maybe George got some of Charlie's bad sushi."

"Yeah, could be—more likely the flu. We got the same two inmates tonight?"

"Yep. With the same standing orders on the guy in A. All right, I'm out of here. No offense, but I hope I don't see you tomorrow."

"None taken."

After grabbing one of the two gym bags sitting on a table near the door of the control room, Cutler headed toward the exit. Once outside he reached into the bag and felt around for a set of keys. He found a single key with a remote entry system built in and pushed the open door button, but nothing happened. *I knew this was going too well*, he thought. He tried several more times and got the same response. *This has got to be the only fricking parking lot for miles—the car's gotta be here.* He searched the bag again and found another set of keys containing a remote. When he activated this one, the lights flashed and the door lock popped on the Civic right in front of him. He hopped in and started it up. *I really shouldn't think negative thoughts.* He turned the lights on, adjusted the heater controls and pulled off. And lookie here, a GPS unit. A hundred yards down the road he came to an electronic sliding gate. There was a control box on the side of the road that took a key. *Would have thought this thing would take a key card, not a real one. Hope one of these keys fits—I'm not sure this little car would break through without some major damage.* Lucky for him, one did, and he drove out of there as soon as the gate slid open far enough for him to get through. As he approached what looked like a main road, he started pushing the presets on the radio until he found something he liked. A couple of miles away he pulled over and searched the bag and the car for a weapon but found none. *Must have been in the locker back there. No problem, I've got my own weapon.*

Twenty minutes into their shift Wilshire remarked, "Hey Harry, is Charlie still in the john?"

"I didn't see him come out."

"I think he's been in there the whole time. You better go check on him before we start the first round. See if he fell in or something," he chuckled.

"Got it," Brookings said as headed toward the bathroom. A few moments later Brookings cried out, "Tom, get in here!"

When Wilshire entered the restroom he saw Hastings sitting on the floor in what looked to him like a yoga position. Then he noticed the blank stare. "What the hell is going on here? Is he okay?"

"He doesn't seem hurt, but he's not responsive. Should we try to wake him or call for help?"

"Hell yeah, we'll try," Wilshire replied as he whacked Hastings upside the head.

Hastings's head turned sideways and remained thus for what seemed like fifteen seconds to his two cohorts, but was actually only a few. When he faced front he shook his head and said, "What am I doing on the floor?"

"I don't like this. He's alright, Harry, and we need to go check on the prisoners."

In short order they determined it was Mavens in the cell and not Cutler, but at least the other prisoner was still there and asleep. Mavens responded to a good shaking and relayed his fainting experience. He started to yell at Hastings until Wilshire explained how they found him in the john. Hastings claimed he didn't remember telling Mavens it was okay to approach the cell or opening the door, nor was he aware of the wardrobe change and subsequent departure of Cutler.

"Holy shit! We've been mind fucked in spite of the precautions we took. The guy somehow hypnotized us into playing right along with his escape plan," Mavens complained. "We gotta get a BOLO out on him. Charlie, go see if he jacked one of our cars so we can include that. Oh fuck, man, the boss is not gonna be happy about this."

Hastings came back in complaining, "He boosted my Civic. Let me write down the description and plate number." He handed the paper to Mavens who was already on the wire putting out the BOLO. All the local jurisdictions and the Virginia State Police would now be on the lookout for a 2005 light blue Honda Civic, with license plate "IHQLD-EM".

"Who wants to call Agent Dunkirk?" asked Mavens.

"I'm the one who opened the door and let him loose. I guess it should be me," offered Hastings. "It's bad enough that I'll probably wake him up, but now I gotta tell him we let his guy escape. Man, I don't know how he got to me—I never got closer than fifteen feet like the man said. I guess the guy is better than they thought."

Mavens didn't argue.

Cutler didn't notice the personalized license plate until he stopped to check the bag and car for weapons: it was hard to miss when he raised the trunk lid. *I gotta ditch this car or at least the plates if I want to get out of here. I don't know how long before they find either of those two idiots. I'll pull over and swap with the first available secluded parked car I see, which should buy me some time.* Although he was driving slow and looking for anything with four wheels, he saw nothing. The GPS finally got him out to Route 15 and indicated Route 50 was about two miles south of his position, but he knew that was too well traveled a road and the chances of being noticed were greater. Not too far north there was a back road which headed west, so he opted for the northerly route. It looked like he could take all back roads to West Virginia and hopefully avoid detection. He was familiar with Charlestown, and thought he could make a few connections there. *Things are looking up.*

CHAPTER FIFTY-FOUR

Sunday, Springfield, Virginia

JT picked up his work cell on the fourth ring and answered with a sleepy, "Yeah, Dunkirk here." Thirty seconds later he was wide awake and bummed, but not surprised. They were dealing with a new kind of criminal here. Since they had already put out the BOLO on Cutler and the vehicle, he had the detention officer describe exactly what had happened. They had not considered the idea implantation trick, probably because Rodriguez had said the psychic ploy couldn't get you to do something you really didn't want to. That certainly changed with the realization Cutler was quite a bit stronger than anyone had anticipated. He woke Carmen up and told her he had to go into the office. He wasn't sure he could do anything other than wait, but he could marshal more resources from there if the need presented itself. On the way in, he phoned Charlie Moffett and woke him up with the bad news.

"Okay then," Moffett said. "Monitor the search for Cutler from the office and let me know if you need authorization for anything or if I need to run any interference for you. How definitive was the BOLO they put out?"

"Possibly armed and dangerous—do not approach—notify DHS at . . . etc.," JT replied.

"I'll call the Virginia and Maryland State Police and the Loudoun and adjacent County Sheriffs' Offices and amend it. I'll also ask them if some of them can get additional manpower on the streets, and give them your contact information. Let me know as soon as you hear something."

Crystal City, Virginia

The watch officer was monitoring the building entrance and opened the office door for JT when he got upstairs. "To what do I

316

owe the pleasure of your company, Agent Dunkirk? At this time of the night, I'm sure it's nothing you're too happy about." Terence Branton had been with the Fusion Team since the beginning, and knew the ropes and the personnel. He had spent a lot of time working as a Secret Service agent, and then later as a White House guard, and was happy to settle in to a less active position with DHS. Although well past retirement age, he was a widower with little else to keep him occupied but work, and made a point of making himself indispensable. Truth be told, he was the source of many of JT's jokes.

"You got that right, Terence. My special prisoner escaped from our detention facility out in Loudoun."

"Anyone hurt?" the watch officer asked.

"No, at least there's that. I'm afraid I'm gonna be here the rest of the night though. You got any coffee made?"

"Right over there," he said pointing to an alcove in the back. "Help yourself."

"Thanks. If you wouldn't mind, could you keep the pot full?"

"You got it. Expecting anyone else tonight?"

"No, but I might need your help monitoring some things, making phone calls, and who knows what all."

"That's what I'm here for."

JT was in the office for only a few minutes when he got a call from a Virginia State Police emergency communications coordinator. She explained how JT could tune in to the real time broadcasts from the officers on patrol. It was a web-based feed requiring special access, and JT set it up on one of the office computers. He asked the operator to read him the cautionary procedures required to deal with Cutler in the BOLO. He could tell the operator thought they were somewhat odd, if not unreasonable. He then called the Loudoun County Sherriff's Office and established the same setup, and soon had two monitors going. He made sure they had the same precautions in their BOLO. He reminded the Sheriff's Office, as he had the State Police, that they would need to patch him into the locating officers so he could advise them firsthand on how to handle the escapee. Neither group was comfortable with this outside assistance, but had received orders from the very top of their organizations. What amazed them both was how quickly this happened, as the suspect had escaped just about an hour ago.

CHAPTER FIFTY-FIVE

Sunday, Loudoun County, Virginia

Cutler was driving north on Route 15 and had seen only one other car, and that one was on the road and headed south. He knew it was very early Sunday morning but thought there should be more traffic, and certainly a few more cars parked alongside of the road. What he didn't realize, but was becoming increasingly apparent, was this part of Virginia was horse country and sparsely populated. The few houses there had long driveways— you often couldn't see them from the road even in the daytime. *Just need to keep looking*, he thought.

Senior Trooper Sherry Sanbridge was parked some thirty feet off the road with her engine running and her interior lights on. She was working on some reports when she saw headlights hit the canopy of trees covering the curve in front of her. A vehicle was heading down her side of the road, so she turned off the overheads to get a better look at it as it passed. It wasn't speeding, and in fact seemed to be going slower than usual—not a bad precaution given the lack of lighting and the local deer population in this area. She was situated so she avoided any headlight glare, and was able to get a good look at the vehicle as it passed her position. It was a light colored compact, maybe a Civic or a Corolla, with a personalized tag: IHQLD-EM. She recognized it from the recent BOLO, and thought tonight might not be as boring as usual after all. She pulled onto the road and quickly caught up with the suspect vehicle. She hit the blue lights and waited for the moment of truth.

"Shit!" Cutler yelled to himself. "You guys just can't leave me alone." He hit the accelerator and kept his foot there until he got up to seventy-five. *This is ridiculous—I can't outrun a police car*. He slammed on the brakes and veered off the road, let up the pressure somewhat, and carefully guided the car into a tree after he slowed to a less dangerous twenty-five miles per hour. He braced himself as the air bag deployed, and it and his upper body slammed into each other. It took him a few moments to shake it off, at which time he realized he was leaning on the horn. In his side mirror he could see that the officer had pulled up slightly behind and beside him, and was just sitting in his vehicle, most likely running the license plate. Cutler just sat there with the horn blaring.

Trooper Sanbridge had called in the pursuit, and now contacted headquarters to report the status.

"The BOLO says the suspect is an escaped federal felon and armed and dangerous—do not approach under any circumstances. We have an ambulance and backup on the way. Sit tight, Trooper." The dispatcher didn't sound convinced and didn't stress the instructions.

Sanbridge saw no movement, and the horn was blaring like the driver was leaning on it. She didn't think that could occur if the air bags deployed. In any event this guy needed help. She approached with her weapon drawn, and saw the suspect leaning on the steering wheel column which was covered by the deployed air bag. She opened the car door carefully with her left hand, her gun in her right. The suspect appeared unconscious, but there was no obvious bleeding anywhere. She decided it wouldn't hurt to push him up straight and off the horn. As she reached down for him she experienced a wave of nausea, tried to straighten up, and then fell over backwards into unconsciousness.

"I'm getting good at this," Cutler said to the supine trooper. "Well, I'll be damned, you're a woman. Sorry about this honey." He reached down and took her service weapon with one hand and gave her a pat on her check with the other.

"Say again, Sherry, I didn't copy that," Cutler heard her dispatcher say as he walked around her toward her vehicle.

Trooper Marvin Kensington was already headed south out of Leesburg on Route 15, when he copied Sanbridge's original contact with the suspect. He now had the 10-20 on her and was only fifteen minutes north, when he heard dispatch having trouble raising her. The road was relatively straight so he bumped it up to eighty. Not six minutes later he saw a northbound unit and knew it had to be the suspect, as anyone else would have been headed towards the incident. He slammed on the brakes, did a one-eighty and called in. "Dispatch, this is Charlie 16. I have sighted a northbound unit on 15, just south of Harmony Church Road. I am in pursuit."

"Roger, Charlie 16. We cannot raise Trooper Sanbridge and believe her vehicle has been commandeered by the suspect. Maintain pursuit but do not attempt to apprehend. I have a federal agent on the line. Stand by."

JT had come on line just a moment before. "Charlie 16, this is Special Agent JT Dunkirk with DHS. What's your name, Trooper?"

"It's Marv Kensington, Sir."

"Okay, Marv. Call me JT. Let's take it easy and we'll catch this guy. I guarantee you he can't drive as good as you, and we've got a road block working." He then directed his comments to Cutler. "Paul, I know you're listening. Running is useless. You know you don't want anyone else to get hurt. Talk to me, Paul." He addressed the dispatcher on a different channel: "Do these guys have voice activated mikes in the cars?"

"Yes—the cars and their shoulder mounts."

"Paul, all you have to do to talk to me is just speak. The mike will pick it up. Just talk to me."

"Dispatch, I mean JT," corrected Trooper Kensington, "the vehicle is slowing down. He's pulling over to the side of the road. I'm pulling in behind him."

"Marv, do not approach the suspect. How far back are you?"

"Two car lengths."

"What's he doing? Talk to me, Marv."

"He's exiting the vehicle. He does not appear to be armed. His arms are extended and he's walking toward me."

"Marv, point your gun at him and tell him to stop."

Kensington got out of his car and complied with JT's request, but Cutler continued approaching him. "He's still walking towards me."

"If he doesn't stop, shot him in the leg, Marv. You hear me? Shoot him in the leg!"

"But he's unarmed!"

"Shoot him, Marv! You CANNOT let him get close to you. Shoot him now!"

Kensington was still hesitating when he heard his supervisor yell, "Shoot the bastard in the leg, Marv!"

Kensington put a bullet in Cutler's upper left thigh, towards the outside. It was a through and through. "He's hit, and he stopped. No wait. He's bleeding, but he's still walking."

"Stop him now, Marv. Put one in his knee."

"He's already hurt."

"DO IT NOW! Shoot him in the knee."

Kensington took aim and hit Cutler in the right knee.

Cutler dropped to the ground and landed on the side which had taken the thigh shot. He was cradling his knee and yelling, "Jesus Christ that hurts! I'm bleeding really bad here. Help me stop this bleeding."

"Don't go near him," cried JT. "Help is on the way. He'll make it until they get there. DO NOT go near him."

Cutler rolled on his stomach and appeared to pass out.

"What's going on?" yelled JT.

"I think the suspect passed out. I see a weapon tucked in his belt at the small of his back. I'm going to disarm him."

"Do not go near him!" shouted JT.

Trooper Kensington approached Cutler and reached for the gun. As he pulled it from Cutler's belt, he felt a wave of nausea, and then dropped down to his knees. Then his head seemed to explode, and he dropped both guns and reached for his temples. He then fell face forward across Cutler's legs.

"Talk to me, Marv. What's going on?"

Cutler struggled onto his side and managed to push the trooper off. He picked up one of the guns. "Agent Dunkirk. How are you this evening?"

"Paul, what did you do to the trooper, is he alright?"

"He's a little under the weather right now. How are Charlie and George doing?"

JT had talked to the two agents from the detention center, both of whom were awake and seemingly okay, but quite embarrassed. "They seem to be none the worse for the wear."

"Well then, I guess the two troopers will be okay shortly as well. Thank goodness for that. That's a little less on my conscience."

"Paul, we got more troopers and EMTs on the way, but you know I can't let them approach you. They're either going to have to wait until you pass out from loss of blood, or taser you again. We may not be able to save you at that point. You gotta work with us here, Man. Give up the gun and let us help you."

"I'm not giving up the gun, JT."

"It will be suicide by cop . . . if you don't bleed to death first. Remember what Rodriguez said—we can work this out."

"No, JT, I remember what Ellis said—you guys will never be able to trust me. I'm not getting out of this, and I'm not going to spend the rest of my life in solitary confinement with very little human interface, and no women. This damn ability I thought was a gift, is actually a curse. Maybe it works for those other folks, but watch out when they get to my level."

"Paul, this is Stan."

JT had called Doctor Rodriguez earlier, and the MENSA program manager was now patched in on the conversation.

"Hey, Doc. How's it hanging?" Cutler asked, chuckling to himself.

"Ellis, myself, and the others with the TGS, Paul, we're at your level or almost, and we can handle it. I'm sure we can come up with a way to overcome your difficulties, but you have to work with us."

"No. That's not going to happen for us MENSA types, Stan. Something is wrong there."

"Help us figure it out, Paul. Talk to me. What's not working?"

Cutler heard the sirens approaching. "I'm out of time, Doc. Tell Arati I'm sorry—I really lost it there. And I'm sorry about Doctor Lee, too. That was an accident. I was just trying to get him to forget what he knew about me, and it got away from me. But I'm telling you, you guys got another problem because somebody tried to kill me. And for the answer to your question about what's wrong, Stan, just ask any aardvark."

"Paul, don't do this. It doesn't have to end this way," pleaded JT.

"Oh, one more thing—Lee's iPad is toast. No, one more—I promise this is it—you guys can have my brain. Goodbye, yellow brick road."

JT heard Cutler laughing, then BLAM!

Crystal City, Virginia
"Shit! Shit! It didn't have to end like this," JT moaned.

"Yeah, it sounded like it did, JT. It sounded like it did," said Branton who had been standing behind him for the entire conversation.

CHAPTER FIFTY-SIX

Tuesday, Crystal City, Virginia

"Okay, everybody, let's figure out where we are on this," said Charlie Moffett. In this case everybody included JT, Juanita, Arati, Doctor Rodriguez and Tom Hanson. In light of yesterday's developments, Moffett wanted to refocus the team's efforts. "I guess our man fell off the mountain, huh JT?"

"I'm afraid he did, Sir," JT responded.

"All right then. First off I'd like to know how everyone whom Cutler had contact with is doing. JT, do you have an update on them?" Moffett asked.

"Yes, Sir. Yesterday Stan and I flew up to Detroit to pick up Cutler. While we were there, the doc checked out our two guys at the border, Roger Finster and Stanley Pommice, and they are showing no ill effects. George Mavens and Charlie Hastings, the two guards at our Loudoun detention facility, were also checked out by the doc when we got back to the CTF. They're not showing any ill effects either, and are on notice to let Stan know if they should develop any. They knew of Cutler's abilities, except for the idea implantation trick, which is our fault for not thinking of and warning them about it. Obviously our ten foot rule was inadequate, and begs the question of how to handle someone with his capabilities." JT looked over at Juanita.

"JT and I have been working with the CTF and TGS staff on some procedural changes. We should have recommendations in a day or two," Juanita offered.

JT continued: "State Trooper Sherry Sanbridge, who thought Cutler was disabled in the accident, appears to have recovered completely, and suggested herself that Cutler used some sort of knockout drug on her, and we didn't disabuse her of that idea. We did ask her to contact Stan if she has any after effects. We used the same ruse on Trooper Marvin Kensington, although I'm pretty sure he didn't buy it. We think the trooper may have a little PTSD from shooting a seemingly helpless Cutler twice, but I'm pretty sure we convinced him of Cutler's intention to use the gun on him. Per protocol, they are both seeing the psychologist for the State Police, who, by the way, are bugging us for more information. So far we've managed to stonewall them with the classification issue. I'll let Arati speak for herself."

"I am doing fine, Sir. Doctors Ellis and Lisbon seem to have removed all ill effects from my encounter with Mr. Cutler."

"I'm glad to hear that; and I'm really sorry about what happened to you, Arati. We'd totally understand if you want to take some time off or get some counseling. There's no shame in accepting a little help," offered Moffett.

"I know, Sir. But I truly believe that under these circumstances that will not be necessary."

"Okay then. JT, where are we on this case?"

"Cutler admitted to killing Doctor Lee—he said it wasn't intentional and in fact it 'got away from him.' And he said Lee's iPad was toast, which says to me he took it to cover his tracks. He also admitted he lost control in the incident with Arati. I'm not a psychiatrist, but indications are that, even with his superior mental abilities, or perhaps because of them, he did indeed have psychological problems he couldn't handle. Further, he said he had to 'adjust her understanding' of the two rape incidents Arati had connected him to—the one in Denver and the one in San Francisco. I'd take that as an admission of guilt in those two cases, and I think we should close them with the locals. But he denied having anything to do with the attempt on his own life. Given his obvious intention to kill himself, I believe this qualifies as a deathbed statement and we need to look elsewhere for the guilty party there and in the Brosard attempt. Perhaps Stan would like to address that issue."

"I would," Rodriguez said. "Brosard believes his boss, Randal Cunningham, was the deep throat behind the original tip that this was an inside job. He also believes Cunningham set up the fake hit on Cutler, using some black ops guys he used to deal with at the Agency, in order to discredit the program. When that didn't work, Brosard is convinced, his boss set up the fake hit on him. These 'operatives' were apparently contractors whom Cunningham still had access to, and paid himself in order to keep the incidents off the books. Unless Brosard is much better than we think, and we have no indication of that, then we really believe he was taken completely by surprise, and only put it together afterwards. He then told us he thought Cunningham was so enamored with himself as the 'premiere polygrapher' in the world, that he'd do anything to protect the integrity of the program and thus his reputation. We're not sure how much credence to put into his accusation, given that he's not real happy with Cunningham at this point; but he does believe it, and Cunningham's actions support it."

"Perhaps I can shed some light here," offered Arati.

Moffett nodded in her direction.

"I looked into the transactions of the financial institution Mr. Moffett asked me to—the one Doctor Ellis 'glimpsed' when he was with Mr. Cunningham. I managed to trace them to a stateside institution, and then back overseas through what appears to be a dummy corporation. I have some more work to do there, but first need to add some data sources to the Tomfoolery program. What I did manage to discover is that the timing of these transactions correlates very closely to messages Mr. Cunningham has sent from his personal computer at home to his 'trading card' friend. As you know, I suspected he was passing information via electronic renditions of those cards, but had no basis for comparison. I went back as far as I could in his emails, but did not find where he had sent any earlier versions of the cards. I looked for the key in the forwarding email, but again to no avail. Then it occurred to me to find an independent version of the cards, but many of the ones available were apparently corrupted by their capture process, as they were not consistent. However, I did find ten which were identical over many copies. Two of those were versions Mr. Cunningham had transmitted recently, and both appear to contain hidden data, but it is encrypted. Although that is probably not a big enough sample, I forwarded them to the NSA anyway and am awaiting a response from them."

"JT, do we not have him under surveillance?" asked Moffett.

"Yes, Sir, on the weekends. But he has done nothing suspicious so far. I guess we should reevaluate that when we get the NSA results and anything else Arati comes up with?"

Moffett nodded. "Did Brosard give us anything else during his interrogation?" he asked.

"He mentioned that he thought Krumski and Rydell were hiding something," Rodriguez responded.

"Based on what?"

"The fact that they were not as forthcoming as the other troops, and he was getting a vibe from them as well—nothing definitive I'm afraid."

"Okay." Moffett was about to say something else but was interrupted.

"There is one other thing, Sir," Arati said with a sheepish grin.

Moffett looked at her expectantly.

"Within twenty-four hours after the 'hits' on Messrs. Cutler and Brosard, there were transactions from the same financial institution mentioned above. These were through an intermediary account to the same account used by Cunningham's Agency to pay their contractors."

"Indeed?" Moffett almost purred. "Perhaps we need to increase our surveillance on him. Thank you, Arati. Keep up the good work. We now need to decide what to do with Brosard. Tom, what do you think our chances are in court?"

Hanson thought about it for a minute before replying. "I don't think we can definitively say he knew Cutler was guilty of murder, so that's off the table. And if he knew about the attempt on Cutler, the only chance we'd have there is if Cunningham verifies that, and even then, without transcripts of phone calls or some other proof, it would be a he said, she said situation. Unfortunately, I believe the same logic applies for the attempt on him. What do Ellis and/or Lisbon think?"

"They believe he was quite certain of Cunningham's involvement; they're just not sure when. They also believe he considers himself guilty for not acting, but not that he was in collusion with Cunningham," replied Moffett. "So, Stan, what do we do with him?"

"I have to admit I'd hate to lose him. I think he can contribute a lot to the program, but I also think he's damaged goods. He already told us he was considering quitting, so let's debrief him and let him go. If he changes his mind, then I say we kick him out."

"Good."

"What are we going to do about the two rape cases?" JT asked Moffett.

"I know your druthers, JT. From all I've heard, we can't say with one hundred percent certainty he did those. If we close those cases it would, I suppose, bring some comfort to the victims, even after the years gone by. But if it wasn't him, closing them would take them out of consideration and possibly prevent their linkage to related cases. We need to let sleeping dogs lie here."

Moffett then paused and looked around the room considering if this was the right audience. "Stan," he said slowly, "what did Cutler mean by his 'ask any aardvark' comment?"

"Cutler was one of the sharper ones of the group; that is, his abilities were better than most, and he held back to our pace. Based on a review of Toshi's notes, and from an inventory of our supplies, I'm convinced Cutler was dosing himself with extra AJ. At first we didn't think we were missing any, but then after examination we realized our entire supply was watered down to about sixty-five percent purity. That explains the lower efficacy of the drug compared to our expectations, and, I believe, the apparent accelerated increase in his abilities. In my opinion this was the cause of his psychotic break. He knew he had a problem, and I believe he shot himself in the heart in order to leave us his brain intact. At least now we can correct our data and change our protocols accordingly. It's a good thing we found out when we did, because with him gone, we may have unknowingly increased the dosage from sixty-five to a hundred and ten or fifteen percent. I'm having second thoughts about using it at all now, since we're combining with TGS and have new methodologies to pursue. That's probably more than you wanted to hear."

"No. That explains a good deal. Tom, I'd like the benefit of your experience while Stan and I stick around and discuss the transfer of TGS to our Department. I want you three," he said indicting JT, Juanita and Arati, "to continue pursuing the Cunningham case."

"Yes, Sir. We're out of here," said JT as the three of them went back to their offices.

CHAPTER FIFTY-SEVEN

Wednesday, Tysons Corner, Virginia

Arati usually worked out of Fusion Team Headquarters in Crystal City, as Hanson had managed to have a SCIF built there. This included the special communications infrastructure required to access the highly classified data bases she needed to accomplish her job. However, there were a few data bases she couldn't access from there, notably some CIA ones, but could from the National Counterterrorism Center located at Tysons Corner. She could have accessed the data at Langley as well, but the NCTC, a sleek, six story, modern white building, with bullet- and blast-proof external windows located on McLean Drive, was easier for her to get to and she also had her own desk there. She wanted to show Charlie Moffett what she had found, and he suggested the NCTC as he had to be in the area anyway on another matter. Arati asked JT and Juanita to join them as well. Moffett drove separately, so JT and Juanita agreed to wait for him in the lobby before proceeding to Arati's work station. The three of them rode the elevator to the fourth floor and rang the buzzer located beside the vault door guarding the entrance to her inner sanctum.

"I am so glad you could join me," she said upon opening the door. "I have some good news which is best illustrated here, and I believe it is imperative you see it for yourself and give me your opinion."

JT knew Arati seldom if ever exaggerated, so this was very likely something good. It was late afternoon, and JT knew she had been at it since early this morning. "Arati, you need to get a life," he chided.

"I have one," she replied. "It just does not happen to coincide with your definition of same. Although, I suspect there is not that much difference," she said with a smile. "Please pull up a chair around my work station here. I want to show you something."

Her area was not very big, so the four of them, with Arati in the center driving her computers, crowded in close together. Moffett and Juanita placed chairs on either side of Arati, and JT stood behind them looking over their shoulders at her console.

"I heard back from the NSA regarding the hidden data in Mr. Cunningham's baseball card images. They could not decipher it with any certitude, but there best bet was that the data represented dates and times and GPS coordinates. On the upper left hand screen I have shown a local map with the two suspected coordinates highlighted, along with their corresponding time stamps. As you can see, the lower one is a roadside stop on the George Washington Memorial Parkway, and the other is a side street in Georgetown. These are both within a few minutes of Langley. From my console here I can track the comings and goings of Mr. Cunningham, by virtue of his agency's pass requirements at their front gate. In the last twelve months he has left the compound at lunch only four times—the dates highlighted on the upper right hand screen. Two of those are on the dates correlated with the GPS coordinates from the NSA data. Further, within twenty-four hours of those two times and dates, as indicated on my center screen, transfers were made to the accounts Mr. Moffett had me check into. My conclusion is that he is physically passing data to his baseball card friend after he sends him a message indicating where and when, and then being paid for his efforts."

JT noticed Arati was beaming. *She is just beautiful*, he thought. *There is something about a happy person that brings out their best qualities*. "Can you call us real time when he goes out on his next run?" he asked.

"If he sends out advance notice with an email, then I should be able to give you as much warning as Mr. Cunningham is giving his friend, or about fourteen or fifteen hours."

"How often has he done this?" asked Moffett.

"Notes to his friend have been quite sporadic; however, over the last year he telegraphed the four lunch excursions I showed you with emails to him. Additionally, they were accompanied by fiscal transfers within the next eighteen to twenty-four hours. I can go back further if you would like, but I believe I have established a definite pattern here."

"Arati, this is fabulous. It would be most helpful if you could get us a location on his friend. JT, given that we're likely to get advance notice of his next run, call off the surveillance on him but be prepared to follow him on short notice. I need to talk to the Secretary about the ramifications here. If there is nothing else, Arati, then I'll be on my way."

"That is all I have for now, Mr. Secretary."

"JT, you could learn some manners from this woman," said Moffett as he grabbed his coat and headed out the door while shaking a figure at JT.

"Juanita, could I talk to you for a few minutes?" asked Arati.

Juanita looked at JT who said, "I'll walk down with Charlie and meet you at the car. I have some calls to make so take your time." He then ran to catch up with the Assistant Secretary.

When JT cleared the door Juanita looked at Arati with question marks in her eyes.

"Could we go to the break room for a moment or two?" Arati asked.

Juanita held out her hand in the direction of the hall way and Arati led the way through the door and down the hallway to the break room.

"Can I buy you a cup of coffee?" Arati asked.

"I wouldn't mind a Diet Coke."

Arati put two dollars in the kitty and grabbed two Diet Cokes from the fridge.

"So what's up?" Juanita asked.

"Tom asked me out yesterday."

"The Boss? That Tom?"

"Yes, and I wanted your advice on whether or not to accept. I have always heard office relationships, especially between a supervisor and a subordinate, are not a good idea, and I know the reasons why. Yet, people do it all the time and he knows this as well, but still he asked."

"Do you like him?"

"Yes. He is a great supervisor and a wonderful person based on everything I know and have heard about him."

"Did you Google him?"

"No—that seemed like an invasion of privacy."

Juanita chuckled. "You do the same thing all the time with dozens of people."

"Yes. But this is different. I am serious."

"I know you are, and I am flattered you asked me. First off, you should look him up. There is nothing wrong with checking people out. If it makes you feel any better, only look him up in the data bases normal folks have access to. But if it were me, I'd check him out in every one I could get into." Arati looked skeptical here, but before she could say anything Juanita continued. "But you don't have to if you'd rather not, because I can tell you you'll find nothing deleterious there. He is not in any serious relationship now, and he is a very nice person. Hell, if people didn't take advantage of the relationships developed in their professional lives, we'd have a whole lot fewer couples, and probably a significant decrease in the population. If something serious develops, you can cross that bridge when you come to it.

For instance, he could move on, or you could be placed in a different section. One of you would have to make a change though, but that's a small price to pay for being with someone you really like."

Arati was pensive and still not convinced. "The thought crossed my mind that his timing was unusual. Perhaps he is only asking me because of my recent experience, and is trying to boost my morale."

"Arati, I can see how you would think so, but I can tell you he has been thinking about it for some time now. I'm surprised it took him this long. Maybe your 'recent experience' was the final incentive he needed. But believe me, he is asking because he really thinks a great deal of you."

"So you are encouraging me?" she asked.

"How many times in your life do you think a well-respected, eligible, handsome, fairly well-off man, whom you know and like, is going to ask you out?"

"That certainly does put it in a clearer light."

"You think?" Juanita asked smiling.

"What do you think JT would say about this?"

"He wouldn't put it in exactly the same words, and no doubt more colloquially, but believe me, the message would be the same. I gotta go, Arati. You do what you think is best. But if you don't agree to go out with him . . ." she said shaking her head and leaving it hanging. As she reached the door to the hall way she looked back and saw Arati smiling.

Juanita met JT in the lobby and they proceeded out to the car. "So what now, Compadre?"

"Sounds like Arati's got it well in hand, so I guess there's not much we can do until we hear Cunningham's on the move. I've got a few things I need to clean up at the office, but then I'm headed home. By the way, what did Arati want?"

"Oh, you are gonna love this."

CHAPTER FIFTY-EIGHT

Friday, Washington, DC

Things had indeed slowed down at the office: Cutler admitted to the Lee murder and then offed himself saving the government some money; Brosard was pretty much a dead end as they had nothing definitive against him; and Cunningham had them in a holding pattern waiting for him to make his next contact. And the timing couldn't have been better—Maryjo was in town. She had arrived at Dulles the evening before and caught a taxi to the Omni Shoreham near DHS headquarters. JT wanted to pick her up, but she insisted he stay at home with Andy since his grandparents were picking him up after school the next day for a weekend stay with them. Her meeting was over by 11:00, and JT had a convenient meeting at DHS headquarters that ended at the exact same time. They tried not to be too effusive in their greeting when she exited the meeting room. Nevertheless, someone did crack "get a room" as he walked by. JT took the individual's advice to heart, and they were back in the hotel within fifteen minutes. Two hours later JT gallantly recommended that Maryjo save the government some money and stay at his place since Andy was gone and Carmen was spending the weekend with her sister. When Maryjo went to check out, the desk clerk wanted to charge her for an extra day, but JT convinced him that wouldn't be good for future government business.

Maryjo had always wanted to see the National Zoo, and JT admitted he hadn't been there since Andy was little. They each had a hot dog when they got there, hoping that would do them until dinner. Maryjo loved the animals and they tried to visit every exhibit before the zoo closed at 6:00, but nonetheless missed a few. JT promised her a return visit. Needless to say they were famished by then, and decided to eat at the Ardeo+Bardeo

Modern American Bistro on Connecticut Avenue. It was nice talking face-to-face rather than on the phone, and they had a wonderful time catching up, drinking wine and relaxing. JT told her what he could of the case, and filled her in on things that had been happening at headquarters while she was gone. She was tickled to learn about Arati and Tom Hanson, and hoped that worked out well for them. In turn, she relayed some of the funnier school stories and the outdoor adventures she undertook in northern California. By 9:30 the waiter was hinting that they had occupied the table long enough, so they headed back to JT's place in Springfield.

Saturday, Springfield, Virginia

"This wasn't exactly what I had in mind when I asked if we could get together this weekend. Not that I'm complaining, mind you—just saying I wasn't expecting this," said Maryjo as she sat at the breakfast table eating an omelet JT had prepared. "You, on the other hand, seem to have had this all planned out: Andy's gone, Carmen's gone, and you're not working. How did you pull that off?"

"Things just fell into place," he explained as he started to cook a second omelet. "After the field trip to the zoo and then that wonderful dinner, it just seemed like the right thing to do."

"Right. That's why Andy and Carmen aren't here."

"Honestly, Carmen had planned on this for a week or two. I thought that Andy would be here, and I was planning on the three of us spending time together. Then at the last minute, Mom and Dad mentioned taking him for the weekend and he was really up for that. And the work thing is very unusual."

"Did your parents know I was coming?"

"Oh, yeah. Now that think about it, I guess I might have mentioned it to Dad."

"Thank goodness for understanding fathers. Speaking of work, can you spill anything else on that CIA mole situation?"

"We think we know how he operates and we're waiting for him to do his thing. Not much else I can tell you at this point. So what do you want to do this weekend?"

"I was hoping we could go to the Torpedo Factory and then over to National Harbor. How does that sound?"

"Great. They have this terrific Mexican Restaurant there."

"I should have known."

"Think you could change to a later flight tomorrow?"

"I tried already with no luck. We can check again in the morning, but I'm not hopeful. And I've got to get back for a Monday class. So how about if I jump in the shower and then we hit the road?"

"Sounds like a plan. Need some help?"

CHAPTER FIFTY-NINE

Monday, Washington, DC

Not only was this the first day of the month, but it was also the beginning of a two week pay period for the Department of Homeland Security—a convenient time to bring on new employees. The DHS Secretary was so impressed with the MENSA program, she allocated a dozen personnel slots for them. Her organizational constraints did not allow her to run as loose a program as DARPA had, and she insisted that all of the principals be DHS employees. Three of the original eight would not be transferring: Paul Cutler was deceased; Bill Brosard had opted out as the The Galactic Society hoped he would; and Randall Thompson was uncomfortable leaving the FBI, and returned to his old job at Quantico. Of the remaining five original program participants, two were detailed from other organizations and three were contract employees. The latter three, Ralph Krumski, Sharon Rydell and Brandy Simmons, readily agreed to become government employees. Their current company, Shurcor, didn't balk, since it retained the support contract which was novated to TGS. The two personnel on loan, Tommy Pacquin from the FBI and Gayle Pennington from the Library of Congress, as it turned out, were delighted to leave their old organizations behind. Since they were down to five participants, Rodriguez suggested bringing the former participant, Julie Stafford, back on board. She had returned to her old job with the Department of the Interior after an extended leave for personal reasons, and was glad to transfer to DHS and get back in the program.

Rodriguez accessed the old MENSA files and looked at the applicants who didn't quite make the first cut, and decided to see if four of the top contenders were still interested in coming on board. That would use up ten of the dozen personnel slots the

Secretary had allocated to the program, and he wanted to use the other two slots for the assistant program manager, Sam Donaldson and the resident techie, Bob Pullman, both of whom were DARPA employees and willing to transfer. He figured that he himself, and Tom Parsons, his lab assistant, could remain Johns Hopkins employees. The DHS Secretary balked, but after a tough negotiation Donaldson and Parsons became DHS employees, and Rodriguez himself remained an IPA, but assigned to DHS rather than DARPA. Technically Rodriguez was not a DHS employee, but in actuality he had wrangled an extra slot out of the Secretary. He would have to borrow IT support folks from someplace since Pullman didn't come; however, Rodriguez didn't feel too bad about the loss of his IT person, especially since JT voiced some reservations about his unpaid gambling markers.

So the august group of six MENSA program participants, including the reinstated Julie Stafford, their program manager and assistant PM, and their lab assistant, were assembled here at The Galactic Society headquarters for a briefing on how the program would change, and how they would interface with the TGS. The four potential new participants probably wouldn't be on-board for another month or two. Although JT had not attended the introductory session ten days ago, Rodriguez felt the federal agent knew the organization almost as well as the others, and had indeed earned the right to know the new arrangements.

In order to make it a cleaner and less traceable break from DoD sponsorship, it was decided to change the name of the program from MENSA to SMART. The latter stood for superior mental aptitude reinforcement technology. Including Rodriguez there were six TGS members physically present, and two participating via teleconference: MIT professor Maureen Fields and U.S. Senator Nancy Hemmingway. Frances Kalani, the white house chief of staff, and Shobha Vipashyin, a Supreme Court justice, were otherwise occupied. The program participants— except Julie—had met the TGS members physically present this time at their last meeting, but they had not met the two present via teleconference. If the attendees were impressed before with meeting ex-astronauts, top business leaders, and an assistant and an undersecretary, they were even more so this time: Senator Hemingway was one of the more prominent politicians in that elite group of 100, and Maureen Fields was the heir apparent to Einstein.

"Everyone but Julie was briefed on the mission and operation of the Society a little over a week ago, and I understand she was brought up to speed by Stan before accepting reinstatement," began Sid Ellis, the Chairman of the Board of Directors for the Society. "At that time we mentioned we'd offer you positions on the Board of Governors, and you would eventually be eligible for Directorships, depending upon your suitability, desire and participation. That still holds, and will also for any new participants. The timing here is fortuitous, as we had only recently decided to begin recruiting, but have not gotten very far along in our efforts. And you all are tailor-made for membership."

The excitement in the room was palpable. Julie in particular was beside herself as this was all so new to her. The others had seen indications of the intellectual power of the TGS members previously, but this time they had their socks blown off. Memory capacity and analytical ability were the capabilities the Society was most interested in, and their demonstrations emphasized this. While the TGS members were good at telekinesis and other paranormal activities, these were not skills they concentrated on; nevertheless, Ellis did a credible job of impressing the SMART members with his group's various extrasensory capabilities.

"For this next demonstration I want us to pair up," said Ellis. This worked out nicely since there were six TGS members physically present, including Stan Rodriguez, and there were six SMART participants, with JT, Donaldson and Parsons being the odd men out. "With your permission, your TGS partner is going to enter your mind, and you his or hers. This will actually be a suitability test, as you will most likely be unable to hide any thoughts suggesting you would not be a good candidate for membership. Is everyone here willing to do this?"

They all nodded, gave thumbs up or otherwise indicated their total concurrence. So each TGS member delved into his SMART partner's mind and communicated telepathically. The SMART group members were duly impressed with the ease of communication, and their ability to read the mind of their TGS partner. Some SMART members were a little hesitant at first when they actually felt themselves being probed, but every one of them took a leap of faith and let go of their inhibitions.

After the show-and-tell, Dee Vipashyin addressed the group: "We are delighted to no end that each of you passed with flying colors, and we heartily welcome you to The Galactic Society. If you didn't realize before the special power you have, and with our mutual help, can improve upon, I'm sure you do now. With that comes a grave responsibility. I know Stan, and Toshi Lee before him, talked about the ethical considerations of using your capabilities, but we've asked Maureen to address the similar, but more definitive, laws of the TGS Board of Governors and Directors."

They all fixated at the screen with Professor Fields' image.

"Being a huge Asimov fan, I developed, and the society has adopted, the three "Laws of Cognitive Extension." Cognitive extension is the term we settled on to describe entering another person's conscious or subconscious mind, either to gain or transmit information, or to otherwise influence their behavior.

We'll ask you to agree to, and live by, these at all times. They are: (1) I will not enter another person's conscious or subconscious mind without their knowledge and consent; (2) I will not use my paranormal abilities to contravene any legally enforceable statute; and (3) I may overrule Law (1) or (2) if in so doing I could prevent serious and immediate harm to myself or others. These are simple but powerful proscriptions. However, there may be times when the application of Law (3) is open to interpretation, and we trust you'll invoke it only in the direst of circumstances. Beyond this, we ask that you support the mission of the Society to the best of your ability. I'm going to ask each of you individually if you can agree to these laws."

Fields addressed each of the potential TGS members in turn, each gave their assent, and a new collaboration was born. Fields and Hemmingway offered their congratulations and then signed off. The assembled group then celebrated with a catered champagne brunch.

Sharon Rydell asked about Cutler, and the circumstances leading to his demise. She and the other SMART members had heard the gist of his departure, but not the details. Stan Rodriguez and Harry Lisbon took turns explaining what they had figured out, and the resulting change in protocols.

Charlie Moffett was seated next to JT, and during a break in the conversation he asked, "So what do you think, JT?"

"I think you are off to a good beginning. These are decent, well-intentioned individuals, and I truly believe this empowerment will make them even better persons. I would like to ask one question that's been on my mind."

"Shoot."

"How did the Board members 'find' each other?"

"I guess it's all Chris Ling's fault. He thought being in space had a lot to do with his abilities, and began talking to other astronauts. In the process he found me, Nancy Hemingway, and

Sid Ellis. We were the founding members of The Galactic Society. Sid suspected Maureen Fields just from her reputation, went to see her at MIT, and I guess you could say it was recognition at first thought. In turn, Maureen was conducting a seminar Harry attended, and that's how they met. Chris was invited to a White House function right after Simmons was elected, and 'discovered' Frances Kalani. Frances consulted Stan on some neurological issues, and recruited him in the process. Dee Vipashyin came to a TGS function Sid was running and they had no trouble 'communicating' during a break. She, of course, recruited her sister Shobha. As you can tell, it was all by personal contact. Which is a nice segue for my next question: How would you like to join us?" Moffett asked.

JT was taken by surprise, and wasn't sure how to respond. Moffett added: "The entire group has agreed to extend an invitation to you."

JT took a minute to chew and swallow his mouth full of food. "I'm flattered you asked, but I don't have any paranormal abilities, so I'm not sure I would fit in."

"You have a fine mind and a healthy dose of skepticism. Our main mission is the improvement of your mental ability—how to better obtain and store the facts you need, analyze them, and reach a reasonable conclusion based on them. We do not necessarily utilize the findings of the MENSA program, but we may in the future, and that would be entirely your choice. Using only TGS protocols, paranormal ability may or may not be a side benefit for you, although we distinctly feel that it would in time. That may very well enhance your ability to read people."

"Couldn't I be 'fooled' by what I 'read'? It seems your guys were not able to correctly interpret Cutler, and perhaps Brosard. I'd be afraid it would interfere with my current method of reading people—their body language, how they react to my questions, my gut feel—my kinesics ability or what makes me a good detective. Isn't that possible?"

"It is."

JT paused and Moffett could see he was thinking about his reply. "Then I think I'll pass. But thank you for considering me. And the group. It means a lot that you asked."

"This doesn't mean you won't be involved, however. I believe this group could be a valuable resource for some of our investigations if circumstances require as much. Additionally, I want you to vet our newcomers."

"I'd be delighted to continue working with the organization. Are you going to, or have you already, made the same offer to Juanita or Arati?"

"We did not think Juanita was ready for this, nor did we think she would be interested. Arati, on the other hand, is basically already here. Sid and Harry were deep into her mind and very impressed. We made the offer, but, in spite of her insistence that she is completely recovered from her experience with Cutler and the subsequent deep probe, she wants to make sure there are no ill effects which might compromise her ability to participate. We're working on her, and think it is only a matter of time before she decides to join us. I did insist it only be part time however. She's too good to not work where she does now. "

"She is a hell of an asset."

"Indeed."

CHAPTER SIXTY

Tuesday, Crystal City, Virginia

Arati felt good. The few times she had been sick, or was worried about her family or some other personal crisis, she used work as a distraction and a therapy. Her confrontation with Cutler, and subsequent probes by Ellis and Lisbon, had occurred two weeks ago, and she was back in the office later that same day. She knew intellectually she should have felt a sense of relief, or satisfaction, or something when Cutler was captured, and then later removed himself from the gene pool, but she didn't; and it did worry her. She discussed this with Doctors Rodriguez and Ellis, who admitted this was new territory for them, and likely an outcome of her deep probe. So she threw herself into determining the relationship between Cunningham and Brosard by delving into their emails, internal memos, personnel evaluations, finances and anything else she could think of and latch on to. It obviously had a good effect, as her sense of unease passed, and she began to feel whole again.

After Arati talked with Juanita about Hanson's invitation to see her socially she felt better about it, but still surprised herself by accepting his offer the next time she saw him. She was seldom so impulsive. Then when Ellis offered her a position on the Board of Governors for The Galactic Society, she knew this was a good sign and her recovery was complete. Nonetheless, she wanted a few days to consider all the ramifications of the move. Her main concern was that it might actually have a deleterious effect on her, as it apparently did on Cutler, even though she wouldn't be a SMART participant per se. She discussed the idea at length with Rodriguez, who informed her of JT's decision and the reasoning behind it. As a TGS member and the MENSA, now SMART, program manager, Doctor Rodriguez was well qualified to tell her The Galactic Society did not use the same protocols as the SMART program. Ultimately, Arati felt she had discovered a new purpose in life and decided to join.

She also discovered she was apparently not a morning person. Her schedule was quite flexible and she was coming in later and later each day, although lately those days were turning out to be ten or twelve hour ones. Thus she found herself monitoring Cunningham's late evening emails real-time. That's when she noticed another trading card message to his friend. It was one she didn't have an original, unaltered card to use as a basis for comparison, so she couldn't get the coded message out if there was one, and most likely couldn't get it decoded in time anyway. She did think it likely, based on past history, that Cunningham was setting up another rendezvous for the next day at lunch. Of course she didn't know where, but hopefully the troops could follow him and catch him in the act if he was doing something illegal. She phoned JT.

"Arati, Arati, tell me you've got good news," said JT as soon as he answered his cell.

"How did you know it was I?"

"The caller ID said it was the office, and I was just hoping it was you."

"Well, I do have good news, I guess. Mr. Cunningham has sent out another message I believe is coded. I could not decipher it, but I suspect it is indicative of another lunch meeting with his friend tomorrow. This is what we have been waiting for, is it not?"

"It is, Arati, and I'm going to raise the troops. Thanks."

JT got on the phone to Moffett and relayed Arati's information.

CHAPTER SIXTY-ONE

Wednesday, Potomac, Maryland

The Team had wanted to put a GPS device on Cunningham's car; however, not only did the Agency frequently scan employee vehicles for electronic devices, but they also required a warrant due to a recent court decision. So by 10:00 JT had an unmanned MAV, or micro air vehicle, eight hundred feet over the Potomac River just north of the Langley CIA complex. They still needed on-the-ground assets, so the Team also stationed cars on the George Washington Memorial Parkway, both north and south of the entrance to the CIA. Arati monitored the gate passes real-time, and let them know precisely when Cunningham had exited, so picking him up when he turned north on the parkway was not difficult. The southbound cars turned around to participate in the multi-vehicle surveillance, and, after a swap-off, one of those was one hundred yards behind Cunningham on the inner loop of the Capital Beltway. He took the first exit on the Maryland side of the American Legion Bridge. The car stationed on the westbound Clara Barton Parkway picked him up as he passed by.

JT loved flying the DARPA developed MAV, which he affectionately called the hummingbird. Today he was driving it from a control room located in the main building of the David Taylor Model Basin in Carderock, located a few miles upriver from the Agency complex. Ronnie Hamilton was "riding" shotgun, and communicating with the Team members on the ground. JT had no trouble keeping up with his quarry, since the bird could do over ninety miles an hour. It had real-time audio and visual reconnaissance with a sixty-power zoom lens, and digitally recorded the audio and video inputs. The bird's hover time was twelve hours and the operating range was over twenty miles, so they were confident they could keep up with

Cunningham, although JT had to hang close so as not to lose the suspect's nondescript car in traffic.

"The subject drove right by me," said JT. "I could've throw a rock and hit him. He's now proceeding west on MacArthur Boulevard."

"Copy that control. This is Nora Three and I'm turning on Brickyard Road and Nora Two is picking up the tail."

"I got you, Two. You're about 200 yards back."

"Roger, Control. Hey, our boy's got his blinker on. He's turning right."

"He's in a parking lot of what looks like a small park. I think there's a restaurant there too. He's out of the car and carrying a bag—heading away from the buildings. I'm losing him under the trees, guys," said JT.

"We're in the lot, Control; I've got eyes on him. Will keep you advised."

Fifteen minutes passed while Cunningham ate the lunch he had brought with him.

"Control, this is Nora One. I'm entering the lot to relieve Nora Two. I've got eyes on the subject now."

"Control, Nora Two—I'm out of here."

"Copy that."

When Cunningham was finished a few minutes later, he put his trash in the white plastic bag with a red circle emblazoned on the side that he had brought with him and got up to leave.

"Subject is moving, Control. He threw his lunch bag in a trash container and is heading for his car."

"Nora Two and Three, follow him back to the Agency and let us know if he makes any other stops, or throws anything out of the window. Be prepared to stop him if I let you know we have action on this end."

"Nora Two, copy that. I have him in sight heading east on MacArthur."

"Control, this is Nora Three, I'll bring up the rear."

Not a minute later, Nora One was back on line: "We've got a white male approaching the trashcan. He retrieved the bag the suspect threw in there. Heading back to his car. We're taking him down."

"Roger, One. Then check the can for similar bags. Let me know what you've got."

Brendon Gotlieb and Charles Burton, two members of the Alpha Unit, approached the vehicle the suspect with the white bag re-entered. When they were four feet away, positioned on either side of the vehicle, the engine turned over. Gotlieb, who was on the driver's side, stood next to the door and pointed to the badge on his belt and yelled to the suspect, "Turn the engine off, now!"

The suspect quickly threw the car into reverse and revved the engine as the car leaped backward. Burton just as quickly put a bullet in each of the passenger side tires. The car lurched to one side and traveled a few more feet before coming to rest. The suspect knew he wasn't going anywhere, and had let up on the gas and put his hands on the steering wheel.

Gotlieb saw the driver had placed his hands on the steering wheel, but he approached cautiously anyway. He opened the driver's door with his free hand and said, "Out of the car. Turn around and put your hands on the roof. Spread eagle." He kicked the suspect's legs outward. Burton was on the driver's side now with his weapon trained on the suspect, so Gotlieb holstered his weapon, cuffed the man, and then moved him away from the car. "So what do we have in the little white bag?" he asked the suspect—rhetorically as it turned out. While Burton watched the suspect, Gotlieb retrieved the bag from the floor on the passenger side and unrolled the folded-over top. "Well, what do you know, a flash drive."

Burton put the suspect in the back seat of the company car and got on the radio, while Gotlieb checked the trash container. "Control, we got a flash drive in the possession of our new found friend here." He turned and looked in Gotlieb's direction, who gave him a thumbs up. "And it's the one he got from Cunningham."

"Fantastic, guys. Read him his rights and bring him in. One of you driving his vehicle?"

"Seems it has two flat tires, Control."

"Stand by," JT said, suppressing a laugh. "Nora Two and Three, do you have Cunningham now?"

"Roger, Control."

"Apprehend him, and get him and his car to the compound."

"Will do."

"Nora Four, go baby sit the disabled car and get it towed back to the compound."

"Copy, Control. We're only a few minutes way."

"Alright, everyone, great work. You know what to do from here. Control out." JT turned to Ronnie, who had been hovering the MAV over the drop site. "As soon as you're sure Nora Two and Three won't need you, bring her home. I've got some phone calls to make."

CHAPTER SIXTY-TWO

Wednesday, Crystal City, Virginia

Moffett knew this would not be taken very well by the Central Intelligence Agency. After all, DHS had arrested one of their employees for compromising classified information. And, indeed, that is what they found on the thumb drive they had confiscated from Cunningham's contact in the parking lot. The drive contained a host of information concerning the Iranian nuclear program: how and where they were getting the material required to build a nuclear processing facility, contacts used, sources of income, and transfer payments for the goods and materials. Whom the information was intended for was anybody's guess, as there were a host of entities which would pay dearly for it. In addition to learning who the intended recipients were, the Agency also wanted to determine the extent of the damage caused by Cunningham over the years, and thus what to do about it. In particular, they were interested in how Cunningham got this compartmented information without being detected. They hoped Cunningham would be willing to divulge his methods, and what other information he had passed on, for some sort of a deal. As anxious as the CIA was to talk to him, the Agency would have to wait their turn—DHS had already notified the FBI, since domestic spying was within their jurisdiction, not to mention the potential conflict of interest within the CIA. Agents were on the way.

JT took the initial crack at Cunningham, but the detainee had clammed up and was awaiting representation and his first appearance before a magistrate. JT insisted he was only interested in Cunningham's knowledge of, or connection to, the Doctor Lee murder, and the apparent shooting attempts on the MENSA participants. At first, the soon to be ex-CIA employee didn't budge from his recalcitrant non-cooperative position. But

JT persisted, assisted by his boss Charlie Moffett and Sid Ellis from TGS, and Cunningham finally decided he had nothing to lose by denying any complicity in those events. Moffett and Ellis were convinced the readings they got from Cunningham confirmed he only had a suspicion regarding the murder, albeit a strong one, but was indeed the architect of the two faked shooting incidents. Given he was caught red handed in selling government secrets, the two TGS members had no compunction in using their paranormal abilities to make this determination.

Ellis also picked up on the fact that Cunningham really didn't know who he was giving his information to. The CIA division chief had never actually met any of his contacts, although he thought he had been working with the same one for over eighteen months now. He either passed on the information they requested if he could get it, or his associates were interested in the information he had to offer. Cunningham set up the meets, after which the funds appeared in his overseas account.

The head of the FBI's Washington Field Office, Morton Santone, had arrived with two agents who would take charge of Cunningham. Since JT and company already had his overseas bank account number, Cunningham was of no further use to them, so they released him into FBI custody. It was too late for the Feebs to get him before a magistrate today, so they would no doubt spend a good deal of time talking "at" the suspect before the courthouse opened tomorrow and their twenty-four hours were up. Moffett and Ellis doubted if the FBI would be interested in their kind of help in the broader espionage case, or if the TGS Board of Directors would agree to that in any event. Ellis took his leave, and JT and Moffett would now take a crack at Cunningham's cohort in crime.

The potential terrorist connection put the disposition of Cunningham's accomplice squarely in DHS's bailiwick. The CIA division chief's contact was one Charles Frampton—at least according to his passport. Arati had checked on its validity, and discovered it was a made up identity. The suspect was not talking, not asking to contact anybody, nor asking for a lawyer. The FBI was, and the CIA would be, extremely interested in whom the suspect was employed by, and JT thought it was just a matter of time before he flipped on his handlers for some consideration. It was late afternoon and only a few hours after they had apprehended Frampton, and JT was working that angle. He had expedited Frampton's meeting with counsel, in spite of the suspected spy's declination of same, and also invited assistant U.S. Attorney Alan Pellman. JT, Charlie Moffett, Frampton, Frampton's attorney-to-be Harold Finnegan, Santone from the FBI, and the AUSA, were gathered in an interrogation room at the Crystal City Fusion Team office. After turning two recorders on, Pellman introduced everyone present, read Frampton his rights, and then outlined a way for the suspect to cooperate.

At first Frampton was indifferent to the proceedings, and seemed to pay no attention to what the AUSA said. He didn't even look concerned when Arati arrived and asked JT and Moffett to step outside for a minute. Pellman nodded at the two DHS men and stopped the recorders.

Outside, Arati explained that, while no one in the states had anything on the man, his prints finally got a hit in Interpol: his real name was Alphonse Devereux, a French citizen Interpol had issued warrants on for weapons trafficking. When JT and Moffett stepped back into the room with smiles on their faces, Frampton, AKA Devereux, looked a little worried. As soon as Moffett passed on the Interpol findings, Devereux stopped the proceedings and asked if he could confer in private with his attorney.

"Take all the time you need," AUSA Pellman offered, as he turned the recorders off once again and they left the room.

Not fifteen minutes later the attorney asked them to return. As soon as everyone was seated and they were on the record again, Devereux exhibited a more attentive attitude. Devereux's now attorney-in-fact said, "Mr. Devereux has decided to cooperate with you for immunity from prosecution for the charge of espionage against the United States," he said, "and for entrance into the witness protection program as a free U.S. citizen. In return, he'll offer up all his contacts and the assets he accumulated in these enterprises."

"And the horse you rode in on," said Pellman. "We'll just turn you over to Interpol and let them deal with the 'enterprises' you pursued on the Continent."

"You don't understand," Devereux protested. "There are some nasty groups out there that will not be happy until I'm out of the picture. I can't just turn over what I know and not be protected from them. I'd be as good as dead."

"Not our problem. However, here's an alternative for you," the AUSA offered. "You tell us everything you know about whom you are working with, relinquish all your ill-gotten gains, and agree to cooperate with us in every way, and we'll consider giving you another identity in a minimum security federal prison."

"How long?" asked public defender Finnegan.

"Possibility for parole in twenty years—no sooner," answered the AUSA.

"Five max!" yelled Devereux. "I'll be fifty-six in twenty years for Christ's sake."

Pellman got up and started walking out, and the others took his cue.

"Ten," pleaded Devereux.

The troops continued to leave.

"All right. All right. How about fifteen years in a warm climate."

"I think that can be arranged. Now start talking. To begin with, how do you communicate with your 'buyers,' and how do you deliver the information?"

"Can we get this deal in writing?" interrupted Finnegan.

"We believe time is of the essence here, Counselor. We'll give you one of the tapes."

Devereux nodded when Finnegan looked at him, so the counselor assented.

"You know I started out in arms trafficking, and that's where I made my name," Devereux began. "People started asking me if I could deliver information in addition to my usual trade. The money was good and I only had to be a middle man. I'm not sure how they flipped the CIA guy, or how long he's been working with them. I've only been working with him for about a year and a half. He sends me a coded message on when and where to meet, and I pick up the stuff. With him it's pretty much been at lunch the next day at some park or the like, not too far from the Agency. They did send me his picture so I at least knew what the hell he looked like."

"How do you get the package to your employers?"

"Same way, but in reverse. I get a coded message from them telling me what to do. Sometimes I mail the stuff, and other times I put it in a public pay locker somewhere. One time I left it on the floor of a taxi."

"So you've never met any of your employers?"

"Like I said, one of the guys I used to deal arms with got me into this; but I doubt if he's handling these exchanges. I pick the package up, transfer it as instructed, and the agreed upon amount pops into my account."

"Could you still deliver this package without arousing your employer's suspicions?" asked Moffett.

"Seems they were in a hurry for this stuff. Standard procedure has been twenty-four to thirty-six hours, but they wanted this stuff in twelve. So I've got until two tomorrow morning. But I have no idea whether or not they were tracking me," said Devereux.

"Well, we have nothing to lose," said Pellman.

"The CIA has already been given a copy of the information on the drive," said Moffett. "Let me make a call and see how the Agency wants to play this. So what were your instructions this time? "

"They asked me to tape it to the inside top of a Washington Examiner newspaper dispenser in Georgetown before two tomorrow morning."

"I'll be right back," said Moffett.

Moffett returned twenty minutes later. "As I suspected, the Langley boys would rather pass on fake information and track the disposition of that, than try to track the physical flow. They're sending us revised data in less than an hour," he announced to the group. "We'll load it on the same drive Cunningham actually used just in case that makes a difference. Then you, Mr. Devereux, will deliver it in your usual fashion, but under our surveillance. Subsequently you do whatever you would normally do, until we're sure you're not followed. Then we'll get you back here. We monitor your account until we see the funds transfer, and then put a hold on it."

"What happens to me then?" Devereux asked.

AUSA Pellman answered: "If everything goes according to plan, then we meet with a magistrate tomorrow morning, and explain the deal. As soon as the funds transfer takes place, then we make good on our part."

"What if they figure out what's going on, or for some other reason things don't work out—then what?"

"Depends on how well we think you handled the situation. But I can tell you this, if it doesn't work out as planned, then we'll have some serious doubts about the level of your cooperation."

"Seems I'm damned if I do, and damned if I don't."

"Only difference will be what level of Hades you end up in," Moffett offered.

CHAPTER SIXTY-THREE

Thursday, Georgetown, Washington, DC

"Okay, we're here now. So what's the plan?" he asked in his best imitation of Al Pacino. The questioner, Salvador Dominico, was a JTTF member on loan to the Fusion Team who liked to think of himself as a "good looking" Pacino. Being a second generation Italian-American who grew up in Little Italy in New York no doubt facilitated his fancy. He was told to meet Brian Canterbury here—a storage room located above a trendy boutique on M Street in Georgetown—but not much more. Canterbury was a DIA employee on assignment to the Fusion Team's Delta Unit. He really enjoyed the work and was on track for a permanent position with DHS. His dark hair, large but not obtrusive mustache and wide sideburns, and prominent nose with high cheekbones gave him a smarmy Mediterranean look. The two of them gave the stakeout team a definite European flavor.

"We're here to observe the Washington Examiner newspaper box across the street," said Canterbury as he turned the lights off and opened the blinds. "Our recently captured foreign agent is going to drop off a doctored thumb drive in the box in accordance with his handler's instructions. The real one was picked up by our guys after a greedy CIA bastard dropped it off for our captured spy. They have the turncoat in custody now and are milking him for information. We'll have a GPS on the spy's car, and our guys will be following him from a distance. We'll also have an agent concealed in the back seat who will be in constant communication with our guys. Our job is to observe the pickup if it happens."

"We gonna follow the guy?"

"Nope. Just report that it took place."

"I hope the buyers fall for it; although, I guess the Company is pretty good at playing the spy versus spy thing.

They're probably passing on just enough good information to really fuck things up for the bad guys. Which are who by the way?"

"Don't know."

"And what do they think they are buying?"

"Don't know that either."

"Okay, so we're just the guys who watch the messenger. Sometimes I think I'd enjoy this job more if I knew more of the details. So what happens after the pickup, we're done?" asked Dominico.

"We keep the box under surveillance until daylight, then check to make sure the pickup was consummated."

"What happens to our spy?"

"They want him to go back to his place like he normally would, where we'll have agents waiting for him. In the morning he leaves for work or whatever just like usual, and we get him back to holding without anyone who might be watching him any the wiser. Then we monitor his account to see if the funds he was promised are transferred, indicating, hopefully, that they bought our little charade."

"What's our spy get out of this?"

"I believe at least fifteen years, but in a minimum security lockup. I'll take the first watch if you're tired. This should go down within the next few hours, but like I said, we're going to be here all night."

The place was sparsely decorated so Dominico was glad he brought a portable cot with him. He unfolded it and stretched out. Twenty minutes later he was still trying to get comfortable when Canterbury remarked, "Our guy is here now making the drop. Pickup is supposed to be around two."

"Who's the agent in the car?" Dominico asked as he strolled over to the window to watch.

"I didn't hear who the lucky guy was—hope he's short. How's your cot?"

"Sucks. Think I'll just stay here and observe with you."

Canterbury was watching the approach from the west, or Key Bridge side of M Street, and Dominico was observing the eastern approach from town. At 1:17 in the morning a guy went by walking his dog, but didn't mess with the box. Slightly before the appointed hour Canterbury remarked, "Time's almost up— maybe they figured out he was nabbed and won't show. Oh, oh. What's this? Got a guy walking up to the box. He's looking around. He's going for it."

"Was it taped to the inside top of the box?"

"Yep."

"Well then, I'd say our man definitely went for it. So we report this now?"

Canterbury was already on the phone. "Roger that," he said as he hung up. "Now we just monitor any other activity until morning."

At slightly past 3:00 a drunk stumbled by but didn't go near the box. No other pedestrian traffic occurred. At 4:27 Dominico noted a Washington Examiner truck approaching.

"I'm going down for a better look to make sure the first guy took it and this guy isn't. Keep an eye on me." He got downstairs and across the street just as the newspaper guy dropped a bundle of papers off the truck. "Good timing on my part," he said as the truck driver eyed him suspiciously.

The driver cut the bundle tie and Canterbury took the top paper. "Nothing like fresh news," the DHS agent said as he casually walked off, seeming to check for something in the paper while still maintaining a visual on the box. The driver gave him a sideways glance, shook his head and put the papers in the box. After the driver left Canterbury checked the box, and the package was indeed gone.

"Okay. We're out of here," Canterbury said when he returned. "I'll call this in from the car. Thanks for your help."

"Anytime," his partner said. "Not the worst surveillance I've ever been on," he remarked as he grabbed his cot and headed out.

CHAPTER SIXTY-FOUR

Thursday, Crystal City, Virginia

Arati was napping fitfully in the lounge when JT arrived at 6:25. She had put monitors on the accounts Cunningham and Devereux had identified as theirs, and where the funds for their facilitating the information transfers were supposed to be deposited. She installed a program which would send a text to her cell phone when her monitoring program got a hit, allowing her to catch a few winks.

JT could see she wasn't sleeping, so he asked, "Did you pull another all-nighter, Arati?"

She roused, shook her head and answered, "Only if you can count sleeping part of the time. I wanted to know as soon as the funds were transferred, so I created an app to text my phone. So far it has not happened. Why are you in so early?"

"Guess I was anxious, too. Anybody else here yet?"

"Nobody who woke me up. Is there any coffee brewing?"

"I was going to do that next," replied JT.

"I will tend to it—I need to move around a little, and, get the juices flowing?" Arati was still learning American idioms. JT often felt like he was corrupting her well-spoken second language, her first being Hindi.

"Yes, you got it right. I'll be in my office," he said smiling as he started down the hall.

Ten minutes later she walked down to his cubicle with a cup of coffee for him. "I found some interesting information last night on some of the MENSA participants. I thought I could go over it with you as soon as Juanita gets here." "Sure. But with Cutler's admission of guilt I guess that would be strictly informational."

"Perhaps."

Juanita rolled in just before 8:00 looking more ebullient than usual. JT had left a message on her phone about the drop last night. She had driven one of the cars that tracked Cunningham to the drop point, and felt like they had put a genuine traitor out of business. Ten hours of shut-eye, the first good night's sleep in weeks, and a hot Swiss mocha latte she'd finished on the way in probably helped her mood as well. "Hey, Partner," she called out as she passed JT's desk.

"Hey," he replied back. "Arati's got something she wants to show us. You want to get some java and head over to the conference room?"

"Yeah. Let me dump my stuff and grab a cup. I'll be right there." JT was already there when she got to the conference room. "So what's up, Arati?"

"I recently expanded my data search to the friends and relatives of the participants, as well as local newspaper articles from their home towns. I found out Gayle Pennington's step father was arrested for domestic abuse of his third wife, the one he married after Gayle's mother. There was no child abuse mentioned, and her mother and step father's divorce papers indicated irreconcilable differences as the only reason.

"You already knew Sharon Rydell had a juvenile criminal record which I was not able to access. I was able to obtain the close-out date of her record, and correlated it with newspaper items from her place of residence for the same time period. One article was on the disappearance of her twin sister, and mentioned the local police considered it a kidnapping or worse, at first, but had no evidence to that effect. The same article hinted, obliquely, that she was a suspect for a time, but no charges were ever brought in the case. I have been unable to determine who she has been forwarding funds to.

"I learned Thomas Pacquin also had a juvenile record, which we did not know before, but it was also unavailable.

Similar searches turned up nothing of any note, but my time frame was much wider and the search more difficult. I believe the FBI was well aware of this in their background investigation of him, and may have had the record expunged. I found nothing of significance on any of his relatives.

"Finally, Brandy Simmons' older step brother did a good deal of community service, apparently as a result of some minor burglaries and drug related offenses, and also went through rehab. He was a juvenile at the time, so some of this information on him is also from secondary sources. He relapsed and died of a drug overdose a few years later."

"That's it, Arati?" JT asked disappointedly.

"I will not fall for your antics this time, Sir. This is good information, whether you think so or not."

JT and Juanita started laughing. "You're right, Arati," JT finally managed to get out. "Good work. And I will go back and bounce it off the other information to see what pops."

"Before we go any further, can you explain to me the entire transfer process between Mr. Cunningham and his accomplices?" Arati asked.

"Sure," JT agreed. "Thanks to you we know Cunningham sent a lot of emails with trading card pictures to Devereux. If Cunningham was the one to initiate the process, that is, if he had info he wasn't sure whether or not they wanted, the hidden message contained a brief synopsis of the data he wanted to sell. Devereux has a trading card website and he would post the card as is. His handlers monitored the site and posted a house for sale notice on a Craig's-List-type real estate website indicating they were willing to deal. As the 'owners' of the real estate, they offered to finance the sale, and listed a down payment amount indicative of what they'd pay for the info. Cunningham would read the posting, and if he liked the deal, he'd send Devereux another trading card email with the drop info."

"So if the handlers are careful and use varying public internet sites, they can't be reached directly or traced via email," offered Juanita.

"The rest of the scenario I think you're already familiar with: Cunningham would make the drop and Devereux the pickup. Devereux would then make a notation on the real estate website, and his handlers would respond with a time and location for him to stash the package, or sometimes he would get that info in the original message. If all went well, then they transferred the promised amount to Cunningham's overseas account, and some percentage of that to Devereux's."

"Why didn't they just go all electronic?" asked Arati.

"Cunningham said he felt not having an electronic trace was safer. His synopses violated that somewhat, but I guess he and the buyers were okay with those procedures," said JT.

"I expect the process worked in reverse if the buyers had information they needed," said Arati.

"Pretty much," said JT. "They'd put a notice on the real estate website, which Devereux monitored. He'd notify Cunningham via trading card email that a listing was posted. If Cunningham thought he could get the data and liked the price, he'd send an email back with his reply and an approximate date; otherwise, he'd decline. When he was ready, he'd send the drop email, and they'd go through the transfer routine."

Shortly after the discussion turned to the possible options they thought would be offered to Cunningham, Arati's cell phone buzzed with a text message.

"Wow!" exclaimed Arati. "Four hundred thousand dollars. Is that the price for betraying your country these days?" The funds were transferred into the overseas account Cunningham had set up for this purpose, and brought the total in the account to $2.36 million. Seems he had been doing this for some time: Arati had traced the account activity back through the several years it had been in existence, and there were no withdrawals over that time. She was hoping this real time information would yield a better chance of tracing the source of the funds. The initial deposit was fifty thousand a little over three years ago. Cunningham could have another account which he didn't mention in his debriefing, although according to him there was only the one, and Ellis had only picked up on one when Cunningham attended the TGS briefing two weeks ago. Cunningham's ill-gotten gains were now the property of DHS, or would be as soon as Arati got permission to transfer them to the department's account. They were required to hand anything over five million to the U.S. Treasury, but usually got to keep lesser amounts.

JT called Moffett and informed him of the transfer. The assistant secretary said he'd call the CIA and let them know. He called JT back a few minutes later. "Did you know Brosard has not been at work since Tuesday?" he asked. "They say he called in sick."

"Oh, not good, Boss. You want us to get a man over to his place to see what's up?"

"Yes. I don't like the sounds of this. I want you and Juanita to get down to Davison pronto and have a chopper ready to roll in case he tries to run. Hopefully we're not too late already. Have the funds been transferred to Devereux's account yet?"

JT looked at Arati and mouthed "Devereux?"

Arati gave him a thumbs up.

"Yes, Sir. Just now."

"Good. I'll call the Army and set you up with a bird. Let me know when you're there."

"Road trip," JT said to Juanita. "I've got to see Hanson and have a surveillance set up, and then we're off to Davison— seems our good friend Brosard is a no-show at work. Charlie is not a very trusting person, is he," JT asked rhetorically. He grabbed his go-bag and told Juanita he'd meet her downstairs as soon as he talked to the boss.

CHAPTER SIXTY-FIVE

Thursday, Fort Belvoir, Virginia

As they were turning off the Fairfax County Parkway into Davison, JT's cell phone rang—it was Josh Paxton, one of the ATF members in JT's Alpha Unit. He and Ronnie Hamilton, also an Alpha Unit member from the ATF, had been assigned the surveillance on Brosard's place. "JT, it's Josh. We're outside the suspect's apartment and someone's definitely in there. Wait. Ronnie's got a bead on him now, and it's definitely your guy. We'll keep you posted if anything develops."

"Okay, thanks, Josh." JT turned to Juanita, who was just pulling into a parking space in front of flight operations, and relayed Paxton's information. "Let's see if they have our bird ready for us."

Once inside, JT asked to speak to whoever was in charge. Captain Reggie Washington said he was the guilty party, and was expecting them. He introduced them to their pilot, Chief Warrant Officer Greg Fosterman, and explained the bird was fueled, preflighted and ready to roll. The bird and pilot were on standby for their use until further notice. Davison provided presidential helicopter support until the Marines took over that function in 1976; but now the 12th Aviation Battalion flew Army helicopters in support of public events, military training missions, and some special operations. The UH-72 Lakota light utility helicopter just recently replaced the venerable UH-60 Blackhawk. The new birds could zip along at over 165 mph and had a range of 425 miles. Moffett hoped that would be sufficient to see where Brosard was headed, if indeed he flew the coop. The Lakota normally had seating for only two—a pilot and a passenger. This one had been modified to seat a third person in a jump seat located in the cargo compartment. Juanita didn't know she was

370

going to be relegated to a fold down airline stewardess seat if they had to fly for this mission.

JT called Moffett, told him they had arrived, and made sure the assistant secretary had Juanita's cell number. The Alpha Team Leader told Moffett he and Juanita would be here until nineteen hundred hours, when Hanson had scheduled another team to take over. "Let's hope something breaks before then," Moffett said.

Twenty minutes later Paxton called JT. "Our boy left his place with a couple of bags and just stopped at a Star Bucks three blocks from his apartment."

"Call Arati now and tell her the address and then call me back," said JT.

Three minutes later Hamilton called him back. "We gave Arati the address and she told me to send Josh in the store and, as best he could, determine exactly what time Brosard did whatever he did if he went online, and then call her back with the info. We'll keep you advised." Twenty-three minutes later she called again. "He did something online and we let Arati know. He's moving again and I think he's headed toward the Beltway. I'll call with an update."

JT filled Juanita in and had just grabbed his phone to call Moffett when it rang: it was Arati. "JT," she said excitedly, "Brosard just transferred the money in Cunningham's account to another overseas account—the whole $2.36 million!"

"Fantastic. I always thought the bastard was involved. Are we absolutely sure it was him? I mean, something that would hold up in court?"

"Since we've got a witness who saw him using that IP address at that time, and he knows Cunningham—yes, I think we do."

"Outstanding, Arati. Do you need to change the account number on the funds transfer request?"

"I will. Oh wait, my other line is ringing—it is Ronnie again—hold on."

JT had no sooner given Juanita this news when Arati got back on the line. "What's going on, Arati?"

"Ronnie thinks he is cleaning out his local bank account. They are in front of a Capital One bank. I have the bank information, and she said Josh and she would sit tight until Brosard comes out. I will keep you advised. Do you want me to call Mr. Moffett and let him know?"

"No, I got it. Thanks. Talk to you later." He dialed Moffett's number.

Twenty-seven minutes later Hamilton called: "Josh checked with the bank and Brosard withdrew all but $500 from his account. I let Arati know. We're behind him now and he's on I-66. He's taking the toll road—he's going to Dulles, JT."

"Roger that. Thanks, and keep on him, Ronnie, but remember, he knows what you look like. Did he see Josh?"

"No."

"Okay. Do you guys have tasers?"

"You betcha—two each of the thirty footers and tranquilizer guns. We'll call from the airport."

JT gave Chief Warrant Officer Fosterman the wheels up sign and called Moffett for the third time. When he hung up he called to Captain Washington, "Can you get us clearance at Dulles as soon as your bird can get us there? And ground transport to the main terminal?"

"You got it. We'll have something waiting for you. You're already cleared here. Go."

Fosterman had the rotors turning when Juanita hopped onboard. She looked at the two front seats, passed through to the cargo section and saw the jump seat. "Damn good thing this is going to be a short trip," she quipped as she buckled in.

"RHIP, Partner."

CHAPTER SIXTY-SIX

Thursday, Dulles International Airport, Virginia

Paxton stopped on the departure ramp and jumped out while Ronnie Hamilton took the driver's seat and drove off to park the car. Paxton quickly walked over to the two airport police watching the parking lot. They had spotted where Brosard had parked his car—right out front in the hourly parking. He introduced himself and asked if they had eyes on the suspect. "With your description of his car, it wasn't difficult," said Officer Ralph Simpson. "He's headed towards the entrance directly below us pulling two bags with a carry-on over his shoulder. Take Officer Taylor with you downstairs there and we'll keep in touch."

Paxton and Officer Taylor took the escalator down and he saw Brosard. "Okay, let's split. He doesn't know me, but it's best if he doesn't see me with the airport police." As Paxton walked away from Brosard, noting the suspect had never even glanced in his direction, his cell rang. It was JT.

"Where are you?"

"I'm behind him on the lower level and we're going up to ticketing, I imagine."

"Keep him in sight, but let him buy a ticket. We'll hang back and wait to hear from you."

Paxton followed Brosard to the upper level where he went to the Air France ticket counter. The DHS agent got in line right behind him. His phone rang and it was Hamilton.

"I'm downstairs with JT and Juanita. Where are you?" asked Hamilton.

"I'm in line right now to buy a ticket, Dear."

"What, are you right behind him?"

"Yes, Sweetheart. Did you talk to Mom yet?"

"What airline?"

"I don't know if Air France does that, but I'll ask."

"Okay. If he buys an overseas ticket, I think we'll have enough to detain him. Let us know."

"Oh, sure. I'll call you back in a few minutes." Paxton showed his badge to the ticket agent as soon as Brosard had walked away and was out of earshot. "Where did the guy in front of me buy a ticket to?" he asked, wanting to verify what he had heard. The agent said he was going to Paris. "Oh, and what name did he use?" Paxton asked, again looking for verification.

"Clyde Fornaut," the agent replied.

"And he had an ID with that name?"

"Well, yes, Sir. Of course," the agent answered indignantly.

Paxton called Hamilton back. "Do you know what I think, Honey? Bill Brosard is not the person who just bought a ticket to Paris."

"What?"

"He's got a fake ID, Ronnie, and he's headed to Concourse B."

Paxton waited until Brosard had cleared security and taken the AeroTrain to the B Concourse. He met up with Ronnie, JT and Juanita, and they bypassed security using their credentials. JT felt like he was back in the FAM service. Bill Brosard was sitting outside the Capitol Grounds Coffee shop near the far end of Concourse B. He had two hours to kill until his flight to Paris. Both his bags were checked, and he had one carry-on sitting in the seat next to him. He had bought the latest issue of The Week magazine and was catching up on current affairs, and wondered if he would care that much about what was happening in the U.S. where he was going. His concentration was broken when he picked up an unusual vibe and looked up from his reading. Much to his dismay, he saw JT standing twenty feet away and just staring at him.

"Mr. Brosard, fancy meeting you here. Going overseas?" JT asked.

"What are you doing here, Agent?"

JT just smiled.

"Something tells me this is not a coincidence. Come sit down and let's chat."

JT had planned to wait until Brosard was away from any other individuals before approaching him, but he was not afforded that luxury. The traffic even at this far end of the concourse was fairly steady, and the person nearest to Brosard was only four seats away. "We're here doing routine passport checks," JT said holding his ground.

Brosard didn't like the way this was going. He didn't see how they could have anything on him since he had been so careful. "They already checked my passport. I don't have to show it to you. What are you really doing here?"

"I really am here checking passports; in particular yours, Mr. Fornaut."

Brosard wasn't prepared for this, and had not prepared a cover story. He blurted out the first thing that came to mind—"I can explain. Fornaut's my real name, and I'm going back home to France because I'm fed up with this place."

"Nice try. But either way, it's a felony, so we'll just have to go back to the ranch and talk about it." Brosard started to get up, so JT held up his hand. "As they say in the movies, we can do this the easy way or the hard way—your choice," he said, showing Brosard the taser he had been holding in his pocket. "And in case you are wondering, I've got three backups behind me, all similarly armed."

Brosard looked around and recognized Juanita, and thought he recognized Hamilton. He figured at least three of the seven or eight people he saw nearby probably were agents. And every one of them could hear what was going on and were looking at them. From the look on her face, Brosard guessed the young woman nearest to him was not an agent, not that it really mattered, and decided to go for her. He put his head down, concentrated, and blew a mind blast as hard as he could at JT. JT was stunned, lost his balance and fell backwards on his ass. The young woman screamed and jumped out of her seat to run. Before she had gone two feet, Brosard caught up with her and wrapped her in a bear hug. "If you don't let me walk out of here then I will literally blow her mind, and you know I can do it. I'm better than that fool Cutler ever was, and I've got too much to lose, so you better believe I'm serious," he yelled at JT, who had shaken off the mental blast, but was still sitting on the floor.

JT stood up and recovered his composure. "That's not going to happen, Bill. Come quietly, and we won't add kidnapping and felony endangerment to the charge of using a fake passport."

Brosard was facing JT and holding the woman in front of him. He saw JT look to his right and caught a glimpse of someone rushing him from behind on that side. *And they thought they were a match for me,* he mused. He shifted his weight and turned to face his attacker and blast him, when he was hit from behind with a force which knocked him and the woman down. He lost his grasp on her, and then felt an agonizing pain throughout his whole body before he passed out.

CHAPTER SIXTY-SEVEN

Thursday, Loudoun County, Virginia

Brosard came to propped up in the back seat of a long bus with his hands cuffed to the bar of the seat in front of him. Twelve seats away were Stan Rodriguez and Sid Ellis from TGS. Several seats in front of them were JT and Juanita. Brosard couldn't make out who was driving: he was still pretty woozy, but could tell they were under way.

"JT, our friend is awake," called Ellis.

JT got up and walked toward Brosard. "How you feeling, Bill?"

"Better. What did you guys use on me? Besides the taser, I mean."

"Just enough propofol to get you situated in the bus here."

"What happened back there? You turned to my left because you saw someone rushing me from that side, but when I turned there was no one there."

"With Stan's help, I practiced envisioning an attack from behind just in case I needed it when dealing with Cutler. Funny thing is, I almost screwed up and looked the wrong way in spite of myself. You know, you didn't leave us a whole lot of choice here—you could have come quietly and saved yourself all of this. Why did you feel like you had to run? You weren't going to do a lot of time for a fake passport."

"I figured you were looking to press some bogus misprision charge or conspiracy to commit assault and who knows what else. I'm not real confident in our justice system."

"Hey, we can discuss that. Feel like talking about it?"

"No way. I've said too much already. And don't bother reading me my rights—I'm getting a lawyer and fighting this. And you two stay out of my mind," he said to Rodriguez and Ellis. Then snidely added: "Which you are obviously not very good at anyway." At that point Brosard gave a deep sigh and seemed to go inside of himself.

"Putting up his defenses," commented Ellis.

"I think I'll read him his rights anyway," said JT. "Who knows, he might talk in his altered mental state, and I wouldn't want to have to forgo anything he did say." JT recited the standard Miranda phrases to a silent Brosard, and told him he'd be detained overnight and be taken before a magistrate in the morning.

Rodriguez stopped JT as he walked back towards his seat and asked, "What's misprision?"

"'Misprision of felony' is having knowledge of an actual commission of a felony, but not revealing what you know to a judge or other person in civil or military authority. It usually results in a fine or a sentence of not more than three years, or both. But it can be tough to prove because it requires active concealment of a known felony, rather than merely failing to report it."

"Makes sense. Are you ready for us?" asked Rodriguez.

"I guess I'm as ready as I'll ever be, Docs," lamented JT.

"This will hurt us more than it will hurt you," Ellis said with a smile. He and Rodriguez then scanned JT to detect any action plans that Brosard may have planted. Brosard had very little chance to plant anything, but JT was in close proximity to the telepath, and they didn't want to take any chances. As best they could tell, he was clear.

For the rest of the ride to the Route 15 detention facility, they discussed the new protocols which had been established for prisoners of this ilk. They didn't want a repeat of the Cutler incident. As they were approaching the front gate, JT's cell rang. "Yes, Miss Arati, what do you have for me?"

"I obtained the requisite permission, and the ill-gotten funds of Mr. Cunningham, subsequently purloined by Mr.

Brosard, now grace the coffers of the Department of Homeland Security."

"Wonderful, Arati. Good work. I'll let the troops know. Anything else? . . . Okay then, thanks. Oh, one more thing—go home." JT immediately had second thoughts about letting Rodriguez or Ellis, or anyone else who might get close to Brosard, know about the funds transfer. He'd save that for later.

After passing through the secure gate, the bus pulled up in front of the facility. JT and Juanita got off and briefed the two agents on duty. They then had the agents and the bus driver join them outside the facility, while JT, Rodriguez and Ellis escorted Brosard to his new temporary home. The recently retrofitted cell now had a teleconferencing facility built into the wall. There would be as little as possible close contact allowed. The guards took over, and JT, Juanita, the driver and Doctors Rodriguez and Ellis reboarded the bus for the trip back.

"Did Brosard try anything on you guys?" asked Juanita.

"No," answered Ellis. "Pretty sure he felt outgunned with JT and the two of us there, and I don't think he believes we have much on him; although, he did sound worried about being ramrodded."

"That remains to be seen," said JT. "We can charge him with possession and use of a fake passport, and now, assault." Then, changing the subject, he said: "So Stan, I guess at least some of your SMART participants are better at hiding their thoughts than you realized."

"Well, to tell the truth, we're not sure. Remember, we never really had a chance to scan Brosard, nor Cutler nor Thompson: they were not at the TGS transfer meeting where the participants let us in. And it is possible that even if Brosard was there, and he agreed to the deep scan, he may still have been able to block us by partitioning his mind and letting us in to most, but not all, levels.

"You mean the ones you did scan could still be hiding something?"

"Possibly. For the purposes of that meeting, we were just not as good as we let on. But we did think if we indicated we could read their deep thoughts, it would unnerve anyone with something to hide, and we'd pick up on that—not necessarily what they were hiding, but the fact they were hiding something. And we didn't get those vibes from any of them. This is a learning process, JT. We need to convince Maureen to get more involved. We're all pretty good, and Sid is great, but she's at least an order of magnitude beyond him. However, she is heavily involved in her theoretical physics, and can't accomplish that very well away from her MIT lab."

"Perhaps you need to figure out a way she can conduct her research from here," commented JT. "Otherwise the mountain will have to go to Mohammed."

Ellis and Rodriguez looked at each other, and it was obvious they were going to give the possibility some thought.

CHAPTER SIXTY-EIGHT

Friday, Crystal City, Virginia

JT had informed Moffett of Brosard's capture last night, and was congratulated by his second-level boss. Moffett did ask JT and the troops to meet him at the Crystal City office around 3:00 for a full debriefing. JT had just gotten back from Brosard's hearing before the magistrate, and Juanita and Arati had been in the office for less than an hour. At JT's request, Arati had put together a list of the evidence against the four people she had recently found additional family data on, as well as Brosard. Based on Rodriguez's comment that they could have missed something in their scans, JT was not convinced Cutler didn't have an accomplice. Sure, he admitted committing the murder and did not mention having any help, but it was obvious the man was despondent and suicidal at the time, probably due in no small measure to his long term overdosing of AJ. They had a couple of hours before Moffett would get there, so JT suggested going over the list before he arrived.

"Before we start, how'd it go with Brosard this morning?" asked Juanita.

"Oh, that was sweet. You heard him lawyer up last night, and he had some attorney he knew meet him at the Route 15 facility. I briefed the guy before he talked to Brosard via the teleconference set up, but I don't think his lawyer friend believed much of what I said. We gave them privacy however, so he settled for the setup, and he talked to Brosard for a good forty minutes. The magistrate was briefed by Moffett, so she was clued in and showed up just before Brosard and his lawyer finished. I mentioned the use of a fake passport and the assault on the lady at the airport, and his lawyer said these were not enough to deny bail. The fact that he was an obvious flight risk had the magistrate wavering, and then I mentioned the theft of

Cunningham's funds and I thought Brosard was gonna shit. All said and done, he'll be in our detention facility without bail until his trail. Now, Arati, what have you got?"

"I will start with Rydell. We know Doctor Lee thought she was conflicted, and was concealing some adverse personal information, maybe whatever is in her juvenile record. She was a suspect in her sister's disappearance, but there was never any proof whatsoever of that. Or perhaps it had something to do with her fiancé's dropped malpractice suit: Rydell's boss suggested somebody may have been paid off, because she thought what was a very good case against Rydell's fiancé was dismissed for no apparent reason. We know that could have been due to Rydell's influence. Lee also thought Rydell and Cutler were stronger than the others. She has no alibi for the time of Doctor Lee's murder, and was there providing medical assistance right after Lee was discovered. She has medical training, so it is possible she intentionally mishandled the defibrillator, and her application of CPR, to assure Doctor Lee was not revived. If I recall correctly, JT, you put her at the top of your list at one time."

JT nodded.

"Simmons' older step-brother died of a drug overdose, but there is no indication she had anything to do with it. Her homecoming king, and boyfriend at the time, impregnated her out of wedlock, and she was married, miscarried and obtained a divorce all before her eighteenth birthday. She was the last one to see Doctor Lee alive, and may therefore have been aware of his intended activities and location during the rest of the evening. However, Doctor Lee had no suspicions of her that we know of. She does have an alibi—watching a movie with two other participants—but we have determined she, or the others, could have used one of their bathroom breaks, or just slipped out unnoticed, to commit the murder.

"Pacquin also had a juvenile record, which has apparently been expunged, and I found no secondary source information to elucidate upon that. He was not on Doctor Lee's list of suspicions persons. He was the one who discovered the body, and he has no alibi for the time of the murder. He could have committed the deed, turned in the alarm, and performed an ineffective CPR. He surprised us, and did not return to Quantico like we thought he would when the program switched to TGS.

"Pennington's step-father was arrested for domestic abuse of his third wife, the one he married after her mother, and it is possible he was abusing her, and is the reason for her mother divorcing him. He died in an altercation during a bar fight within a year after her mother's divorce. His attacker claimed self-defense, and this was substantiated by several witnesses. We know she is gay. She is also one of those with the less-than-adequate movie alibi, but was not on Doctor Lee's list either.

"Now, for Brosard. We know Doctor Lee thought he was a megalomaniac who was underplaying his abilities. He is a womanizer and a gambler, yet Lee suspecting him of nothing untoward, other than using his abilities at the tables. He has a PhD in psychology and his parents were brilliant as well. He is head of the Psionics Research Branch at the Agency, and I personally feel he is capable of almost anything—mentally, I mean, not necessarily wrongdoing. He does not have an alibi other than his call to his boss, a weak one at best, and we know how truthful Mr. Cunningham has been. It is possible Doctor Lee found out about Brosard playing his boss, or at least was aware of what his boss was doing. And we are fairly confident Brosard knew what Cutler had done, yet did not mention it at the time.

"The only participants left are Krumski and Randall. I have nothing new on either of them, except Randall has returned to his FBI job."

"Excellent, Arati. I know you hate to speculate, but what possible motives does this data support?" asked JT. "Ones strong enough to warrant murder?"

"If Sharon Rydell was somehow involved in her sister's disappearance, perhaps her death, she may want to hide that. Or if she influenced the individual who brought the malpractice suit against her fiancé, that could be sufficient reason, but a weak one I believe. Simmons would not want it known if she was somehow the cause of her step-brother's death, or if she knew who was and did not reveal it. Tommy Pacquin's juvenile record may have held a reason for motive, but it is not available. If Pennington was abused, or in retribution for the abuse of her mother, she may have set up the fight her former step-dad perished in. I do not think her sexual orientation was reason enough for a murder, since it was fairly well known. Brosard could have been aware of his boss' selling of classified information, and been waiting for a more opportune time to cash in. Or he could have been blackmailing, or planning to blackmail, Cutler, over the rapes or other misdeeds."

"My money's on Rydell," said Juanita. I think the sister theory is weak, but I wouldn't put it past her to 'convince' her boyfriend's accuser to drop the suit. I think it was Lee who said she was conflicted and vulnerable, and susceptible to manipulation, and I think the shame of having this come out would be too much for her. How about you, Arati?"

"As JT mentioned, I hesitate to speculate. All of these seem plausible, but we have no convincing evidence. And the guilty party could have a motive we have not been clever enough to unearth yet. What do you think, JT?"

"From the data we have, the strongest suspects in my opinion are Brosard and Rydell. But let me run this by you. The idea of an accomplice just isn't sitting well with me—these people all think they are too smart to need help. What if this was a crime of opportunity?"

"How so?" asked Arati. She paused for a minute as JT smiled. She then offered: "I see where you are going with this. What if Cutler later thought his attempt at murder was not successful? In his possibly befuddled state of mind, caused by the additional AJ, plus being worried about being discovered, and upset over the idea of taking another's life, he may have thought he misinterpreted Lee's state. What if he caused a serious, but non-fatal stroke? He goes back to his room, broadcasting his terrible misdeed on the way, and his thoughts are picked up by another participant. Brosard admitted as much, and may not have been the only one. The 'accomplice' goes to check on Lee, sees he is incapacitated but still alive, and burkes him to finish the deed. He or she then goes back to whatever they were doing, or pulls the fire alarm, or hangs around close enough to show up and prevent resuscitation."

"Wow," was Juanita's only comment.

"That's pretty much what I had in mind, Arati. It fits the facts reasonably well. The only trouble I had with it is the fortuitous timing for the second perpetrator: being able to get down to Lee, commit the deed, and return all without being noticed. Then I thought, what if Cutler transmitted his intentions ahead of time. It makes the timeline more believable."

"So what do we do with this?" asked Juanita. "Unless we can prove some of our suppositions, we really don't have anything except maybe some places to concentrate on." A smile then crept over her face and she said, "I have a scathingly brilliant idea."

Juanita's odd phrasing and intonation engendered a quizzical look by Arati.

"It's a line from an old Disney movie," said JT. "I think I know what you're going to say, but go ahead."

"Why don't we assume each of the aforementioned scenarios, submit them as uncovered facts to our suspects, individually of course, and see what kind of reaction we get?"

"They will see through your charade," offered Arati.

"Not if I . . ."

"Not you, but me," interrupted JT. "You were going to suggest we have the idea firmly implanted in our mind, so we believe it. And I can't ask you to do that. I think it's risky and I have already worked with Stan on some of this. So it will have to be me, and you'll have to sit out the interview."

"Another RHIP situation I suppose," bemoaned Juanita. "You get to have all the fun. You know we were lucky the other day when you faked out Brosard, and he looked in the direction you wanted him to. He didn't notice me looking the other way at Josh rushing him."

"Sometimes you get lucky."

"I would not mind being the guinea pig in this endeavor, JT," said Arati. "I have been extensively probed with no ill effects, and have no qualms about your suggested procedure."

"Thanks, Arati, but I think it needs to be one of us with a badge. I will have Stan or Sid, or both, there for control purposes, just in case. It'll be fine."

They were discussing exactly how to phrase the misinformation when Moffett arrived.

JT briefed Moffett, including his proposed idea of baiting the suspects. Moffett was okay with the plan, as long as Stan and Sid were there, but he did insist upon an additional safeguard he would not disclose. When JT was through briefing his second level supervisor, he asked him about the disposition of Cunningham and Devereux.

"Cunningham is spilling his guts," said Moffett. "He is telling them every bit of information he sold over the years, but unfortunately he really doesn't seem to know who his buyers were. At least the Agency will know what information has been compromised. Apparently he had some scruples, as he never divulged any agent names, even though he said he was asked to, or so he says. Information he did give probably had the same effect in some cases, and they think he was well aware of that. Nonetheless, they intend to set up a retirement story for him, hold him incognito until they get through with him, he goes to trial and is sentenced. I don't think he'll be out of jail in time to collect much of his social security."

"What about those supposed hits on Cutler and Brosard?" Juanita asked.

"He copped to those as well. Said he hired some 'contractors' to carry out both of those—ones he had dealt with while holding another position in the Agency,"
"Because? . . ." Juanita asked.

"Claims he was trying to discredit the MENSA program because, and I quote: 'It is nothing but a waste of funds on an unscientific boondoggle which might usurp the validity of polygraphy.'"

JT laughed out loud at this.

"A real altruist," Juanita said. "More likely he knew he could hide his misdeeds during a polygraph examination, being such an expert on them, but was afraid he wouldn't be able to fool an ESP-capable investigator, and wanted to delay the program until he had a big enough stash built up."

"Certainly more of a motive than his explanation," said JT. "I presume he totally denied having anything to do with Lee's murder?"

"Yes, he did, and we believe him," answered Moffett.

"What did Cunningham have to say about Brosard?"

"He said Brosard did not know what he was doing, and was in no way complicit with his nefarious activities—claims his employee did nothing more than keep him abreast of what was happening at the CTF. I'm sure he believes as much, but I'm also sure Brosard was a whole lot smarter than Cunningham thought he was. Devereux is another interesting story. The FBI plans to have him pass a note to his handlers saying Cunningham is retiring, and is no longer a source of information for them. They then plan on faking Devereux's death, giving him a new identity, and putting him on trial for treason. He'll go to prison for some time. He did give up two overseas bank accounts, but who knows if those were all of them. Arati, I'd like you to check into the possibility of other accounts in your spare time, if you would. Unless there is something else, I've got a meeting in the Pentagon."

"Who gets to keep Devereux's money?" asked Arati.

"I'm pretty sure they are going to let us keep the funds from both Devereux and Cunningham, since the total is less than five million. The CIA was a little miffed we transferred the money from Cunningham's account—said it might be a giveaway, which is why they wanted to come up with a reason for him to transfer it. They placed a silent hold on both of Devereux's accounts, and told us to keep the money there until they give us the okay to transfer it."

JT looked at Juanita and Arati and then said, "I guess we're done, Boss."

"Keep me advised, Guys."

CHAPTER SIXTY-NINE

Monday, Chantilly, Virginia

JT was nervous—not the kind of nervousness you get when you are worried something isn't going to go as planned, but rather the kind that pumps you up when you are about to do something really exciting and you can't wait to get to it. He had spent many hours over the weekend with Stan Rodriguez and Sid Ellis, preparing his mind with hopefully plausible scenarios he could spring on several of the suspects in Doctor Lee's murder. The three of them had decided William Brosard was going to spend a considerable amount of time in jail, and he likely wouldn't fall for the ruse in any event. His only discernible motives for killing Lee were if the doctor thought he was blackmailing Cutler, which he apparently wasn't, or if he was aware of, and waiting to cash in on, his boss' misdeeds. The former made no sense due to Cutler's financial position; the latter would be impossible to prove, as he had made no overt moves to establish knowledge of Cunningham's crimes. They might revisit these possibilities if none of their other suspects worked out. They had nothing on Tommy Pacquin to trap him with—any scenarios they came up with would be pure supposition, with no thread to any actual events. Rydell, Pennington and Simmons were the most likely suspects left.

Yesterday the staff had closed off the fourth level of the CTF, blaming annual maintenance: pool and sauna cleaning, installation of some new equipment in the theater, and refinishing the gym floor. JT, Sid and Stan entered the building without being seen, and had set up shop in the theater. They planned on having each of the three suspects down individually for an interview. Gayle Pennington was first.

She was escorted to the lower level by Doctor Rodriguez, who told her he needed her help on a special project. She cast

Rodriguez a suspicious glance when he pushed the L4 button in the elevator, but said nothing. When she entered the theater and saw JT and Ellis, she asked Rodriguez, "So what nefarious reason did you bring me down here to meet with Special Agent JT Dunkirk and TGS Chairman Sidney Ellis and yourself?"

JT motioned her to sit down and took the seat next to her. Ellis and Rodriguez were seated at the other side of the table. JT answered her: "Some additional information has come to light in the case of Doctor Lee's death and we were hoping you could help us explain it. We did a deep background investigation, based on a letter Doctor Lee sent to his daughter Chrissie, which she didn't open and read until after his death. In it, Lee expressed grave concerns about some information he had come upon, quite inadvertently, from one of the program participants. Apparently they 'leaked' this information to him unknowingly during one of the procedures where they were very distracted and thus vulnerable to 'broadcasting.' And we believe this information would provide sufficient motive for Doctor Lee's homicide."

"And this information was about me?" Pennington asked. It was obvious to JT that she didn't really believe this, or was putting on an excellent act.

"Yes. We've looked into it and it seems very plausible, and perhaps provable."

"And it is? . . ." Pennington pressed.

JT looked her straight in the eye, concentrated, and said, "That you set up the murder of your step-father in the bar fight because he had been abusing you."

"What! You're insane! Doctor Lee can't have believed that because it never happened."

"You don't believe me?" asked JT. "Then read my mind."

"I don't care what you believe, because it's just not true. And I don't believe Doctor Lee ever said as much, either. This is just a bunch of horse shit, pardon my French. I'm out of here and

I'm calling a lawyer," she huffed as she stood up and knocked her chair over backwards.

Neither JT nor Rodriguez had ever seen Pennington this animated. JT looked over at Rodriguez and Ellis who were both shaking their head.

"Okay, Gayle," said Rodriguez, "you're right. Calm down and sit down for a minute and let me explain, please." He said it calmly, but with enough conviction that Pennington righted her chair and sat down. He then proceeded to give her the details and purpose of their little charade. "Would you mind if we probe you to determine the veracity of what you say?"

Pennington paused and decided she understood their need to take this tact under the circumstances. After a few moments, she accepted the explanation graciously, and said, "I have nothing to hide."

Neither he nor Ellis picked up any negative feedback from her, nor any attempt to read JT's mind earlier. They were confident she was innocent of their fabricated charges and Lee's murder, or it was beyond their ability to determine differently. They told her as far as they were concerned, she was not guilty of the charges and thus had no motive to murder Doctor Lee that they knew of.

"So, JT," she asked coquettishly when they were through, "would you have really let me read your mind?"

"Feel free," he replied. "Stan and Sid planted a doozy of a scenario in there."

"Actually, I think I'll pass. No offense."

"Hey, none taken. I'm sorry if I upset you at all."

Pennington nodded and smiled as Rodriguez got up to escort her back upstairs. On the way he asked for her discretion, as they had another interview or two. He then escorted Sharon Rydell down to the theater.

Rydell's reaction to the trio of interrogators was quite different: "What the hell's going on here—a secret meeting with two mind readers and a federal agent?"

"Don't be so suspicious," said JT calmly. He then gave her the same lead-in he had given to Pennington. That seemed to calm her down, at least until he got to the specific part. "So, Sharon, Doctor Lee thought you had something to do with your sister's disappearance, *and* you used your abilities to convince your fiancé's accuser to drop the malpractice suit."

Rydell squeezed her fists tightly, drew in a deep breath, her eyes spitting daggers at JT. She held the breath for ten or so seconds, as she glanced at Rodriguez and Ellis, and then released it slowly. As her composure recovered she asked, "Are we being recorded?"

"No," JT responded.

She sat for a minute, apparently collecting her thoughts. Then: "Charlie has never been aware of my psychic abilities. He told me about the charges without me asking, and he said they were basically true. He also said he apologized to the lady, offered to help her get a better position, and she agreed to a small settlement under those circumstances. I believed him at first, but then had nagging doubts, based on some scuttlebutt I heard from a few of my nursing friends. My boss even suggested Charlie bribed the lawyer involved, offering him a higher payoff than he would have gotten with a larger settlement amount, although I don't know where he would have gotten the funds for that. I was tempted to probe Charlie to determine if this was true, but could not bring myself to violate my promise to myself to never mind-read someone I was romantically involved with—it seemed so sordid and like I was cheating on him. So I relied on my gut feeling that he wasn't being honest with me, and I broke off our engagement just a few days ago. You can probe me if you want, but I'm telling the truth."

"Let's hear your response to the other charge before we do anything," said Rodriguez.

Rydell drew another deep breath and then started to tear up. She took a few minutes to compose herself. "This is not easy, and I have told no one of this. You will only hear it if I get a solemn promise that it will not leave this room." She looked at JT.

"If it in any way relates to a felony which is still prosecutable, I cannot promise. Otherwise, I agree."

"Fair enough—I have no problem with that. My sister had a drug habit. I tried to convince her she was destroying her superior mental capacities we both knew we had. She said she had more than enough to spare, and she could control it. I started to confiscate her drugs and cut them in order to reduce their potency, hoping to wean her off of them. It was exceptionally difficult not to let her know what was going on—and she tried to find out, but I was able to resist her probes. This pissed her off, but we had both agreed to a no-unsolicited-probes pact. I also tried to figure out who her supplier was so I could turn them in and stop the madness. I don't think she figured out what I was doing, but rather thought her supplier was ripping her off. In any event, I believe she lit out after him one night, and I didn't hear from her again for over a year, and only then to say she was 'disappearing.' I have blamed myself for this estrangement, even though I know I was trying to do the right thing."

"Is this related to your juvenile record?" asked JT.

"Yes. The authorities searched our rooms and found some drugs I had tampered with, and thus had my prints on. She apparently hid them and I didn't find them when I searched her room. They charged me with possession, and I got off with community service since I tested clean."

"And whom are you sending money to out on the west coast?" JT queried.

Rydell was caught off guard, paused, and then started shaking her head very slowly. "Let's just say that person turned state's evidence, and I am not supposed to know where she is."

"Under these circumstances, I can probably find out whether or not she's in witness protection, but not of course, where she is. And if that's the case, you shouldn't know either and may be putting her in danger."

"I forward the funds to a government organization."

"So Arati tells me," JT said chuckling. "You learn something new every day, don't you? Would you allow Stan and Sid to do a probe for verification?"

"Yes. Yes. And then I want you to honor your promise of silence. Further, I want to know that I am no longer suspect."

Rydell "tested clean," and neither Rodriguez nor Ellis found any indication of prevarication, nor any effort by her to read JT's mind when confronted with the accusations. As best they could tell, she was not guilty of the new charges or Lee's murder. Rodriguez escorted her back upstairs and then asked Simmons to accompany him back down.

"Strike two," JT said after Rodriguez left the room. "And she didn't try to probe me either, did she?"

"No. As we said earlier, that would be less likely if they were innocent rather than guilty, but not definitive. With their reactions and our readings, Stan and I believe they are both innocent of all charges. If Simmons is a bust, too, as I suspect she will be, then we'll have to come up with another idea. We'll just need some more good old fashion detective work, concentrating perhaps on Brosard and Pacquin."

JT nodded and got up to stretch and clear his mind. He walked around the table several times before Rodriguez returned with Brandy Simmons.

"Well hello, JT, and Doctor Ellis, too. I gather this has something to do with Doctor Lee's case, right?"

"You're right on as usual, Brandy. And I'll get right to an explanation," JT said as he and Simmons took their seats. He gave her the same preamble as the two former suspects, during which time Simmons remained as upbeat as normal. When JT got to the "leaked information" part, he thought he detected a slight change in her demeanor. Before he got to the last word of "you murdered your step-brother," Simmons stood up abruptly, placed both hands on her head, and stared intently at JT.

JT felt a surge of electricity throughout his entire body. It was like he had been hit with a taser, but it didn't hurt; he was conscious, but couldn't move. The two TGS Directors, who were on the other side of the table, had assumed the same position as Simmons and were staring intently at her.

Simmons lowered her hands and turned her gaze from JT to them. "This is not going to work," she said. "I'm walking out of here and you all are not stopping me." She then turned back toward JT.

JT couldn't help but think of the gun holstered under his sport jacket.

"I don't need your weapon, Agent." In spite of Rodriguez's and Ellis' efforts to control her, she turned around and headed toward the exit. As she opened the door, she saw Maureen Fields sitting there calmly in her wheel chair. "Good evening, Doctor," she said pleasantly; then growled, "Get out of my way." Then Simmons backed up and said, "No, you can't do this to me. Get out of my mind."

"Release JT," Fields said calmly.

"I . . . I . . . okay."

JT felt himself go limp, then regained control of his body and stood up. Fields had moved into the room and JT went over and closed the door. "How very, very nice to see you, Professor

Fields." Her presence there was a surprise to JT—a precaution thought of by Moffett he didn't want JT aware of. "Brandy, why don't you sit back down?"

"Sit down," Fields echoed.

"I didn't do those things," Simmons said as she took her seat.

"Brandy, look at me," JT said.

But Simmons couldn't take her eyes off Fields. "I heard you were strong, but you surprised me. Take this, Fields," she yelled as she closed her eyes. The noted astrophysicist, MIT professor and prominent member of The Galactic Society didn't blink. "You can't keep this up," she said, straining with the effort. After a period Simmons thought lasted forever, but was actually only seventeen seconds, she relaxed.

"Brandy, if you are innocent, then why did you react the way you did? You read my mind to make sure I was telling the truth, and then you zapped me and decided to leave. That screams guilty to me," said JT.

"This will not hold up in a court of law—you have no proof," she shot back.

Fields responded, "But Brandy, we have the truth: you gave your step-brother an overdose of drugs after he raped you; and when you figured out Doctor Lee was on to you, you murdered him."

JT added: "We know what happened, Brandy. How long do you think it will take us to prove it working backwards? You've carried this guilt around way too long. Come clean and we'll work something out."

"Yeah, like you worked something out for Paul and Bill?"

"You are way too valuable to this program, Brandy," said Rodriguez. "You are obviously the strongest one of all the participants. We *can* work something out. Give us a chance to help you."

"Help? You can't help me. I know what you did to Paul—he ended up killing himself rather than go back to an isolation cell. And now you've got Bill in the same situation—afraid to let him near anybody. You think I can live the rest of my life under those conditions? What, are you going to have Fields here next to me for the whole process? I'm sure the good doctor has better things to do with her life than babysit me. More likely I'll end up drugged out of my mind." Then Simmons screamed and gave a powerful, concentrated blast and at the same time reached for JT's gun.

JT and the three TGS members were caught off guard. Simmons got her hand on JT's weapon, but stopped before removing it from the holster.

"My finger's on the trigger, Fields, and the gun is pointed into his gut."

Field's concentration caused bulges on her forehead, and Rodriguez and Ellis looked like they were staring a million miles into space. Simmons was struggling with all her might. She could not pull the trigger. Her head was aching with a thousand pins and needles piercing every part.

"I . . . will . . . kill . . . him," she verbalized very slowly and with great effort. "I . . . I'm . . . sorry," she said as she collapsed and the gun went off.

CHAPTER SEVENTY

Monday, Chantilly, Virginia

Simmons was lying on the floor unconscious at JT's feet. Rodriguez and Ellis were rushing around to JT's side of the table. Fields was looking into JT's eyes, which were open—wide open. "You appear none the worse for the wear, Agent. Do we need to call for medical assistance?" she asked.

JT reached his right hand down and ran it all over his side and thigh. "Apparently not," he said with great relief. "The bullet missed me completely. However, the chair's kind of a mess and there appears to be a hole in the floor. That was a close one."

Rodriguez and Ellis let out deep sighs. They reached down and lifted Simmons into a chair.

"Don't you have a safety on the damn thing?" Fields asked.

"Most law enforcement hand guns don't have safeties."

"And you had a round in the chamber?"

"Departmental SOP requires a round to be in the chamber at all times while you are on duty."

"Well, that was indeed a close one, and I apologize," said the MIT professor. "I regained control of her after she surprised me, and did manage to keep her from pulling the trigger, at least intentionally. When she fainted and fell, the motion must have forced her finger up against the trigger. I was not as prepared as I should have been, and I am sincerely sorry."

"Doc, this was my idea and we got the result we wanted. You have nothing to be sorry about. What kind of condition is she in?"

Rodriguez pulled a hypo from his pocket and administered a tranquilizer to her. "Physically, she's okay, although it looks like she may have a bruise on her face where she landed. We'll have to wait until she regains consciousness to determine her mental condition."

"Can't you do to her what you did to Arati?" JT asked.

Ellis answered: "We were sure Cutler intended to hurt her, and Harry and I felt we couldn't wait. What we did was untried and dangerous, and only done in desperation. The three of us here were merely trying to contain Simmons. It would be far safer to wait until she is cognizant of our probing. I'm afraid she was right about her future—isolation and probably drugs; that is, if we can indeed prove it."

"She is now guilty of assault on a federal officer, and with what we all witnessed, we could hook her on attempted murder. Doctor Fields, do you know exactly what else she is guilty of?"

"I got a pretty clear image of her sitting on top of Toshi, and also of her step-brother raping her. I hope I never have to experience anything similar ever again—vicariously, it was bad enough; the real deal had to be horrendous. I can't be positive of her culpability in his death by overdose, but she certainly believes she gave him a sufficient amount to kill him."

"Wow. When do you think she'll be coherent enough for me to talk to?"

"It was a light dose, and she should be coming around in a few minutes; however, I do not believe she'll have the same control when she does, and in fact will be docile. In any event, we should be prepared for anything," Rodriguez said.

"Do you think maybe she was taking some of the juiced up AJ?" JT asked.

Rodriguez answered: "I don't know, JT. We know how much was missing and how much we recovered, but we don't know how much of the difference Cutler himself imbibed, or hid away in some other place. She was obviously more brilliant than we knew. Toshi noted her significant improvement, but thought she started from a lower level than the others. She must have had him fooled, just as she did me. I can't believe he was aware of her step-brother's crime, or her responsibility for his death, and didn't report it. Perhaps she'll fill us in."

Simmons was coming around. Rodriguez called her name but got no response. He grabbed her by the shoulders and gently shook her, and called her name again. He tried rousing her several times.

Finally: "Doctor Rodriguez, what's going on? I feel very fuzzy. I can't concentrate. Doctor Fields, what are you doing here?"

"Do you remember coming down here with me, Brandy?"

"Yes, I think so. I remember seeing JT and Doctor Ellis, but then I don't remember anything subsequent, or how I ended up sitting in this chair."

"Do you mind if Doctor Fields probes you, to see if we can figure out what happened?"

"What did happen?"

"You passed out, and we think you may have had a stroke."

"You're kidding me."

Rodriguez shook his head.

"Well, go ahead, then."

Maureen Fields nodded at her two TGS cohorts, and then looked into Simmons' eyes and began concentrating. The wheelchair-bound professor didn't find any recollection of the recent events, any guilt associated with her step-brother or Doctor Lee, nor, in fact, any special abilities whatsoever in Simmons. After a few minutes, she asked, "Brandy, can you tell me what I'm thinking of?"

"Ah, no. And I should be able to shouldn't I?"

"You used to be able to. Perhaps you should go get some rest."

"Good idea. I am really beat for some reason. Should I see a doctor?" Simmons looked at Rodriguez. "I'm sorry, no offense. It's just . . ."

"You are right. I'll give you something to help you sleep so you can get some rest. Then we'll schedule some tests to clear this up." Rodriguez then escorted her back to her room, and gave her a strong sedative. He waited until she dozed off. He then told Sam Donaldson to have her monitored continually, and to notify him when she woke up. He headed back to the theater.

"I presume you've been discussing what to do now," he said to the group upon his return.

"I was not trying to wipe her mind," said Fields. "As if I knew how to do that anyway. But apparently that was the result. I am convinced this is a permanent loss, not something like temporary amnesia after a traumatic event. What do you two think after being in there?"

"I agree," said Ellis. "I do know I was concentrating like hell and projecting as much as I could. Maybe we went too far."

"Same here," said Rodriguez. "But I don't see as how we had another choice under the circumstances. I guess the question now is where she stands legally," he said as he looked at JT.

"Hey, this is new ground for me. We're sure she's guilty of two murders, but currently have no evidence we could use in court. And I think we'd have to agree, she knew what she was doing at the time, probably ruling out any insanity defense. However, she may be able to use it on the attempted murder charge, given the circumstances accompanying our questioning and Doctor Fields' actions. I don't know. If she gets a good attorney, I believe she could skate on the latter charge; and unless we get hard evidence, we likely won't even be able to charge her with the murders. Doc, can you give me any details which might help—something we can check into on either murder?"

"I can only say for sure she gave her step-brother what she thought was an overdose, and she was on top of Toshi in the gym holding the barbell in her lap—for the extra weight required to insure a successful burking, I presume. I didn't have a chance to get anything further. I'm afraid we may have ruined a beautiful mind."

"That didn't happen to Arati after Cutler's attack. Maybe it didn't here either, and maybe she's faking again," offered JT.

"Those were different circumstances," said Ellis, "and we don't know what Cutler tried to do, or what he was capable of. Plus, Harry and I went in and effected what we thought was damage control. As far as Brandy's current state goes—I think she's lost it. How about you, Maureen?"

"I really don't think she's faking, nor do I think she'll recover her abilities, at least not without a lot of time and effort. I definitely got the impression we destroyed cells, not disabled them. But then, I have no good reason to believe I'm that much stronger than her, or that I'm infallible in this. Perhaps, if Stan and Sid weren't here helping, we'd have failed miserably. Where the hell do we go from here?"

JT thought a minute before replying. "I think we keep her sedated until we can get her out to the Route 15 facility. Then we charge her with the attempted murder so we can detain her. We'll get some psychiatrists to examine her, and they'll either find her competent for trial or not. If she's found sane and goes to trial, we live with the results whether or not she still has her special abilities. Either way she's probably not a flight risk unless she's found guilty. In the mean time, we try to get evidence for her other crimes. If she's found incompetent, she'll go to a mental facility. If she improves, she goes to trial; if she doesn't improve, she stays there. The third possibility here, is that she really has all her faculties, is faking being insane, and escapes from the mental facility."

"We're coping with new world realities with old world rules," said Rodriguez. "We need to get a handle on this because it is happening, whether the world is ready for it or not."

"I think it's time we got serious about the committee on ethical psychic behavior," said Fields. "For our own benefit, if not everyone else's. JT, would you be willing to be a law enforcement resource for us?"

"Charlie Moffett has already asked me the same thing. So if you think I would really be of some benefit to you, then sure."

"Oh, I think you will be," said Rodriguez. "We obviously need a better vetting mechanism for the SMART program, and probably for TGS, as well. If we had had the benefit of your input earlier, we likely would not have accepted some of these candidates. As it is, we're down to five, including Julie—three of our originals turn out to be deviants of some sort, and one decides to go back to the FBI rather than transfer to TGS sponsorship. We need to look much more closely at this next group of candidates. We are hoping you can help us do that, JT."

"I am flattered. Since I don't see it as a full time job, and therefore I still get to chase terrorists and crooks, I'd be delighted."

"Have you given any consideration to our recent offer, Maureen?" Ellis asked.

"Actually, I came here ready to turn it down—which I felt I should do in person. After today, however, I've changed my mind. I will look into getting a part time job at one of the local universities, and devote more time to TGS and SMART business. I might have to write another book to make up for the income loss, but hey, you do what you have to do."

All three of them laughed at her mood-lightening remark.

"I've got to talk to Charlie Moffett and let him know what happened here. Then I have to get with the AUSA to see if I was right about how we handle Simmons. I wish we had more closure on Lee's murder, but it is what it is. At least for now. Stan, can you keep an eye on our suspect until I can arrange for her transport out to Loudoun?"

"Will do. Don't beat yourself up on this, JT. It was a good idea. I think we got a good deal of closure."

"I agree, but at what cost?"

"Like you said, it is what it is. And only with 20-20 hindsight do I believe we would have done anything different," offered Rodriguez.

"Yeah, you're probably right. If you'll excuse me now, Gentlemen, Professor, I've got some phone calls to make."

EPILOGUE

Doctor William Brosard was convicted of assault, grand theft, money laundering, and fraudulent use of a passport, and was sentenced to fifteen to twenty years in federal prison. He escaped from the courthouse on his last trial date, and is currently at large.

Randal Cunningham was convicted on seventeen counts of treason, and is serving a life-without-parole sentence in a maximum security federal prison. To the outside world, it appears as though he retired and moved to the South Seas.

Alphonse Devereux, AKA Charles Frampton, was convicted on three counts of espionage, and is serving a fifteen year sentence in a federal penitentiary under an assumed name. When released, he will be deported to France to stand trial on charges of illegal arms trafficking.

Professor Maureen Fields moved to Georgetown and is teaching at the nearby university. She developed a telepathic contact method of neuronal enhancement, significantly improving the field strength and acting distance of the SMART program participants and her TGS cohorts.

Doctor Arati Jabornae is the Chief Information Officer for DHS, and the Human Capital Director of The Galactic Society. She is responsible for vetting new members of the SMART program and TGS.

Doctor Ralph Krumski left the SMART program and reopened his psychiatric practice. He testified at Brandy Simmons' competency hearing. He remains an active participant in The Galactic Society.

Tommy Pacquin replaced Sam Donaldson as the Assistant Program Manager for the SMART program. He occasionally subs as a polygrapher for DHS. He admitted his juvenile record was for burning down an outhouse.

Gayle Pennington joined the Rainbow Coalition, and counsels their members on gender confusion issues. She remains an active participant in The Galactic Society.

Doctor Stanley Rodriguez gave up his Johns Hopkins medical practice, and works full time for TGS in the SMART program. He developed the accepted standard on ethical psychic behavior.

Sharon Rydell, now Doctor Rydell, earned a PhD in neuroscience, and is the vice-chair of the Board of Directors of The Galactic Society.

Brandy Simmons was declared incompetent to stand trial, and was remanded to a secure mental institute. She became catatonic after two months in the facility, and is not expected to recover.